Vince Sgambati
SANCTUARIES

Sanctuaries

Copyright 2022 by Vince Sgambati

All rights reserved—Reproduction without express permission of the author or publisher is prohibited.

First printing 2022

$18.00

Standing Stone Books is an imprint of **Standing Stone Studios,**
an organization dedicated to the promotion of the literary and visual arts.

Mailing address:
1897 State Route 91, Fabius, New York 13063

Web address:
standingstonebooks.net

Email:
standingstonebooks@gmail.com

Distributor:
Small Press Distribution
1341 Seventh Avenue
Berkeley, California 94710-1409
Spdbooks.org

ISBN: 979-8-88896-565-8

Library of Congress Control Number: 2022950688

Book Design by Adam Rozum

Standing Stone Books is a member of the Community of Literary Magazines and Presses
Clmp.org

Vince Sgambati
SANCTUARIES

For My Son, Jesse

ACKNOWLEDGMENTS

Thank you to Robert Colley and Adam Rozum. I am honored to be published by Standing Stone Books. Major kudos to Adam—the cover is stellar. To my editor, Nancy Keefe Rhodes, for ongoing support and inspiration. Nancy is Syracuse's own Gertrude Stein. To my first readers, Anne Marie Voutsinas and Susie Weiss. And to Anne Marie for readily reading a second and third time. To Phil Memmer & Georgia Popoff from the Downtown Writers Center. To Miriam Camerini for her course *Two People, one womb: The Jews of Italy*. Miriam kindly corresponded with me via zoom and through emails regarding my character Raffaella Tedeschi. I am also indebted to Centro Primo Levi New York and to organizations and individuals that have preserved archival images, transcripts, and videos regarding the Stonewall era, including the West Village, Christopher Street Piers, and early Pride events. A special thankyou to pioneering photojournalists Kay Tobin Lahusen and Diana Davies. The New York Public Library's exhibit *Love & Resistance: Stonewall 50* was outstanding. Thank you to the Sisters of Mercy at Angel Guardian Home for generously opening the campus for me to take in its grounds and buildings and to listen to ghost memories, possibly my own. My deepest gratitude to Susie Weiss for sharing the personal memoir her mother wrote. Susie's mom, Atalia Weiss, was a Holocaust Survivor. After many aborted attempts and through tears, I read her words. May her memory be a blessing.

Naming the hurt is how we begin to repair our broken parts.
　　　　　　　　　　　　–Desmond Tutu

PROLOGUE

On the landing outside Gianni's family's second-floor apartment, above his parents' bakery, his cousin Michael said, "You're not our *real* cousin."

Next, his cousin Peter said, "Our mom said you were adopted."

They took turns bearing their bad news. Michael consoling. Peter taunting.

"Uncle Liberato and Aunt Fina aren't your *real* parents. They adopted you," Michael said—kindly but smug.

"Because your *real* mom didn't want you," Peter said.

And then in unison, "That's why you're not our *real* cousin."

And, for Gianni, having been adopted became synonymous with being unreal or imaginary. He clinched his fists, gnashed his teeth so hard that his jaw felt as if it might snap, and he pressed his bare toe against a crack in the tile floor until an abyss separated him from his not-real cousins. *I'm not real* is what Gianni will remember.

A door opened on the landing above them. A young woman stood at the open door. The pregnant bulge beneath her nightgown parted her pink chenille robe. But motherhood, chenille, and pink were ruses disguising her greed and cruelty.

"What are you two doing?" she said. "I told you to stay away from him."

Gianni's not-real cousins looked at their mother and shrugged, and then Michael looked at Gianni and reached for his arm. Consoling? Or condescending?

"Upstairs now!" Cigarette smoke signaled the woman's anger.

In his apartment, Gianni stared at the twelve-inch television screen—rounded corners, an *RCA Victor*. Mr. Green Jeans planted seeds in a flower pot while Frank Sinatra sang *High Hopes*. Gianni threw himself across the emerald green Queen Ann sofa—his legs wrapped over the scrolled arm, his head tilted backward off the seat cushions. The room turned upside down, and the floor became the ceiling. Rugs and furniture defied gravity, rules blurred, and possibilities inspired.

Yesterday Gianni's uncle had banged at the door to his family's apartment. His father and uncle exchanged heated words, and then Gianni's mother stepped between them to keep the men from punching each other. Gianni's aunt stood on the hallway stairs. She wore the same pink chenille bathrobe, which parted at her baby bump. Gianni couldn't see her, but he heard the exaggerated sound of spitting, and then her words, viler than the antipathy in her voice: "That's your son under my feet."

Most details of yesterday's fight had already burrowed deep within the folds of Gianni's brain, where children hide what frightens them. Only the spitting sound and his aunt's words lingered like niggling vibrations. Gianni didn't know what he had done wrong or at least he couldn't remember, but an adult's anger is always the child's fault.

Gianni not only liked looking at the upside-down room, but he liked singing upside down. He sang along with Frank Sinatra. "Just what makes that little ole ant think he'll move that rubber tree plant…" When you're upside down, tears dampen your forehead instead of your chin.

That night, Gianni and his parents watched the *Ed Sullivan Show* and, during a commercial break, Fina stopped knitting, leaned forward in her rocking chair, and poked Liberato, who stood and turned the television's sound down to a murmur. He returned to the couch. Gianni frowned. His Davey Crockett hat sat askew on his head, and he wore the same pajamas he had worn earlier when he sang aloud with Frank Sinatra.

"Do I have to go to bed already? It's not over yet."

"No, no you don't have to go to bed," Liberato said. "You're a big boy, Gianni."

Gianni nodded. His hat's raccoon tail tickled his neck.

"Third grade already," Liberato said.

Gianni nodded again. He scratched at his neck.

"Do you know what adoption means?"

Gianni nodded a third time, and the chicken cutlet and mashed potatoes he ate for supper rose like lava from his stomach into his throat.

Fina fidgeted with her knitting needles. She and Liberato knew that their sister-in-law Liviana would use Gianni's adoption as revenge for yesterday's fight, but they had underestimated how quickly she'd strike. Had Fina witnessed what took place earlier in the hallway, she'd have smacked Liviana. But for Liviana's baby bump, Fina would have knocked her down the stairs. She had shown restraint the day before when Liviana spit and said, "That's your son under my feet." But Fina would seek revenge in other ways. Every customer in the bakery and neighbor will learn from Fina how despicable Liviana is.

"When you were a tiny baby," Liberato said. He paused and took a deep breath. "Mama and I adopted you."

Fina pulled a tissue from her sleeve. She blew her nose. Liberato took another deep breath and pressed his lips together.

There was the faint sound of, "Plop, Plop, Fizz, Fizz. Oh what a relief it is." Gianni glanced at the black and white image of Speedy standing next to a bubbling glass of water.

In 1959, children were seen and not heard. If heard, they said what pleased and appeased adults, especially adults who were sad.

"It's just that the wrong lady had me," Gianni said. "Can we please turn the television back up?"

Liberato turned up the volume. Father, mother, and son stared red-eyed at Erich Brenn spinning five glass bowls atop tall sticks. Not one of them crashed and shattered. He made it look so easy, but then Brenn wasn't a boy in third grade.

The following week, Gianni's Aunt Liviana and his cousins left to stay with Liviana's parents. A month later, a moving van parked in front of the bakery. Burly men chewing on unlit cigar stubs emptied the third-floor apartment. Gianni sat at the bakery's front window and watched the men load the van: the living room furniture he and his cousins had tied sheets to and made tents, the television where they watched *Lassie*, cartoons, and *Zacherle's Shock Theater*, the double bed where the three of them slept, the kitchen table they had once crawled underneath and tied his uncle's shoelaces together, and then got scolded when his uncle stood and fell, and the crib where the baby bump would soon sleep.

Fina tied a red string around a small white box with the words Paganucci's Bakery on top. She glared out the bakery window. "That bitch thought she was too good to live over a storefront and wanted her own fancy house. That's why she made all this trouble."

Liberato nodded. He turned off the bread slicing machine and looked at his son. "Hey, Gianni, how about we go to a movie on Sunday?"

Gianni looked at his father and smiled. He thought of the last movie they'd seen together, *Pinocchio*. Michael and Peter had joined them. When the theater went dark the boys shot popcorn at each other, and Liberato pretended not to notice. What was it the Blue Fairy had said? "Prove yourself brave, truthful, and unselfish, and someday you will be a real boy."

PART 1

When I was a child, I spoke, thought, and reasoned as a child.
　　　　1 Corinthians 13:11

CHAPTER 1

Gianni froze. Had he erased too much of Sister's perfect cursive from the blackboard? Did chalky water drip from the sponge onto the floor? Was his fly open or his nose running? Could Sister read his thoughts about Sean Doyle? Sean's ears stuck out like twin moons. Why would moon ears make Gianni smile when the moon didn't? But how wonderful, Gianni thought, to sit behind Sean and stare at his moon-shaped ears.

Sister puckered her lips, shook her head, and sighed a second time. Her white wimple fluttered like a sail struggling in the wind.

"She didn't like Catholics, you know," Sister said.

"Who, Sister?"

"Eleanor Roosevelt, child of grace. Your essay is about Eleanor Roosevelt. It's a very good essay, including correct capitalization and punctuation, and your cursive is improving, but Mrs. Roosevelt didn't like Catholics."

"Why didn't Mrs. Roosevelt like Catholics, Sister?"

"I really don't know." Sister returned to making tidy marks on the tidy stack of papers on her tidy desk. Behind her, a statue of the Blessed Virgin Mary stood on a shelf and gazed euphorically at the American flag. A fly buzzed round Mary's crown, landed on her praying hands and, in that jerky stop-and-go way flies walk on three pair of legs, as if each pair has a mind of its own, it lurched down the plaster folds of Mary's blue mantle to her bare and dainty serpent-crushing feet.

Portraits hung on either side of the Virgin Mary. John F. Kennedy and Pope John XXIII. The nuns at Saint Mary Gate of Heaven Elementary

School adored President Kennedy almost as much as they adored Jesus. Gianni's father once said that the Kennedy boys were skirt chasers like their old man. Gianni didn't know what that meant, but it didn't sound like something the Virgin Mary or Pope John would approve of. He didn't mention Liberato's comment to Sister Joan Marie.

Each morning, after reciting ten Hail Marys, which generated a sea of bobbing heads whenever the holy name of Jesus was spoken, Gianni's classmates placed their right hands over their hearts, recited the pledge of allegiance, and then Sister closed her eyes as if she were about to be kissed by Cary Grant or Clark Gable in one of the films on the *Million Dollar Movie*. Gianni and Liberato were great fans of the *Million Dollar Movie*.

"Dear Jesus," Sister said, "keep our President Kennedy in your good graces and help him show that wretched Mr. Khrushchev the errors of Communism."

Wretched was one of Sister's favorite words, especially when talking about lost souls. There seemed to be a lot of them. Sister also loved the word languish, which is what wretched souls did while they waited for Jesus, like when Gianni's mother played solitaire while she waited for the macaroni water to boil.

Gianni said, "Maybe Mrs. Roosevelt was mad at Catholics because being a Protestant she couldn't go to Heaven."

Sister clicked her rosary beads, and if she prayed aloud, Gianni would follow her, "…blessed is the fruit of thy womb Jesus," with a bow of his head and, "Holy Mary, Mother of God…"

Like skirt-chaser, wretched, and languish, Gianni also found "fruit of thy womb" confusing. Fruit of the vine often meant grapes, and there were many arbors in Gianni's neighborhood. He wondered if Mary might have had grapes in her womb. However, he really didn't know where Mary's womb was anyway, so he prayed the rosary without too much thought.

Sister clicked but didn't pray aloud and neither did Gianni, but he continued to ponder Mrs. Roosevelt's grievous sin of disliking Catholics. Surely, her soul must have been wretched and she now languished in purgatory. Gianni fretted over such matters. He once spit out a bite of a perfectly good Nathan's hot dog because he remembered it was Friday. He wore a scapular—even while taking a bath or shower—until the two faded patches of limp rag hung from the frayed string around his neck.

Wearing a scapular guaranteed a speedy entrance into heaven, should he happen to fall and crack his head open in the porcelain tub, which his mother always told him to be careful not to do. Porcelain tubs were a death trap for distractable children like Gianni. And for his twelfth birthday, he asked his parents for an Extreme Unction Crucifix used to give last rites. His parents agreed, though Fina said it would bring bad luck. Liberato reminded her that their dresser, crowded with statues of saints and vigil candles, resembled a medieval shrine.

"That's different!" Fina had said.

Sister stopped clicking and looked up from her papers. "Times are changing. We now have a Catholic President."

Feeling the need to defend Eleanor Roosevelt's honor, if for no other reason than he had written an essay about her, Gianni said, "But Sister, Mrs. Roosevelt said it's better to light a candle rather than curse the darkness."

Sister squared her shoulders, and the crucifix tucked in her apron bib poked out like a joey in a mother roo's pouch. "That's a very nice sentiment, but I'm not sure Mrs. Roosevelt was the first to say it, and of course it's always a sin to curse."

Having ended his essay with the candle quote, and now learning that Mrs. Roosevelt may have plagiarized it, Gianni gave up all hope for a favorable grade. He took a deep breath and, instead of imagining Sean Doyle's moon-shaped ears, he imagined Eleanor Roosevelt standing outside of Heaven's gates. Saint Peter frowned at her. He forbid Mrs. Roosevelt entrance and held up Gianni's essay with a big red F scrawled across the page. Not only was Gianni one of those distractible children at risk of cracking his head open in a porcelain tub, but he was prone to daydreaming.

"Gianni, you're daydreaming again," Sister said—sometimes three or four times in a day.

Tired of Mary's foot, the fly buzzed around Gianni's nose. He swatted at it with the wet sponge, and droplets of chalky water splattered across the back of Sister's gray woolen habit but fortunately went unnoticed.

Outside the classroom door, Colleen Elizabeth Murphy waved her hands as if chasing away mosquitos. Gianni ignored her and resumed washing the blackboards and sills.

"Cleanliness is next to Godliness," Sister Joan Marie always said after he finished, and Gianni smiled and nodded. Unlike Gianni who placed nuns on a pedestal, Colleen didn't like nuns and never smiled at them—not since she'd auditioned four years ago for the part of Mary in a Christmas pageant, and Sister Kathleen Theresa, a third-grade teacher, told Colleen she was too plump to play the Holy Mother.

Colleen Elizabeth held grudges. One nun was as mean as another as far as she was concerned. To make matters worse, when Colleen was in fifth grade another nun overheard her sing: "Give a cheer, give a cheer for the nuns who drink the beer in the cellars of SMGH. They are brave, they are bold for the liquor that they hold in the cellars of SMGH. For it's guzzle, guzzle, guzzle as the beer goes down their muzzle, and you hear their favorite cheer. More Beer!" A full week's detention for that faux pas sealed Colleen's dislike of nuns. Her oldest sister, Pat, tried to temper Colleen's opinions. Pat gave up her own religious calling to care for her younger siblings after their mother passed. Colleen was a toddler at the time and Pat's most spirited challenge.

"Hurry up!" Colleen whispered loud enough for Sister to hear.

"Colleen Elizabeth," Sister said without looking up from her papers, "if a job's worth doing it's worth doing well."

Colleen mouthed Sister's words and shook her ample bottom back and forth. Forgetting that he was holding a wet sponge, Gianni brought his hand to his face to conceal his smile. He stuck out his tongue and gagged.

"All done, Sister Joan Marie," Gianni said. "I just have to empty the bucket."

"Well done, child of grace."

"Yes, Sister." Gianni said. In the hallway, he spit the taste of chalky water into the bucket. Colleen laughed and followed him to the boys' room.

The Kentile floors shone like a mirror. Not a trace of scuff marks or leftover green sawdust that Mr. Murry, the school janitor, used to soak up daily accidents. Pre-Vatican II Catholic children had tiny bladders and weak stomachs. In first-grade classrooms, urine barely trickled beneath the book cubbies and under desk-seats before Mr. Murry miraculously appeared and mopped up the impending puddles and, in hallways, his green sawdust hit the floor before a student's vomit.

Truly an extraordinary janitor. He buffed and burnished the floors with the grace of Fred Astaire dancing across a stage, the floor buffer being his Ginger Rogers.

Gianni stepped from the hallway into the boys' bathroom and told Colleen, "You can't come in here."

"I'm just standing by the door. Who wants to go in your stinky bathroom anyway? Look, I have money for Italian ice." Colleen took off her Buster Browns and held out a shoe, which resembled the open draw of a cash register.

"How can you walk around with money in your shoe?"

"I don't have a choice." Colleen's navy-blue jumper with a pleated skirt had no pockets. "There's no place to put money in these stupid uniforms. At least your pants have pockets. If I had big bazookas like Linda Esposito, I could put money in my bra. She could hide a gazillion dollars in hers."

Sister Joan Marie, her finger pressed to her lips, stepped behind Colleen. With her other hand, she pointed to the open door across the hall.

"Shh…Sister Alphonse is working. You're disturbing her. And, child of grace," Sister looked over her glasses at Colleen, "use appropriate language."

They crossed the hall, peeked into the classroom, and found the ancient Sister Alphonse sitting at her desk and snoring. Her head drooped over an open attendance book. She often fell asleep in the middle of a lesson. Her students would sit perfectly still, waiting for her false teeth to slip, which always woke her. In fifth grade, Colleen bet Joey Colombo that the next time Sister Alphonse dozed, she'd sleep for at least five minutes. At four minutes and forty-eight seconds, Sister's false teeth slipped, and Colleen lost her ice cream money.

"Our dear Sister Alphonse must have been up late last night grading papers," Sister Joan Marie said. "She's a very dedicated teacher,"

Colleen poked Gianni's ribs. Sister took the empty bucket from Gianni. "Thank you. You two can go now."

Ezra Weiss sat at the curb waiting for Gianni and Colleen. An ant carried a crumb of doughnut three times its size, and then paused when it reached the rubber toe of Ezra's high top Keds. Ezra lifted his left then his right foot. The ant passed undisturbed.

"Hey Ezra," Colleen shouted. "Time for Italian ice."

Gianni shook his head. "I don't believe your sister gave you that money. You took it from your Lenten offering box."

Each year, on Ash Wednesday, the nuns at Gate of Heaven gave their students Lenten offering boxes, where the students placed money not spent on treats they gave up for Lent. A fundraiser for mission children. Despite her six older siblings' donations, Colleen usually lost hers or turned in a near empty box. The only thing she gave up for Lent was pretending to give up anything for Lent.

"No, I didn't!" Colleen snapped. "My sister Pat gave me money for washing dishes."

"You don't know how to wash dishes. Whenever there's a party and it's time to clean up, you say you have to go home. Tell her Ezra. Did you ever see Colleen pick up a dirty dish?"

Ezra shrugged his shoulders.

"How many times do I have to tell you my sister gave me the money?"

"You need to put that money in the collection box in church," said Gianni.

Colleen puffed out her cheeks and squinted her eyes. "Fine! I'll put the money for your ice in the collection box, and I'll keep enough money for me and Ezra."

Gianni shook his head a second time. "Come on Ezra, let's follow her and make sure she doesn't steal the collection box."

They ran across 104th Street, beyond Gate of Heaven's large iron gates, through the parking lot, past the rectory, up the stone steps to the church's side entrance. Then with an exaggerated grunt, Colleen pulled open the massive wooden door. They entered the church's cool, quiet nave. The antithesis of the surrounding sundrenched and noisy neighborhood, Gate of Heaven loomed above the two-story houses lining side streets, the second-and-third-floor apartments above storefronts on avenues, and the El where trains rattled from Queens, inbound to Brooklyn and Manhattan or outbound to the Rockaways.

Colleen cupped her hand over a collection box.

"There! You satisfied? Now let's go get some ice."

Gianni asked Ezra if he had heard coins drop. Again, Ezra shrugged his shoulders. Something he often did, given Colleen and Gianni's gift for gab.

"See," Colleen said. "Ezra heard them."

Gianni knelt before the marble altar railing. A larger-than-life crucifix hung above the main altar. During Lent, with the exception of the crucifix, purple cloth covered all icons.

"Oh, now he's gonna pray. It'll be Christmas by the time we get out of here." Colleen grabbed Ezra's hand. "Come on, let's see if we can make Jesus open his eyes."

In fifth grade, Sister Alphonse had shown the film *The Miracle of Our Lady of Fatima*. She slept through most of it, but the story of the Blessed Mother appearing to three peasant children mesmerized Gianni. The following week, he watched *The Song of Bernadette* with Jennifer Jones on the *Million Dollar Movie*. When the movie ended, he telephoned Colleen to exclaim, "The Blessed Mother appeared to Bernadette just like she appeared to the Children of Fatima."

Colleen claimed that once she saw President Kennedy yawn while Sister Alphonse went on and on about diagraming sentences.

Gianni laughed: "That wasn't a miracle. You thought he yawned because you were bored and stared at his picture. Anyway, President Kennedy's not a saint. My father said he's a skirt-chaser."

"What's that?"

"I don't know, but it doesn't sound like something a saint would do."

The next day, Gianni and Colleen entered church hoping to be Ozone Park's version of the Children of Fatima.

"That's Saint Ann," Gianni said. "You can tell because she's holding baby Mary. And that's Saint Theresa, The Little Flower, holding a crucifix and roses, and that's Saint Theresa of Avila. She always looks like she has a migraine."

"What's a migraine?"

"A bad headache like my mother gets."

Colleen rolled her eyes, unimpressed with Gianni's expertise regarding saints. "Just pick one."

Each day, either Colleen or Gianni picked another statue to kneel before and stare. Nothing. Colleen suggested they give the larger-than-life crucifix a try.

Maybe it was the way they had strained their heads backward to look up at the crucifix, or the downward tilt of Jesus' head, or the afternoon light playing peek-a-boo through the stained-glass windows, but Colleen poked Gianni—her mouth agape. At the same moment, Gianni saw Jesus' left eye open. Gianni screamed. Colleen screamed. They tripped over each other, ran out of church, and pushed open the massive side door as if it were made of plywood. Once outside, they panted a cloud of condensed breath. Gianni brought his hand to his chin the way his father did when he was about to say something important.

"That wasn't a real miracle," Gianni said.

"What do ya mean? Didn't you see his eyes open?"

"Yes! But it was like when you were staring at the picture of President Kennedy. If you stare too hard things get all blurry and start to jump around."

"So how do you know that's not what happened to those kids in Fatima?"

"That's different. They weren't staring at a statue. The Blessed Mother just appeared to them on a rock."

"So, now you're saying we should stare at rocks?"

Since that day in fifth grade, whenever Colleen and Gianni grew tired of bike riding or roller skating or stoopball or marbles or whatever they were doing, they climbed Gate of Heaven's side steps, knelt beneath the crucifix over the main altar, and stared until Jesus opened his eyes, or shifted the tilt of his head. Once Colleen said he stuck his tongue out, but Gianni said she was lying.

Colleen told Ezra to kneel next to her and stare up at Jesus. Gianni frowned.

"We're getting too old to play this game."

"Don't listen to him, Ezra. Just keep staring."

The trio stared without blinking. Ezra, whose ears grew faster than the rest of him, had a head full of cowlicks. Colleen, round faced and splattered with freckles. And Gianni, who most resembled Jennifer Jones in *The Song of Bernadette*, with his dark brown eyes and black curly hair. Often raising a single eyebrow and smirking, Gianni appeared ethereal, and one could imagine him far from the city in a forest playing panpipes and dancing on cloven feet.

Colleen tugged at Ezra's sleeve. "Do you see anything yet?"

"No."

"Maybe it's not working because you're Jewish."

Gianni smacked his palm against his forehead. "That doesn't make sense. Jesus was Jewish."

"But then he discovered Catholics," Colleen snapped. "It's because Ezra didn't see either movie, and he's not doing it right."

Colleen pressed the palms of her chubby hands together, tilted her head to the right, and lifted her eyes up to the left. A perfect tableau of the Mary statues in all of Gate of Heaven's classrooms, proving that Colleen was actually the perfect choice to play the Blessed Mother in the third-grade Christmas pageant. Sister Kathleen's casting blunder.

"See, Ezra, you have to do it like this."

"Or we're not seeing anything because we're getting too old for this stupid game," Gianni said.

Colleen twisted her mouth to the side. "You're the one who knelt down first."

"I was praying for Jesus to forgive you for stealing money from the Lenten offertory box."

"I told you, I didn't steal any money. My father gave me money."

"You said your sister gave it to you."

"Shh…" Ezra stared wide-eyed at the crucifix. "I think he just winked at me."

A loud creak startled them. Light faded at the far end of the nave. A door closed slowly behind the silhouette of a tall woman wearing a dark dress.

The children's gaze followed her. She approached a small altar to their right. Her stride proud and confident. She lifted a black lace mantilla from her shoulders and covered her dark wavy hair. But for a brief glance at Gianni, so brief that Gianni maybe imagined it, her eyes stayed on the altar. Gianni recognized her from his parents' bakery. The almond biscotti lady.

She dropped coins in the collection box. The clang echoed in the near-empty church. Gianni thought to mention this to Colleen. Why were Colleen's coins silent?

Like a prima ballerina, the biscotti lady held her head erect atop squared shoulders. She lowered one of the lighting sticks into a flame. Her large hoop earrings glinted. Rows of flickering candles in red glass illuminated and exaggerated her formidable features: large dark eyes, a Greek nose, full red lips. Her skin was alabaster like the faces of marble Madonnas.

In the bakery she was just another customer. But now Gianni wondered, *Do my eyes resemble hers?* Not just in color and shape but as if eyes showed emotions. *That's what carrying the weight of the world on your shoulders looks like,* he thought.

After Gianni's cousins told him he wasn't real, at least that's what he remembered, and then his parents told him he was adopted, people, including strangers, said he looked as if *he* carried the weight of the world on *his* shoulders. But when he looked in a mirror, he saw only his familiar face. Now, staring at the biscotti lady's large, mournful eyes, larger and sadder in the candlelight, he saw what people had seen in him. A chill spread across his shoulders and down his arms.

She didn't kneel before the altar railing or fold her hands in prayer. She simply stood for a few moments of silence, and then turned. No doubt, this time she glanced at Gianni. More than a glance. A recognition of sorrow, which lingered in Gianni's fractured frames of memory: Michael and Peter standing on the landing outside his door, Aunt Liviana wrapped in smoke and looking down at him, moving men loading a van in the shadows beneath the El outside his parents' bakery.

The biscotti lady walked toward the same heavy door she had entered moments earlier.

Ezra whispered, "She goes to my synagogue."

CHAPTER 2

Liberato woke at 4:00, began baking at 4:30, opened the shop at 6:30, and Fina, after making Gianni's breakfast and doing a bit of housework, took charge in the bakery at 10:00 while Liberato went back up to their apartment and napped until noon. Tuesday through Saturday, they closed at 7:00pm, Sunday at 2:00pm, and on Mondays Paganucci's was closed all day.

On Sunday evenings Liberato and Gianni took in a double feature at one of the three neighborhood movie theaters. The Casino, on Liberty Avenue was seven blocks from their bakery. The Lefferts, another twelve blocks away. Or the Crossbay, in the opposite direction on Rockaway Boulevard. Weather permitting, they walked, but if it rained or was too cold, they took the A train: one stop inbound for the Casino, two stops for the Lefferts, or one stop outbound for the Crossbay. Sometimes Fina joined them. It depended on her mood, her migraines, and whether or not she had the patience to sit through a double feature. Mostly, she left after the first movie or came late for the second, depending on which movie interested her.

Their apartment, one floor above the bakery in a three-story building, faced the elevated A train at the corner of Liberty Avenue and 104th Street, Ozone Park, Queens, New York. Next to the bakery, in a dark and narrow shop, the ancient Mr. and Mrs. Friedman and their elderly daughter sold penny candy from display cases smudged from snotty noses and the tiny prints of grimy fingers. Colleen often dreamt that the bent and shriveled couple, each barely five feet tall, chased her through the neighborhood pushing their "ginormous daughter" in a stroller. But nightmares never stopped Colleen from joining Gianni to buy ten cents worth of malted balls (Gianni's favorite) or Bit-o-Honey (Colleen's favorite). Should they have the windfall of a quarter or more between them, they added candy buttons, atomic fireballs, and bottle caps to their pickings.

Beyond Friedman's Candy Store, Mrs. Jack from Jack's Dry Cleaners smoked more than the pressing machine. Next, Bill's hardware pushed everything a do-it-yourselfer might need, including Bill's advice about what his customers were doing wrong, even when they didn't ask, which they mostly didn't. Finally, a laundromat stood at the corner of Liberty Avenue and 105th Street. Above each storefront the windows in second and third floor apartments rattled in their frames when the A train passed along the El. This was often, especially during rush hours. The train's predictable shriek of iron against iron reminded neighbors that, no matter the challenge, life goes on. Another station, another stop—as reassuring and irritating as morning sunlight peeking through closed blinds or around yellowed window shades.

The El shaded the shorter expanse of Paganucci's Bakery windows, which looked out on Liberty Avenue. Over the longer expanse of windows along 104th Street, Liberato lowered a canvas awning on sunny days to protect his baked goods, but also to protect his framed movie posters from fading. A cinephile, with a bias for Italian cinema, Liberato had posters that included films by Visconti, Fellini, De Sica, Rossellini, and also directors less familiar to American audiences, like Mario Mattoli. Liberato once suggested to Fina that they change the bakery's name from Paganucci's to Fellini's or De Sica's. Fina, a sober woman, waved an open hand at her whimsical husband and said, "Changing the name of the bakery will not make you a director. You'll still be stuffing ricotta filling into cannoli shells."

On the white tile wall, directly behind the showcase displaying pasticciotti—Liberato's signature pastry—hung three posters from films starring Anna Magnani: Mattoli's *Assunta Spina*, Visconti's *Bellissima*, and—though not directed by an Italian—Daniel Mann's *The Rose Tattoo*.

When *The Rose Tattoo* aired on the *Million Dollar Movie*. Fina argued that Gianni was too young to watch it. Liberato thought otherwise. "Last year you said he was too young to see Fellini's *La Strata*, but Gianni loved it."

"Don't remind me," Fina said. What other boy names his gold fish Gelsimona, the clownish but soulful character played by Fellini's wife, Giulietta Masina? Fina wiped her fingers on her apron, leaving a glaze of powdered sugar. She threw up her hands. "Do what you want. You'll make that boy as crazy as you. All I need are two jadrools thinking they're Fellini."

Gianni loved *The Rose Tattoo*. When Magnani yelled at Lancaster and threw him out of her house, Gianni whispered to Liberato, "Anna Magnani is funny. She reminds me of Mama."

Liberato chuckled. "That's why I married Mama, but let's keep that between you and me." Given Liberato woke at 4:00, he went to bed as soon as the movie ended, and Gianni asked Fina if Anna Magnani was his birth-mother. Since he had learned he was adopted, fantasy birth mothers from the *Million Dollar Movie* tropes cluttered his daydreams—from distraught women in rags leaving their babies in baskets to fairy tale princesses whose infants were spirited away. Why not a famous Italian actress? It would explain why his father blathered on so about Magnani.

Slicing peppers to fry with sausages and onions for the following night's supper, Fina held out the knife. It's sharp edge glinted with bits of red pepper. Gianni jumped back.

"Who put that crazy idea in your head. Anna Magnani is a puttana. Your mother was a good woman. Even good women make mistakes."

Gianni let the matter drop. He had obviously struck a nerve.

The next morning when Fina entered the bakery she glared at the framed poster of Magnani embracing Burt Lancaster above the pasticciotti. "Ooh! I'm sick of looking at that puttana."

Now, Liberato jumped. He dropped the piece of crumb cake he was dunking into his coffee.

"Do you know what Gianni asked me last night after you went to bed? If that whore is his mother." Fina pointed to the Magnani posters. "Maybe we should light vigil candles and genuflect in front of Madonna Puttana."

"You know how kids are." Liberato attempted to rescue his crumb cake, but it had turned to mush.

"Not all kids think their mother is Anna Magnani. And not all fathers allow their sons to watch these stupid movies. Why can't you take him to a baseball game like a normal father?"

Liberato dumped his coffee into the trash.

Fina slipped a bib apron over her head, wrapped the apron strings around her waist, and tied them in the front. "If not for your brother's bitch of a wife, we wouldn't have had to tell Gianni he was adopted."

"Well, someday we would have—"

Fina cut Liberato off. "These movies give him crazy ideas. He's always asking about his birth mother. A few weeks ago, he asked me if Barbara Stanwick was his mother."

Liberato nodded, "Must have been *Stella Dallas*. It was on the *Million Dollar Movie*. A real tear jerker."

"See! You put all these crazy ideas in his head. Most boys his age don't even know who Barbara Stanwick is, never mind Anna Magnani. They're watching *Bonanza*, not *Stella Dallas* and *The Rose Tattoo*."

"You're his mother," Liberato said.

At this, Fina deflated like a punctured balloon. Her eyes filled.

"Why doesn't he ask who his father was? He wants to replace me."

"That's not it, Fina. You're right, it's the movies and children's stories about motherless little ones. Fathers don't even figure."

Fina took little consolation in Liberato's comments. "In school, Sister said he's barely passing. He was at the top of his class in third grade, before your brother's bitch of a wife made all this trouble. She couldn't stand that he was smarter than the morons she had. Now she's getting exactly what she wanted. Since the fight his grades have been going down and down. That miserable witch put the Malocchio on Gianni."

"You don't believe in that nonsense."

"No, but she does. Because she's an imbecile. An evil imbecile."

The front door to the bakery opened, and a small bell rang. A tall woman entered. Her dark hair, though pinned up, refused to be tamed, and she swept a few unruly strands away from her face. An earring fell from its pierced lobe and caught on her blouse, just above her left breast.

"Ciao, Raffaella," Fina said.

"Buona giornata, Fina."

"Due biscotti coming up, Raffaella," Liberato said. He glanced at the fortunate earring. "I saved the best for you."

Fina rolled her eyes.

Liberato lifted two almond biscotti with a square of wax paper and placed them in a white paper bag, while Raffaella tugged at her earlobe and secured the gold hoop

"Grazie, Liberato." Raffaella smiled, opened her pocketbook, and removed a small beaded change purse.

Twice a week, after Raffaella Tedeschi finished her work at the Saint Mary Gate of Heaven convent, assisting nuns with laundry, house cleaning, and cooking, or whatever chores they required, she walked to Paganucci's bakery, bought biscotti, which Liberato took great care in selecting, and then she climbed the El steps to the Oxford Avenue Station, rode the A train to Boyd, where she changed for the F to Manhattan's Lower East Side.

En route, she encountered at least one, sometimes two or three, subway philanderers. At age forty-two, Raffaella had much experience with unsolicited male attention and had long become expert at ignoring both their unwanted gaze and their crude remarks—more lurid when she approached a pack of them working construction sites, as if steel and reinforced concrete elevated the male libido. No sense getting upset. It will pass like bad weather or a touch of indigestion. Raffaella had endured and survived much more than a lascivious gaze or word.

In her purse, she carried a stainless-steel nail file, pointy enough to eviscerate a pig. Her eyes focused on the words and sentences on whatever page of whatever book she happened to be reading. She rode the subway undisturbed.

At Delancey and Essex, she exited and walked five blocks to The Orchard Cinema, passing street vendors trumpeting the many bargains hanging from outdoor racks or piled in pushcarts. She inhaled the pungent smells rising from crates of produce, barrels of pickles in brine, and trays of fish splayed across shaved ice.

Despite its cracked and crumbling rococo and its peeling blue ceiling with white puffy clouds, The Orchard turned enchanted when the theater went dark and lights shone through countless punctures in the ceiling. A celestial dome of twinkling stars above the surrounding silhouettes of opulent Churrigueresque facades. A woebegone, miniature replica of the Loew's Wonder Theaters, where with little effort Raffaella imagined herself sitting in an exotic courtyard. A refuge from subway philanderers, construction workers, and more.

Despite the small, uncomfortable, horsehair seats, where Raffaella sat with her long legs turned to the side and her ankles crossed, she thought The Orchard a magical place. The smell of mold and popcorn replaced the smells of Delancey Street. Beneath the starlit dome, to the purr of a reel-to-reel projector, Raffaella's ghosts hushed. The more glamourous and extravagant the movie, the more her own story faded.

Hanns Schein managed The Orchard—a Jewish émigré from Austria, barely twenty years old when he came to America. Like many European filmmakers and actors of the time, Hanns settled in Los Angeles. He made a modest living, playing bit parts in Hollywood movies. But mostly he worked box office at a neighborhood theater, until his wife of twenty years died in a car accident and a friend in New York City convinced Hanns to move east.

"Hollywood is dying with the crap they're cranking out now," Saul Rosenthal told him. "Revival theaters are catching on in New York City, and you're just the man to make one work. I found the perfect building. Used to be a Yiddish Theater, but the old timers are gone and their children moved to Long Island. They wouldn't know a herring from a hot dog. Some disrepair in the theater. It's been vacant for years. Maybe a little facelift. Not much. We'll see once we make a little money. In the meantime, we'll keep the lights low. You pick the films and manage the day-to-day affairs, and I'll make you a half-partner. I'll put up the seed money, keep the books, and handle the finances. It's a good thing, Hanns. We'll preserve something we once loved. They don't make movies like they used to."

Hanns knew Hollywood films, and he was a quick study. He learned about New York City's fast-rising Repertory Theaters. The New Yorker, the Bleeker Street Theater, and the long-standing Thalia. He'd stay clear of avant-garde or lesser-known films. The Orchard's niche would be strictly revival, with a focus on Hollywood's Golden Age. He had rubbed elbows with the writers, directors, cinematographers, and actors whose films The Orchard would show. He had Los Angeles connections to help him locate what company or person owned even the most obscure vintage American film. Occasionally he'd show a foreign film, especially Italian cinema for flavor.

Ninotchka, staring Greta Garbo, first lured Raffaella to The Orchard and eventually to Hanns. By then, The Orchard had a fair number of regular customers—mostly people who lived on the Lower East Side who weren't comfortable frequenting the trendier revival theaters in the Village or Uptown. Some films also attracted students from Columbia and seasoned cinephiles. In the small lobby, a display of photographs boasted of Hanns's connections and also hid the stained and faded wallpaper. There he worked the box office beside the candy and popcorn counter.

Raffaella purchased her ticket, and looked at the picture of Hanns standing between Greta Garbo and the writer Mercedes de Acosta.

"Is that you?"

"Yes, it is."

In the black and white photograph, a much younger Hanns, sporting a pencil-thin mustache, grinned like a school boy. The way Garbo leaned into him suggested they had been lovers. Hanns didn't mention that Garbo was more interested in de Acosta than she was in him.

Raffaella reminded Hanns of women he had met at Salk Viertel's salons in Santa Monica. Viertel, the well-known salonaere, entertained Hollywood notables like Garbo as well as unknown emigres from Europe, and she treated all of her guests like fine crystal. Beneath Raffaella's confidence lingered a vulnerability reminiscent of the Jewish emigres at Viertel's—women and men who fled to America after the unimaginable had already consumed Europe.

"Here, you're with Billy Wilder. Yes?"

Charmed by Raffaella's allure and her Italian accent, Hanns stepped from behind the candy counter, pretending to take a closer look though he knew the picture well.

"Correct, that's Billy and me. He has a great sense of humor." Hanns pointed to more pictures and dropped names. Some Raffaella knew. Some she didn't.

"I better find a seat before the movie starts." Raffaella stepped around Hanns and made her way through the doors between the lobby and the theater.

Her presence at The Orchard became routine and, running out of small talk, Hanns asked what she carried in the little white paper bag. "Just curious," he said. He blushed like the young Hanns posing with Garbo almost thirty years ago.

"Biscotti. Would you like to try?" Raffaella held out the open bag. He removed one and took a bite. "Delicious!"

The next time Liberato said, "Due biscotti coming up," Raffaella help up three fingers.

"Tre."

Liberato selected three of the largest biscotti. "Ahh...so you've found an admirer who also likes my baking?"

Raffaella smiled, and an hour later, before she entered The Orchard's theater to see *It Happened One Night* with Claudette Colbert and Clark Gable, she held out the open paper bag to Hanns. "I bought an extra today, if you'd like."

"She goes to my synagogue, not often but occasionally on the High Holy Days, Rosh Hashanah and Yom Kippur," Ezra had said. Ezra's mom knew Raffaella, but then Golda Weiss knew everyone at their synagogue. She was one of those go-to-people if you wanted something done.

Gianni pondered Ezra's words while he helped Liberato carry trays of warm rolls, coffee cake, and Danish from the large kitchen behind the bakery to their respective display cases. He wondered why a Jewish woman would light a candle in a Catholic Church. If she went to Ezra's synagogue, she must Jewish. Maybe? Maybe not? Ezra was Jewish and he too was in Gate of Heaven. Of course that was different. He didn't enter the church of his own accord, and he certainly didn't choose to kneel at the altar railing. That was Colleen's doing. The woman neither knelt nor made the sign of the cross, both customary after lighting a candle. She simply stood for a few moments and appeared to be more in thought than prayer. All very confusing. Gianni recalled the weight in her eyes, as painful as the weight of the world. And his memory included more than picturing her dark, mournful eyes; it was visceral. He felt her sorrow, even though he didn't know what pained her so, as if he understood without knowing. Sometimes understanding has little to do with knowing. You may know a lot of information, but if it never moves from your head to your heart you'll never understand. And sometimes an expression, a tilt of the head, a heaviness in the eyes goes right to your heart, and you understand without knowing anything. Lost in these thoughts and feelings, Gianni carried a tray of jelly doughnuts and backed out through the swinging door from the kitchen into the bakery. Liberato carried a wire basket of warm Kaiser rolls. He pushed through the same swinging door.

"Papa, you know that lady who always buys biscotti?"

"Yes, what about her?" Liberato dumped the rolls into a larger basket on a shelf behind the counter. Poppy seeds scattered on the tile floor.

"I saw her in church yesterday. She lit a candle before a statue of the Blessed Mother, but Ezra said she goes to his synagogue."

"Is that a problem?" Liberato brushed seeds from his apron.

Gianni considered his father's question and shrugged his shoulders. He didn't think it was a problem, but merely a curiosity. Something to wonder about, but then wondering seemed to be something adults had little time for. The bakery's front door flew open.

"Looocy, I'm home!"

Gianni glanced at the large round clock above the Anna Magnani posters while Colleen laughed at her imitation of Ricky Ricardo.

"About time. We're gonna be late for Mass, and Sister's gonna be mad."

During Lent, the nuns at Saint Mary Gate of Heaven expected their students to attend Mass each morning before class. To ensure one hundred percent attendance, Sister Joan Marie wielded peer pressure.

After the pledge of allegiance, morning prayers, including a supplication for the protection of President Kennedy and the demise of Communism, and before Sister taught a lesson from the Baltimore Catechism, when she asked questions like "Why did God make us?" for which there was only one correct answer, Sister Joan Marie stood before the classroom world map and held out her wooden pointer.

"Children of grace, do we see any classmates who weren't at Mass today?" She already knew the answer since she took attendance at Mass, and woe to the child who overslept but was foolish enough to come to school. Better to feign a terminal illness than face Sister's scowl and the wrath of Catholic children suffering Lenten sugar withdrawal. Then Sister placed another gold star on the map, forming a trail from New York City to Haiti, as if she and her students were missionaries charting their course to a place where, according to Sister, there were many wretched souls in need of saving. Should the gold-star trail reach Haiti before Easter vacation, students could bring in treats for a party on the last school day before the long break. Gianni and his classmates loved class parties, and they loved Sister's mission stories, especially stories about zombies or mothers who sacrificed their newborn infants on blood-altars and levitated above the abominations they had committed.

Colleen eyed the baked goods. "We have plenty of time to get to church."

As he did every morning, Liberato told her to pick whatever she wanted, and she chose a jelly doughnut from the tray Gianni held.

"You'll get powdered sugar all over your uniform," Gianni said.

"Will not." Colleen bit into the doughnut and proved Gianni right.

"Come on. You can finish that on the way." Gianni placed the tray of doughnuts on a shelf in a display case and grabbed his bookbag. "See you later, Papa."

"Geez—goodbye, Mr. Paganucci. Thanks for the jelly doughnut," Colleen mumbled with a mouth full of doughnut, and more powdered sugar rained down on her navy-blue uniform.

Mass had already begun when Gianni and Colleen slipped into the pew behind Sister Joan Marie. Several girls with fancy handkerchiefs pinned to their white blouses and sparkly barrettes in their hair looked aghast at Colleen's uniform. Obviously Colleen hadn't given up sweets for Lent. She brushed at the powdered sugar with the palms of her hands, making matters worse, and then stuck her tongue out at the girls.

In their classroom, Sister led the pledge of allegiance, then morning prayers, and finally she picked up her wooden pointer and approached the gold-star map.

"We have another gold star today, but let's remember, children of grace, there is a time for everything under heaven, and when it's time to attend Mass, we must be punctual. Being late is rude to Jesus."

Sister bowed her head, as did all thirty-seven of her students. When Sister turned to press the gold star to the map, most of the class frowned at Gianni and Colleen. Gianni sank low in his seat, but then smiled when Sean Doyle turned around, looked at him, and winked. Maybe Gianni should be late for Mass more often. Colleen looked around the room as if she had no idea why her classmates were frowning.

Despite Eleanor Roosevelt's dislike for Catholics, Gianni did well on his essay—ninety-five percent and a gold star. Startled, Gianni looked at Sister Joan Marie. She smiled and said, "God has given you a gift. Treasure it."

He wasn't sure what Sister meant by gift. *My writing or my grade?* Gianni thought.

Fina taped it to one of the large refrigerators in the bakery kitchen, next to a personal narrative Gianni had written about Fina having had a hysterectomy last summer. So laden with grief were his words that Sister Joan Marie thought Fina passed away and was much relieved when Fina showed up at parent-teacher conferences looking remarkably robust for a dead woman. Watching *Million Dollar Movies* gave Gianni a flair for embellishment. Writing remained the exception to what, since fourth grade, his teachers referred to as underachievement.

"Very good." Fina poured Gianni a glass of milk. "Words matter. Maybe someday you'll write for a newspaper." She handed Gianni the glass, lifted a broom, and swept the spotless black and white dot-mosaic tile floor.

On the butcher block counter, a tray of oblong choux pastry shells waited to become eclairs.

Gianni sat on a stool next to the pastry shells and considered Fina's words.

"You mean like Cary Grant?"

Fina swept invisible crumbs onto a dustpan. "Cary Grant?"

"Yeah, like in *His Girl Friday*, with Rosalind Russell."

Fina sighed. "You have the Seder dinner tonight at Ezra's. I put your dress clothes on your bed. Change out of your school clothes before you go. Do you have homework?"

While Gianni finished his milk he recalled Cary Grant and Rosalind Russell's perfectly timed quips.

"Yes, Mama, I think I'd like to be a journalist. That's what Cary Grant called them. Journalists. Did you know that Eleanor Roosevelt didn't like Catholics?"

"Did Cary Grant tell you that too?" Fina dumped the empty dust pan into the trash.

"No. Sister Joan Marie said so. But she still gave me ninety-five percent and a gold star."

"Well you deserved your grade. I have to go back in the bakery so your father can fill the eclairs. Did you hear me when I mentioned that your clothes for tonight are on your bed?"

Gianni nodded. Seconds after Fina pushed her way out of the kitchen through the swinging doors, Liberato pushed his way in.

"Hi, Gianni. Good day at school?" Liberato opened one of the refrigerators, removed a large bowl of vanilla custard, and placed it on the counter next to the tray of pastry shells. "Mama said you're going to a Seder tonight. Is Colleen going?"

"No, she made up some stupid excuse. She didn't like it last year. She said all that reading and having to sit still and listen felt like school. And she got too hungry with all the waiting. I knew she wouldn't go again. She said that she has to help her sister do laundry, which I know is a lie."

Liberato chuckled. He pressed his fingertips against a pastry shell, cool from the breeze coming through the screen door and open windows.

Outside, in postage-stamp gardens, daffodils bowed before concrete Marys, windowpanes displayed cardboard cutouts of colorful Easter eggs and jovial bunnies, and Mezuzahs were affixed to several doorposts. Neighbors along 104th Street valued tradition.

Gianni stood, grabbed his schoolbag, and placed his empty glass in the sink. "I almost forgot. Sister Joan Marie asked if I would help some lady who works in the convent."

With the precision of a pâtissier, Liberato sliced each pastry shell lengthwise.

"But she said I have to ask you first if it's okay."

"Where does she live?"

Gianni held out a slip of paper. Liberato glanced at Sister Joan Marie's perfect cursive.

"You know who this is. Miss Tedeschi. Raffaella Tedeschi. You said you saw her lighting a candle in church. Sure, you can help her. She's a nice woman."

Gianni looked at the paper. He hadn't read it before showing it to Liberato, not that he would have recognized the name. He smiled at the name Raffaella Tedeschi. The sound of it went well with *starring* or *featuring* or *introducing*.

CHAPTER 3

Behind Paganucci's stood eight attached row houses. Each with a bay of three windows on the first and second floor flats facing 104th Street. Rear windows looked out on small yards. Next, double row houses shared internal walls. Windows along external sidewalls looked across narrow driveways at the neighboring row house. Across 104th Street were more doubles, with the exception of two free-standing houses closer to 103rd Avenue. One, an old farmhouse converted into a two-family and the other a dilapidated wood-framed bungalow, which the neighborhood children called the spook house.

On warm afternoons, the spook house's octogenarian owner sat on his dilapidated porch, in an even more dilapidated cane rocking chair. His bottom poked through the frayed webbing while he ate hard boiled eggs and rye bread and drank seltzer water from green glass siphon bottles delivered by the case. A line of empty bottles stood on the porch next to a screen door with more holes than screen.

A parrot, perhaps as old as the man, perched on the back of his chair. The foul-mouthed bird screeched a torrent of curse words whenever the neighborhood children came too close, which they often did when summer daylight exhausted their creativity. When the parrot dropped f-bombs, they'd fall to the ground laughing.

Norway maples—whitewashed each spring to deter boring insects and pruned up high enough for firetrucks and mobile amusement rides like sky swings, Ferris wheels, and whips to pass under—arched over 104th Street and shaded the row houses, the old converted farmhouse, the dilapidated wood-framed bungalow, the old man, his parrot, and the mischievous children rolling in hysterics on the concrete sidewalks.

Ezra's family lived in one of the double row houses midway between Liberty Avenue and 103rd Ave. The neighbor's house and family mirrored Ezra's. First floor: husband, wife, and younger children. Second floor: widowed grandmother and older grandchildren. In Ezra's house, the widowed grandmother was Mr. Weiss's mother. In the Conti household, the widowed grandmother, Anna Ricci, was Mrs. Conti's mother. The Weisses were Russian Jews, the Contis Italian Catholics.

On summer afternoons, the two matriarchs, Esther Weiss and Anna Ricci, sat on web-strap beach chairs in front of their attached row houses. They chatted and eyed passersby rushing to and from the corner train station—a geriatric neighborhood watch. In summer evenings, the number of neighbors sitting with them grew and spanned generations. Fresh coffee, half and half, sugar, and hot cups were plentiful.

Women disagreed about how to make the best lasagna or brisket or corned beef, while men argued about clapboard versus shingles versus vinyl siding versus brick, and whether or not the Mets would ever win a game. Everyone agreed that life wasn't what it used to be.

Fina rarely engaged in stoop-sitting or neighborhood chatter, but Liberato occasionally indulged, bearing a box of cookies—assorted Italian and a few rugelach—and steered conversations toward topics that engaged the men and women. Children played ringolevio, red light green light, hide and seek, or Simon Says. Teenagers played Johnny on a Pony or gathered around stoops in a cloud of cigarette smoke.

When Esther Weiss opened the front door, Gianni handed her a box of macaroons tied with red string.

"Come in, come in."

Gianni followed her down the long hallway, past the staircase to the second-floor apartment, and into a galley kitchen. Beyond the old woman's puff of white hair, resembling a dandelion gone to seed, Ezra's mother, Golda, spooned matzah balls from a pot of boiling saltwater into the adjacent pot of chicken soup.

"Look what such a handsome young man in a nice suit and tie brought us," the older Mrs. Weiss said. She held out the box of cookies. Golda looked above her steam-fogged glasses.

"Papa made them," Gianni said. "They're macaroons."

"Thank you, Gianni. And no doubt delicious. We're about to sit down."

People sat or stood around the dining room table, extended with leaves and a card table into the living room and just short of Ezra and his younger brother Jeffrey's bedroom—once a screened porch but closed in during the 1950's residential air conditioner boom. The dining room and living room throbbed with boisterous conversations.

Ezra called Gianni to sit next to him. "Why are you all dressed up?"

"My mother's idea." Gianni tugged at his tie.

He recognized most of the folks present, including Mr. Weiss's brother, sister-in-law, and twin daughters—redheads like their mother. Ezra's cousins looked nothing like Ezra and his siblings, who more resembled Gianni—dark hair and eyes, olive complexions. Ezra's uncle, whose voice boomed above everyone else's, worked in the diamond district in Manhattan. His wife reminded Gianni of Rita Hayworth in the movie *Gilda*. The twins, miniature versions of their mother, wore identical frocks and jingly charm bracelets.

Joseph Weiss, no resemblance to his brother in appearance or tone, asked everyone to take their seats, and Golda, about as different from Rita Hayworth as a woman could be, carried a box of matches into the dining room. Gianni recognized a few other guests, with the exception of an elderly couple Golda introduced as Mr. and Mrs. Leichtman, friends from their synagogue. Golda and her oldest daughter lit the two candles on the credenza, brought their hands to their faces, and prayed, "Baruch Atah Ado-nai, Elo-heinu—"

Joseph extended his hand and spoke of the food on the Seder plate symbolizing the harshness of slavery, tears, sacrifice, and ultimately hope and renewal. He then held up his glass of wine. Everyone followed. The children held up glasses of grape juice and recited the Kiddush blessing in Hebrew. Golda paused after each word so little Jeffrey could follow. Gianni whispered along, reading the English translation in his copy of the Haddagah: "Blessed are You, Lord our God—"

A soft-spoken, understated man, Joseph grew more animated as he proceeded with the Passover Seder. He encouraged the children to question. They not only asked questions but also questioned answers, and Joseph smiled and nodded. *Maybe he's a teacher*, Gianni thought. He had never asked Ezra about his father's work.

Gianni had told Sister Joan Marie that he was going to a Seder, and she explained that years ago Father Marlo, the assistant pastor at Saint Mary Gate of Heaven, once helped Jews gather for Seders in secret. Sister shook her head. "He was in Italy. A very dark time and many Jews lived in hiding." She didn't elaborate, but Gianni recalled Sister's mournful look. He wanted to ask Joseph Weiss what Sister had meant by a dark time, but he felt foolish raising his hand and didn't know how else to interrupt the rhythm of questions and answers.

Joseph spoke of the ten plagues, and Gianni recalled Charleston Heston in the movie *The Ten Commandments*. He imagined Joseph, slight of build, growing in height and brawn, threatening Yul Brynner, and turning a staff into snakes or lowering his staff into the Nile and turning the river to blood. Tension built. To engage the young children, Joseph reached into a paper bag and tossed small rubber frogs, and vermin, and locusts onto the table. When he spoke of the slaying of the first born, Gianni stared at the shag carpet fearing green smoke, which symbolized the angel of death in the Paramount movie. Tension broke when everyone sang, "Dai, da-ye-nu," and Gianni felt much relieved.

Ezra leaned close to Gianni. "Last year I thought Colleen would explode."

Gianni chuckled, and Golda smiled at the boys. Jeffrey sat on her lap eating matzah, but most of the matzah crumbs fell on Golda's white, cotton blouse while he played with the plastic toys Joseph had tossed on to the table. *She's prettier than Rita Hayworth*, Gianni thought. *Like a lot of the mothers on 104th Street. Pretty without being fancy.* He pictured Raffaella lighting the candle in Gate of Heaven.

After eating small sandwiches of matzah, maror, and charoset, Joseph said, "In life we have sweet moments of blessings and bitter moments of challenges." Gianni coughed from having added too much horseradish to his. The Rita Hayworth twins giggled. Dinner was served.

Again, the dining and living rooms bubbled with talk. Golda and her daughters served matzah ball soup, followed by gefilte fish, and then the main course: brisket, roasted chicken, potato kugel, tzimmes (made with sweet potatoes, carrots, and prunes). Ezra and Gianni passed on the gefilte fish, but made up for it with potato kugel. During dessert, everyone praised Liberato's macaroons, which the older Mrs. Weiss had arranged on a silver platter. The Rita Hayworth sister-in-law brought a red fingernail to her red lips and said the cookies were scrumptious.

"You should taste his rugelach," the old Mrs. Weiss said. "Better than Dombrowski's on 114th Street. I never liked Dombrowski anyway." She wrinkled her nose and mouth and pushed her hands forward as if hitting a volleyball.

Joseph laughed. "And what do you have against poor Mr. Dombrowski? I worked for him when I was a boy. Remember?"

"Yes! And that's why I don't like him. He worked you like a mule. Not even a piece of bread did he offer you—Hannah, eat a macaroon."

Hannah Leichtman reached for a cookie, her crepey skin speckled like a robin's egg. Above her thin wrist, speckles became numbers. Gianni blinked several times, and then looked to her left at her husband. His hands were folded on his lap.

"Mmm." Hannah nodded and smiled. "A beautiful Seder." She looked at Gianni and stretched out her arm, speckled and numbered, her fingertips holding a remaining piece of macaroon. "Beautiful." Gianni heard, *Do this in memory of me.*

Hannah's husband slowly moved his head, looking from one face to the next, as if he just noticed the people around him. "Gut Yontif," he said wishing all a good holiday. His voice cracked. He brought a linen napkin to his eyes. His jacket receded. Above his wrist were numbers similar to his wife's.

As if he'd witnessed something he shouldn't, Gianni looked away, but then found himself studying everyone's arms, including little Jeffrey's. Were these numbers a secret code Ezra never told Gianni about? Little Jeffrey lay still. He had fallen asleep with his head pressed against Golda's breast, his arms free of numbers. Just little boy scratches from playing with sticks, climbing monkey bars, or falling off park swings.

After welcoming Elijah and downing the fourth glass of grape juice, Gianni excused himself and thanked Golda and Joseph Weiss for inviting him. Old Mrs. Weiss gave him a hug. "Such a handsome boy," she said. Gianni chewed the corner of his lip.

Ezra walked him to the front door. A stray cat sat on the stoop. "Go away. You're not Elijah."

"The Seder was fun," Gianni said.

Ezra shrugged his shoulders. "I like the kugel and the charoset."

"Me too, and that stuff with the sweet potatoes."
"Tzimmes."
"Yeah, that. How do you remember all those names?"
"Same way you remember cannoli and pasticciotti."
"True, but you also know all those prayers in Hebrew."
"It's like when you became an altar boy and had to learn Latin."
Gianni brought his hand to his chin. "They're gonna change all that. No more Latin."
"How come?"
"I dunno. Guess they wanna make it easier to be a Catholic. Maybe they'll make it easier to be Jewish too."
"I doubt it."
The cat ran under Ezra's uncle's Cadillac Seville, parked in front of the house. It watched Gianni leave Ezra's stoop and approach the sidewalk.
"Oh! I just remembered." Gianni paused, turned and caught Ezra's attention before Ezra closed the front door.
"Remember that woman we saw in church. You said she goes to your synagogue."
"Yes."
"I'm going to be helping her with something. Not sure what. Is she a nice lady?"
"I don't know. I've only seen her a few times. Never talked to her. I can ask my mom."
"Nah, it's okay. I was just wondering. See you later."
Walking home, Gianni replayed scenes from the Seder: Golda ladling matzah balls from the pot of saltwater into the soup, Joseph tossing rubber vermin, Jeffrey dropping matzah crumbs on his mother's blouse, the old woman holding out the piece of macaroon, the old man patting his eyes with a napkin. *How could it be that only Catholics go to heaven?* Gianni thought. *Mr. Weiss knows a lot about God. Wasn't the Last Supper a Seder? Even Sister Joan Marie said Father Marlo had helped with Seders. What fun would heaven be without Ezra? Maybe Colleen won't be there, but that's for other reasons.*

Gianni spotted his mother. Her hair in rollers and wrapped in toilet paper, Fina sat at an open window above the bakery kitchen looking out on 104th Street. Her elbows pressed into a pillow on the window's sill. Gianni looked up through his thoughts and waved.

"Papa's sleeping. Don't ring the doorbell, I'll just buzz you in."

Gianni turned the corner onto Liberty Avenue. He barely heard the buzzer over the racket of a passing train, but he pushed open the door between the bakery and Friedman's candy store, stepped into the tiny vestibule, and pushed open the second door. Standing on the landing outside their apartment, Fina pressed her finger to her lips.

Gianni removed his jacket and tie, sat at the kitchen table, and listed the events of the evening to Fina.

"Remember to tell Papa they liked his cookies." Fina poured half and half in her coffee.

"I will." The A train passed, and Gianni stared at the flashing lights through the kitchen window.

"There was something I forgot to ask Ezra. The two people from their church, I mean their synagogue. It looked like they had numbers on their arms. They were old, at least as old as Ezra's grandma. Maybe older."

Fina lowered her cup of coffee and pushed her glasses up on her nose. By now the train was a distant rumble.

"Where are they from?" Fina said.

"I don't know. They sounded like Ezra's grandma except more. I mean their accent was stronger. You know like when people who just come from Italy have more of an accent than people who are here for a while. But they didn't have an Italian accent."

"They had probably been in the camps."

Gianni furrowed his brow. "The camps?"

"Yes." Considering Gianni's age, Fina measured her words. In short, Fina said that six million Jews were murdered by Nazis in World War II. Millions of the six million in concentration camps. Millions in gas chambers.

Gianni scratched at his cheek until his fingertips remained pressed against his parted lips.

"Mr. Weiss mentioned the Holocaust and Pogroms after he talked about Moses bringing the Jews out of slavery in Egypt, but I didn't understand everything he said."

Fina removed her glasses and rubbed the tiny pink imprints on either side of her nose.

"Mama, how could this happen?"

"Nazis! Hitler!" Fina wore the same disgusted expression she had worn when she said Anna Magnani was a puttana. "But a lot of people allowed it. A lot of people looked the other way. That's always the problem. No matter how evil one man is, he can do only so much damage. Hitler didn't murder six million Jews by himself. Your grandpa, my father, had a lot of Jewish friends. Terrible stories. Many terrible stories."

"What religion were Nazis?"

"I don't know. Christians, I guess. It's hard to think that a Nazi could be a religious person. But not all religious people are good people, Gianni. That doesn't sound right, but it's true."

"Were some Nazis Catholic?"

"Maybe. I don't know."

"Can Jews go to heaven, Mama?"

Liberato entered the kitchen bleary eyed and carrying an empty glass. His slippers scuffed against the linoleum.

"Did we wake you?" Fina said.

"No. I had to go to the bathroom, and now I want some water." He turned on the faucet and let the water run cold.

"Your son has a question," Fina said.

"Did you have a nice time tonight, Gianni?"

"Papa, can Jews go to heaven?"

Liberato filled his glass and looked at Fina.

She raised her eyebrows and shook her clasped hands. Sign language for *He's your son with all these crazy questions.*

Liberato took a sip of water, another, and then another. He brought his free hand to his chin. "Did Jesus, Mary, and Joseph go to heaven?" He took a final sip of water, said goodnight, and then shuffled back to his bedroom.

Gianni, eyes wide and mouth open, looked from his father shuffling out of the kitchen to his mother finishing her coffee, and then placing the empty cup back in a saucer, as if nothing of importance had just been said.

Papa's right! Gianni thought. *Of course Jesus, Mary, and Joseph went to heaven. And the apostles. Probably not Judas, but so did John the Baptist, and Moses. Jews can go to heaven, and so did Eleanor Roosevelt.* He watched Fina carry her cup to the sink. *And you're not my real mother. And Papa's not my real father.*

Gianni no longer wanted to think about the Holocaust, or the numbers on the old couple's arms. He especially didn't want to think about the night Liberato said, "Mama and I adopted you." One question leads to another. That's what's unsettling about questions. They pester you until what you once thought was true becomes a lie.

The nuns at Gate of Heaven had taught Gianni that in order to go to heaven people must be baptized or their souls will linger in limbo. *So all the Jews who weren't baptized, but then murdered by people who were baptized, were now in limbo*, Gianni thought. *More lies.*

Desperately wanting to change the subject, Gianni said, "Mama, did Papa tell you that I'm going to help Miss Tedeschi? You know, the lady who buys biscotti. I'm not sure what I'll be doing, but I guess she needs help moving boxes or something."

"Yes, he did tell me. A good thing to do."

Gianni's breathing calmed.

CHAPTER 4

A deep porch traversed the back of the convent and overlooked a garden where a brick path meandered through burgeoning pale green leaves dappled with yellow forsythias, narcissus, and daffodils. Soon tulips would add bolder colors to the tranquil space, then peonies, irises, roses, daylilies, and hydrangeas. A perennial bouquet that had awakened not long ago to snowdrops and crocuses and come late autumn would doze under frost-covered mums and a lingering rose or two until winter's deep sleep. On a bench, amid the flowers, near a small statue of St. Francis with a tiny bird perched on his shoulder and a wolf curled at his feet, sat an elderly nun. Asleep, her head tilted left and her white wimple shined luminous in the sun.

Gianni followed Sister Joan Marie past the sleeping nun and under a clothesline stretched between the trunk of a gnarly pear tree with clusters of paperwhite blossoms and the deep porch where Raffaella Tedeschi leaned over the railing and hung sheets with wooden clothespins. A procession of white sails welcomed the mild breeze.

In her bib apron like those Gianni's parents wore in the bakery, and a kerchief covering her hair and tied at the nape of her neck, Raffaella reminded Gianni of the women in photographs from the old country. "Old country" were the words Fina used when speaking of family in Italy.

Sister Joan Marie placed her hand on Gianni's shoulder. "Miss Tedeschi, this is Gianni Paganucci, the boy I recommended to help you with your move. I know he won't disappoint me."

Raffaella cocked her head slightly, and then smiled. "Yes, the baker's son."

"I'll leave you two to become acquainted." Sister took her bag from Gianni and disappeared into the dark cool of the convent. Gianni watched her leave. He wondered what she thought about when she wasn't saying the rosary or grading papers.

"Let me hang this last sheet and we'll talk," Raffaella said.

Despite her kerchief and apron, Raffaella held herself like royalty. In Saint Mary Gate of Heaven's flickering candlelight, Gianni felt he could look at Raffaella forever and never tire. He felt the same way on this sundrenched porch. Was it her height, her posture, something about her features, or something beyond the physical? A confidence, like a leading actress who could meet the challenge of any role.

"Finito!" Raffaella removed her apron. The top buttons of her dress had opened, and Gianni looked away while she fastened them. He recalled a poster hanging in his family's bakery, the De Sica/Ponti film *Two Women*, which showed the ravaged Sophia Loren crouched and crying. Her dark dress torn at the shoulders. In the background, her young daughter cowered. Another movie that Fina had said Gianni was too young to see. But again Liberato disagreed. When Gianni asked his father what the allied Moroccan soldiers had done to the mother and daughter, Liberato said, "Something decent men would never do to a woman. Only animals act like that."

"Do some men act like animals?" Gianni had said.

Liberato answered yes. "Yes, men who are brutes."

Raffaella removed her kerchief and twisted her hair into a bun. She sat on a wicker rocking chair and motioned to another for Gianni to sit. "Sedere!"

He sat and held his book bag on his lap.

"I'm moving from my second-floor apartment to the first floor. Silly, yes? But the kitchen door opens to the yard, and I can have a garden. You like gardens?"

Gianni nodded.

"The landlord said I can plant whatever I want. Now the yard is filled with weeds and babbaluci." As if directing an orchestra, Raffaella talked with her hands. Fina did the same, but mostly when angry.

"Sister said you're a good worker. Your father makes you work in the bakery? Yes?"

Gianni nodded again.

"Good. Too many children sit in the house and watch television."

"Oh, I do that too. So does my father."

Raffaella laughed. "Me too. You can't work all the time. The moving men come on Friday to carry my furniture downstairs, but you can help me carry boxes. You look like a strong boy."

Heat rose in Gianni's neck and ears. "Yes, I can carry boxes."

"Good! And your parents? They are good with you helping me?"

"Oh, yes. My father said you are a very nice lady."

Raffaella smiled and reached for the empty laundry basket. Gianni noticed purple numbers on her left forearm, more distinct than the numbers on the Leichtman's diaphanous skin. Gianni's stomach turned. He lowered his eyes.

Raffaella stood. "Friday, after school. Si?"

"Si." Gianni said.

"You speak Italian?"

"No, not really. Just a few words."

"Bene! A few words are better than no words. Ciao." Raffaella propped the empty wicker basket against her hip. The basket swayed as she walked. She entered the convent, closed the French doors behind her and, like Sister, disappeared into the convent's cool darkness.

The sleeping nun awoke when Gianni rushed past her, and he barely mumbled, "Good afternoon, Sister Alphonse." He feared he might vomit.

Once out of the yard, Gianni ran home. Out of breath, he slammed open the screen door to the bakery kitchen.

Startled, Liberato dropped a cannoli shell and squirted ricotta filling on the butcher block counter. "Gianni, what's the matter?"

Gianni threw down his book bag, ran to his father, wrapped his arms around him, and sobbed.

"Gianni, Gianni, what's the matter? What happened?"

"Mama told me about the Nazis. How can they do that?"

"Do what, Gianni? That was a long time ago."

Fina pushed open the swinging doors, one foot on either side of the threshold, so she could keep an eye on the bakery.

Between sobs, Gianni uttered, "Miss Tedeschi—I went to meet Miss Tedeschi after school—She has numbers on her arm, Papa—Numbers like the old people at the Seder—Was she in the camps too, Papa?"

Liberato looked at Fina. She clasped her hands together and shook them.

"That all took place in other countries," Liberato said. "World War II ended a long time ago—Miss Tedeschi is safe now. She came to America and no one will hurt her here."

Gianni heard Sophia Loren's screams in the movie *Two Women*. He saw her torn dress. *Something no decent man would ever do. Only animals. Only brutes.* Gianni threw up on Liberato's apron.

"Minga!" Fina let go of the door and ran to the sink. She soaked a towel with cool water, embraced Gianni, and wiped his face.

The bell rang in the bakery. Liberato removed his soiled apron and peeked out through the swinging doors. "Aspetta! We'll be there in a minute."

That night, Gianni lay in bed struggling to understand. After Fina had first told him about the camps, he looked up Holocaust and Nazis and antisemitism and Hitler and Auschwitz in their *Encyclopedia Britannica*, and one reference led to another like a serial horror story.

He fell asleep but woke to the sound of the A train rumbling past his bedroom window. He heard the cries of Jews—men, women, and children calling out for him to help them. Half-asleep and terrified, he stumbled out of bed, looked out his window, and saw faces pressed against the train's blood-streaked windows, mouths agape and twisted. Faces turned familiar: old Mrs. Weiss, Golda, Joseph, Ezra and his sisters, even little Jeffrey cried for Gianni to help him. *They're taking us to the gas chambers*, they screamed. But all he could do was pray. *God, why didn't you hear their prayers?* he thought. "Jews are God's chosen people," he remembered Joseph saying. But what kind of God allows his chosen people to be murdered?

Gianni climbed back into bed, buried his face in his pillow. Eventually, he fell back asleep, only to wake again in the middle of another nightmare where Raffaella lit a candle in Gate of Heaven church, and soldiers wearing red bands with swastikas on their arms grabbed her and dragged her away. She screamed, *Gianni, help me!* Nazis floated above him and stared down with terrifying grins and all around him lay the horrible abominations Nazis had committed. Gianni screamed. The light went on in his bedroom. Liberato and Fina sat at the edge of his bed. Fina pressed him to her breast and Liberato smoothed back Gianni's sweat-soaked curls.

CHAPTER 5

Waiters dropped cloth napkins and silverware on tables and yelled orders from the narrow dining room to the kitchen where Mama Luna added basilico, cut fresh from Mama's herb garden, to the gravy. Raffaella sipped chianti from a jelly glass.

"Per favore! What time is it?"

The waiter looked at his watch. "Five minutes past seven, signora."

She massaged the knot in her neck. Had Raffaella met Hanns someplace other than The Orchard, where movies lightened her spirit and lowered her guard, would she have said yes to dinner? Buying him biscotti, she may have encouraged his interest. She knew better. She finished her glass of wine, opened her purse, and removed a few dollars from her wallet to leave for the waiter.

"Sorry I'm late. Saul's son was supposed to cover the box office for me, but you know how boys are." Hanns wore a dark blue blazer and smelled of aftershave.

Yes, Raffaella knew how boys are. Boys with noble and not so noble ideas. She knew boys who hated Fascism and boys who loved it. Boys who thought Mussolini and his efficient fascist regime were the best thing to happen to Italy. And she also knew boys who gave their lives resisting Mussolini and all that he stood for. Boys like Marcello, with his gypsy eyes and a sculptor's hands. She once melted at Marcello's touch and at his scent of almond blossoms and earth. But there were also the fair-haired boys of the Third Reich with baby faces but brutish hearts. Raffaella knew only too well how boys are.

She slipped the money back into her purse.

"Saul?" she said.

"Yes, my partner's son." Hanns sat and pulled his chair toward the table.

Raffaella stared at him the way men stared at her. She didn't lower her eyes when he stared back. *Distinguished might be the best way to describe him. James Mason in A Star is Born.* But Mason had also played Erwin Rommel in *The Dessert Fox*. In life, Rommel's relationship to Nazism was at best ambiguous. Raffaella disliked the Mason resemblance. She disliked the name Hanns. She especially disliked Hanns's accent. Why hadn't she realized this at The Orchard? *This was a mistake*, she thought.

A short stocky waiter, looking more as if he were about to step into a prize fighter's ring than wait on them, distracted her. He dropped two menus on the table.

"Chianti?" He looked at Hanns.

"Yes, please."

The waiter banged a jelly glass on the table in front of Hanns and filled it. He looked at Raffaella. "More?" he said.

She pushed her glass toward him without answering.

"Just leave the decanter," Hanns said.

"You're the boss, mister." The waiter walked away.

"The gnocchi are delicious. Do you like gnocchi? I don't even know if you like Italian food. I just assumed."

"Italian food?" Raffaella said, the tone in her voice a bit cool. "In Italy cooking is very regional. But, yes, I like gnocchi."

Hanns cleared his throat. "Good. Good that you like gnocchi. Homemade. Luna makes all the pasta from scratch. At least that's what the menu says. Did it take you some time to get used to food in America?"

"Not really. Three things to remember. Put salt, pepper, and butter on the dinner table. It seems that Americans season their food after they cook it, and they eat bread and butter with everything."

"True," Hann said. "I never thought of that." He smiled, and then raised his glass. "To *Ninotchka*."

Reluctantly, Raffaella also raised her glass. "Why *Ninotchka*?"

"It was playing the first time you came to The Orchard."

"Ahh—To *Ninotchka*."

Raffaella felt more at ease. So what if she transposed the calm and safety she felt at The Orchard onto Hanns. What difference did it make? Who knew the reasons for feeling more comfortable with some people than others? The knot in Raffaella's neck subsided. Aside from the nuns at Gate of Heaven, Raffaella could barely remember when she last felt at peace around anyone, especially men. Maybe she was finally moving on with her life as Sister Joan Marie had been telling her to do for years.

"The war is over, Raffaella," Sister sometimes said. "Forgiveness is crucial." But Sister Joan Marie had no idea what she was asking Raffaella to forgive. Even a crucifixion paled when compared to what Raffaella had seen and experienced.

They ordered antipasto for two and gnocchi with marinara sauce.

Hanns talked about when he first came to America, his life in L.A., some of the films he had appeared in, such as *Confessions of a Nazi Spy*, Warner Brothers' effort to expose Nazi aggression at a time when America favored isolationism and downplayed the dangers of the pro-Nazi German American Bund. He talked about meeting Edward G. Robinson and Paul Lucas who had starred in the film, and also of actors he met in other films and those he met at Salka Viertel's salons.

"Remember, I told you about the salons. That's where I met Garbo, at Salka's. They were friends and she helped write several scripts for Garbo's movies. You would have liked Salka, and she would have loved you."

Raffaella took in a long, deep comfortable breath. The stories of Hollywood and films and salons and famous people relaxed her. She enjoyed his tale of a Jewish man who had left Europe's dark world for a world of bright lights and story making. He had escaped what millions hadn't, but she didn't begrudge him his good fortune. In fact, she admired him for his foresight. What good were Marcello's heroics once a bullet ended his short life?

After antipasto and halfway through the gnocchi, Hanns paused. "Enough about me. How about you?"

"What's there to tell." She shrugged her shoulders. "After the war, I worked with nuns to care for war orphans. There were many. And in America, I also work with nuns but in a convent. My life is not glamorous." She popped another gnocchi into her mouth as if it were a period at the end of a sentence.

"I might have made myself sound more important than I am. It's a marketing strategy at The Orchard to make up for the shabby theater. I had bit parts in movies. Mostly walk-ons. Sometimes a couple of lines, but mostly I was a face in a crowd. Caring for war orphans is more important than the make-believe world I was a part of."

Raffaella brought a cloth napkin to the corner of her mouth and wiped a spot of sauce. "Don't think poorly about what you've done. What you do now. You make magic. I couldn't bring magic into the lives of those poor children in Italy. What they saw. What they lost. There was no make believe for them."

Hanns stared quietly at Raffaella. Her neck began to stiffen. She felt relieved when he finally spoke again.

"How did you come to work in a convent in America?"

"I met Father Marlo in Italy when I worked in the orphanage in Rome. He's the assistant pastor at Saint Mary Gate of Heaven where I work now."

"Do you like the work?"

Raffaella laughed. "It pays my bills. And I like the nuns. At times I feel as if I'm one of them."

"A Jewish nun?" Now Hanns laughed.

Raffaella didn't. "When I came to America, I felt safe in the convent. Safer than I had felt in years. The nuns were kind and polite. They rarely spoke of their lives before vows. As if that's when their lives had begun again, and they had forgotten all that had happened before. I envied that. I wanted to forget. To start over."

"Are you able to?"

Raffaella took a few moments to answer. She pondered his question and with her fork prodded at the single gnocchi remaining on her plate. "I don't know."

Hanns poured himself a little more wine. Raffaella placed her hand over her glass. "Grazie, no."

After Hanns took a sip of wine and a few moments of awkward silence passed, he resumed talking. "When things got bad, I left Austria for Paris. From Paris, I came to America. Most of my family including my parents and sister perished in the camps."

Raffaella had met other Jews who had emigrated to America before the German stranglehold on Europe. Jews she didn't know, but because of the numbers on her arm they told her of their loss. Some asked her many questions, expecting her to describe the fear, the humiliation, the hunger, the smell, the desperation. She found it perplexing that those who didn't know struggled to remember, and those who knew struggled to forget.

"And you feel guilty," Raffaella said with neither comfort nor scorn in her voice. It wasn't an accusation. She said it with the same tone and inflection that she might have said *And you feel tired*. Which was exactly how she felt when he had asked, "Now how about you, Raffaella?" She knew he wanted her to tell him about life before America, before the war ended, and maybe before the war. But she didn't know him well enough. She might never know him or anyone in America well enough for that. How do you explain hell to those who have never been there? There are no words.

"Coffee? Dessert?" The waiter took the empty plates from the table.

"No grazie," Raffaella said.

The waiter looked at Hanns.

"We'll just take the check."

The waiter scribbled a few numbers on a slip of paper, dropped it in front of Hanns, and left.

"You're right, Raffaella. I do feel guilt, but that's not all that I feel."

Raffaella nodded.

They left the restaurant. Raffaella draped her embroidered shawl with metallic flecks across her shoulders. It glittered beneath the colored lights that arched over Mulberry Street. She slipped her arm through Hanns's, which made it easier for the two of them to walk without getting separated among the throngs of people. All of the tables at the sidewalk cafes were full. Each restaurant they passed boasted a recording by an Italian singer: Mario Lanza, singing *O Sole Mio*, Louie Prima, singing *Che La Luna*, Connie Francis, singing *Mama*.

"I should have been Italian," Hanns said.

Raffaella nodded again.

"I have to do the last box office shift at The Orchard, but if you want to see the movie maybe we could get coffee after. Do you like screwball comedies?"

"Si. Very much."

"*My Man Godfrey* with Carole Lombard and William Powell. It's a gem."

On their way to The Orchard, they spoke of favorite films, favorite songs, and favorite food—including desserts. They had much in common. No more questions about the past.

Raffaella settled into the cramped seat in the theater. As soon as the film began, her neck, arms, and hands went limp, as if she were suddenly immersed in a pool of warm water. She loved Lombard's wise cracks and her glamourous dresses. She laughed at the silly storyline but appreciated the subtle critique of the novelty-chasing, spoiled upper class versus the "forgotten men" during the Depression.

What would Marcello have thought of the movie? Certainly he would have mocked the wealthy and thought that the men living in the city dump should rise up against them. He would have disliked the film, and back then, seeing it through his eyes, Raffaella would have agreed. That was the price for loving Marcello. There was no other way to love him, but to agree with him. Raffaella thought of the boy Sister Joan Marie had introduced her to a few days ago. The dreamy, sad-eyed Gianni, tall for his age, with thick dark black curls. Raffaella had seen Gianni many times in the bakery. Looked for him. Buying biscotti had become her excuse. A young Marcello or Marcello's son, had their son survived.

Carole Lombard's quips drew Raffaella away from her musings about Marcello and Gianni and back to the movie.

"I went to Venice, and one night I went for a ride in one of those rowboats that the man pushes with a stick. Not a matador. That was in Spain. But it's something like a matador," Lombard said.

Raffaella threw her head back and released a full belly laugh. She no longer cared what Marcello would have thought of the movie. She loved it.

When the lights went up, Hanns stood by the doors to the lobby. He smiled and exchanged words with customers as they left. Raffaella waited for the theater to empty, and then approached Hanns.

"Did you like the film?"

"Yes, very, very much."

"Me too."

Something else they had in common.

"Once I lock up we can get coffee. If you're still up for it."

"It's late, and I have to take the subway."

Hanns looked at his watch. "I'll take the subway with you and see you home."

Raffaella laughed. "A gentleman, like Godfrey, but I'm not like that scatterbrain Irene Bullock in the movie. I can manage the subway alone."

"Then at least let me walk you to the station."

Raffaella waited outside the theater while Hanns locked up. Again she wrapped her shawl around her shoulders and slipped her arm through his—glad she had said yes to his dinner invitation.

CHAPTER 6

Fina usually preferred cooking, cleaning, or waiting on customers in the bakery to watching movies on television. Now, she put aside her knitting and ignored the sound of the faucet dripping in the kitchen. *Watch on the Rhine* was the *Million Dollar Movie*, and Fina, Liberato, and Gianni sat with their eyes riveted on the small RCA screen. Paul Lucas played a German anti-Fascist working for the European underground to fight the rising Nazi threat. Bette Davis played his American wife. At the end of the movie, ailing Lucas returns to Europe without Davis and their children. He carries twenty thousand dollars to free fellow anti-Fascists,

Fina pulled a tissue from her sleeve and patted her eyes. Liberato often teared up over movies, but Fina rarely sat still long enough to follow the plot, never mind become emotional.

"Like my father," Fina said.

She looked at Gianni. "Sad that you never met your grandfather. Pictures don't describe a person. He believed in a better world. Our small apartment in East Harlem was always filled with all kinds of people. Different religions. Different backgrounds. Different races. What they had in common was they wanted a just world. Once, the great Paul Robeson came to our apartment."

Fina had mentioned Paul Robeson before, but Gianni had no idea who he was. She also referred to herself as a red diaper baby. Gianni assumed that this meant his grandparents dressed her in red diapers. It seemed silly, but Fina spoke without elaborating. She assumed her listeners had the required background information to understand what she said. And if they didn't have it, they should inquire. Unlike Fina, Liberato included the most trivial details when telling even the most insignificant story.

The next day, in school, Gianni imagined his grandfather playing the Lucas role, and he and his grandfather, to save anti-Fascists, spirited money across border checks throughout Europe.

"You're daydreaming again. This is the third time today." Sister Joan Marie tapped her knuckles against Gianni's desk.

But Sister didn't understand. Today he was to help Raffaella move boxes from her apartment on the second floor to her new apartment on the first floor. Raffaella, who had numbers on her arm like the old couple at Ezra's Seder. Raffaella, who had been in a concentration camp. Raffaella, who had lit a candle in Gate of Heaven and who had an Italian last name, was Jewish, and maybe the Nazis were after her to bring her back to the camps. Liberato's promise that there were no Nazis in America didn't comfort Gianni. "Never again!" were the words Ezra's father had said at the Seder. "We must always be vigilant." That didn't sound as if Nazis were gone. Imagining himself courageous soothed Gianni's rumbling stomach. He had to daydream and conquer monsters, or he wouldn't be able to help Raffaella.

Despite his imagination or because of it, after school he asked Colleen to walk with him to Raffaella's house just in case Nazis hid in the basement or closets or under the bed—places monsters like to hide—but he didn't mention his fear to Colleen.

Raffaella stood at the open door. She fanned herself with her hand.

"This is my friend, Colleen. She wanted to meet you."

"Hello, Colleen."

"We saw you in church the other day. You looked very pretty and lit a candle. See you later, Gianni."

Red-faced that Colleen mentioned they saw Raffaella in church, Gianni followed Raffaella up the hallway stairs to the second floor in the small two-family house. The elderly landlady who had lived on the first floor recently passed away. Her children planned to keep the house as a rental, and they offered the first floor to Raffaella before they sought a second renter.

"The movers were here earlier. My furniture is already downstairs." Raffaella said. She opened the door to her old apartment. "I've been packing boxes all day. You can start with those." She pointed to a stack of boxes. "I wrote the room on each box."

Gianni almost dropped the first box he lifted, which had living room written across the front in black magic marker.

"Those are books. I packed them in small boxes, but they're still heavy. The door downstairs is unlocked."

For over an hour, Gianni placed boxes in the three-room apartment—kitchen, living room, and bedroom.

Raffaella handed him a glass of water. "Sister Joan Marie was right. You are a hard worker."

"Thank you." Gianni gulped the water.

"Sister also said you're a daydreamer."

"Yes."

"Nothing wrong with dreaming."

"That's what my father says, but my mother said I might get hit by a bus."

Raffaella laughed. "So your mother is not a dreamer?"

"Oh, no. She says, she's a doer, and if it wasn't for her my father and I would starve. She says my father is garrulous by nature."

"Garrulous?"

"I think it means he talks a lot, which he does."

Raffaella laughed again.

"Sometimes when a customer doesn't know what to buy, my father and the customer go on and on while the line gets longer, and my mother says, 'Buy a cheese ring. It goes with everything. Next!'" Now Gianni *and* Raffaella laughed so hard he almost dropped the glass, but Raffaella grabbed the empty glass before it slipped from his hand.

"Thank you," Gianni said.

"Prego. Some people are both dreamers and doers. If you don't dream, how do you know what to do?" Raffaella raised her hands and shrugged her shoulders. The poppies on her housedress danced to a breeze that flowed through the kitchen window.

Gianni thought she looked like spring. He brought his hand to his chin and recalled a time when he was very little and fell off his tricycle. He lay on the sidewalk mesmerized by sunlight twinkling through the quivering green leaves of a Norway maple. A passerby startled him: "Are you alright, little boy?" He nodded but remained staring up into the leaves. He didn't mention this to Raffaella. Nor did he mention how often he felt suspended in a cloud, especially when he's in school. Everything turns white. When this happens, Sister's voice becomes a distant whisper until she raps her knuckles against the blackboard or on his desk and says, "Gianni! You're daydreaming again." *But Raffaella is right*, he thought. *If you don't dream how do you know what to do?*

The sound of Raffaella closing the refrigerator door startled him.

"I made this earlier. By the time it's ready, we should be finished working. I'll help you carry. I'm done packing." Raffaella placed the pizza from the refrigerator into the oven.

Gianni lifted one of the open boxes in the bedroom. Two framed black and white photographs lay on top. One of a man and one of a much younger Raffaella holding a baby. At least Gianni thought it was Raffaella. He was too embarrassed to ask.

Alone in the downstairs bedroom, he picked up one of the photographs and held it in the light of a window. *Definitely Raffaella.* Gianni thought. He looked at the photo of the young man. Like Gianni, the man had dark curly hair. There were also other similarities. Their eyes or something about the man's smile.

Raffaella's voice came from the kitchen. "A few more boxes, and then pizza time. I hope you like pizza."

"Yes, I do." Gianni put both photographs back in the box.

Three more trips up and down stairs. The final trip Gianni made alone, while Raffaella took the pizza out of the oven. Again, Gianni lifted the photo of the young man, looked at his own reflection in the mirror above the dresser, and then looked back at the photograph. Since Gianni had learned that he was adopted, he scrutinized customers' features, he took notice of people he passed on the street. He sought answers to questions he had yet to form.

Gianni stretched out his arm to see the young man's image at a distance, then slowly brought the photograph closer, and then again studied his own reflection. He tilted his head to the right and smiled, imitating the young man's pose and expression. *He's an older me.*

"Gianni," Raffaella called. "I brought the pizza downstairs."

He dropped the photograph and the glass cracked. *Stupid! Stupid!*

If he said nothing, Raffaella would assume it cracked in the move, or he could say he dropped another box on it, but that would be a lie.

Raffaella pressed a pizza cutter into the hot pie.

"Look what happened." Gianni held out the framed photograph with the cracked glass. His eyes twitched.

Raffaella looked up. "My fault. I should have wrapped it in newspaper."

He pressed his lips together, nodded, and propped the photograph on the enamel table, next to the pizza.

Raffaella opened several boxes. "Bene! I found the plates and glasses. Gianni, there's a bottle of Nehi orange soda in the refrigerator. You like orange soda?"

"Yes, thank you."

She placed two plates on the table, and then pointed a blue Soreno glass toward the refrigerator. "Get the soda, and we're ready. Now, where's the bottle opener. Ahh—I found it."

Gianni blew on his slice of pizza. He looked from Raffaella to the photo and back again.

She folded her slice and took a bite. "Ooh, mama mia. Too hot. Be careful."

The doorbell rang.

"Must be one of those Jehovah Bible people. Gianni, please answer it. Tell them I already met Jesus." Raffaella took a small bite of the pizza.

Gianni wondered if Sister Joan Marie had in fact told Raffaella about Jesus. Working in a convent it would be hard to miss him.

Colleen and Ezra stood on the front stoop.

"What are you doing here?"

"I figured you were done," Colleen said.

"I'm not. We're eating pizza."

Colleen's eyes widened. "I like pizza."

"I can't just invite you in."

"So we'll wait in the hallway until you're done. Come on, Ezra." Colleen grabbed Ezra's hand, and they brushed past Gianni.

"Ok, wait here and be quiet. I'm all finished working. I just have to finish eating."

Gianni found Raffaella staring at the photograph behind the cracked glass. She wore the same weight-of-the-world expression she had worn in church. *Who is he?* Gianni thought. *Why do I look like him? Why do you look so sad?*

Cheese stretched between the pizza crust and Raffaella's lips.

"It was just my friends," Gianni said. "You met Colleen. She's kind of pushy. They'll wait until I'm done."

"No—no. Tell them to come in. They can't wait for you outside."

"They're not exactly outside." Gianni waved them in.

"Miss Tedeschi, this is Ezra. You already met Colleen."

Raffaella placed two more plates and glasses on the table. She looked at Ezra.

"I'm Golda's son," he said as if he read Raffaella's thoughts.

"Yes, of course. But you look like your father."

Raffaella pushed the plates toward the children. "Mangia! Mangia!"

"She means eat," Gianni said.

Colleen took a slice of pizza and put it on a plate. "I know what mangia means. Your mother says it all the time." Colleen took another slice of pizza, placed it on a plate and handed it to Ezra. "Mangia, Ezra."

Gianni shook his head and Raffaella laughed.

"Who's that?' Colleen said, mozzarella stretching from her full mouth to her chin. She pointed to the photograph. Gianni wanted to push the whole slice into her mouth.

"Marcello," Raffaella said.

"You mean like that guy on the posters in Gianni's bakery."

"That's Marcello Mastroianni," Gianni said. "He's an actor. How can they be the same people?"

"I don't know. They kinda look alike."

"They don't look anything alike. Eat your pizza."

Again, Raffaella laughed and this time choked a little on her soda. "Are you sure you're friends?"

"Yeah, we're best friends." Colleen licked sauce from her fingers.

"Bene! But that's not Marcello Mastroianni. It's a picture of a boy I knew a long time ago in Italy."

"Who broke the glass?"

Afraid Colleen wouldn't stop asking questions that were none of her business, Gianni stood up. "Come on, Colleen, you can finish that on the way home."

"Aspetta un minuto. I almost forgot," Raffaella said. She reached into her pocket and retrieved a small brown envelope. "Here, Gianni, for you. Grazie! You did a great job. When I plant my vegetable garden, you will help. Yes?"

"I'd love to."

After they left Raffaella's apartment, Colleen mimicked what Gianni had said to Raffaella, "I'd luuuve to." Gianni told her to shut up.

"How much did she give you?"

"I don't know." Gianni slipped the envelope into his pocket.

"Aren't you curious?"

"No, I have other things on my mind."

"You always have things on your mind."

Ezra lagged behind, kicking stones to the side.

"Ezra, hurry up. We're going to Friedman's."

Gianni frowned. "Who said we're going to Friedman's?"

"If Ezra or I had money, we'd go to Friedman's and buy you candy. Isn't that right, Ezra?"

Ezra shrugged his shoulders.

"See, even Ezra said we'd go to Friedman's."

"Ezra didn't say anything. You don't give him a chance to say anything. Anyway, I have to tell my parents I'm home."

Mrs. Friedman shook open a small brown paper bag while the children stared through the glass display case at the assortment of penny candy. Colleen pressed her fingers against the glass.

Mrs. Friedman's jowls shook. "You smudge the glass. How many times I have to tell you the same thing. You're not a little girl no more."

"Sorry, Mrs. Friedman. I'm just excited because Gianni has a lot of money."

"I don't have a lot of money," Gianni said, though he was surprised to find more money in the envelope than he had expected to earn.

They picked out the usual: malted balls for Gianni, Bit-O-Honey for Colleen, and red licorice wheels for Ezra. Given his windfall, Gianni also bought each of them wax lips, bubblegum, and a four-pack of the tiny wax bottles filled with sweet liquid called Nik-L-Nip.

Outside, Colleen took a Spaldeen from her pocket. "Ya wanna play stoop ball?"

"It's getting too dark, plus I'm tired. I must have gone up and down stairs a hundred times. Let's just sit on your stoop."

"Let's sit on Ezra's stoop. If my brothers see us, they'll take my candy."

Moths gathered around the light above Ezra's front door, and Gianni divvied up the candy.

In between munching malted balls and biting open the wax bottles to drink the sweet liquid, Gianni mentioned the photographs.

With her fingernail, Colleen scraped the sticky candy from between her teeth. "You mean the picture in the kitchen?"

"That was one of them. Who do you think the guy in the picture looked like?"

"That guy on the poster in the bakery, Marcello Macaroni. I already said that."

"His name's not macaroni." Gianni sighed. "There was also a picture of Miss Tedeschi holding a baby. Miss Tedeschi looked like a teenager in the picture. Wouldn't it be weird if she turned out to be my real mother?"

Ezra unrolled a licorice. "What do you mean, your real mother?"

"You know I was adopted. I mean suppose that little baby was me. I mean suppose she had a baby when she was young and had to give it up. Maybe she was poor or something. You know like in the movies."

Colleen unwrapped another Bit-O-Honey. "You mean like in the *Hunchback of Notre Dame*? Maybe you're Quasimodo?"

"And you're the bride of Frankenstein," Gianni said.

Ezra held up his hand. "You said Miss Tedeschi has numbers on her arm. That means she was in the concentration camps. The camps were liberated in 1944. You weren't born in Europe, and if she had a baby back then he'd be at least twenty years old by now."

"I hadn't thought of that." Gianni rested his chin on the palm of his hand.

Colleen popped the Bit-O-Honey into her mouth. "What does liberated mean?"

"To be freed," Ezra said.

Gianni crunched another malted ball. "Suppose she had a baby after the camp. Maybe she was a little girl during World War ll. And maybe she had the baby in America."

Ezra unrolled another licorice wheel. "You're the same age as me, which means you were born in 1950. So if she was a teenager when she had the baby, let's say sixteen, then she'd be twenty-nine now."

"Maybe she is twenty-nine."

Ezra shook his head. "I don't think so."

"How do you know how old she is?" Gianni crushed the empty bag.

Ezra shrugged his shoulders and glanced up at the moths flying around the stoop light above them.

"I don't think she's your mother," Colleen said. "You don't look like her. I look like my ma. That's what Pop says. He says we all look like her."

"But I kinda look like the guy in the picture."

Ezra ran his hand across his forehead. "So you think he's your father?"

"I don't know. Guess I'm just wondering why I like being with her so much."

"Maybe you have a crush on her," Ezra said.

Colleen choked on a Nik-L-Nip. "Eww, that's gross. She's old."

"She's not old." Gianni threw the crushed bag at Colleen.

"Don't get mad at me. Ezra said you have a crush on her. Not me. Why don't you ask your mother?"

"I can't do that. When I asked her if Anna Magnani was my mother, she got mad and called her a puttana."

"What's that?" Colleen and Ezra said in unison.

"I don't know, but the way she said it, I think it means something bad. I don't want her to call Miss Tedeschi a puttana."

Ezra looked back up at the moths. "I wonder why moths are attracted to light, even flames. I wonder if they ever get burned."

CHAPTER 7

Yellow wooden sawhorses with the words POLICE LINE DO NOT CROSS blocked 104th Street where it met Jerome Avenue. Saint Mary Gate of Heaven students stood in single file rows for the annual May crowning before the larger-than-life statue of Mary, while construction workers building a convent next to the school ceased working and either leaned against the new convent or sat on the sidewalk curb, hard hats in hand. Father Marlo, Father Werner (most of the seventh and eighth grade girls had a crush on him as did a couple of the boys), and Father Kelly (no one had a crush on him) stood in front of the construction workers. Last week, one of the workers was fired for exposing himself to eighth-grade girls on the playground. Should there be a copy-cat flasher, the priests were ready to spread their cassock skirts, block the offender, and Mary's crowning would proceed unsullied.

Sister Mary Delores, the choir director, rolled up her sleeves, raised her hands, and students, nuns, and priests sang, "Tis the month of our mo-o-ther. A blessed and beautiful month. All hail to Thee dear Ma-a-a-ry, the guardian of—"

First grader Mary Katherine Elizabeth O'Malley carried a crown of flowers. Despite the numerous rehearsals, she hesitated when she reached the ladder next to the statue. With one hand, Sister Mary Delores directed the singing and, with the other, she steadied the ladder. She jerked her head to the right, motioning for Mary Katherine Elizabeth to ascend. This confused some of the students who then held vowels longer than rehearsed, which caused great dissonance.

Some students sang, "—joy to the erring," others sang, "—sinful and sorrowful," yet others, "—a glorious goal."

Sister Mary Delores yelled, "Silence!" As if someone had pulled a plug, all seven hundred and twenty students and their teachers went silent.

Pastor Sadowski walked among the seventh and eighth grade boys, tapping a rolled *Tablet* (*Catholic News and Opinion From Brooklyn and Queens*) against his broad palm. The boys heeded his warning. Many of them knew the sting of Father Sadowski's *News and Opinion* against the back of their heads for being unruly during Mass or Benediction. Rumor had it that Father Sadowski was once an amateur boxer. Evidence being his flat nose, skewed to the left.

Finally, Mary Katherine Elizabeth climbed the ladder one cautious step at a time. She plopped the crown of flowers on Mary's head, albeit lopsided. The Blessed Mother looked as if she had just stumbled out of a local bar.

Next, Sister Joan Marie led praying the Rosary aloud. Nuns pressed their thumbs against large black rosary beads. Most of students also had rosaries, especially the girls. Colleen could never find hers. After the Lord's Prayer, Sister Joan Marie began, "Hail Mary full of grace the Lord is with Thee," and everyone followed with, "Blessed art thou amongst women and blessed is the fruit of thy womb, Jesus—" Speaking the holy name of Jesus, a sea of heads bobbed while Sister Mary Delores stretched up her arm and, with the tip of her music baton, straightened Mary's crown of flowers. Ten Hail Marys were followed by a Glory Be, another Lord's Prayer, and then another ten Hail Marys, Glory Be, Lord's Prayer, etcetera, etcetera, etcetera.

Gianni spotted Raffaella, her hands folded loosely in front of her, and she looked toward the statue of Mary. She wore the same dark dress with buttons down the front that she had on when they first met at the convent. Occasionally she unfolded her hands and wiped a strand of her hair away from her face. Her skirt ruffled in the mild breeze.

Since helping Raffaella move, Gianni also helped her install a wire fence with angle steel posts, and he helped her plant a vegetable garden: tomatoes, squash, eggplant, peppers, and several herbs. Viewing life through a *Million Dollar Movie* lens, Gianni still entertained thoughts of Raffaella being his mother and Marcello his father. Anything is possible on the silver screen.

Sister Gertrude Jerome, the school principal, clicked her clicker and the students snapped out of their Rosary malaise and stood at attention. Avant-garde dog trainers had attempted to promote clicker training in the 1940s and 50s with little success, but it worked wonders on Catholic children. Then Sister Gertrude Jerome clapped her hands twice—a clicker encore—and said, "Wonderful, children. Now please follow your teachers back to your classrooms in single file."

Gianni watched Raffaella cross the street and walk toward the convent. He bumped into Sean Doyle with the moon-shaped ears. Sean turned around and laughed.

"Sorry," Gianni said. He suddenly felt light headed.

"Hey, no problem, Gianni."

Gianni spent the rest of the morning and afternoon daydreaming about bumping into Sean Doyle.

That evening, Fina's screech cut through the sound of the television news and startled Gianni. He was imagining ways to bump into Sean at school tomorrow. He rarely paid attention to the news—just white noise.

"Jesus, Mary and Joseph. They're children," Fina said. She held out her hand and dropped her knitting. "Vergogna!"

Gianni's eyes widened. Police officers sicced German shepherds on Black youth or slammed them against brick walls with pressure hoses strong enough to rip the bark off trees. Several children looked younger than Gianni.

Gianni's brow tightened. "Why Mama? What did they do wrong?"

"Nothing! They did nothing wrong."

"Papa, you said there are no Nazis in America. I don't understand. Will they send those children to camps?"

"No, Gianni. No one will send them to camps. I told you. That was years ago in Germany. This is in the South where colored people are not allowed to do certain things with white people."

"Like what, Papa?"

The news went to a commercial—a cartoon of white children marching and singing, "Oh, I love to be an Oscar Meyer Weiner. That is what I truly like to be-e-e. Cause if I were an Oscar Meyer Weiner, everyone would be in love with me." Gianni glanced back and forth between the commercial and Liberato.

"Like eat at the same lunch counter, or drink out of the same water fountain, or go to the same school."

"There are no colored children in my school."

Fina stood and left her knitting on the seat of her rocking chair. "I need a cup of coffee."

"Just a minute Fina. I'll tell Gianni about our trip to Virginia."

Fina paused and nodded. "Yes, good idea."

"When you were about two or three years old—"

"Two years old," Fina said.

"Okay, two years old. We took a little vacation to Virginia Beach. Not long, maybe four days all together. I don't like to close the bakery for too many days. You, me, and Mama walked along the boardwalk. It was hot and you wanted an ice cream, so Mama went up to a little beach shack and ordered three ice cream cones. Mama had—"

"Minga, Liberato. You're not making a movie. Get to the point."

"Okay, the colored woman at the counter stared at Mama for a few minutes. Mama repeated what she wanted, and the woman shrugged her shoulders and got Mama the ice cream cones. Everyone passing stared at us like we were schifoso, and then I noticed the sign over the shop window. It said, *Coloreds Only*. A few yards away another window had a sign that said, *Whites Only*."

Gianni looked at Fina. "But the woman gave you the ice cream?"

"Yes. But what Papa is trying to say is if a colored family went to the *Whites Only* window, they wouldn't get served. Who knows? They'd probably get arrested. If you ask me, the schifoso were those white people staring at us. I'm just glad we didn't get that poor woman in trouble. See, that's what this news is about. People trying to change those stupid rules. But too many people don't want to change. Whatever! I gotta get my coffee before the movie comes on."

Liberato went back to reading his newspaper. Gianni scratched his head. It baffled him how his parents could speak of horrible things, and then just go back to doing whatever they were doing.

Liberato looked up. "Hurry up, Fina. The movie is starting."

Gianni looked from his father to his mother, and back at his father, but they just looked at the television. He then succumbed to *Tara's Theme*, the black and white images of Manhattan, and soon *Million*

Dollar Movie spelled out in lights.

It Happened One Night was a romantic comedy about a spoiled heiress, played by Claudette Colbert, and a cocky newspaper reporter, played by Clark Gable. It turned out to be a light hearted distraction from the horrible events on the evening news, but in an early scene a Black actor stood at a train station ringing a bell and shouting, "Yass Sir. Red hot sausages." Before tonight, this scene would have slipped into Gianni's unconscious and joined memories of other not-so-subtle Hollywood stereotypes. But tonight he looked at his parents, expecting them to comment. Instead, Liberato's eyes focused on the television, and Fina glanced at the television between sips of coffee and knit 1, purl 2.

Gianni thought about the few times he had seen Black actors in bit parts—bug-eyed, saying things like yass'm, and always playing maids or butlers, chauffeurs or shoeshiners. Black customers in Paganucci's and the Black people Gianni saw daily running up and down the stairs to catch the A train to and from work at the Oxford Avenue station didn't behave like Black people in movies. Who were these Black actors portraying? Occasionally Gianni became lost in Colbert and Gable's antics, but then the unforgettable images of German shepherds tearing children's clothes or biting their thighs returned, along with images of police officers hosing down Black children as if they were flames to be extinguished. Gianni learned from his parents to seek the help of a police officer if he were lost or in trouble. He wondered what Black parents told their children. Certainly they didn't tell them to ask police officers for help.

After that evening, Gianni no longer daydreamed through the news. He paid attention, and he returned to the family encyclopedia, this time for information about Black Americans. He wondered why the nuns at Saint Mary Gate of Heaven went on and on about the missions, devil worshipers, saving wretched souls for Jesus, and showing pictures of poor starving Black children with distended bellies, but they never spoke of slavery, or Jim Crow, or lynching, or segregation, barely any of the topics the encyclopedia touched upon. They never explained why the only Black children in Saint Mary Gate of Heaven were in slides of the missions or in *National Geographic* magazines. Gianni became a regular at the neighborhood library, devouring information his teachers never taught him.

On August 28th, Gianni and his parents listened to Dr. Martin Luther King's "I Have A Dream" speech.

"There are always people on the side of angels," Fina said. Gianni wanted to be one of those people.

Come September, Gianni and Raffaella picked the last tomatoes in her vegetable garden. They put the green ones in paper bags to ripen off the vine.

A robin perched on a tomato cage. "You're still here?" Raffaella said. "Silly bird. Summer's almost over."

Gianni counted the spots on a ladybug's wings. He recalled a jingle, but was too embarrassed to sing it aloud. *Ladybug Ladybug fly away—*.

From a radio on a small table beneath the open kitchen window, an announcer interrupted Connie Francis's sentimental *Al di la*: "This morning, in Birmingham, Alabama, a bomb blast at the Sixteenth Street Baptist Church killed four little negro girls during church services and injured seventeen other negro congregants."

Gianni dropped a bag of green tomatoes, flew toward the radio, and turned up the volume. Raffaella looked up from the clumps of parsley she cut with gardening shears.

"This was the third bombing in eleven days, after a federal court order to desegregate Alabama schools. The bodies of fourteen-year-old Addie Mae Collins, Cynthia Wesley, Carole Robertson, and eleven-year-old Denise McNair were found beneath the rubble in the church basement."

"What is it, Gianni?"

"They killed four little girls."

"Who killed four little girls?"

"I don't know." Gianni's voice cracked. He feared he might cry. "The Klan probably killed them."

Raffaella slipped the shears into her apron pocket and joined Gianni at the table. "The Klan?"

"Were you ever in a building when it was bombed?"

Raffaella ran her finger tips along the table top—a mosaic of clusters of pink and purple grapes against a background of green leaves. Gianni remained silent and struggled to hold back tears.

"Gianni, I lived in Italy during the war. There was a lot of bombing."

"That's what they did. They bombed a church in Birmingham and killed four little girls. Four girls who did nothing to them. My father says there are no Nazis in America, but we have the Ku Klux Klan. What difference does it make what you call hateful people? They all do terrible things."

Raffaella sat up straight. She squared her shoulders and twisted the top button of her blouse. "We had Fascists, and then we had Nazis. But you're right. It makes no difference what we call them."

Gianni wiped the back of his hand across his damp cheek. "I hate them all. Did you hate the Fascists?"

"Yes. I hated the Fascists, and then I hated the Nazis."

"Sister Joan Marie said it's a sin to hate."

"Sister Joan Marie is a good woman, but maybe—how do you say? A little naive."

Like bumper cars in Coney Island, Gianni's thoughts crashed into each other—random and chaotic. "Did Marcello hate Fascists?" spilled from Gianni's lips as if his words had a mind of their own, and all he could do was listen to them. It was the first he had mentioned Marcello's name. "Did you love Marcello?"

Raffaella looked back toward the spent vegetable garden. "Very much. I loved him very much. That was a long time ago in Italy. I was barely seventeen. That's an age when love and hate come easy." She looked back at Gianni and smiled. "You'll find out."

"I already hate men who blow up a church and murder little girls." Gianni paused for a few moments. He struggled to sort out his thoughts. Again, accidental words slipped from his lips. "Did you know I was adopted?"

"No, I didn't know that."

Raffaella looked as if she were not only carrying the weight of the world, but the weight of the universe, while the radio announcer explained that the Ford Fairlane is built for family comfort.

Gianni regretted mentioning Marcello. He regretted asking if she had loved him. He especially regretted mentioning adoption. *Ezra was right*, Gianni thought. *Raffaella knew Marcello in Italy, before the camps, over twenty years ago. She couldn't be my mother. Maybe the baby in the picture wasn't even hers, or maybe the baby was killed in the camps. What does any of this have to do with four little girls killed in a bombing? What could four little girls do to be so hated?*

Raffaella placed her hand over Gianni's trembling hands. "Those poor little girls. May their memory be a blessing." She stood, took the shears from her pocket, and returned to the garden.

Like Gianni's parents, Raffaella appeared to transition easily from speaking of something horrible to doing what's ordinary. He didn't understand this about adults, as if emotions were like a faucet to be turned off at will.

May their memory be a blessing. Old Mrs. Weiss had said that when a neighbor's baby died from what adults called crib death. Gianni didn't know what crib death was, and he didn't understand how the memory of a baby dying or four little girls being murdered could be a blessing. He recalled standing on the landing with his not-real cousins four years ago. That was when his world fell apart, and since then he glued his world back together with stories of goodness the nuns and priests at Gate of Heaven told, with church and statues and crucifixes and rosaries, with *Million Dollar Movies* and television sitcoms with fathers who smoked pipes, and mothers who wore frilly aprons, and always smiling children. There were no television shows with Black children under the rubble of a bombed-out church or hosed down by police officers. In fact there were rarely Black children at all, except on the news or in Gate of Heaven's slides on the missions. The glue began to feel like lies. It dried and cracked and no longer held.

CHAPTER 8

Five stories above Mulberry Street, they dined at an intimate rooftop restaurant. Wrought iron railings with elaborately detailed balusters topped the building's parapet. Italian planters and jardinieres contained dwarf cypress, hasta, and bluestar juniper, mixed with colorful annuals, and meandered about tables for two draped in white linen beneath an arbor of vines heavy with grapes. Tiny white lights reflected in the lacquered sheen of a baby grand piano. A lavish setting befitting a Zeffirelli production. Below were the festivities of the San Gennaro Feast—distant enough to enhance, rather than distract.

A young waiter with features more finely sculpted than Michelangelo's David poured glasses of prosecco, first for Raffaella, and then for Hanns. A pianist played *Three Coins In The Fountain*. In this restaurant for lovers, Raffaella and Hanns looked the part. She wore a simple black crepe dress from a vintage shop in Greenwich Village. Something Jean Harlow might have worn in *Dinner At Eight* that blurred the lines between clothing and lingerie. She had pinned her hair up. Black beaded earrings embellished her graceful neck. Dapper in his tan linen suit, pale blue shirt, and blue linen tie, Hanns toasted the evening, "To magic." But to say Raffaella and Hanns were in fact lovers was an exaggeration, at least from Raffaella's perspective.

She enjoyed spending time with him—dining together before a movie at The Orchard, walks in Central Park, a ferry ride around Manhattan Island, long summer days sunning on the sand or jumping the waves at Coney Island, followed by amusement park rides, and hot dogs and knishes at Nathan's. Raffaella was very fond of Hanns, but neither passionate nor romantic. Years ago, she left such feelings in Italy, before everything changed. But she was grateful to be at ease with a man, something she thought would never happen again. Gratitude best described what she felt for Hanns.

Given Hanns was a widower and a dozen years her senior, Raffaella hoped he sought companionship over love. He spoke of film and people he had met, not of his feelings for her, and Raffaella never tired of his stories—delicious distractions from her own grim tale. Who wouldn't want to hear about laughter, satin dresses, and Champagne and caviar rather than eyes too dry to cry, stars or triangles stitched on coarse uniforms, and boiled potatoes with rutabaga and groats? She took delight in Hanns's talk of studio set gossip, bloopers that wound up on editors' floors, and lively salons. What she didn't know was that the ping of his glass against hers spoke of more than fine crystal or prosecco or companionship and certainly more than Hollywood stories, no matter how entertaining. Hanns was mad about Raffaella. He had never felt this way, not even for his wife of twenty years whom he loved dearly.

On two small plates, the David poured olive oil and sprinkled the oil with fresh ground pepper and grated cheese. Next, in the center of the table, he placed a basket of warm crusty semolina bread, a bowl of oven roasted garlic, and a small platter of roasted red peppers with pignoli, capers, and raisins.

"Buon Appetito!" The David flashed a smile at Raffaella before he left.

They took turns preparing their plates and pinched cloves of roasted garlic, which melted into the warm bread. Raffaella dipped the bread in the oil and took a bite. She tilted her head. A beaded earring brushed her left shoulder. "Good that we're both eating garlic, or we'd have to sit on opposite sides of the roof."

"I love garlic," Hanns said.

Raffaella laughed. "You already told me you should have been Italian. No need to convince me. How did you hear about this place?"

"A friend from L.A."

"It seems a lot of your L.A. friends wound up in New York City."

"Yes, you only hear about the Jews who made it big in Hollywood. Not everyone became Louis B. Mayer." Hanns pointed to the bowl of roasted garlic. "Speaking of Mayer, did you know that the first theater he bought was a rundown burlesque theater called the Garlic Box?"

"It doesn't sound like a place I'd want to go," Raffaella said.

"Mostly poor Italian immigrants saw shows there. But he fixed it up and called it the Orpheum. Amazing, his family fled the pogroms in Russia, and he grew up to become a key player in movies like *Gone With the Wind*. But that's not every Jew's story."

"No, it's not," Raffaella took another sip of prosecco. "I have a young friend who doesn't like that movie."

"*Gone With the Wind*?"

"Yes, I never saw it, but he said it made slaves look happy. How can anyone be happy in slavery? He said the only realistic scene was when a white woman slapped a Black woman and got away with it. I think her name was Scarlet."

"Vivien Leigh played Scarlet. She won an academy award for best actress." Hanns took his last forkful of roasted peppers.

"Do you know the names of the actresses who played the slaves?"

"You mean Hatti McDaniel and Butterfly McQueen?"

"Yes. They weren't permitted to go to the premiere in Atlanta because of Jim Crow laws. I never heard of Jim Crow laws, but Gianni, my young friend, explained them to me."

"Is your friend a film critic?"

Raffaella smiled. "No, he's only a boy, but he's very sensitive, and he's sometimes very serious—beyond his years."

Two wandering mandolinists accompanied the pianist. They played *Torna Sorrento*. They paused at Hanns and Raffaella's table.

The taller one with a pencil thin mustache placed a rose in a vial of water on the table before Raffaella. "Che bella."

Raffaella lifted the rose and inhaled its aroma. "Grazie."

"He's right," Hanns said. "You are beautiful."

Raffaella lowered her eyes and returned the rose to the table. Hanns refilled their glasses with prosecco.

The David replaced their appetizers with carbonara for Raffaella and parmesan risotto with roasted shrimp for Hanns. After dinner, they ordered espresso but postponed dessert until they joined the merrymakers at the San Gennaro's feast where Raffaella turned many heads as she and Hanns walked arm and arm through the throng of feastgoers.

"Zeppole?" Hanns said.

Raffaella pressed her hand to her stomach. "Just one for San Gennaro."

A man as round as the vat of hot oil where he dropped dollops of dough yelled, "Fresh zeppole!" The dollops sizzled and spat until they puffed into golden orbs. The round man scooped them out with a large slotted ladle and tossed them onto a wire mesh.

The feastgoers shouted their orders while two women behind the counter filled brown paper bags with hot zeppole, dusted them with powdered sugar, and shook the bags. "Next!"

Hanns raised his hand and caught the eye of the older of the two women with a mole sprouting hair that resembled a spider. "Half dozen? Dozen? How many?" she yelled.

Hanns looked at Raffaella, and she moved in closer. She held up two fingers. "Due!"

The woman frowned. Her lips formed an arch over the spider mole. "We don't sell two."

"And I can't eat a half dozen," Raffaella said.

The round man looked at Raffaella and let out a hearty laugh. His belly shook. "Give the pretty lady two."

The old woman shoved a bag with two zeppole at Raffaella.

"How much?" Hanns asked.

The round man shook his head. His cheeks jiggled like a bulldog's jowls. "Go! Come back when your pretty wife has a better appetite."

"Grazie!" Raffaella smiled at the round man, took Hanns's arm and directed him away from the vendor.

"They're no good the next day." She held open the bag for Hanns and, not to get powdered sugar on their clothes, they both leaned forward and took bites.

"Va bene!" Raffaella said. "Just enough."

Hanns swallowed his last bite of zeppole. "Delicious. I didn't know you could be so persuasive. You should work at The Orchard."

Raffaella raised her eyebrows. "Hmm…is that an offer?"

When they reached Canal Street, Hanns stepped off the curb to hail a cab. "Tonight, please let me take you home. You can't take the subway dressed like that. You're wearing high heels."

"I got here by subway."

"Raffaella. It's late."

She shrugged her shoulders. A cab stopped. Hanns opened the door and waited. She stepped from the curb into the street and ducked into the cab. A quiet ride to Queens. Raffaella was relieved when the cab pulled up to her house, and Hanns told the driver to wait.

He walked her to the door, drew her toward him, and pressed his lips against hers. Startled, Raffaella neither resisted nor responded. Until now, a kiss goodnight was little more than a peck.

Still holding her, Hanns said, "Raffaella, when I joked about you working at The Orchard, you said, 'Is that an offer?' I hope you think this is a better offer, but I don't want you to answer me now. Will you marry me?"

Raffaella looked away. She glanced at cigarette smoke rising above the cabdriver's open window.

"Just think about it, Raffaella. Please. Either way, this night rivaled the best Hollywood movies. Buona notte, Raffaella."

She leaned against the stoop railing and watched Hanns step into the cab. *The war is over, Raffaella.* She recalled Sister Joan Marie's words, and then considered Hanns's proposal. *Will you marry me?* Marcello had never asked her to marry him. They had married when she became pregnant. His mother insisted. Marcello loved and hated with equal passion. But romance? Too sentimental. Who had time for romance when Europe was being swallowed by monsters?

Hanns waved from the open cab window.

Raffaella returned his wave with the slight flutter of her fingertips.

What would Marcello think of Hanns? she thought. She searched her purse for her key, and then laughed, "Basta! Who cares what you'd think of him? He asked me to marry him, not you."

CHAPTER 9

The Friday after Thanksgiving and two weeks after President Kennedy's assassination, Gianni washed the blackboards while Sister Mary Delores, his eighth-grade teacher, straightened Kennedy's black draped photograph, which hung next to Pope John the XXIII's photograph, also draped in black. No photograph of slain civil rights activist Medgar Evers, who died nine days after Pope John and, like Kennedy, was assassinated and left young children behind. Not even a mention of Evers or the NAACP. The only Black people the nuns perpetually spoke of were wretched souls in need of saving. One-dimensional characters like the Black actors in Hollywood movies. They were props in the Saint Mary Gate of Heaven's productions of benevolent white missionaries.

Sister looked from the photograph of the Pope to the photograph of Kennedy and back again, and then she made the sign of the cross. Gianni recalled that he and his mother did the same when they first learned of Kennedy's death.

The day Kennedy was assassinated, Sister Gertrude Jerome entered Gianni's classroom, spoke quietly to Sister Mary Delores, and then turned to the class. "Our beloved President Kennedy has been shot."

The two nuns prayed the rosary aloud, and the startled students followed the nuns' "Hail Mary full of grace," with "the Lord is with thee—"

Like many students who lived close to school, Gianni went home for lunch. He sat at the butcher block counter eating a grilled cheese sandwich when Fina tuned up the volume on the radio: "A flash from Dallas. Two priests who were with President Kennedy say he is dead of bullet wounds. This is the latest information we have from Dallas. I will repeat with the greatest regret—"

Fina made the sign of the cross. Gianni did the same. A Catholic reflex.

"Are you almost done?" Sister glanced at the clock, and then at Gianni who was running a sponge along the blackboard sills. "Never mind that. I'll finish. You'll be late for your meeting with Father Kelly."

Gianni frowned.

On the first day of school, Sister assigned an essay: "What Do I Want To Be When I Grow Up?" A ploy to unearth children with a religious calling, no matter how tenuous. Gianni wrote that he wanted to become a priest but now he was more interested in making movies. Since film was not a part of Saint Mary Gate of Heaven's curriculum, Sister suggested that Gianni join the other boys who wrote about the priesthood and meet with Father Kelly. Meetings took place monthly in the cafetorium and included boys in grades six through eight. The first two meetings put to rest Gianni's already waning interest in the priesthood. However, Sean Doyle's presence in the group made Father Kelly's droll lectures tolerable.

During the first meeting, "Avoid Impure Thoughts," Father Kelly advised the boys not to linger in the bathroom, especially the shower. "Never look at your nude body in a mirror or the bathroom tiles."

Gianni never thought of doing that. He tried that night after he showered and the steam cleared, but all he could see were water-beaded pink and green tiles. He dried the tiles with a towel. Still no luck. He figured that the tiles in the rectory must be polished for viewing.

The second meeting, "The Legion of Decency," rated the suitability of motion pictures as A, B, or C (for condemned). Gianni made the most grievous error of asking, "What if you like the actors and actresses who are in a movie rated B or C?"

Without looking at Gianni, Father raised his hand as if he were about to swat at a pesky bug. "It is a sin for Catholics to see movies that are condemned. Period!"

At dinner that night, Gianni told Liberato what Father Kelly had said about movies. Liberato dunked the heel of semolina bread into his beans and escarole. "Ask Father Kelly if it's a sin that the garbage can outside of the rectory is always filled with empty whiskey bottles on Monday morning?"

Fina didn't comment, but Gianni caught her grin. Neither of his parents liked the idea of him becoming a priest. The only person in Gianni's family who joined a religious order was Fina's first cousin, Annunciata.

According to Fina, after her Aunt Luisa died in childbirth, Annunciata didn't want to care for her younger siblings. "That's why she entered the convent," Fina told him. "Her poor father had to work to put food on the table and take care of four children, one of them a toddler. Now Annunciata's a big shot mother superior, but she couldn't be mother to her own siblings. Family comes before strangers."

Gianni left Sister Mary Delores to finish washing the sills. Given he was late for the session, he sat at a table near the entrance to the cafetorium.

Father Kelly fiddled with a slide projector. "Today I will talk about mission work."

The boys looked at each other and smiled. A few mumbled, "Yes!" Not that they felt a calling to be missionaries, but they loved the stories of zombies and devil worshipers, just as Gianni did before he saw white police officers hose down Black children on the news, read about the Freedom Riders and Ruby Bridges and The Greensboro Four, noticed more and more distorted images of Black people in movies, and grew sick of the nuns' stories about good white missionaries who helped poor Black people, "—with wretched souls."

Once obsessed with the gory stories of martyrs like Saint Isaac Jogues who was killed with a tomahawk by the Mohawks, Gianni began to understand that for every white missionary killed, there were thousands of Indians slaughtered, but no one spoke of that. And it wasn't Indians who lynched Black people, but white church-going Americans. The nuns at Gate of Heaven didn't shy away from gory stories. After all, a crucifix hung in every classroom, including first grade. They simply selected which gory stories to tell—victims were always some combination of white, Catholic, and clergy. Stories filled with distortions and omissions.

Father Kelly turned off the lights, and Gianni's mind wandered. His family hadn't gone to Liberato's favorite revival theater in months, but tonight The Orchard was showing *It Started In Naples* with Sophia Loren and Clark Gable. Not a vintage movie, but Liberato missed it when it first came out a few years ago. He spoke of Sophia Loren almost as much as he spoke of Anna Magnani. Given the movie was a romantic comedy, featuring a child actor playing a major role, Liberato agreed when Gianni asked if he could invite Ezra and Colleen. Had the sound of a slide projector click not startled Gianni, he would have continued to daydream about the evening ahead.

Slides flashed to the projector's click, click, click. Father listed the names of a makeshift school house (click), hospital (click), and church (click). He also mentioned the names of the white priests and nuns.

"Father McKenna helped raise the money to build the hospital—Father Le Blanc was a medic in World War II—Sister Clair has a background in nutrition."

Black people also have names, Gianni thought. Given Father Kelly's response to his question about movies, he remained silent and resumed daydreaming until the cafetorium went bright.

Leaving, Gianni designed ways to intentionally bump into Sean Doyle on the way out, something he fantasized doing many times since he accidently bumped into him at last spring's May crowning. But actualizing his fantasies took nerve. Gianni preferred daydreaming.

Hanns called out when Gianni's family and friends entered The Orchard. "It's been too long, Liberato, Fina, and your little cinephile, Gianni."

Liberato and Gianni shook hands with Hanns. Fina forced a smile.

"But you missed the first feature," Hanns said.

"That's alright. We came for this movie."

"Then half price."

"Thank you. Very generous of you." Liberato handed Hanns the cost of the tickets, and then made introductions. "Colleen and Ezra, this is Mister Schein. He knows more about movies than anyone. See that's a picture of him with Greta Garbo." Liberato pointed to the photograph.

Colleen and Ezra looked for a moment, and then Colleen shrugged her shoulders.

"She was a famous actress," Gianni said.

Colleen shrugged her shoulders again and turned toward the candy counter.

Fina opened her purse. "A small popcorn and one candy each."

The movie's opening sequence had begun. Not to disturb anyone, Fina took a seat in the last row, followed by Gianni, Colleen, Ezra, and Liberato. Fina took her crocheting out of a mesh bag—quieter than knitting.

The three children laughed aloud at the cigarette-smoking, wine-guzzling ten-year-old Nando's antics and wisecracks. They also laughed when Sophia Loren did her tongue-and-cheek dance while singing, "Tu vuò fà l'americano" (You Want To Be American).

Liberato leaned across Colleen and Ezra to Gianni. "Father Kelly wouldn't approve."

Gianni laughed, and Fina shushed them.

When the lights went up, Fina stood as if an alarm had gone off. Liberato turned to the children. "Did you like the movie?"

They all nodded, and Colleen looked at Gianni, "Nando looks like you."

"You think everyone who's Italian looks like me."

"Not true. Your parents are Italian, and they don't look like you."

As if a director yelled, "Cut!" everyone except Colleen froze. She turned her bag of popcorn upside down to make sure it was empty.

Ezra broke the awkward silence. "Thank you, Mr. and Mrs. Paganucci." Colleen followed.

"You're welcome, children," Liberato and Fina said.

Hanns waved above the crowd in the lobby. "Liberato come meet the future Mrs. Schein.

In the crowd, Gianni didn't notice Raffaella until he and his family neared Hanns.

"Raffaella, this is Liberato. If I were ever to open another theater, I'd put this man in charge. And this is his wife—"

Raffaella interrupted him. "I know the Paganuccis." She held out the empty white paper bag as evidence.

Liberato patted Hanns's shoulder. "So you're the third biscotti. Congratulations!"

"I didn't know you're a baker," Hanns said.

Fina let out a humph, insinuating that Hanns talks too much and only about himself. Of course he didn't know Liberato was a baker.

Raffaella placed her hand on Gianni's shoulder. "This is my young movie critic I told you about."

"You mean the one who doesn't like *Gone With The Wind*?"

Liberato turned to Gianni. "Since when don't you like *Gone With the Wind*?"

But all Gianni heard over and over was *meet the future Mrs. Schein.*

At some point, after planting Raffaella's vegetable garden, but before the harvest, Gianni no longer needed an excuse to visit. Their friendship, albeit unconventional, took root. On those long summer evenings, Gianni told her about the latest news on television or what he was reading in the family encyclopedia or at the library. Horrible injustices that disturbed him deeply. He also talked more about adoption and that someday he might search for his birthparents, but the thought of it made him feel guilty.

"It's not that I don't love my parents," Gianni said.

"You're a curious boy," Raffaella said. "How could you not be curious about your own beginnings?"

Raffaella spoke of being a little girl in Turin, that she was also an only child and loved to read. She spoke of picnics in parks along the Po River and vacations in the Alps.

"I had what I think you'd call a charmed childhood. There was sorrow but also much love."

Her mother died when Raffaella was nine years old, and her father, a brilliant scholar whose students at the University of Turin loved him, accepted a professorship at the University of Padua.

"Memories of my mother were too painful for him," Raffaella said. "They were very much in love. My mother's family, especially my grandmother, wanted me to stay with them, but I wanted to go with my father, and he allowed me to choose. From very early, my father treated me as someone to make my own decisions."

On one such evening, when words flowed between Gianni and Raffaella and a single citronella candle glowed on the small mosaic table, Gianni recalled the spring afternoon when he and Ezra and Colleen knelt before the crucifix in Saint Mary Gate of Heaven, and

Raffaella entered the church.

"Remember you lit a candle?" Gianni said.

Raffaella nodded. They drank their espresso. Raffaella's with a of drop of anisette. Gianni's with a lot of milk and sugar. Raffaella dipped a biscotti in hers and took a bite.

"Did you light the candle for Marcello?"

"No, Marcello would have laughed at such superstition."

"Do you think it's superstition?"

"No, not superstition. Remembering a loss. But it wasn't the loss of Marcello."

Raffaella didn't explain. Weight returned to her eyes, and Gianni remained quiet for a while. He changed the subject (somewhat) and asked why she didn't have shabbat candles or a menorah.

"My father was secular, and he didn't partake in such traditions."

"Secular?"

"We weren't practicing Jews. Had I stayed with my mother's family, I would have had a different upbringing."

Gianni recalled that Ezra had said this about Raffaella.

"I didn't think any more about being Jewish than I thought about being tall or having dark hair but, when Mussolini enforced the racial laws, that changed. We went from being Italians who happened to be Jewish to being Jews who no longer had a country. But this didn't happen just in Italy, nor just in Germany. You've told me about Jim Crow. Maybe these laws were Hitler's version of the Jim Crow. And there were similar laws against Jews long before Hitler. Jews have a long history of being—what would be the word? Evicted."

"Ezra said that sometimes you go to his synagogue."

"Sometimes. Golda Weiss, Ezra's mother, was very kind to me when I first came to America. Father Marlo introduced me to her."

That night much was left unsaid. Gianni understood that some feelings need time to become words, especially spoken words. He often had feelings he couldn't express.

They moved on to other topics. They talked and listened and talked some more until fireflies appeared above the vegetable garden, and the surrounding buildings and trees became silhouettes against the summer twilight, like the silhouettes of facades against the starlit dome at The Orchard.

On evenings when their conversations strayed back to Marcello or

Italy, Raffaella would inevitably pause, look away, her dark eyes grew darker, and that's how Gianni knew she had said enough. At least for now.

So the evening Gianni sat at Raffaella's kitchen table drinking a Nehi orange soda, and Raffaella stood at the stove frying breaded eggplant, and Gianni asked if she loved Hanns, she wasn't surprised or put off by his question. Instead of answering immediately, she lifted the cast iron frying pan, turned toward the table where Gianni had placed three rows of paper towels and, with a fork, she lifted each golden slice. She'd learned to let Gianni's questions sit like unfinished thoughts in need of clarification, and sometimes questions left unanswered floated away and vanished, and Gianni switched topics. This was not one of those times.

"I mean, how much do you love Mr. Schein?" Gianni said.

"Much? That's a funny word to use for love. Either you love someone or you don't, but there are different kinds of love."

She set the frying pan back on the stove and added five more slices of breaded eggplant, which spat as they hit the hot oil.

"I know that. I mean falling in love." Gianni thought of Sean Doyle.

Raffaella turned the sizzling slices. "Drink your soda. What do you know about falling in love? Your mother is right. You watch too many movies."

"I know I don't want to be a priest."

Raffaella turned off the stove. She set the last five slices of golden eggplant on the paper towels, which turned damp with oil. "Good! Don't become a priest. Your parents will be happy."

Together they prepared the parmigiana, adding sauce, layers of eggplant, and mozzarella in two Pyrex baking dishes. Raffaella covered each one with foil. One for Gianni to take home.

"Your mother won't have to cook tonight. All she has to do is bake this a little in the oven."

"Does Mr. Schein like eggplant parmigiana?"

"Dio mio!" Raffaella laughed. "Again with Mr. Schein. Don't worry about what Mr. Schein likes and doesn't like."

But, while walking home, Gianni did worry. How could Raffaella marry if she still loved Marcello? The parmigiana's aroma and Gianni's empty stomach competed with his concerns about Raffaella marrying Hanns. He walked faster.

He found his father hanging another poster on the tile walls in bakery, this one advertising Rossellini's movie *Rome, Open City*.

"Where did you get that?" Gianni said.

"Mr. Schein. He had it rolled up in a closet collecting dust. I had it framed in a shop near Lefferts Boulevard. The one I used to use closed."

"Mr. Schein, Mr. Schein. All of a sudden everyone loves Mr. Schein."

Liberato stepped back, and he looked through the adjacent L shapes he made with his hands, thumbs touching as if he were about to shoot a scene. He tilted the poster to the left.

"I said he gave me this poster. I didn't say I love him. What's got you in a fuss?"

"Nothing!" Gianni looked at what appeared to be a portrait of Anna Magani wearing a red scarf and, in the background, barbed wire and a silhouette of Rome's skyline.

"Mama's not going to like looking at another picture of Anna Magani."

"No, Mama liked this movie. It's about the resistance against the Italian Fascists and the German Nazis in occupied Rome."

"What resistance?"

"Not all Italians supported Mussolini and once he got mixed up with Hitler, many who had supported him, turned against him. Whatever you're holding smells good."

"Eggplant. Raffaella made it. But how could they fight the Fascists?"

Liberato tilted his head back and forth. "A lot of ways. Maybe the movie will play at The Orchard again. We'll go see it."

"I wonder if Raffaella ever met anyone in the resistance."

"I'm sure she met many. She was an anti-Fascist and involved in the resistance."

Gianni nearly dropped the eggplant parmigiana. "What? Who told you that?"

"Mama. Ezra's mother told her."

Filomena Lasante entered the bakery. She and her husband owned the neighborhood Italian-American Grocery Store. "Filomena! Your cassata is ready. Best I ever made. Just for you."

During supper Gianni prodded his parents with questions about the resistance in Italy. Mostly Fina responded.

"Like any dictator, Mussolini fed the people a bunch of silly stories about being a superior people. You know, ancient Rome nonsense. Why must any people be superior to other people? Do you want more grated cheese?"

Fina put another tablespoon of grated cheese on Gianni's eggplant.

"And then that stupid Il Duce was made a fool of by Hitler who knew how to play the superiority game better. Italians fell for all that national pride nonsense until Mussolini became too chummy with Hitler. Did you tell Raffaella thank you for the eggplant?"

"Yes, Mama." Gianni rolled his eyes. He wanted to hear about the Italian resistance, not eggplant parmigiana, but Fina had her own agenda and ways of weaving stories.

"Not bad, the eggplant. Raffaella's from the north. She must have learned how to make this from a Neapolitan. Anyway, there were Italians who saw through Mussolini's braggadocio and hated Fascism from the beginning and resisted. Some had fought Franco's regime in Spain. Italian Communists were the most organized. Eat your food before it gets cold. The good news is an Italian Communist partisan finally shot the jackass."

"Who?" Gianni said. His head was spinning.

"Mussolini. Who do you think? They should have shot him sooner and Hitler too. Bury them both in the same hole for the worms to eat. Poor worms. They'll suffer terrible agita from eating such spazzatura."

Liberato finished his glass of wine. "I thought there's still debate about how Mussolini died."

Fina shrugged her shoulders. "Whatever. He's dead. That's what's important. You want more eggplant?"

Gianni left dinner with more questions than answers. Back to the encyclopedia. Mussolini? Italian resistance? Partisan? Franco? Communism? All he knew about Communism was that Sister Joan Marie had her students pray for the demise of the wretched Mr. Khrushchev. The next day, after school, Gianni returned to the library.

CHAPTER 10

"Since it's your first marriage, would you like to get married by a Rabbi and in a synagogue, maybe a small reception afterward?" Hanns said. "Whatever you want."

Raffaella unfolded a linen napkin and placed it on her lap. She and Hanns had become regulars at Luna's in Little Italy. "It's not my first marriage. We were very young and impulsive."

Hanns dropped his napkin on the floor. "What happened?"

"He died."

"The camps?"

"Before the camps." Raffaella pressed the edge of her fork into a tender cut of veal. "A justice of the peace is fine."

Hanns let the matter drop, and after dinner, rather than stopping next door at Ferrara for espresso and pastry, which had become routine, they walked to The Orchard to see Hitchcock's *Rebecca* with Laurence Olivier and Joan Fontaine, and then rode the subway back to Raffaella's apartment.

Hanns sat at the kitchen table while Raffaella made espresso. Once the water boiled, she removed the pot from the stove, flipped it over, placed it on a hot plate on the enamel table between two demitasse cups, and sat across from Hanns. Light from the circline ceiling fixture reflected on the Star of David dangling at the end of the thin gold chain Raffaella wore. A gift from Hanns. As if it were a talisman to bring about healing, Raffaella brought the star to her chin, and rubbed it between her fingers.

"Hanns, I haven't been with a man in a very long time."

"You already told me you were married. I understand. No need to explain."

"But you don't understand." Raffaella poured the espresso. She found strength in its pungent aroma. "I haven't been with a man because I don't know that I can. I'm not talking about having been married. I'm talking about Buchenwald."

Hanns passed the palm of his hand over the steam rising from his cup. "I said I understand."

Raffaella's eyes flashed. "Stop saying that!"

Hanns's cheek twitched. Raffaella took his hand.

"It's not your fault. There's no way you can understand, so please stop trying."

She stood, still holding his hand. "If we're to be married, we first need to know if I can be your wife."

Their coffees untouched, Hanns followed Raffaella into the bedroom. She turned down the coverlet, and then returned to the kitchen to turn out the light. They didn't speak. They undressed. Their eyes adjusted to the dark. In bed, Hanns slipped one arm under Raffaella's shoulders. He pressed his lips to hers. He stroked her breast. She grew tense. He withdrew his hand.

Recalling The Orchard—the dome of stars, the hum of the movie projector, the solace she felt when watching a film, the magic, the peace—Raffaella silenced her ghosts. Her breaths slowed. She reached for his hand and brought it back to her breast. She inhaled his faint scent of tobacco and aftershave, not the stench of sausage and sardines mixed with vodka or whatever liquor Nazi guards had confiscated from the latest arrival of Jews. The smells of ouzo, brandy, sambuca, and rum spoke of the varied countries Jews had lived before their national identities had been erased, before Buchenwald. They were a diverse people from many countries made one by Hitler. Hanns caressed and kissed Raffaella, tender and deliberate. Not brutal like the men in the camps who behaved like vultures and she was the roadkill they devoured until she was nothing but bones.

She moved beneath Hanns and, as his passion increased, she remembered Marcello. He had been a generous lover. His hands calloused but attentive. His body hard but limber. His scent strong but seductive. A cheating of the mind? Maybe Hanns also thought of his wife. Raffaella took small comfort in that possibility.

She was grateful when it was over. Not because it was over, but that the ghosts she had struggled to contain didn't win. Pleasure? Maybe in time, but for now gratitude was enough. She smiled and held Hanns to her breast.

"Hanns."

"Yes, my love."

Raffaella mulled over his words and the gentle way he said them. Not since her father had anyone spoken to Raffaella so lovingly. Marcello was a man of raw passion, be it in his hatred of Mussolini and Fascism or his love and lust for Raffaella. He had often called Raffaella mi amore, but in a tone that made the words sound like comrade, rather than a term of endearment.

"Hanns, you didn't have children in your first marriage. Are you wanting children in a second marriage?"

Hanns chuckled. "Raffaella, I'm not a young man."

"No matter. But you need to know one more thing and then no more. They performed horrible surgeries. I can't—"

"You said, no more, Raffaella. And I agree. It's time for us both to let go of the past. For me to let go of my guilt for having left Europe before things got so bad and for you to let go of the unimaginable pain you suffered. At least as much as it's possible to let go of such pain. You are here with me now. That's all I need to know. I love you, Raffaella. If someday you feel for me even a smidgen of what I feel for you, I'll be the happiest man alive."

They lay in each other's arms. No longer speaking. Soon Raffaella heard his slumberous breaths. Two photographs sat in shadows on her dresser. Tomorrow, in a drawer and beneath sweaters rarely worn, she'll place the photograph of Marcello and the one of her holding their infant son.

They were married on June 21st, 1964, by a justice of the peace at the New York City Marriage Bureau in Tribeca. Hanns had reserved a room for their wedding night at the Plaza Hotel. Driving uptown from City Hall, the cabbie turned on the radio. A broadcaster announced: "Andrew Goodman, James Earl Chaney, and Michael Henry

Schwerner are missing. Two of the men worked for the Congress of Racial Equality, the third was a voter registration volunteer as a part of the 1964 Mississippi Summer Project."

Raffaella looked at Hanns. He looked out the window. He glanced at his watch, distracted and oblivious to what had been announced on the radio.

"I hope our room is ready. We have dinner reservations at 6:00, and then a horse-drawn carriage ride through Central Park." He leaned over and kissed Raffaella's cheek. "I love you Mrs. Schein."

Raffaella smiled. The small bouquet of gardenias Hanns had bought for her sat on her lap. How lovely they looked against the ivory tulle of her dress and its faint peach lining. She thought of Gianni and how he would rant about the radio announcement. She also thought of Marcello who, unless the disappeared men were immediately found and alive, would strategize ways to blow up a Mississippi police station.

The cab pulled into the Plaza's circle drive at Central Park South. A doorman approached the cab. He wore a cape with gold piping matching the gold embellishments on the iconic hotel.

"Welcome to the Plaza." He opened Raffaella's door. She stepped out of the cab, and recalled the movie she had last seen at The Orchard. *Midnight* with Claudette Colbert. She imagined Colbert wearing the shimmering silver dress she wore in *Midnight* and stepping out of one of the limos in the circle drive. Hanns took Raffaella's hand and made a slight bow. "A golden-era evening awaits you, Mrs. Schein."

Raffaella smiled. "Thank you, Mr. Schein."

PART 2

The wrestling had some deep meaning to them
—an unfinished meaning.

—D.H. Lawrence

CHAPTER 11

High school was a blur. Gianni feigned illness, cut classes, and played hooky. Done with Catholic School, he joined Ezra at Thomas Jefferson High School, two blocks from the bakery. The instruction was even more vapid than it was at Saint Mary Gate of Heaven. At least the nuns spoke of poverty. If not for reading newspapers and watching the news on television, Gianni would have spent four years of high school without hearing of the Black Panthers, and no teacher hung a picture of Malcom X or Dr. Martin Luther King draped in black after they were assassinated. For that matter, neither did they hang a picture of Robert Kennedy when he was assassinated shortly before Gianni's graduation. High school instruction focused on the distant past. At best, teachers perpetuated what Gianni now thought of as white Christian myths. At worst, they told outright lies. Bussing from surrounding neighborhoods brought in Black students, and Gianni wondered how they endured the hostile instruction, which, except for inventing the cotton gin, insinuated that anything worth doing white people had done.

College, he assumed, would be no different, but his parents expected him to go. His grandparents' generation immigrated to America, his parents' generation worked as laborers or owned a mom-and-pop business, and his generation should go to college and enter the professional class.

Ezra was accepted at Columbia and Colleen at a small community college in Upstate New York. Gianni barely eked out passing grades in high school. Daydreaming remained his favorite subject, and he maintained the academic status of underachiever, the backhanded compliment Gate of Heaven nuns assigned to him from 4th grade on. Short hand for you're smart, but we'd never know it because you're so damn lazy.

You've changed, his teachers and parents said, but no one thought to ask why, as if, after his aunt spit on the floor and said he was dirt under her feet, he changed of his own volition to prove her right. His fault.

"He reads at a seventh-grade level," Gianni's fourth-grade teacher once said at a parent-teacher conference. "But there's a steady decline in his work."

By fifth grade, Gianni passed on probation—meaning his grade average fell short of seventy-five percent.

In the neighborhood library, where Gianni learned what teachers never taught him, Fina researched colleges with lenient acceptance practices. Come fall, Gianni attended Lyndon State College in the Northeast Kingdom of Vermont.

In late August, Liberato and Fina waved goodbye to Gianni, returned to their Buick, and cried their way back to Queens. Loneliness overwhelmed Gianni. Something in his parents' tears and their departure triggered feelings that he later described to a therapist as a sense of abandonment. The feelings persisted and intensified when he entered his sterile dorm room—white walls, a blond wood desk and wardrobe, and a thin Vinyl mattress. The feelings lingered when he met his two roommates and unpacked his clothes. In the cafeteria, at dinner, he wondered if the other freshmen felt the same way.

Homesickness, he told himself. *To be expected. Stop being such a wimp.* He smiled, introduced himself to others, and pretended to be excited.

Where one grew up influenced initial friendships, and Gianni befriended a Black girl from Brooklyn named Renee. She grew up four A train stops away from Paganucci's. During orientation week, after a talking heads lecture on making the most of freshman year, Gianni and Renee walked down the hill from Lyndon State into town.

Renee wore her hair in a large afro. She wore an ankle length dashiki. Gianni, his face framed by long Cat Stevens curls, wore a tie dye T-shirt, torn jeans, and granny glasses.

An ancient man approached them. His mouth a whiskered sinkhole between his bulbous nose, spidered with broken blood vessels, and his near absent chin. He stared at Renee with kind eyes, but he looked confused. Seconds passed, and Gianni thought, *What the fuck are you looking at?* Finally, the old man, standing inches from Renee, his breath reeking of alcohol, slurred: "Are you a clown?"

Renee said, "No."

They left the old man in his stupor.

"Wow! Welcome to Vermont," Gianni said.

"You mean, welcome to America."

They stopped in the only diner on main street and ordered French fries with gravy. A first for both of them. A week later, Renee straightened her hair and wore sweatshirts that read Lyndon State College. Two weeks after that, she left Lyndon and returned to Brooklyn.

Though not listed in the syllabus, pairing off was a requirement for college freshman. Gianni met a girl from Massachusetts. They had sex. Another requirement. A dispassionate voice within Gianni directed the scene. More than once, it yelled, *Cut! The audience will see through this farce.* Their relationship didn't last.

One evening in late September, just when Barnabus from *Dark Shadows* was about to do something diabolical, the television in the lobby adjoining the boys' and girls' dorms went blank. The disgruntled students hissed and booed. One student kicked the side of the television, but Barnabus was gone.

Gianni suggested a game of charades. That's how he met Maura Silberman and Owen West. Maura—assertive, opinionated, and from Long Island—reminded Gianni of home. Owen, a Vermonter, reminded Gianni of the pastoral Vermont he had imagined. They became an unbeatable team. Maura's and Gianni's skill made up for Owen's faux pas. A queue of students waited to compete against them. Charades was short lived—a new television appeared and *Dark Shadows*, *Laugh In*, and *Get Smart* took precedence—but the threesome's friendship continued. For Gianni, Vermont came temporarily alive. He was comforted by the familiar feeling of being one of a trio. His friendship with Colleen and Ezra revisited, but not quite.

With her dark brown hair and eyes, and slender form, Maura held no resemblance to Colleen. Their personalities were somewhat alike, but Maura more resolute. Owen was the opposite of Ezra: fair hair and complexion, athletic, and not at all scholarly. Maura and Owen were also lovers, and there were times Gianni felt the trio was more of a duo plus one. The one, Gianni, being the sympathetic ear for the duo's complicated relationship. Maura promised to marry a childhood sweetheart, Jimmy, before she left for college and met Owen. The wedding was set to take place before Jimmy's deployment to Vietnam.

As if he stepped onto a real-life set for Romeo and Juliet, as if he were Benvolio, Romeo's loyal friend, Gianni feared this Romeo would be hurt. In Gianni's emptiness, he welcomed the deep love and protection he felt for both Maura and Owen. To further complicate matters, Gianni fell in love with Owen. He wondered if Benvolio had also fallen in love with his Romeo. A story Shakespeare hid.

Owen's creamy complexion flushed easily in the cold. His thick blond hair, parted and neatly combed, sometimes fell before his blue eyes, which appeared lit from within and could be spotted across a room. Affable to a fault, Owen talked with his arm wrapped around Gianni's shoulder and leaned his athletic skier's body against Gianni. When watching television, Owen's head or feet rested in Gianni's lap. Whenever they were together, some part of Owen rested upon or pressed against Gianni.

Being guarded with Owen was like being guarded with a puppy. Short of tethering him, little could be done but to accept being snuggled and nuzzled and wrestled with.

Owen treated life the same way he treated people—with enthusiasm. "What a day!" "Can you believe it?" "That's amazing!" And with this enthusiasm, *he* had fallen in love with Maura. He had never met anyone like her, just as he had never seen a day as wonderful as today or a sunrise as awesome as the current morning's sunrise.

He embraced his friendship with Gianni with the same enthusiasm. Like ancient Olympiads in loincloths, they wrestled in nothing more than their underpants, their friendship a merging of spirits and bodies. Strength against strength, flesh against flesh, a carnal connection, and not about winning or losing. Should either boy overpower the other to the point that there be a danger of harm, he, being Gianni or Owen, would lower the other gently and release him. Protection the end goal. As if to say: *No matter what, I'll always have your back. Your safety is my only prize.*

Owen wrote Gianni poetry, expressing how he had found a brother in Gianni. But therein lay the problem. Gianni's feelings for Owen grew beyond the fraternal. Since his crush on Sean Doyle in elementary school, Gianni had other crushes, even on a few girls he had dated, but this was different. Owen overcame the boundaries Gianni had created since he first realized he desired boys—boundaries of shame to ensure that crushes never became love. Owen crashed through them, turned them to rubble, and love is exactly what Gianni's crush on Owen became.

As often as he could, Gianni spent time with either Maura or Owen, or Maura and Owen. He had other friends, wrote articles for the Lyndon State Gazette, even acted in a play, but nothing compared to being with them.

The end of summer yielded to autumn and, after a brief flash of color, autumn surrendered to winter. The trio spent much of their time in Vail Manor, the architectural center piece of the otherwise monotonous campus. A rambling hodgepodge of interconnected buildings—several living quarters, barns, and carriage houses—once the rural home of Theodore Vail, the founder of the Bell System. What it lacked in symmetry, it made up for in aesthetics: leaded mullion windows, built-in window seats and bookcases, balconies and curved staircases, numerous stone fireplaces, stained and shellacked wood trim, wide planked floors, wainscoting, and paneled ceilings. The horse stalls in the carriage houses had intricate ironwork, and the huge barn, though drafty, made for a great theater. In contrast, the recently built campus buildings—utilitarian dorms, cafeteria, library, and gym—brought a gulag to mind.

The trio explored Vail Manor's balconies, their hands outstretched, feeling for cold spaces said to be ghosts. They held seances using a Ouija board in the many remote rooms. They often ended their evenings curled up in one of the two, huge, deep-winged, and canopied, porter-styled chairs—the only two pieces of original furniture—before a fire in the fireplace in the main drawing room. The chairs were rumored to have been custom made for President William Harding Taft's visit with Vail at the manor. Each man weighed over three-hundred pounds.

Owen and Gianni pressed next to each other. Maura curled onto their laps.

They listened for the phantom sounds. The most notorious of the many ghost stories about Vail manor involved ladies of the night who traveled by sleigh from Lyndonville after respectable townies had turned out their lights. Up the hill to the manor, they went to entertain Vail's influential guests. Gianni, Maura, and Owen listened for the sounds of shaft chimes on horse drawn carriages, for giggles and sounds of passion, for mournful whispers or cries. As the stories went, sometimes sex had turned violent, and the ghosts of the hapless prostitutes returned to tell of their sadistic deaths at the hands of a powerful man.

"Did you hear that?" Owen would say, reminiscent of Gianni kneeling beneath the Crucifix with Colleen and Ezra waiting for Jesus to wink or smile at them.

Curled up in the huge porter-styled chair, they spoke of everything and nothing: the latest paper they were assigned, the latest song released, the latest movie seen, Owen teaching Gianni to ski, how the administration insisted a visiting blues-rock singer wear a bra before they'd allow her on stage; and their favorite topic—themselves and how glad they were to meet. Eventually they fell asleep and woke to a few embers remaining in the fire place. Outside the hint of sunrise turned the sky pink and the snow lavender.

Maura and Owen's drama eclipsed Gianni's unspoken yearnings, and Gianni's loneliness turned into despair, anxiety into phobia, sorrow into depression. People appeared distant, as if he viewed them through the wrong end of a telescope. The campus buildings and the surrounding trees and hills turned flat and wan. Facades on a studio back lot. Life became a movie that mattered less and less. The characters distant, the plot irrelevant. If the celluloid snapped or bubbled and burned and the screen suddenly went blank, so be it.

During Thanksgiving break, Liberato and Fina sensed a change in Gianni. When he stepped into the cab to ride to Port Authority and catch the bus back to Vermont, Liberato and Fina stood at the curb, their hands raised, positioned to wave, but Gianni didn't look back.

He would have, had he thought to, but instead he watched shadow follow light and light follow shadow, and so on and so forth, beneath the El's train tracks. By Christmas, the change in Gianni was blatantly obvious.

"I don't know," Gianni said when his parents questioned him. "I just don't feel like me. In fact I don't feel at all, except a little frightened."

Maybe the small campus, isolated on a hill above a small town where everyone looked and sounded and acted the same, surrounded by more hills, woods, farms, and a modest ski slope was too much of a leap for the pensive city boy. At home, his bedroom window looked out on the screeching A train, where streetlights illuminated the nights and delivery trucks greeted the mornings, where crowds of people with varied accents poured over goods and groceries and fruits and vegetables and fresh flowers and iced fish. Though he fancied the pastoral photographs and homey articles in *Vermont Life*, and the small-town settings in movies like *Little Women*, Lyndonville's provincial ways crawled up the hill to the college campus and, to Gianni, it felt claustrophobic and surreal—the product of Rod Serling's imagination rather than George Cukor's.

His grades arrived in the mail, worse than high school. Even if he wanted to, Gianni couldn't return to Lyndon State for the spring semester. Had his feelings not turned numb, he would have felt relief.

He slept during the day and, at night, he stared at the television until the screen turned to white fuzz and noise. Occasionally, he thought to call Raffaella. Maybe they could watch a movie together at The Orchard. But just thinking about it overwhelmed him. He no longer read or watched the news. What difference did knowing anything make? Paying attention didn't save Vietnamese children from crying. It didn't save American youth from coming home in caskets.

Come February, Fina hurt her back, or so she said. Liberato needed Gianni's help in the bakery. Given Gianni's sleep habits, the first day or two were grueling, but he soon fell asleep by 8:00 pm, woke at 4:00 am, felt his way through the dark, and followed his father down the creaking steps to the bakery's kitchen where he squinted against the florescent lights and the glare of white tile walls. He slipped a hairnet over his long hair.

Liberato turned on the ovens in what had long been his private world, but he welcomed his son gladly. Like an apprentice in a Dickens novel, minus the harsh master, Gianni studied his father's routine. Under Liberato's tender guidance, he learned quickly. He performed his tasks as thoroughly as he once washed blackboards in Gate of Heaven.

He kneaded dough until his neck and shoulders turned pliant, drew heat from the ovens, inhaled the aroma of Kaiser rolls, semolina bread, brioche, and croissants. He iced cinnamon buns, pastry rings, and Danish with the care of a potter glazing porcelain. And within a few weeks, he found pride as well as solace in the work.

On some mornings he and Liberato spoke of Vermont.

"Maybe it was too much of a shock," Liberato said. "You know, the change from living in a city to the country."

Gianni sprinkled flour on the butcher block counter, and then turned out another round of dough. "I thought I'd like it, but I was wrong."

He sprinkled more flour on top, patted the dough down, and then cut it into even sized pieces. "I felt lonely. There were plenty of people around me. I mean I lived in a dorm and had two roommates, but it was as if they were all on the other side of a window or a fence that I couldn't climb."

"Homesickness," Liberato said.

"Maybe, but now homesickness has followed me home. Something's changed. There's a numbness that I can't seem to shake. Sometimes it scares me."

Liberato mixed cream cheese, sugar, egg yolks, and vanilla extract in a stainless-steel bowl. "Mama mentioned that maybe you should to talk with someone. Maybe a doctor or a priest?"

"Definitely not a priest," Gianni laughed.

During the early, groggy, and healing hours, while the neighborhood slept, words flowed unencumbered between father and son. They were of one mind, simply thinking aloud. But once the sun rose and the bakery buzzed with customers, and in the evenings, when Gianni, Fina, and Liberato sat together for dinner, or watched television before an early bedtime, they never spoke of Vermont.

Fina returned to the bakery. Gianni no longer mixed-up days and nights. He continued to assist his father with early morning baking, which helped quiet the nagging loneliness in his head. But he was glad to no longer wait on customers and explain why he had left college.

Fina ignored intrusive questions and whenever a nosey customer persisted, her eyes narrowed and her chest heaved. "I only have a few days to live, and Gianni came home to help. Now tell me what you want before I drop dead in front of you."

Early April, while the family watched the *Red Skelton Hour*, the phone rang. Fina jumped up to answer it.

She handed Gianni the receiver. "It's Maura."

Maura had married Jimmy on December 27th, two weeks before he left for Vietnam. Owen and Maura returned to Lyndon for the spring semester, their interactions a spiral of battles and transient truces, including forgiveness leading to sex.

"I'm home. In Island Park," Maura said. "Jimmy's helicopter was shot down over Hanoi."

"Is he missing?"

"He's dead," Maura said, the way she might have said it's raining––a statement of fact, with a slight edge of annoyance in her voice.

Red Skelton laughed his way through one of his monologues.

When Gianni approached Jimmy's casket, Maura whispered: "Tell that fool to leave before there's a second funeral." But Gianni knew that Owen wouldn't listen. The next morning, under a gray sky and to a bugle's lament, Owen and Gianni stood behind scores of mourners, before rows of open graves waiting to be fed.

Weeks after the funeral and back at Lyndon State, Maura did her best to ignore Owen, but the frequency in which their paths crossed suggested intent on Owen's part. Grieving, confused, angry, Owen drove the three-hundred-plus miles from Lyndon State to the corner of Liberty Avenue and 104th Street only to return to Vermont the next day. The weekly midnight shower of pebbles against Gianni's bedroom window became routine.

"He's going through a rough time," was all Gianni said to his parents. They didn't ask questions.

In mid-May, again the sound of pebbles against glass, again Owen standing in his usual spot like a lost puppy beneath the streetlight outside the bakery, and again Gianni stretched his arm out into the night and dropped keys for Owen to let himself in. They sat at the edge of

Gianni's bed in a tunnel of posters—civil rights and antiwar activists, pop artists, peace signs and antiwar slogans—and bookshelves housing left-leaning books, magazines, and pamphlets that he and Owen never discussed. While at Lyndon, Gianni helped organize anti-war rallies, which Owen never joined. Before them, an angry Malcom X chastised a stoned Janice Joplin.

Owen leaned forward, his elbows on his knees, and his fingers splayed against his forehead.

"She hates me."

Gianni didn't respond.

"Really hates me, I'm not kidding. She said if I bother her anymore, she'll report me for stalking her. Even call the police."

"She wouldn't do that."

Owen looked at Gianni as if to say, *We're talking about the same Maura, right?*

To the staccato of steel against steel, the A train lights strobed Gianni's room. The train screeched to a stop, then again steel against steel until the sound faded then vanished.

Owen raked his fingers through his thick blond hair. "I'm done with college."

No point in Gianni trying to convince him otherwise. And who was Gianni to lecture anyone about school? He agreed to drive back to Vermont with Owen and help him pack.

They undressed down to their skivvies, slipped under the sheets in Gianni's twin bed, and continued talking until they fell asleep.

Gianni woke to the bed shaking. Owen crouched at its foot and, as if he were buried under a pile of debris, his voice sounded muffled: "Gonna jump…gonna jump."

Gianni tried getting him to lie down without waking him, but Owen's eyes shot open, wide and fearful. His drenched skin shone in the muted light.

"You must have had a nightmare."

Owen collapsed onto Gianni's lap and sobbed. Gianni stiffened.

"Jimmy didn't make it!" Owen cried.

Burning and sweat soaked, Owen inched up from Gianni's lap and slid against his bare chest. A meld of shadow and light, Owen rose above Gianni and pressed Gianni's wrists against the bed, as if unsure what to do next. Gianni broke free and pulled Owen down onto him.

They locked their arms around each other. Their clinched fists pressed into each other's backs. Their muscles straining and cocks grinding. Their bodies twisted and undulated like a chrysalis wrestling to become. Then the call of another train; again lights strobed the room. A brief pause, and like the jumpy frames in a silent movie, Gianni and Owen appeared, vanished, reappeared, until the train passed, and in its wake they lay tangled and redolent of sex.

Silence, except for the sound of their hearts and breaths. Gianni felt more alive than he had felt in months, maybe years. He had finally left his lone seat in the theater and stepped into the screen. He savored the taste of being real, but he feared that Owen might think this had been a mistake.

He whispered, "Owen, are you..." Owen pressed his fingers against Gianni's lips. Owen fell asleep. Gianni glanced at the clock. His father would already be turning on ovens and cutting dough into even squares.

Liberato looked up. "Owen show up again last night?"

"Yup! He's quitting college."

"Too bad. Do his parents know?"

"Not yet. I don't think so. I'm driving back up with him today and help him pack."

"Then you better get some sleep. I'm okay here. Mama will be down later to help in the shop."

"Thanks, Papa." Gianni thought better than to give Liberato a kiss on the cheek. The smell of Owen's heat lingered on his skin.

Back in his room, Gianni undressed and slipped into bed next to Owen. Usually they slept with their backs to each other but, this time, he placed his arm around Owen and pressed his cheek against Owens's shoulder. They slept until 11:00. When they woke, Gianni asked Owen if he still wanted him to drive back to Vermont with him.

"Of course. Why wouldn't I?"

Gianni didn't answer. They showered, dressed, grabbed coffees and doughnuts from the bakery, and took turns driving Owen's Volkswagen back Vermont.

Patches of snow lingered beneath evergreens along Route 7, and detour signs warned of washed-out roads. They talked about Maura, about Owen leaving college, about his parents' probable reaction, about Owen joining the reserves, about Gianni's 4F status for hypertension. They mentioned nothing of Owen's nightmare or what they did afterward.

Upon arriving, Gianni helped Owen pack. They stuffed dirty clothes into plastic bags, stripped a few posters from the walls, boxed books. Owen didn't have any records, just a radio—then they loaded Owen's Volkswagen Beetle. He strapped his two pair of skis to the ski rack.

Owen said good-bye to friends while Gianni visited with Maura. He spotted her sitting alone in a window seat in Vail Manor. She stared at the twilight through leaded mullion windows. Last Gianni had seen her, she wore the black dress and held a folded tri-cornered American Flag.

"How are you?"

Maura turned and glanced at Gianni. "Don't be ridiculous."

She then looked back through the window, as if Gianni were merely a mirage. The sun dawdled and Philip Roth's *Portnoy's Complaint* sat unopened on her lap. "I have a report due tomorrow," she said—her tone indifferent. She shrugged her shoulders and sighed, "No worries. Professors cut war widows a lot of slack."

Silent moments passed before Maura looked back up at Gianni. "Are you here to help Owen leave?"

Gianni nodded.

News about Owen leaving school had traveled fast. His behavior—what Maura called his insanity—drew a lot of attention. Maura told Gianni that if Owen didn't leave college on his own, she believed college administrators would force him to take a leave of absence or he'd be expelled. Students noticed him staring zombie-like at Maura in the cafeteria or walking to and from classes. Some claimed they saw him peeking in her first-floor dorm window. Hoping to humiliate him and force him to stop stalking her, Maura had screamed at him several times in front of other students.

"It didn't work," she said.

"Are you afraid of him?" Gianni asked.

"No, but it's time for him to grow up. What's done is done."

Maura stood and hugged Gianni. They wandered through Vail

Manor until they settled in a quiet spot on the balcony above the drawing room, where not long-ago Owen, Maura, and Gianni cuddled in the huge, deep-winged, and canopied, porter-styled chair, like triplets in a womb, oblivious to causalities and grief and guilt. Gianni glanced at the chair through the balusters. He sat on the floor, his back against the dark wainscoting, his legs crisscrossed. Maura rested her head in his lap. He recalled Owen moving from his lap and pressing against him, but didn't mention this to Maura. They no longer spoke of Owen, or of Jimmy, or of anything that was no more. Maura updated Gianni on silly campus gossip. Gianni told her he found baking to be healing.

"Maybe I'll try it," Maura said. "I'll learn to make challah."

Mostly they were quiet. As if Maura were a child needing sleep, Gianni stroked her long dark hair to the lullaby of the manor's creeks and moans.

"Do you think you'll go back to college?"

"Maybe. I don't know. But not back here."

"No, not back here. I thought about finishing in a college on Long Island. But there's the hassle of applying and transferring credits. Too much trouble."

A few friends who hadn't seen Gianni since he left Lyndon spotted him with Maura, but they didn't interrupt. At most they nodded and Gianni nodded back.

Gianni and Maura walked back to the dorm arm-in-arm under the dome of stars against the velvety black Vermont sky.

"Looks like The Orchard," Gianni said.

"What's that?"

"Nothing. Just a movie theater I used to go to."

Gianni told Maura that he loved her. "I know. I love you too."

A hug then a kiss. Maura turned, opened the door to her dorm, and Gianni watched until the door closed behind her.

Back in Owen's car, he discouraged Owen's questions about Maura. "What do you want me to say? You know how she feels."

"But—"

"Let go of it, Owen."

"But—"

"Owen—"

Owen finally fell asleep. Gianni stopped for gas, for cups of black coffee, for stolen moments to watch Owen sleep, and then he continued the long, mournful drive back to Ozone Park.

When they stepped out of the Volkswagen in front of the bakery, rush-hour passengers climbed the metal steps to the El and the A train passed overhead.

They hugged. Owen repeated several times before Gianni could hear him, "I think I'll just drive back home—I have a lot to tell my folks."

Gianni recalled Maura's words. *What's done is done.*

CHAPTER 12

Weeks passed before Gianni no longer woke to the sound of phantom pebbles against glass. He'd stare out his bedroom window at the sidewalk below and yearn for one of the lone shadowy commuters rushing to or from the El to pause under the streetlight and look up with Owen's buoyant smile and blue-lit eyes. In dreams, Gianni returned to Vermont. He floated through Vail Manor's labyrinth of halls and stairways and balconies in search of ghosts. He trekked through woods silenced by snow-heavy boughs where a cushion of white crunched beneath his boots and the peppery air stung his nostrils. He drove along dark, meandering roads through small, grimy towns where the sporadic glow from windows intensified his loneliness. When adrift in the surreal world between sleep and wakefulness, should the A train careen past his bedroom window and its lights quicken, Owen appeared, vanished, and reappeared until Gianni's room pulsated with light and heat, and, when the A train came to a screeching halt, Gianni awakened drenched in sweat and smelling of his own semen.

Moving forward requires taking a step, and a step often requires the tug of those who care. Ezra and Colleen had called or stopped in the bakery numerous times during Christmas break and again since the spring semester had ended. Until now, Gianni concocted hackneyed excuses about why he wasn't available. Finally Gianni yielded.

They hadn't been in each other's company since Gianni left for Vermont, Colleen for the small community college in Utica, and Ezra began classes at Columbia. Ezra suggested they meet around 5:00 at Figaro's in Greenwich Village, after he got out of work.

"The coffee's great," Ezra said. "A groovy spot and Colleen will already be in Manhattan for whatever she said she has to do. Plus you'll get out of Queens."

During high school, the trio's friendship ebbed and flowed. Colleen drifted toward new friends she made at Christ The King, which was a bus ride away in Middle Village. Gianni kept his neighborhood friends. They were older but also went to the same high school, including two of Colleen's brothers. Ezra, even more studious than he had been in elementary school, rarely joined the neighborhood teenagers sitting on stoops along 104th Street, listening to the jukebox and lingering over egg creams and French fries at H&B's Ice Cream Parlor, playing pool in the parlor above the pet shop on Liberty Avenue, or bowling at the Ozone Park Alleys on Rockaway Boulevard. But no matter how much time passed, when Gianni, Ezra, and Collen got together, they fell into instant rapport. Still kids pressing their noses against the display case in Friedman's Candy Store. Gianni missed that sense of the familiar.

Le Figaro Café stood at the corner of Bleeker and MacDougal Streets. In summer, waiters opened the glass, bifold doors, and the crowded tables inside the café spilled onto the more crowded sidewalk where troupes of colorful young people, their hair and clothing spurning convention, gathered to be seen and heard. Gianni sat at an inside table with a clear view. He thought of Renee, the first friend he had made at Lyndon. Here, her large afro and long dashiki would not attract stares. Here, she would be one of hundreds of youths proudly wearing their politics.

In cutoff jeans, an Indian gauze blouse with thin straps, and a feather boa, which accentuated her Joplin likeness, Colleen crossed Bleeker Street. She had let her hair grow long. It frizzed in the humid heat. She waved to Gianni.

Ezra appeared next to her—stoop shouldered and intense, with a mustache and goatee. He carried a backpack heavy with books and a folder with newspapers and fliers under one arm. They nudged their way past Figaro's patrons, and then wedged themselves into chairs around the small marble-top table where Gianni already sat.

"You have some splaining to do." Colleen resurrected her silly Ricky Ricardo imitation.

Ezra stuffed his backpack and folder under his chair. "It's great to see you, Gianni. Been too long."

Gianni ignored Colleen's comment. In the din of chatter and china and silverware, he steered their conversation away from the personal and toward music and politics—Sly and the Family Stone's album *Stand*, John Lennon and Yoko Ono's *Give Peace A Chance,* and Jimmy Hendrix getting busted for heroin. Talk of politics began with trashing Nixon, then the electoral college, and finally the Vietnam War. In between topics they ordered three cappuccinos. Gianni ordered a sfogliatelle and Colleen and Ezra ordered cannolis.

Colleen took a bite. "Not like Paganucci's. Ok, enough blabber. So, Ezra, who'd ya blow to get a newspaper job?"

"It's hardly a newspaper job. I'm an errand boy. There were fliers about summer work tacked to a bulletin board in the library. I applied to a few and got this job at *The Voice*. No big deal but kind of cool."

"Are you interested in journalism?"

"Maybe." Ezra reached under his seat, pulled two newspapers from his folder and handed one to Gianni and one to Colleen. "Just came out today. Hot off the presses, to coin a phrase."

"Errand boy or not, I think it's pretty cool." Colleen said. "I'm working at the A&P on Liberty Ave. It's a drag. How about you, Gianni?"

Gianni scanned *The Village Voice's* front page—a photograph of young people. Beneath the photo were the words *In Front Of The Stonewall.* To the right a photograph of graffiti GAY PROHIBITION CORUPT$ COP$ FEED$ MAFIA and, beneath the graffiti picture, the headlines *Gay Power Comes To Sheridan Square* and *Full Moon Over The Stonewall*. He turned the paper over. Colleen poked him.

"You gonna work at the bakery all summer?"

"Probably. Maybe take a class. I don't know." Gianni drank what was left of his cappuccino.

"Are you going back to Lyndon State in the fall?"

Since December, Gianni thought only of getting from one day to the next, and then in May, his thoughts turned to Owen. Now thoughts of the photographs and headlines in *The Village Voice* loomed. The idea of returning to Lyndon State was as remote to Gianni as space travel.

He looked at Colleen. "No."

Ezra twisted his goatee. "NYU has an awesome film school. A guy at *The Voice* goes there. You always liked film."

"I haven't thought about going back to school full time. I haven't thought about much of anything. Actually, I like baking. It's honest work. I'm tired of school bullshit. Tired of the lies." He glanced at the back page of *The Voice*.

Ezra nodded. "I hear you man. It's all a part of the system. The trick is using the system, without believing in it or becoming a part of it."

To keep from repeatedly glancing at *The Voice*, Gianni slipped it under his butt on the seat of his chair. His hands trembled and he folded them on his lap. He leaned into the table, his words barely audible. "Something broke inside of me. I don't know how to explain it. Like not only was Lyndon State unfamiliar, but I became unfamiliar to myself. Like all my life I had been going at 45 RPMs and suddenly I'm going at 33 RPMs, or my needle got stuck in a different groove. Even now when I look at things, like trees and houses and you guys." Gianni looked from Ezra to Colleen and back to Ezra. "You look unfamiliar. I mean I know it's you. I recognize you, but it's like you're not real. Like it's a cardboard cutout of you."

Gianni shook his head. "Sorry, guys. I don't mean to be such a downer. This is why I've been making up excuses not to get together." Gianni's eyes darted around the packed cafe.

Colleen placed her hand over Gianni's. "Don't worry, only Ezra and I heard what you said."

Ezra placed his hand over Colleen's. "Everyone here is deep into their own shit, but we hear you."

"Thank you." Gianni forced a weak smile. "When my parents left me at Lyndon, I know this is going to sound weird, but it was like I was back at Angel Guardian. Like I knew someday I'd be back in an orphanage, even though I have no memory of the place. At least no conscious memory. Like I expected it. I'd be alone. The word 'abandoned' kept coming into my head. Here my parents are paying for me to go to college, and they're in tears leaving me, and I'm feeling as if they abandoned me."

Ezra nodded. "I get it man. You went through some pretty fucked up shit and it finally caught up with you."

"What?"

The three leaned in closer, their elbows propped on the table.

Ezra cupped his hand over his goatee. "Your aunt, man. She dumped some pretty heavy shit on you. I don't know what it's like to be adopted, but I can imagine what it would have been like to suddenly not have my brother and sisters. To have had someone take them away."

"What are you talking about?" Gianni said.

Ezra picked up the check. "Let's get out of here, and we'll talk more outside."

They split the check three ways and headed down MacDougal toward Washington Square. Ezra on one side of Gianni and Colleen on the other.

"You and your cousins were like brothers, man. You lived in the same building. Wasn't Michael your age?"

"A month older and Peter was a year older than us."

"Bummer. You guys were tight. Your mom told my mom you used to eat with each other and do sleepovers and stuff."

Gianni stopped walking. "My mom talked to your mom about this stuff?"

"Sure, she told my mom plenty."

"About the fight?"

"Yup, she said it was about greed. Your aunt wanted your grandfather to leave more money to your uncle than your father. Some shit like that."

"Yeah, I overheard my parents talking about that stuff. Something about Liviana saying I wasn't a real grandchild."

"She was one evil bitch," Colleen said. "I remember once we were riding our bikes and you moved Michael's a little so we could lean ours against the building. Your aunt started screaming at you from the window, right in front of everyone. She told you to get your filthy hands off Michael's bike. Your mother heard her and came out of the bakery. I swear if your mother could have reached up the three stories, she would have killed her.

Next Ezra said, "And there was the day your aunt piled us all in her car to go to Rockaway beach and left you standing on the sidewalk."

Colleen grabbed Gianni's arm. "I remember that too. Come on Gianni. Let's walk."

Gianni bit his lip and stared off to the left. He stumbled a bit as Colleen pulled him. "I kind of remember the beach thing. My mom left my father in the bakery, and she and I took the train to Rockaway––116th Street."

"Yup," Ezra said. "She told my mom that she wasn't going to let you stand there and watch everyone go to the beach without you. When my mom found out that your aunt didn't take you she got pissed at me for going, but I didn't know your aunt wasn't taking you."

Colleen pulled Gianni toward an open patch of grass in Washington Square. "Me neither. I thought we were all going. Hurry up before someone takes that spot. No sense sitting around the fountain or looking for a bench. It's more crowded here than Figaro's."

Scores of young people in various levels of undress lay on the grass. Some on blankets. Others splashed in the Jacob Wrey Mould fountain. Its center geyser made mini rainbows above a cornucopia of wet bodies, swaying to the sounds of flutes and guitars and drums. The air heavy with cannabis and incense, as if a surfeit of skunks carrying frankincense and myrrh meandered about the square.

Colleen sat with her legs crisscrossed on the grass, Gianni and Ezra followed, Ezra took a joint from his bag. "This is good shit."

He lit it, took a toke, and passed it to Gianni. It made the rounds several times.

"Hey, Colleen!" A voice came from a girl wearing only panties and a bra, and at least a pound of beads. Her hair, like a bejeweled lion's mane, sparkled in the sunlight.

Colleen looked up. "Unreal! I'll be right back, guys."

Ezra shrugged his shoulders. "So as I was saying. What was I saying?"

"Something about going to the beach."

"Oh yeah, all I'm saying is she took your brothers away from you. Man, it's like not only did you find out you were adopted, but your brothers disappeared. You had the rug pulled out from under you twice in the same week. It's like you were eight years old and your whole fucking world turned upside down."

Gianni's jaw went slack. "You're right. But I didn't get it. I guess I felt it. You know, like you can feel stuff but not have the words to explain it."

Ezra swayed back and forth as if he were about to pray. "Heavy shit, man. Ya know why your aunt had to get out of the neighborhood so fast? Your mom told everyone what she did. I guess she said some pretty wiped-out shit when they were fighting."

Gianni leaned over on the grass and rested his head on his hand. He recalled the sound of her spitting and her words, *that's your son under my feet.* "I remember some of it. But not all of it. I don't even know what the fucking fight was about. One minute there was a knock at the door, and the next minute my dad and uncle are swinging at each other. My mom got between them."

"Lucky for your fucking aunt, man. I know I wouldn't want to mess with your mom. Even if you don't remember everything, it still was traumatic. Maybe that's why you don't remember much."

"Traumatic? I didn't go to Vietnam, Ezra. Going to war is traumatic. Aren't we kind of blowing things a little out of proportion?"

"Think about it, man. Your mom told my mom that you were top of your class, and after the fight your grades dropped like a fucking bomb. In high school, you were out more than you were there. I don't know how you got away with playing hooky so much. So it's like you were a pressure cooker, man, and at Lyndon you finally blew your lid. Guess I'm just saying that what you're going through now makes sense. You've probably been going through it a lot longer than you think. Ya know, like you been treading water, but now you need a fucking lifesaver."

"Ya know, you're right. You were right about Raffaella and you're right about this."

"Huh?"

"You said Raffaella wasn't my mother. You were right about that, and now you're right about this. I did go through some pretty heavy shit. I mean my cousins and I used to make tents and watch scary movies and take baths together. Especially Michael and I were really close. We'd even sit with each other in the bathroom when taking a crap. Imagine being that close with someone. No wonder I'm so fucked up."

Ezra laughed. "Now that's fucking close."

"Yup. Since they moved, I haven't seen them. Like they just vanished. Sometimes my father sees my uncle. After all, they're brothers. But I haven't seen my cousins. Not once. Even when my grandfather died. My mom said it would be better if I didn't go to his funeral. Guess Vermont just put me over the edge. Like I'd been standing at the edge for a long time, and all those fucking mountains, and trees, and cows just pushed me into this funk. Kind a like cow tipping."

"What?"

"Cow tipping. I never saw it done, but townies told me that for fun they sneak up on a sleeping cow and tip it over. Imagine doing something like that to a poor cow who's nice enough to give you milk."

Ezra removed his shirt. "Bummer. Sounds like some fucked up shit to me. Let's catch some rays." His shirt caught on the band tying his hair back. He freed the band, lay back on the grass, closed his eyes, and folded his hands behind his head. "Poor cows, man."

His long hair fanned out on the grass, and Gianni's eyes wandered from the top of Ezra's head, to the line of hair below Ezra's navel, which stopped at his jeans below his protruding pelvis. No elastic band cut across his waist. Ezra didn't wear underwear. Being stoned gave Gianni a different appreciation for his brainy friend, no longer a timid little boy. Gianni had never thought about Ezra's body. When Ezra held his arm around Gianni's shoulder as they walked to Washington Square, it felt more like something Owen would do.

Gianni also removed his shirt, his shoulders broader and body thicker and more muscular than Ezra's. He lay back in the grass. His shoulder touched the underside of Ezra's arm. Ezra stretched. His left arm fell across Gianni's chest, and Ezra's musk mixed with the lingering scent of pot. Gianni grabbed his shirt and dropped it over his crotch to conceal his rising erection.

As if floating, Gianni looked down on his eight-year-old self, sitting near the bakery window. He saw the moving men carry furniture across the sidewalk and lift each piece into a large truck: the couch and chairs where he and his cousins spread blankets to make tents, the beds they shared on sleepovers, the RCA television where they watched *Zacherley's Shock Theater*. He heard his father say, "Hey, Gianni, how about we go to a movie on Sunday?"

"Far out!"

Gianni and Ezra opened their eyes. Colleen stood above them, indistinct in a halo of sunlight.

"That was this kiss-up I knew in high school. Boy, has she changed. So, Ezra, did you diagnose Gianni's shit?"

"Yup, we decided his mother was frightened by a cow while she was pregnant and Vermont brought up a prenatal memory. Prognosis is fair as long as he stays away from ice cream."

The three of them laughed.

Gianni sat up and Ezra's arm fell to the side.

"If that's the treatment there's little hope for me," Gianni said. "I was just thinking of when my dad took me to see the *Seventh Voyage of Sinbad*. I think. Or was it *Cat On A Hot Tin Roof*? Another movie my mother thought I was too young to see. Father Kelly wouldn't have liked it either. Whatever. They were both good movies."

Colleen squatted, "Father Kelly. What the fuck made you think of him?" She pulled on Ezra's pant leg. "Sit up, now it's my turn to tell you guys something."

They resumed a tight circle, leaning into each other like three poles supporting a tepee. The full effect of their cannabis high had kicked in.

"I'm telling you this because Gianni was so honest, and then it's your turn Ezra. Three months ago I had an abortion." Their foreheads pressed together, and Colleen cried. Ezra and Gianni wrapped their arms around her.

"Weird. It's one of the few times I missed my ma. Strange how you can miss someone you don't even remember."

Ezra and Gianni held Colleen a little closer.

"I'm okay, really. It would have been stupid to have a baby, but sometimes it still hurts."

Ezra nodded. "Damn right! Of course it does."

Gianni pulled on Ezra's goatee. "Ezra, you're like fucking Sigmund Freud."

"I told you guys this because sometimes you go through stuff and you gotta talk to someone about it. There was this counselor at school. A far-out woman and she really helped me. Not sure what I would have done if I didn't have her to talk to. It was like there was this place I could blow off steam so I wouldn't explode. Just saying, Gianni, you should find someone like that you can talk to."

"You mean like Ezra."

"No! A real therapist, jackass. Ezra, it's your turn to tell us a secret."

"Hmm…let's see." Ezra sucked on his top lip. "Got it! I like pussy and dick."

Colleen burst out laughing. "Far out."

Gianni yawned. "Who are they?"

The three fell over laughing, curled up on the grass, their bodies entwined like puppies. They drifted off to someone strumming a guitar and the sound of a crystalline soprano voice,

What was said in Washington Square stayed in Washington Square, or Ezra's joint had a powerful amnesiac effect. But on the train ride back to Queens, no one mentioned Gianni's aunt, Colleen's abortion, or Ezra's sexual preferences. Once home, Gianni remembered *The Village Voice* headlines. He had forgotten the newspaper on the chair at Figaro's, and there was no mention of Stonewall on television or in the newspaper his father read, but he remembered reading Christopher Street. Two weeks later, Gianni took the A train back to Greenwich Village.

Saturday night on Christopher Street, summer of 1969, resembled a Hollywood studio lot where Westerns shared the set with the Ziegfeld Follies. Men, some wearing Stetson hats and unbuttoned flannel shirts, or no shirts at all, and drag queens in Dolly Parton wigs, eyed Gianni as if he were an angel come to Sodom and they could smell the newbie on him. He plodded along several blocks with his hands stuffed in his pockets, then stopped at a pizzeria. He leaned against a counter before the front window, and blew across his slice of pizza. An audience of three gathered. One man wearing cutoff blue jeans and a T-shirt hanging from his back pocket sang: "How Much Is That Doggie In The Window…," sounding very much like Patti Page. He ended the song with a howl. His friends laughed, and the three moved on in search of a more appreciative pretty-boy to serenade. Gianni blushed, finished his pizza, and tossed the rest of his soda in the trash.

Beyond Christopher Street, and on the other side of the Westside Highway, were the Christopher Street Piers. Temples to homoeroticism crumbling into the Hudson River. Among the shadowy bones, human silhouettes swelled and dwindled like the waves lapping at the piles below. Gianni knew the silhouettes weren't gazing at the river. He recalled summers during his high-school years at Rockaway Beach when boys and girls disappeared into the streaks of shadow and sunlight beneath the boardwalk. A few times he partook, yielding to peer pressure rather than passion.

Now what? Retreat back up Christopher Street? Enter one of the bars he had passed, or join the silhouettes on the piers?

He walked back across West Street, under the highway, turned south, past bordered up buildings, and thought to turn left at the next corner and head back to the subway.

At West and Barrow, a rusted, partially lit neon sign "HOTEL" hugged the corner of a six-story building like a dog in heat. Once a swank river-front hotel in the heyday of cargo ships and transatlantic cruise lines, turned home for itinerant seamen, turned welfare hotel, and now as abandoned and neglected and seedy as every riverfront building for a mile in either direction.

The flickering first three neon letters of the hotel sign "HOT.." winked at Gianni. Two men entered the door below the sign. Gianni bit his lip, glanced at the pack of motorcycles parked along Barrow Street, and followed the men into the bar.

A bouncer, huge with patches of vitiligo on his left cheek like isles on a moonlit sea, leaned against a stool just inside the open door. Gianni paused and pressed his hands further into his pockets.

"What the fuck, boy? You comin' or goin'?"

Gianni entered. His eyes lowered and, careful not to step on anyone's sneakers, boots, or stilettos, he slipped past hot, sweaty men and grew dizzy with the smell of musk, poppers, and cologne. But for a few white tourists, Black men reigned in this bar. "Excuse me," went unheard given the din of voices, pinball machines, a cue ball busting a rack, and the soulful Etta James rendition of *At Last* coming from a jukebox. The crowd opened around one of the pool tables and Gianni, his back against the wall, raised his eyes, met another's glance, and then looked away. The frontpage photograph in *The Village Voice* had shown people around his age. Here men were at least thirty years old or older. Maybe there were a few guys in their late twenties, but Gianni was clearly the youngest.

Leaning against the bar, beneath strands of colored lights and wearing a shimmering white stretchy romper, unzipped to just below his muscular chest, a man stared at Gianni. His Vaselined ebony skin shone like Rodin's Adam. Gianni noticed, looked away, their eyes met again and again and again, until Gianni stared back more out of defiance than acquiescence. Out swept the man's hand. His pointer finger made longer by a fingernail polished white stood erect then curved. Summoned, Gianni stepped away from the wall, paused briefly, not to interrupt a pool player's angle shot, and then found his way around the pool table.

"Welcome to Keller's. I'm Gabriel."

"Thank you. I'm Gianni." He held out his hand, and Gabriel looked at it as if he had no idea what to do.

"Oh, you are green aren't you?" Gabriel's voice was gruff but breathy, like a prizefighter channeling Marilyn Monroe. He lowered his outstretched fingers onto Gianni's hand. Unsure if he should shake or kiss Gabriel's hand, Gianni gave a little squeeze. He took full notice of the surroundings. Hypermasculine men with arms and chests bulging from athletic T-shirts or leather vests juxtaposed to hyperfeminine men wearing makeup, wigs, and stilettos, but among them, like walk-ons with bit-parts on a Hollywood studio set, most men wore T-shirts or button downs with jeans or khakis and looked like guys Gianni saw every day on the subway or walking around the streets of New York City. But Gabriel was an enigma. Despite the breathiness of his voice and his fluid motions, he had the body of Atlas, which he flexed boldly beneath his skintight romper. The weight of the world meant little to Gabriel. At least upon first appearances.

A man wearing leather chaps, his bare buttocks exposed, caught Gianni's eye. The man ran his pink tongue across parted lips. Gianni immediately looked back at Gabriel.

"So tell me, child, what brings you to a Black leather bar?"

Gianni's ears tuned red. "I didn't know…"

Gabriel opened his muscular arms and tilted his head as if he were about to lip sync *I'd Rather Go Blind,* the Etta James song now playing. "Well, child, in case you didn't notice, I'm Black." Gabriel made a sweeping motion with his hand. "They're Black, including that stud who just licked his lips at you. You know, the one wearing leather chaps. Clue…Black, leather bar."

Gianni's eye twitched. He turned away from Gabriel, about to leave, but Gabriel placed his hand on Gianni's shoulder. "Okay, child, no more teasing. Tell Gabriel what's going on. I won't bite, unless you want me to."

Keeping one hand on Gianni, Gabriel called to the bartender. "Derrick, get my child a beer and put it on that gentleman's tab." Gabriel pointed to and winked at an older white man sitting at the other end of the bar who had been eying Gabriel for the past hour.

Derrick placed an open beer bottle on the bar in front of Gianni.

"Here, child, drink up. You are old enough to drink, right?"

"Nineteen."

"Then you're ancient. Down South, I used to sneak my old lady's bootleg when I was ten."

Gianni took a sip. "Where down South?"

"Some backwater in Mississippi, but that's enough about me. Okay, talk."

"Not sure what to say. I've never been to Christopher Street. Didn't even know it existed, but my friend works for *The Village Voice*, and I saw an article about Stonewall."

"Fat Tony's dump."

"What?"

"Fat Tony? Honey, Gabriel knows plenty. The mob owns most of the gay bars in the Village. What they don't own, they still get their cut. And the pigs get their cut. Only difference between the mob and the pigs is the mob wears sharkskin and the pigs wear blue. It's all about drag, child. And when they have hissy fits, us fags get fucked. And not in a good way. The queens at Stonewall had enough bullshit. Can't blame 'em. Girls can only take so much nonsense."

"Did you see it? The riot, I mean."

"You mean revolt, child. Sure I saw it. Word spreads fast. I headed up there. Continued for almost a week." Gabriel inhaled; his huge pectorals strained against his romper. He flexed his biceps. "Gabriel can take care of Gabriel…Anyway, so you saw it in *The Voice*. Made you curious?"

"I guess." Gianni took a swig of beer. "Pretty sure I'm gay."

"Welcome to the club." Gabriel kissed Gianni on the cheek. Gianni's ears grew warm.

"Ever have a lover?"

"No. I might have been in love. Maybe I still am. And we kind of were together once, but not really."

"Not really. How does one not really have sex?"

Gianni shrugged and placed his half-empty bottle back on the bar.

"Well, Owen. That's his name. One night…" And Gianni, surprised by his own words, explained to Gabriel what had happened.

Gabriel's eyes went soft, and the corners of Gabriel's lips turned up, just a tad. "First love is always the hardest. No pun intended."

Gianni laughed.

"I like the sound of your laugh, child. Don't let nobody's shit get you down. That's for them to figure out."

Gianni leaned in and hugged Gabriel. He didn't know why. For a moment, Gabriel froze, but then wrapped his arms around Gianni. "You'll be okay, child. I got a feeling you're going be better than okay, and Gabriel knows plenty."

Outside, Gianni walked back toward Christopher Street. A man climbed down out of the shadows of an open box truck. He paused and zipped up his fly. Several guys around Gianni's age crossed West Street and headed under the highway to the piers. Gianni stopped at the corner of Christopher and West. He looked at his watch—1:00 am, too late to go home and sleep. By the time he fell asleep, it would be time to wake and help Liberato with the day's baking. He had told his parents he was going to a party with Ezra in Manhattan and not to wait up. The subway ride home would take an hour, so he had at least another hour to spare. He ran his fingers through his curly black hair, took a deep breath, crossed West Street, passed under the highway's shadows, and joined the silhouettes on the piers.

CHAPTER 13

Raffaella became the Salk Viertel of The Orchard. Not only did she engage with customers but, like a dowser finding underground springs, she discovered the opinions, tastes, and feelings of even the most arid moviegoers—their favorite and least favorite films, actors, and directors—and she introduced them to like-minded fans then stepped away so friendships could flourish. Regulars adored her, and the infrequent customers became regulars, including uptown cinephiles, professors, and university students. Viertel's salon had been an oasis for the movie-makers in Hollywood's Golden Age, many having fled the Nazi's encroaching grip on Europe. The Orchard became an oasis for the movie-lovers of those now vintage films.

Given The Orchard's financial boom, Hanns increased trips to Los Angeles and expanded his connections for films difficult to find. He planned weekly festivals and advanced sales for season or festival passes. He scheduled talkback nights and hosted guest speakers—experts with knowledge of particular films or genres.

On a Tuesday evening during a Labor Film Festival, showing John Ford's *How Green Was My Valley*, Herbert Biberman's *Salt of the Earth*, Elia Kazan's *On The Waterfront*, and several lesser-known films, Raffaella looked up from sealing a roll of quarters.

"I'll take one ticket please."

Raffaella's breath quickened. A boy on the cusp of becoming a man changes a lot in a year. This was the first she had seen Gianni since he had left for college. *Marcello*, she thought.

She tore a ticket in half, placed half on the counter for him to take and pushed away his hand holding out money. "How wonderful to see you."

"Thank you. It's wonderful to see you, too." He pointed to what was once the wall of L.A. photographs, but now an archway opened to a spacious parlor. "Wow!"

"Saul Rosenthal bought the building next door," Raffaella said. "But I can explain all that later. The movie already started."

Gianni picked at his week's growth of beard. "Will you have time to talk later?"

"Of course. This is the last show and not so many people. Go watch your movie." Raffaella waved her hands, shooing away Gianni while stifling tears.

She tried unsuccessfully to count the day's earnings.. *Eleven, twelve...no that's a five.* Memories competed with numbers. *Seventeen...*memories of making love in the shade of an almond tree, *eighteen...*labor pains followed by the cry of her beautiful infant, *nineteen...*a Carabinieri points a gun at Marcello. Raffaella pressed the palms of her hands against her ears to hush the sound of a shot. "Basta! Enough! Enough!"

She recalled Gianni's frequent visits to The Orchard during his high-school years and, as if having changed the reels on a movie projector to more pleasant memories, she sighed and lowered her hands. Better to remember Gianni's complaints about school, his youthful angst and anger about current events, and the repose he found in whatever movie he had just watched at The Orchard. Sometimes they sat and watched movies together, and then talked for hours about what they had liked or disliked.

Hanns had disapproved of Gianni skipping school, and he and Raffaella often had words.

"Don't you think it's wrong that Gianni comes here instead of going to his classes?"

"No, I don't think it's wrong. I wish he would go to school, but it's better he comes here than gets into trouble."

"If he didn't have The Orchard and you maybe he'd go to school more often."

"There's a sadness in Gianni. What's the word? Melancholy. That's it. He feels too much. Like he's carrying something very heavy. No, I don't think he'd go to school if he didn't have The Orchard. Who knows where he might go and what trouble he might get into?"

"Shouldn't you tell his parents?"

Raffaella's eyes flashed whenever Hanns suggested this. "And what should I tell them? That they should see their son's sadness. That they should ask him what's wrong and stop blaming him. Not that he'd be able to tell them. But just because someone doesn't know why, especially a young person, doesn't mean they're not troubled. It takes years to understand, and even then…" Raffaella would pause in mid-sentence as if lost in her own thoughts, but then end with, "If I tell them he comes here instead of school, he'll just go somewhere else."

Their words varied, but this was the general tenor of their dispute. In time, Hanns let the matter drop. He didn't understand his wife's relationship with the boy, but then he never saw the picture of Marcello, nor did he know that Raffaella had had a son.

Counting seventeen, eighteen, nineteen, and so forth, and then filling out the bank slip, Raffaella entertained the pleasant memories of moving from Ozone Park to Chelsea. A yard had been her only demand. After Hanns bought a brownstone in need of renovations, he had the second and third floors renovated for rentals, and the first and sub-level, a tad below street level, renovated for them to live in.

The first-floor renovation included an office, which could also serve as a guest room on the street side of the brownstone. At the back of the building was their master suite: a bedroom, small sitting area, and bathroom. The sub-level, with the exception of a second bathroom, incorporated an open design: a kitchen, next a dining area, and finally a living room with a row of French doors, which opened to a deep narrow yard including a sunny patio, large enough for two to enjoy breakfast, a late afternoon cup of espresso, or an evening glass of wine at Raffaella's mosaic topped table. Beyond the small patio, a curved stone path led to a second slightly larger brick patio covered by a grape arbor and, beyond this, a fenced rectangle of earth bore vegetables in fall.

Gianni was still in high school when Raffaella moved to Chelsea, and he helped her select and plant perennials at her new home. In the library on Liberty Avenue, where he had learned what he wasn't taught in school, he asked the librarian for books on gardening. The stout librarian with too much blue rinse in her gray hair looked from Gianni to Raffaella and smiled.

"Follow me. I'm glad to see that your son is finally researching a more agreeable topic. He's here a lot, which is good, but his interests are terribly glum for such a young fellow."

Raffaella winked at Gianni. The librarian stood before a walnut card catalogue and opened one of the drawers. "Unless you have a specific author or title in mind, your best bet is to look for books under the subject heading of gardening. There will be a description of the book on the card. For example, urban or rural gardening, geographical location, books about perennials, biennials, or annuals. Etcetera, etcetera, etcetera."

She handed Raffaella two stubby pencils and yellow paper. "The number on the left-hand corner of the card will match the number on the spine of the book. Of course, your son already knows that, but most gardening books are over there, on the other side of the sansevieria."

"Grazie. I mean thank you."

"Oh, you're an Italian." The librarian dragged out the I as if she were about to say Irish. "My favorite is veal piccata."

Raffaella smiled and nodded. Not to laugh, Gianni sucked at his cheeks.

They skimmed cards, wrote titles and numbers on the yellow papers, retrieved numerous books, and, on a worn cherrywood table, they thumbed through pages of the books and listed a variety of perennials ensuring blossoms from spring until fall.

Raffaella sighed. "Enough! I have to go home and make veal piccata for the librarian."

Gianni had put his hand over his mouth to muffle a laugh.

Raffaella smiled at the memory of Gianni's laughter. She leaned against a stool and became lost in her book until the movie ended.

In the otherwise dark parlor addition to The Orchard, track lighting illuminated Hanns's black and white Los Angeles snapshots and autographed photographs of various movie stars. There were also posters similar to those in Paganucci's bakery, but mostly celebrating Hollywood's Golden Age rather than Italian cinema: Kate Hepburn's and Cary Grant's stunning faces above a cartoon of them feeding a leopard in Howard Hawks' *Bringing up Baby*, Mae West seducing Cary Grant in Lowell Sherman's *She Done Him Wrong*, Humphrey Bogart cheek to cheek with Ingrid Bergman in Michael Curtiz's *Casablanca*, Charlie Chaplin hugging a small boy in his silent film *The Kid*. These and numerous other posters left very little wall space. The only poster not depicting a Hollywood movie was an Art Nouveau graphic of sky scrapers soaring in Fritz Lang's urban dystopia *Metropolis*. Lang was one of the Europeans Hanns had cordially befriended while in Los Angeles. He played minor roles in several of Lang's films noir. Next to the *Metropolis* poster hung a black and white photograph of Hanns with Lang sporting a monocle, taken at one of Viertel's salons,.

Gianni followed Raffaella through a shadowy mismatch of upholstered chairs, settees, and small round ice cream parlor tables and chairs that Saul acquired at auctions. Several times Gianni's shoe scraped against the leg of a table. Raffaella paused before two worn leather club chairs.

"Siediti." Raffaella pulled the chain on a table lamp with frosted glass and beaded fringe. They sat in the pool of lamplight.

"Did you like the movies?"

"Yes, very much. Especially *On The Waterfront*."

Her elbow on the arm of the chair, and her chin propped on the back of her hand, Raffaella waited out the awkward silence.

"Sorry I stopped answering your letters and cards when I was at Lyndon," Gianni said. "They meant a lot to me."

"You were busy."

Gianni shook his head. "No. I was a lot of things but not busy. In December, I left school. More like I flunked out. I didn't want to go back anyway."

Again, silence.

"Something's wrong with me."

"I can see you're sad, but I've known that for a long time."

"That's what Ezra said. Not exactly, but he wasn't surprised when I told him that I felt as if something inside of me broke. Guess he thinks all that stuff with my aunt and cousins messed me up. I told you about that. Maybe he's right. He and Colleen remember a lot of stuff I had forgotten or didn't want to remember."

Gianni nodded toward a poster of *The Rose Tattoo*. "My father has that poster hanging in the bakery. He has several posters with Anna Magnani. I don't think my mother likes her. Once I asked Mama if Anna Magnani was my mother. She had a fit. Called her a puttana. Back then I didn't know what that word meant. But I knew it wasn't good."

In the lamp-light's glow, Gianni's eyes met Raffaella's.

"I once thought you were my mother. Silly, but when you looked at me in church—that time I was with Colleen and Ezra—at least I think you looked at me, it felt like you recognized me. And I felt real, maybe for the first time since my cousins told me I wasn't. Well, they said I wasn't their real cousin, which meant I wasn't their parents' real nephew, which also meant I wasn't my parents' real son. Boy, that's a mouthful. It just made me feel as if I wasn't real, period."

"I did recognize you," Raffaella said. "From the bakery."

"But you never looked at me in the bakery."

"Of course I did. I looked at you many times. And I was pleasantly surprised when Sister introduced us. I was glad that you would be the one to help me move. Once, I remember—it might have been the third or fourth time I shopped in your bakery, you sat on the ledge at the front window staring at a moving truck. I bought bread and, while your father put it in a bag, I looked at you. It was the first time I saw your sadness. As if someone broke your heart. I wanted to sit next to you and ask what was wrong, but of course it wasn't my place to do that, and I might have frightened you."

"That was the day they moved. You know, my cousins. I mean, they already left, and were staying with their grandmother, but the moving truck made it final."

Raffaella nodded. Moments passed, then Raffaella broke the silence. "Gianni, I once had a son."

"The baby in the picture?"

"Yes."

"What happened?"

Raffaella opened her hands, palms up, and shrugged her shoulders. "What happened? The Fascists. The war. The Nazis."

"And I look like Marcello."

Raffaella nodded. "Yes, and you look like Marcello."

"Is that why you looked at me in the bakery?"

"Yes."

"As if you were seeing Marcello's and your son."

"Maybe." Again Raffaella shrugged. "As if I were seeing what could have been." The lamp's glow reflected in the sheen of Raffaella's eyes.

"The weird thing is you also looked familiar to me," Gianni said. "Not that you resembled someone I knew. It was more like I recognized something in you that others saw in me. After I learned I was adopted and my cousins moved, people, even strangers, would say I looked like I was carrying the weight of the world on my shoulders. I didn't know what that meant until I saw you in church."

Gianni leaned forward and lowered his voice, though only the posters and photographs would overhear what he was about to say.

"When I saw you, I thought that's what it must look like to carry the weight of the world. Maybe it wasn't just Marcello or your son that you saw in me. Maybe you also saw your sorrow. Like you were looking in a mirror."

Slowly Raffaella ran the fingers of one hand over the palm of another tracing what a psychic would call parallel lifelines. "Everyone carries sorrow and loss, Gianni."

"But not everyone sees another's sorrow. It's kind of a gift to recognize sorrow in someone else. It makes you feel less alone."

"Do you feel alone?"

"Yes. At least I did when I was at Lyndon and when I first came home. Maybe a little less now. It comes and goes in waves. Surely you've felt alone. I mean with what you've been through."

As if traversing a minefield, they proceeded gingerly, pausing between comments and questions.

"Was Marcello a Communist?"

Raffaella shrugged. "He called himself a Marxist."

"What's the difference?"

Again Raffaella shrugged and raised her open palms.

Gianni thought of Anna Magnani in *A Rose Tattoo* and of Fina. "Were you a Marxist?"

"I was a foolish girl."

The lamplight exaggerated Gianni's frown. "Why do you say that? You were a part of the resistance against Fascism. Nothing foolish about that."

Raffaella smiled. "And who told you that?"

"I don't remember. Ezra or my mom or someone. No, I think it was my dad. In America, anyone who protests the Vietnam War or wants racial and economic justice is called a Communist. We're all called Communists. Even people who don't know anything about Communism."

"That was also true in Italy. If you were against Fascism, you must be a Communist. Hanns said, even in Hollywood that became a big problem. A lot of careers were destroyed because of accusations."

"When I was a kid, my mom used to say she was a red diaper baby. I didn't know then, but it meant her parents were Communists, or at least her father was. And she always spoke well of him. Most of the time anyway. But the nuns in my school acted as if all Communists were from hell."

Another stillness settled between them. Hepburn and Grant, and Bergman and Bogart, and Chaplin and Coogan, and an array of other actors waited patiently for someone to speak the next lines.

"Is it not knowing that makes you sad, Gianni?"

"Not knowing what?"

"Who gave birth to you."

"Maybe, but Ezra thinks it's more than that. The things my aunt said and did, and then losing my cousins. He said what happened traumatized me. Who knows? Once, I looked through metal boxes in my parents' closet and found my adoption papers. My name was written above another penciled-out name, but I didn't look closely enough to see what was crossed out." Gianni shifted in his chair and looked around the parlor. "You said Hanns's partner Saul did all this."

"Saul bought the building and rents the upstairs apartments, but since more people were coming to The Orchard—long lines outside—Hanns came up with ideas on how to use this space. During festivals, people sit here and chat between films, or they come early. Sometimes Hanns schedules guest lecturers. We had an Elia Kazan festival, including the film you just saw, and Hanns got Kazan to speak. Do you know Thelma Ritter or Ruth Gordon and Garson Kanin? They've also done what Hanns calls talkbacks."

Gianni shook his head. "Not sure I know who they are, but that's pretty cool."

"No wonder Saul wanted Hanns for a partner. He's very good at making ideas real, but I'll let Hanns tell you about all that. I'm probably forgetting some of the speakers. What have you been doing since you left college?"

"Helping out in the bakery. Mostly in the kitchen, helping with baking. I actually like it. It relaxes me or at least distracts me. Gets me out of my head, which isn't such a great place to be."

"Honest work. Nothing wrong with that."

"I said the same thing to Ezra." Gianni's eyes grew narrow. "It's better than staring at a television all day. Maybe I'll go back to school. I don't know."

Again, Raffaella waited out Gianni's silence.

"Did you see *On the Waterfront*?"

Raffaella nodded.

"There's a scene when Brando's talking with his brother, Rod Steiger, about regrets. Remember, his brother made him throw a fight? The first time I saw *On The Waterfront* was on the *Million Dollar Movies*, and my dad said, 'I coulda been a contender,' was one of Brando's famous lines. That and when he screamed, 'Stella!' in *Streetcar*. I'm not making any sense, but this time I kind of got what Brando meant. I mean not exactly. But he lost his chance." Gianni shook his head. "Never mind. I don't know what I'm talking about."

"You're barely twenty, Gianni. You'll have many chances. First, you need time to heal."

"But how do I heal when I don't know why I'm hurting? I don't know if it's adoption or what Ezra said. Or it could also be because..." Gianni stopped. His eyes filled, and Raffaella leaned forward and grasped his hand between hers. The lamp light caught the burgundy folds in Raffaella's silk blouse, the contrast between Gianni's sun-browned arms and his sea-green T-shirt, and the sheen in their deep brown eyes. The posters surrounding them and the brilliant films they represented suddenly paled in comparison.

"You'll find your way, Gianni."

"I'm a wimp. Guys my age are dying in Vietnam, and I'm—"

Raffaella tightened her grasp on his hand. "No! Don't compare wounds. All wounds must heal."

"I know you're not religious, and I don't know what I am anymore. I mean, what I believe in. But do you—" Gianni paused, his eyes searching for the next words.

Raffaella sat back. She was used to conversations with Gianni sometimes feeling like a game of whack-a-mole, and she gave Gianni time to clarify his question.

"I guess what I'm asking is how do you think about being Jewish if you're not religious. I mean you told me your father was secular and you don't do shabbat or the kinds of things Ezra's family does."

Now it was Raffaella's turn to take pause. "I told you, when I was young, I didn't think about being Jewish any more than I thought about being tall. But then being Jewish defined me. First losing my mother at a young age defined me, then being a girl defined me—though I was fortunate to have a father who raised me to think for myself. Then the racial laws and the war. Mussolini, then Hitler, and I became a part of a living history of Jewish people. So it's true, I'm not religious and I'm definitely not a Jewish scholar. But whether or not I believe in God or hold Jewish laws as sacred, I'm Jewish." Again, Raffaella paused. Then she said, "I know persecution and I know what it is to live in—I guess the best word is diaspora. Jews were Russian, but not quite. Polish, but not quite. German, but not quite. I was Italian, but not quite. Again, it's the history of Jewish people—never really having a home. So that's how I'm Jewish. I know what Jews know firsthand. Does that make sense?"

Gianni thought for a while. Several times, he began to speak but stopped as if the words had slipped away. Finally, he spoke. "A few minutes ago, you asked if not knowing makes me sad. You know, not knowing who gave birth to me. I'm not saying that I'll never search to find my birth parents, but even if I do find them it won't change who I am. There's something they could never understand, just as there's something my adopted parents can't understand. But I think you just told me what that is. I'm also of a people who live in diaspora. I mean, isn't that exactly what an adoptee's story is? We just don't have the rituals to acknowledge it. I don't know anyone else who was adopted. Maybe that's what I miss. Someone else who really gets it without me having to explain. Not that having been adopted is good or bad. Just that it is."

Raffaella leaned forward again. She placed her hand on Gianni's arm.

"I love you, Raffaella. I've loved you from that first time you looked at me in church. At first, I thought it was because you were my mother. Then I thought I had a crush on you. At least Ezra thought that.

But I was just trying to find a way to understand what I felt."

"Maybe some things even Ezra can't explain," Raffaella said.

Gianni laughed. "He'd disagree."

Raffaella smiled. She released his arm. "I have an idea. You said you like baking or at least it helps you to relax. Why don't you sell coffee and biscotti here. It would be something to do—something new, different. Get you out of your head and out of your house. You'll also make some money. Build your confidence. That's the word. Yes? Confidence. And you can see all the movies you want. I'll talk to Hanns. As I said, he's good at making ideas real."

"Wow! I kind of like that idea."

Raffaella cast her eyes on the surrounding posters. "There's magic at The Orchard. The old films under a sky of stars. It's make-believe, but sometimes we need make-believe to heal. It was a safe place for you when you were in high school. It could be that again, at least until you are ready to move on. And you will move on. I promise you that. This will just be a little rest, while you find your confidence. A sanctuary."

"Sanctuary!" Gianni said. He pointed to the poster of Charles Laughton in *The Hunchback of Notre Dame*."

"Yes," Raffaella said. "But don't pour molten gold on the customers."

They both laughed.

Hanns agreed. If having Gianni around made Raffaella happy, so be it. Sure, Gianni probably had a crush on his wife, but who didn't? Most likely Gianni reminded her of someone special from her past, a childhood friend or a boy in the orphanage where she once worked. Hanns envied the ease of their long conversations. Nothing more.

Saul thought it was a great idea. But then Saul acted as if everything Raffaella suggested was brilliant. His school-boy crush on Raffaella once irritated Hanns. But hadn't Hanns been enchanted by Raffaella when they first met? She didn't become invisible once they married. He got used to Saul's crush, he got used to heads turning wherever they went, he got used to men staring at Raffaella while purchasing movie tickets at The Orchard and trying to make silly small talk with her. Whenever he mentioned to Raffaella that a particular man went overboard, she shrugged and said, "In time it will change." But, at fifty, that time hadn't yet arrived. Hanns doubted that it ever would. Much of Raffaella's charm was her indifference to her appeal. Not that she didn't attend to her appearance, but she wasn't one to primp or fuss—her taste understated, except for earrings. Her earrings and hair suggested a hint of gypsy.

Once, Hanns asked her why she wasn't vain.

"About what? Everything has its advantages and disadvantages. If someone is very tall they can see more than others, but they also bang their head a lot."

Hanns chuckled, but then shuddered at the thought of Raffaella in the camps. Better to be invisible.

Hanns, Saul, Raffaella, and Gianni met to come up with a plan for a modest coffee and dessert stand. Saul hired the same contractors who did the original renovations.

In the back of the parlor, they updated wiring and outlets, installed shelves and a counter above a display case, and Saul purchased a secondhand refrigerator and coffee makers. Raffaella had a small neon sign made: *Sanctuary.*

Fina and Liberato bought Gianni a used delivery van and had the words *Sanctuary: Paganucci's Pastries* scripted on both sides. Liberato suggested painting images of a belfry or gargoyles. "Maybe the Hunchback of Notre Dame yelling, 'Sanctuary!'" Liberato said.

"While you're at it," Fina said, "you can also paint a picture of Anna Magnani yelling, 'Jackass!'"

Liberato decided *Sanctuary: Paganucci's Pastries* was sufficient.

Gianni already knew his way around the kitchen and the basics of baking. Now Liberato taught him how to make a variety of biscotti: mixing the simple cookie dough, including extracts (always a little vanilla, but also almond or anise), adding slivered almonds, chips of chocolate, or pistachios, rolling out the dough logs, baking, slicing, baking again, and the final touch—drizzle with chocolate.

For cannoli, Liberato taught Gianni how to whisk the ricotta until smooth and beat heavy cream until firm, then fold the two together.

"Go light on sugar and other ingredients," Liberato said. "You want to enhance the flavor of the ricotta cream, not overwhelm it. Sometimes a few chips of chocolate. Up to you. Some customers like them. Some don't."

Making the shells was more complicated and took longer. Gianni soon mastered rolling out the dough until thin, cutting small circles, wrapping each dough circle around a mold, and then the frying. Tedious. Unlike mixing and kneading and rolling-out, frying cannoli shells was not a task Gianni found relaxing.

Liberato stressed not to fill the shells until ready to sell them. "Nothing worse than soggy cannoli. We'll wait and see how the biscotti and cannoli sell. If sales are good, then I'll teach you how to make sfogiatelle and pasticciotti, my signature pastry. That's why I display them in my star showcase beneath the posters of Anna Magnani."

Gianni told his father that the new room at The Orchard also has a lot of movie posters, including one of Anna Magnani.

"Only one?" Liberato frowned and shook his head.

The last week in September, Gianni opened *Sanctuary*: Thursdays and Fridays, 4:00 pm until midnight, Saturdays, 2:00 pm until midnight. And Sundays, 2:00 pm until 9:00 pm.

Sanctuary was open for over a month and doing well when The Orchard commenced a Lena Horne Festival, showing William Nolte and Ralph Cooper's *The Duke Is Tops*, Andrew Stone's *Stormy Weather*, and Vincente Minnelli and Busby Berkeley's *Cabin In The Sky*. The festival began on a Friday evening with *Cabin In The Sky*, and a talkback by a film professor from City College.

The audience filed out of the theater, through the lobby, and into the parlor for the talkback. Raffaella stepped behind the counter to help Gianni. She often did this on busy nights, especially when there were talkbacks. Like Fina, when a customer had difficulty deciding what kind of biscotti they wanted or maybe a cannoli, she made up their mind for them. Sometimes Ezra also worked. Gianni paid him for his hours, including travel time.

A tall Black man tapped a long glossy fingernail on the display case. "I'll take that one right there. I am partial to chocolate."

"This one?" Raffaella lifted the biscotti with the most chocolate, placed it on a paper plate, and handed it to Gabriel.

Gianni almost dropped the cup of coffee he was pouring for a customer. Gabriel looked at him, but Gianni kept his eyes on the stack of paper cups next to a full Silex.

"Coffee?" He said, keeping his eyes on an empty paper cup.

"Yes, please. I like mine light and sweet, child."

Without looking up, Gianni handed Gabriel a cup of coffee.

"Thank you, child."

When most of the audience was seated, Raffaella left Gianni and Ezra to wait on the remaining customers, and she resumed her role as The Orchard's Salk Viertel. She greeted regulars and welcomed newcomers. There were more first timers than the usual, including several African Americans. You could count the number of The Orchard's regular Black patrons on one hand.

Raffaella introduced herself to Gabriel and Gabriel's two friends. They sat on each side of Gabriel like understudies in the wings waiting for the star to miss a line, but Gabriel was in true form: witty, campy, and gregarious. He pointed to an empty chair at the small round table. Raffaella joined them.

"A cannoli and coffee please," an elderly man repeated for the second time.

"What?" Gianni said, louder than he meant to.

"A cannoli and coffee, young man."

"Yes, of course. I'm sorry."

Lost in thought, Gianni didn't hear Hanns introduce the guest lecturer. He struggled to listen to the small professor with a billowing red pocket handkerchief speak. At what appeared to be staged intervals, the professor removed the handkerchief, wiped his brow, and then stuffed it back into his pocket with aplomb. More of a theatrical gesture than necessity, given he didn't appear to perspire.

To focus on the speaker and stop worrying about what Gabriel might tell Raffaella, Gianni pinched himself. A trick he had practiced in high school to help him pay attention, especially when he had a teacher whose pedagogy was to lecture from bell to bell.

The professor took a sip of water, wiped his brow with his red handkerchief, and then said, "Unlike *Cabin In The Sky*, in which Lena Horne had a prominent role, she was given minor roles in numerous Hollywood films. She usually played a cabaret singer in scenes that could easily be cut before a movie was shown in southern theaters. She refused to play a maid—that was the role most Black actresses got at the time in mainstream movies."

Did Gabriel tell Raffaella that she met me in a gay bar? Gianni blew out his cheeks and pinched his arm.

"Horne was passed over for the role of Julie in *Showboat* because of racism, and therefore the role went to Ava Gardner. Despite that, their friendship endured." Red handkerchief, wipe. "Horne and Gardner are both no-nonsense women and remain the best of friends to this day."

Gianni heard little of the rest of the professor's lecture, nor did he pay attention to the questions and answers. He was ashamed he hadn't said hello or even made eye contact with Gabriel. *But I pretended not to know Gabriel for other reasons. It's not about race*, he kept telling himself. *As if that's any better. I'm as full of shit as all those film editors who left Black actors on the cutting room floor.*

Applause startled him. People began to leave.

"You okay here, Ezra, in case someone wants something to go? There's something I have to do."

"Sure. No problem."

Gianni walked around the display case, approached the table where Gabriel, his friends, and Raffaella had resumed their conversation. He paused. They looked up at him.

"Hello Gabriel. It's nice to see you again."

Someone called to Raffaella, and she excused herself. Gabriel propped an elbow on the table, and rested his chin in the palm of his hand. He tapped his glossy fingernails against his strong jawline. He smiled.

"I'm sorry," Gianni said.

"For what, child?"

"For not saying hello sooner."

"No need to apologize, child. Gabriel is nothing if not discrete. I've been arrested by cops who I've blown the night before. A lady never tells. Right, girls?"

Gabriel's friends nodded in agreement. He stood, and then pushed his chair back to the table. "Now if you'll excuse us. Girls need our beauty rest. Delores and Tammy, this is Gianni. By the way, child, Tammy does a great Lena Horne. Better than Lena."

Gianni turned to Tammy. "Maybe someday I'll see your show."

Gabriel placed his hand on Tammy's arm and said, "Yes. Someday he will. Some children just need a little time to figure things out." Gabriel smiled at Gianni. "By the way, your mother is lovely."

"My mother?"

Gabriel pointed to Raffaella.

"Oh, she's not my mother."

"Well, whoever she is. She's a doll. Tell her I said thank you for the welcome. And don't worry. What happens in Keller's stays in Keller's. Or is that Vegas? Same difference. Ta-ta!"

"Bye Gabriel, and it was nice meeting—" By the time Gianni finished his words, Gabriel and his friends had already turned and were leaving. Gabriel waved his long fingers over his broad shoulders. Track lighting reflected on the gloss of his fingernails.

Gianni rapped his knuckles against a table top and mumbled to himself, "Fuck me!"

Hanns escorted the professor to the front door. Raffaella said goodnight to the few regulars who lingered to talk with her. There were always a few.

She gathered empty paper cups and plates while Gianni swept and Ezra scrubbed the Silex coffee pots.

Hanns picked up stray napkins from the floor. "Another great night. Couldn't have gone better. And Sanctuary really added to the evening. You're doing a great job, Gianni."

"Thank you."

"Raffaella, you were pretty chummy with those guys sitting over there." Hanns pointed to the table where Gabriel and his friends sat.

"Yes. Fans of Lena Horne. They knew a lot about her. Probably more than your professor. You should have had them speak."

Gianni stopped sweeping.

"Don't get me wrong," Hanns cleared his throat. "There were plenty of guys like that in Hollywood. Maybe a little more discrete. But everyone knew."

Raffaella crushed a paper cup in her fist. She looked at Hanns. "Yes, we also had people *like that* at Buchenwald." Raffaella exaggerated the words *like that*. Her tone icy. "But it was hard to be discrete when you had a pink triangle sewn on your shirt."

Gianni's hand tightened around the broom. Neither he nor Hanns responded. Ezra looked up from a soapy coffeepot. Even the actors on the vintage posters looked startled.

Gianni knew that Raffaella wouldn't ask him how he knew Gabriel. Knowing what not to ask had become an unspoken rule in their friendship.

PART 3

My silences had not protected me. Your silence will not protect you.
—Audre Lorde

CHAPTER 14

First and second graders from Saint Mary Gate of Heaven and P.S. 62 searched the curbs and sidewalks and small front gardens along 104th Street. Their mission was to find the perfect fallen leaves for classroom bulletin boards. Most prized were the bright reds from Mrs. Basilio's sugar maple, but children had to rise early for such pickings. She was quick to sweep up and bag debris. Occasionally one of the many Norway maples shed a bright gold or orange leaf. These were second best. Soon most of the children tired of their task and jumped in the hillocks of leaves their parents or grandparents had raked up, scattering them back across sidewalks. Ezra crossed the street on his way to Paganucci's and nearly stumbled over a little guy rolling in leaves.

Liberato and Fina waited on customers, but they motioned to Ezra that Gianni was in the kitchen.

"Morning, Baker Man!" Ezra used the nickname he gave Gianni after Sanctuary caught on at The Orchard.

"Hey, Ezra." Gianni rolled dough through a pasta maker, decreasing the setting each time until the dough was thin enough to make sfogliatelle shells. He had practiced this all winter and perfected it in time for Sanctuary's first anniversary.

Ezra sat on a stool at the butcher block counter across from Gianni, his jacket open, exposing a T-shirt with the words "THEY CAN'T KILL US ALL!" The same words he and friends had painted on a sheet they hung from an NYU dorm window after the Kent State massacre back in May.

"Did you hear about Joplin?" Ezra said. "First Hendrix. Now Joplin. What the fuck. What a bummer."

"Yup, definitely a downer." Gianni stretched out the paper-thin dough on the counter, greased it with butter, and slowly rolled it into a log.

"They performed at Woodstock," Ezra said. "Out of sight. Sure they were stoned, but so was I. So was everyone. I'm sitting in the mud, butt naked and I hear Joplin belt out *Summertime*. Thought I was trippin'. She was amazing. Then again, I probably was trippin'. You should have gone with me."

"Um, I was kind of a mess that summer. Remember?" *Stretch, grease, roll. Stretch, grease, roll.*

"Boy, you really get into that shit."

"It relaxes me. Baker's yoga. Jamming the heels of my hands into dough or going after nuts with a knife."

"As long you don't go after *my* nuts with a knife."

They both laughed. *Stretch, grease, roll.*

"My shrink says it's because I'm in control. Could be." *Stretch, grease, roll.* "Elavil helps too. Kind of a quack, my shrink, but whatever. Looks like a Freud-wannabe."

Ezra pulled a flier from his backpack where he kept an endless supply of them: meetings, protests, boycotts, concerts. Whatever progressive event about to take place in Manhattan, Ezra had a flier for it. He was a walking kiosk.

"Remember that time you went to that group therapy and got the hots for a lesbian?"

"I didn't get the hots for a lesbian. I said I thought she was cute, and it was interesting that she turned out to be a lesbian."

Gianni never brought up Ezra's comment in Washington Square about liking pussy and dick. Once he started college, Ezra took on a flower-child persona with his crystals, chamomile tea enemas, daily transcendental meditation, and following a guru, Maharishi something or other. Ezra's dramatic transformation and his stoned proclamation that summer day about his sexual preferences might have had more to do with espousing free-love than declaring himself bisexual. Either way, Gianni wasn't about to ask him. Ezra occasionally spoke of girls he dated or at least fucked, but he never asked Gianni about his absent love-life. This was fine with Gianni. Whenever Gianni's parents asked about girls, he responded: "I have enough trouble dealing with me right now, never mind trying to figure someone else out. Plus working keeps me busy." This was true. Baking and managing Sanctuary took up a lot of his time, with the exception of sporadic, clandestine escapes to the Village.

Ezra pushed the flier toward Gianni.

Done stretching, greasing, and rolling, Gianni wrapped the loaf of dough in wax paper and put it in the refrigerator. Tomorrow he'll slice it, gently press his thumb into each round and form a cone shape, careful not to separate the ribs of dough, add two tablespoons of ricotta cream, press the open edge together, place each on a greased tray, and bake until they transform into golden sfogliatelles. Their surface light and crispy—inside, sweet and creamy.

Back at the counter, Gianni read the flier.

Ezra twisted the edges of his beard. "Know anyone who might be interested?"

"You're not thinking Raffaella?"

"You read my mind, Baker Man. She's exactly who I'm thinking of. I know the girl making the film. A friend at NYU Tisch. I met her at *The Voice*. Probably mentioned Jennie to you before. Her parents are Holocaust survivors. It's her senior project, but of course much more than that. No agenda. Just survivors telling their stories. And Raffaella has an important story to tell. She was involved in the resistance before the camps. She and many others tried to take down those mother fuckers. Someone must tell those stories. Too many folks think Jews just sat around waiting for Nazis to come get them."

Gianni read the words on Ezra's T-shirt "THEY CAN'T KILL US ALL!" Except for those few moments in Washington Square, Gianni had never thought of Ezra physically. He was just Ezra. Handsome? Not particularly, but a man can be attractive without being handsome, especially when he speaks of something he believes in. Clearly Ezra believed in this film.

"I don't know," Gianni said. "Raffaella doesn't talk much about the past. Especially Europe. Especially the camps. Once in a while she'll mention something, but I've learned not to push. She kind of freezes and gets this faraway look. A heavy look like she's carrying the weight of the world."

"Like you do."

Gianni nodded.

"No harm in asking. And my friend's only a junior. This isn't due until the end of her senior year, but she's beginning to get her ducks in a row. Ya know, it's a big project, so Raffaella would have time to think about it."

Ezra stood and walked to one of the windows. "Look at those crazy kids jumping in leaves. Makes me think of when we were kids. We used to do that."

Gianni stared at Ezra. "Funny, the literal meaning of sfogliatelle, the pastries I just made the dough for, is little leaves. They do kind of resemble a miniature stack of leaves."

Ezra turned from looking out the window and met Gianni's eyes. "I'm glad you came back from Vermont, Baker Man. I'm sorry you had such a hard time, but for what it's worth, I'm glad you're here."

Unsure how to respond, Gianni simply held Ezra's gaze. Ezra broke the silence. "Sanctuary is pretty cool. Like you once said, baking is honest work. It's all good, man. All good."

"I've gotta go. I have a paper due tomorrow. Think about asking Raffaella if she's interested. See ya later, Baker Man."

"See ya later, Ezra."

His backpack hanging from one shoulder, Ezra stepped out of the hot bakery kitchen into the breezy autumn day. Gianni thought of Owen. Nothing about Ezra reminded him of Owen, but in the course of most any day, thoughts of Owen came and went—skiing with Owen, wrestling with Owen, Owen's head in his lap while sitting by a fire, and Owen's hot, sweaty body sliding up against his, their gasps muffled by the passing A train. Maybe Ezra's nostalgic tone or the word Vermont triggered thoughts of Owen. Gianni wondered if he'd ever stop thinking of him. If he'd ever stop missing him. If he'd ever stop loving him.

Fina startled Gianni. "Ezra left already?"

"Yup, he had a paper to write."

"I had some rugelach for him to take to his grandmother." She held out a paper bag and looked at the clock. "Shouldn't you be leaving soon?"

"Pretty soon." Gianni stacked several Tupperware filled with biscotti.

Fina took a cookie from the bag, took a bite, and again held out the open bag to Gianni. She lifted the flier from the counter. "What's this?"

"Ezra wants me to give it to Raffaella. A friend of his is making a film about Holocaust survivors."

Fina wiped rugelach crumbs from her bib apron with the flier and made the sign of the cross with her free hand. "You want help carrying the Tupperwares to your van?"

"No, there are only a few. But thanks." Gianni slipped on his denim jacket, festooned with decals and buttons. "Years ago, Papa told me Raffaella was involved in the resistance against Fascism in Italy. Later that night, I asked you about the resistance, but I didn't mention Raffaella."

Fina nodded. "Yes, I remember. Golda told me about Raffaella. Not a lot. Just that she was involved."

"Are there other things she told you? I mean about Raffaella. She doesn't talk much about what she's been through."

"Knits and purls." Fina placed the bag on the butcher-block counter, then folded her arms, and leaned forward. She rested her elbows next to the paper bag, the way she sometimes leaned on a pillow at a windowsill, waiting for Gianni to come home. "Some stories are easier told in knits and purls, like when I knit an afghan or a sweater. A little of this and a little of that. Maybe that's how she remembers it. Too much to remember all of it at once. You already know Raffaella was in the camps. What's there to say about concentration camps? Too terrible to imagine. After the war, she went back to Italy and worked in an orphanage. That's how she met Father Marlo. She didn't have any family here when she came to America. Father Marlo sponsored her, or vouched for her—not sure what they call it. Anyway, she lived at the convent for about a year before she found an apartment. When she first arrived, Father Marlo called the rabbi at Golda's synagogue, the rabbi called Golda, and Golda called me. She thought I could help with translating, but Raffaella already knew a lot of English, and what she didn't know, she learned fast. She talks better than me. I think her father was a professor." Fina shrugged. "That's it. Before she came here, I know she was in the resistance and then in Buchenwald. Nothing else."

"Do you know about Marcello, or—" Gianni paused, afraid he might betray the little confidence Raffaella had entrusted in him.

"Who's Marcello?" Fina took another rugelach from the bag.

"He was a man Raffaella knew in Italy."

Fina waved her hand. "I don't know any personal stuff. Golda's not a gossip. One of the things I like about her, unlike most of the women in this neighborhood. And some of the men."

"I'm not sure about showing this flier to Raffaella. Like you said, maybe she has to remember in knits and purls. Remembering all at once might be too painful."

Fina placed her hands on her broad hips. "You're a twenty-year-old boy in America. We have enough food to eat, a good business, a good place to live." She pointed to the windows. "No black shirts or brown shirts coming to take us to a prison or a concentration camp. You're a good boy. Like my father, your grandfather, injustice troubles you. But Raffaella's a grown woman who's been through things we can't begin to imagine. For you to try and protect her is an insult. Show her the flier. Tell her what Ezra told you. She'll make her own decision."

Gianni hugged Fina. "I'm glad Anna Magnani's not my mother. She can't compare to you."

Fina laughed and messed Gianni's hair. "I'm glad too. And I agree."

Gianni folded the flier, slipped it in his back pocket, and lifted the three Tupperwares of biscotti. Fina set the bag of rugelach on top. "Give these to Raffaella before I eat them all. Hopefully she likes more than biscotti. Papa and I will see you later. After we close the store we're going to The Orchard to see *La Strada*. Papa's seen it so many times he can recite every line by heart. But you know Papa when it comes to Fellini." Fina shook her head and wiped more rugelach crumbs from her apron.

Gianni arranged biscotti in the showcase. Several customers sat at tables or in club chairs. They sipped coffee and munched on biscotti or pastry. They chatted and read the Sunday paper. One woman chewed the edge of her already mangled pencil and read clues in *The New York Times* crossword puzzle.

Not a full house, but an ample crowd showed up for the *La*

Strada matinee. Once the movie began, Gianni's customers entered the theater—except for the cruciverbalist devouring her pencil stub. Gianni wiped down the empty tables and smiled at the words Sanctuary at The Orchard stenciled across the front window. Hanns had commissioned a local artist to do the work. Outside, leaves and trash swirled. The window pane shuddered.

Sanctuary was now the neighborhood place to go. Not the same clientele who frequented Figaro's on MacDougal and Bleecker and, fortunately, not the large numbers. That would be too much, too soon. But enough customers to maintain a steady buzz and turn a profit.

On talkback nights, Gianni locked the street door and hung a sign in the window: "Talkback." In time, regulars learned what this meant. Regardless, they were miffed to have walked a few blocks for a cup of coffee, dessert, and distraction only to find the door locked, so now Gianni posted the talkback schedule in advance.

"Lyceum! Done!" The sole remaining customer said and folded her *New York Times*, stuffed it in a satchel already bursting with books and papers, stuck what was left of her pencil stub behind her ear, and trudged lopsided toward the front door. Her heavy satchel bumped against her left ankle. She opened the front door. Ginkgo leaves blew in on a gust of wind and rustled among the empty tables and chairs.

Raffaella joined Gianni in the parlor and poured herself a cup of coffee.

"A good turnout?" Gianni asked. He swept up the leaves and dumped them in a trash can.

Raffaella rocked her hand back and forth. "Cosi cosi."

Gianni busied himself pushing chairs closer to tables. *Let's get this over with*, he thought and slipped the flier out of his back pocket.

"A friend of Ezra's is making a film about survivors. I mean Holocaust survivors."

He handed Raffaella the flier. She unfolded it. Across the top were the words "Never Again." Beneath the bolded title was a description of the project and contact information.

Hanns entered the parlor. "Saul's nephew just stopped by. While he watches out front, I thought I'd grab a coffee." He noticed Raffaella's expression. "Is something wrong?"

Gianni cleared his throat. "Ezra has this friend making a film about Holocaust survivors. He wondered if Raffaella might be interested in being interviewed. I didn't think it was a good idea, but—"

"Raffaella, you don't have to do this. Gianni, if you didn't think it was a good idea, then why—"

Raffaella shot a glance at Hanns. "Stop!"

The front door opened, and Raffaella held up her hand. "Un momento!" The customer froze, his hand holding the door open. The parlor turned cold.

Raffaella looked back at the flier, appearing unsure of what she had just read. She glanced back at the customer. "Close the door!"

She turned, walked to the lobby, entered the theater, and sat in the last row. She took in the masterful Italian actress Giulietta Masina's heart-rending portrayal of the forlorn clown, Gelsomina. The mournful cries for compassion coming from Gelsomina's trumpet tore at the wounds in Raffaella's heart. The flier sat open on her lap. Darkness obscured not only "Never Again" but the tears streaking down Raffaella's face.

That night Sanctuary closed at 9:00, but Gianni waited the extra twenty minutes for *La Strada* to end so he could drive his parents home. He knew Fina wouldn't sit through the second film.

"Cozy but better than the subway," Fina said.

Gianni's van didn't have a back seat—more room to transport baked goods and other supplies—so Fina, Liberato, and Gianni sat crammed together on the front bench seat. Gianni turned right on Delancey and drove toward the Williamsburg Bridge.

"Did you enjoy the film?"

"Fellini!" Liberato raised his hand as if he were about to direct an orchestra. "What's not to enjoy!"

Fina shrugged her shoulders. "Giulietta Masina is wonderful, but I don't like Anthony Quinn. Faccia bruta!"

Liberato laughed. "That's because you don't like the character he played."

"True, that big blow-hard Zampano. Masina should have smacked him in the head with her trumpet."

"That would have been out of character for Gelsomina."

"Maybe in Fellini's version. Not in mine."

"The two of you are more entertaining than *La Strada*," Gianni

laughed. "Fellini should make a movie called *I Forni*. (The Bakers)
 They all laughed at that.

At a stop light, a homeless man approached the van and wiped the windshield with a dirty rag. Gianni rolled down the driver's window and handed him a dollar.

"God bless you," the man said, expelling the stench of alcohol.

Fina shook her head. "In Manhattan, some people live in penthouses and others in the gutter."

"But he'll probably just buy alcohol," Liberato said.

"You think people in penthouses don't spend their money on alcohol?"

"True."

Headlights shone from varying directions as Gianni turned onto the Williamsburg Bridge. With folks returning home to Brooklyn or Queens after an afternoon and evening in Manhattan, traffic slowed to a stop, then go, then stop again.

"You know, Mama, you were right."

"Of course."

"You didn't give him a chance to tell you what you were right about." Liberato shook his head and laughed. "Did you know this was once the longest suspension bridge in the world? That was back when America did everything first. Now we're first at everything falling apart."

"No, I didn't know that, Papa. But as I was saying, Mama, you were right about letting Raffaella make her own decision about the Holocaust film. When I showed her the flier, Hanns came in to the parlor and asked about it. I mentioned that I didn't think it was a good idea, and he told Raffaella that she didn't have to do it. She just froze. I don't know if it was the thought of doing this interview or if she got angry at Hanns and me for what we said. She even shouted at some poor customer who was coming in. Then she went to sit in the theater. Hanns said she had just seen the movie a few days ago. But I guess she wanted to be alone or just away from us. She left without a word to Hanns or me."

"Humph! So to get away from the two of you she had to watch Zampano bully Gelsomina again," Fina said.

"Are you saying we tried to bully Raffaella?"

"Worse. You tried to take her choice away. You tried to protect her from something neither one of you know anything about. You assumed you knew better than her about what she could handle. No doubt she dealt with plenty. Something only women know about war."

Gianni pictured the *Two Women* poster hanging in the bakery. His stomach knotted. "But I didn't mean to—"

"You're a good boy, Gianni. No you're a good man. Like my father, you hate injustice, and you want the world to be better. But it's not better. When I was young, our apartment was always filled with men talking, arguing, shouting about big important ideas. Sometimes there was a woman or two who outshouted the men. And then there was my poor mother, a good and kind woman. She served coffee and wine and Strega. And after they all left, she emptied ashtrays and washed dishes. So for all the talk about injustice, they treated my mother like their servant. When I brought Papa home to meet my parents, my father wasn't impressed. 'What do you want with him?' My father said. 'A merchant. Small-minded bourgeoisie,' he said. I said, 'At least he hears me. With him, I can speak for myself, and we don't have to agree to respect each other.' For the first time ever, my father, with all his lofty opinions, shut up. As I said, like my father, you hate injustice. That's not bad. But don't be like him in thinking you always know what's better. Let others think for themselves. Raffaella survived more than any of us can understand. She doesn't need your protection."

Contradictions stirred within Gianni. He resented what Fina said. And before he understood why, he blurted out, "Did you ever think about protecting me?"

"What?"

As if someone else spoke using his voice, someone who understood what he didn't, someone who had the words to clarify his feelings, Gianni continued. "When the two of you fought with Uncle Leo and Aunt Liviana."

"Liviana! Her parents should have named her Brutta. That bitch!"

"Yes, that bitch. That's always what you say, Mama. You can't see beyond your own hate. But you didn't think of me."

"A fight between adults has nothing to do with the children."

"Really? Did you ever think that not trying to appease Liviana, no matter how much of a bitch she was, not trying to patch things up with her made me lose the closest thing I had to brothers?"

"Gianni—"

"No, Papa. Mama just spoke about the importance of being heard, and she's right. I insulted Raffaella. And I hope she forgives me. But now I want you to hear me. Yes, Aunt Liviana was a horrible woman! But maybe, for me, for my sake, you should have put up with her. Maybe I should have been more important than hating her. And if I always knew I was adopted, she wouldn't have had any ammunition. You gave her that power. In third grade, everything I thought was real suddenly became a lie. And then you want to know why my grades dropped, why things got worse in high school and college? Why I'm still so fucked up? You acted as if it were all my fault. As if I intentionally made bad choices or didn't try hard enough. One day I'm playing with my brothers, together with my family, and the next day my brothers are snatched away from me, and I find out my family is not really my family. I guess trying to protect Raffaella was treating her like a child. And that's wrong. But I was a child. I was fucking eight years old, Mama. Eight years old. I needed protection."

Gianni could barely see through his tears. His hands shook.

"Do you want me to drive?" Liberato said in a soft faraway voice.

"No! I'm fine. Like your father, Mama. I'll shut up now."

Silence: driving home, parking the van, walking up the stairs to their apartment.

After Gianni climbed into bed, Liberato appeared at his door. "Goodnight, Gianni."

"Goodnight."

Gianni pulled the chain to the lamp on the night stand next to his bed. He turned away from Liberato. He heard a soft whimper and assumed it was Fina. In the distance the A train called, and then it roared. Like Coney Island bumper cars, Gianni's anger crashed against regret, backed up, and crashed again, backed up again, crashed again, backed up, crashed, again, and again. What Fina said was true, but no truer than what Gianni said. He thought of Ezra's words that day in Le Figaro's Café, *You went through some pretty fucked up shit and it finally caught up with you.* Knowing he hurt his mother, Gianni's heart broke. Yet he also felt oddly relieved, as if he purged himself of a truth he didn't understand until now. He felt a little more real, a little more visible, even if just to himself.

The next morning, being Monday, Paganucci's was closed, but Liberato wasn't about to disappoint the neighborhood children on Halloween. He floured the butcher block counter, rolled out cookie dough ¼-inch thick, pressed a cookie cutter into the dough over and over, and transferred the pumpkin shapes onto a parchment lined baking sheet. A lone oven, set at 375 degrees, waited to bake Liberato's Halloween cookies.

After school and into early evening, trick-or-treaters will line up at the bakery door for a wax bag containing two large pumpkin-shaped sugar cookies glazed with royal icing.

His black lashes dusted with sleep and hair tangled, Gianni poured himself a cup of coffee. Since opening Sanctuary, he no longer helped Liberato with morning baking.

"You're up early," Liberato said. He placed the baking sheet in the oven and sprinkled more flour on the counter for the next batch of cookies.

Gianni yawned. "I woke up and couldn't get back to sleep." He held the Silex pot toward his father. "More coffee?"

The aroma of fresh coffee and cookies baking, the sound of the A train passing, and black windows slowly turning gray, spoke of any morning. But it wasn't any morning. Words were said last night that couldn't be ignored today.

Fina and Gianni could be hot-headed. During his early teenage years, Gianni pushed boundaries like any teenager. Tempers flared, but come morning all was forgiven, forgotten, and nothing had changed, like when seeds fall from a Kaiser roll or loaf of semolina bread, the flavor and texture remain the same. But more than a few stray seeds fell last night. Liberato, ever the peacemaker, asked Gianni to please sit down. "I have a few things to say about what happened."

Gianni filled his father's empty cup with coffee, and then sat on a stool at the butcher-block counter.

Liberato pressed the heel of his hand into another ball of dough. "Thank you for the coffee," he said.

"You're welcome."

Liberato floured the large wooden rolling pin. "You were almost a year old when we adopted you. They told us that because of our age, we'd get a toddler, two or three years old, and it would take a year or two, but in less than a month Angel Guardian called and said a baby had suddenly come available." Liberato pressed the rolling pin into the dough. He pressed and rolled in various directions. "We had nothing. No crib, no clothes, no baby bottles, but we closed the store and drove right to Angel Guardian." Press, roll, press. "A nun told us your parents were good people and healthy. She told us a story. She said a baby had been placed with a couple, but during visits, the social worker noticed the husband was very attentive, but the wife was distant." Press, roll. "In time the social worker learned the husband wanted to adopt a baby, but the wife didn't. And they took the baby back from the couple." Roll, roll. "I don't know if you were that baby. All I know is they said you suddenly became available. That's how adoption was talked about or not talked about back then."

"In knits and purls." Gianni said.

"What?"

Gianni shook his head and sipped his coffee. "Nothing. Just remembering something Mama once said."

Liberato pushed the rolling pin aside and wiped the flour from his hands and his eyes met Gianni's. "We didn't know anyone who had adopted. The nun said it was up to us, but she recommended that we not tell you. 'Raise him as your own,' Sister said. And as soon as we held you, you became our own. As if you were always our own."

Frost on the gray windowpanes melted into tears. Liberato took a handkerchief from his pocket and blew his nose. His eyes filled. "Gianni, please check the cookies in the oven."

"Done." Gianni removed the tray of golden sugar cookies, set the tray on the far end of the counter, and returned to the stool.

Liberato pressed more rows of pumpkin shapes. "So, should we have raised you knowing you were adopted?" He shrugged his shoulders. "Different times, Gianni. Even Mama's cousin Dr. De Britta said we should tell you later or not at all. I'm not saying it was right. Just saying it was different times. I think people thought if you tell a little one he's adopted, it's like saying he's not yours. Better to wait until they're older and can understand things."

Liberato looked up from the rows of pumpkin shapes and looked at Gianni. "All I can tell you is that the day Mama and I brought you home from Angel Guardian was the happiest day of our lives. Did we do some things wrong? Sure. All parents do things wrong, but it's not because they don't love their children. And we certainly never meant to hurt you."

Liberato lifted the pumpkin shapes and placed them on parchment in another tray. "To be honest, we were also afraid. Afraid that, if you knew you were adopted, you wouldn't want us. We knew we wanted you, but how could we know what you would want? And after we told you, that fear came true, at least for Mama. You were always asking about who your mother was. Remember you even asked if Anna Magnani was your mother." Liberato chuckled.

Gianni didn't laugh. He just listened. This was the longest either of his parents had spoken of his adoption.

"Of course you were curious. It's only natural, but Mama thought you were trying to replace her. As if she wasn't good enough. Even your friendship with Raffaella. Mama doesn't mention this, but I think she feels that you wish Raffaella was your mother instead of her."

Liberato placed the cookie tray in the oven.

Gianni's eyes filled.

Liberato wiped flour from his hands onto his bib apron. "About Liviana. What can I say? We knew she hurt you. That's why Mama hates her so much. True, sometimes your mother has a hard time seeing the good in people. But even a saint would be hard pressed to find the good in Liviana. I don't want to bad mouth the woman. I don't even remember half of what she did. She's a bullshit artist. Always has to be better than everyone else. She didn't like that you were smarter than her kids. You always got better grades. In second or third grade, the school did what they called acceleration. You'd have to ask Mama. I don't remember what it was about, but you were put in the half-day acceleration class for kids who learned faster. Michael was put in the full day. Liviana didn't like that. And she didn't like living over a bakery. My brother was what we used to call henpecked. I don't even remember what the fight was about, but I'm sure Liviana stirred something up for my brother to come down and bang on our door. What difference does all that make now? Except it hurt you. And I'm very sorry, but there was no peace with that woman. However, you're right. We gave her power she should have never had. It wasn't her place to decide how and when you'd find out you were adopted. That was our fault."

How easy for Gianni to hug Liberato and say it was okay, that last night he spoke in anger. Pretend it didn't matter, but it did matter. When his parents told him he was adopted, his response was, "It's just that the wrong lady had me." Eight years old and he was already protecting his parents' feelings at the expense of his own. No more.

He watched Liberato press the heels of his hands into another ball of dough. He bit his lip and clenched his fists to keep from hugging his father. His words were angry, but true. He didn't know how true until he said them. Even now he could say more. But why?

It wasn't about punishing his parents. It was about understanding himself. Understanding that though Fina blamed him for changing, it wasn't his fault. She said more times than he could recall, "You're too smart to be getting such poor grades. You didn't used to be like this."

In high school when he feigned illness and she picked him up in the nurse's office, she said: "There's nothing wrong with you. You look healthier than most of the kids in the hallways."

But grief can be as debilitating as any virus—more painful. Liberato and Fina didn't see it. But Raffaella did.

"I can see you're sad, but I've known that for a long time." Those were Raffaella's words. Words his parents had never said. Didn't they see it?

Gianni didn't wish Raffaella was his mother, but he was grateful that they had found each other. For years he had felt guilty when Fina said he changed. He wasn't about to feel guilty about befriending Raffaella. She had been right when she said, "Don't compare your wounds to others. All wounds must heal."

Gianni's therapist said that losing his cousins so suddenly and learning he was adopted was traumatic. And before her, Ezra had said the same. The day Gianni's cousins said he wasn't real, he became an only child. The day he watched the moving men empty his cousins' apartment, his loneliness was sealed. He kept his feelings of loss locked in a closet, unaware that they were even there, unaware that they seeped out beneath the locked door and eventually made him a stranger even to himself. And though he heard and considered his therapist's and Ezra's words, he didn't quite get it until last night.

Yes, it would be easy for Gianni to hug Liberato and say everything is okay, to protect them from his hurt the way he tried to when he was eight years old. But everything wasn't okay then or now. And he grew weary of pretending and protecting.

One closet door finally smashed open, but there was another. He was loathe to open that door to others, except to his therapist, Gabriel, and the random men he occasionally met on the Christopher Street piers. Not yet.

Gianni stood, brought his cup to the sink, washed it and put it back on its shelf. He slipped on an apron, washed his hands, removed another ball of dough from the refrigerator, and together father and son pressed the heels of their hands into the cool balls of dough, until they were warm and pliant.

Later that day, Gianni painted his face to look ghoulish and gave out pumpkin cookies to the neighborhood children. At the dinner table that night, Gianni, Liberato, and Fina spoke of the children and their costumes over bowls of steaming pasta e piselli. Fina cut a slice of semolina bread for Gianni. A few seeds fell on her blouse. She brushed them away, and then handed Gianni the chunk of bread.

When Hanns arrived home on the night Gianni had shown Raffaella the flier, Maya Angelou's *I Know Why the Caged Bird Sings* lay open on an ottoman before a rosewood lounge chair. Next to the chair, on an end table, sat an empty Meissen porcelain demitasse cup, one of a set of eight Hanns gave Raffaella on their first anniversary, along with a dozen long-stemmed red roses. The outside lights were on, and Hanns found Raffaella wrapped in a heavy sweater and crouched in a flowerbed pruning and mulching the heirloom roses she and Gianni planted five years ago. Tea roses were her favorite.

"It's cold out here, my love."

Raffaella looked up. Garden lights reflected the few rebellious coils of silver in her unruly hair. Puffiness around her eyes spoke of tears. "I'll be in soon."

Hanns returned to the living room and sat in the matching rosewood lounge chair next to Raffaella's open book. He thought better than to make a cup of espresso. Too late for caffeine. He dozed, then woke to a kiss on his forehead. Raffaella sat on the ottoman. Two photographs lay face down on her lap.

"I hope you didn't argue with Gianni."

"Nothing serious."

"Hanns, you once said it's time for both of us to let go of the past, but should I decide to do this interview, there are things you must know."

"You already told me that—"

"I know what I already told you, but there's a lot I didn't tell you, and should have. You've been a good husband, Hanns. You've given me a second chance at life."

"You don't have to do this, Raffaella."

"Yes, I do. I mean, at least I need to tell you. Later I'll decide about the interview. But this is a first step. I owe you this."

"You owe me nothing. You've also given me a life I never dreamed possible."

"Then we're even. But please, listen now. Keeping this to myself, I'm tired of the loneliness."

Raffaella had turned out the garden lights, but a full moon illuminated the yard, and a breeze ruffled the grape arbor vines and the Japanese red maple branches, casting ghostly shadows upon the row of French doors. Shadows appeared, vanished, and reappeared, as if anxious to overhear what Raffaella might tell. So many stories. Surely, she wouldn't share them all. Surely, she didn't remember them all. Surely, some were impossible to unearth.

"My mother died when I was young. My father was a university professor. Literature, especially poetic forms from the Sicilian School. You've heard of Dante. *La divina commedia.* Yes?"

Hanns nodded.

"My father was a brilliant man, not only accademici, but in life. He never trusted Mussolini. Even when many Italians, including Jews, joined the Fascist party. My father said Mussolini was a despot.

"In the summer of 1938 the Manifesto of Race was published, and my father knew what would soon follow. I was sixteen. He sent me south to live with Catholic friends in the Tuscan countryside. Signora Noti, a widow, and her two children. In childhood, my father and her husband were friends. Like my father, he also hated Mussolini and Fascism. When I was younger, we visited with them for a few days each summer. A beautiful place. A large stone house, vineyards and olive groves. Even some livestock. Angelina was my age, and Marcello was two years older. After their father died, we no longer visited.

"I didn't want to leave home, but my father insisted. He said we'd communicate through mutual friends. No letters. After the manifesto was published, one law after another stripped Jews of any rights. We went from being Italians who happened to also be Jewish to being Jews without a country. By the end of the summer, my father lost his position at the university."

Hanns fidgeted with the buttons on his cardigan sweater, his lips taut and nostrils flared.

"Angelina and Marcello were part of the resistance against Fascism. Marcello more so. Much more so. I knew little, except that envelopes and packages were passed among partisans in the surrounding mountains. But I joined Angelina, riding our bikes short distances, one house to another, or one cave to another. We delivered packages where Marcello told us to.

"Signora Noti, I'm sure, surmised what was going on, but never said anything. She spent much of her days in church saying rosaries.

"Marcello disappeared sometimes for a week. But when he was home, what can I say? I make no excuse. He was like no one I ever knew. I found myself pregnant and Signora Noti insisted we marry. The priest didn't know I was Jewish, or he didn't let on. Italians are very good at ignoring what we don't want to see."

Raffaella placed the picture of Marcello on Hanns's lap. He lifted his reading glasses, which hung from a lanyard around his neck. Then Raffaella handed Hanns the picture of her holding her son.

He looked from one picture to the other. The corners of his lips turned up. A faint smile. His eyes filled with tears.

"A beautiful young mother and baby," he said, his voice cracking.

He looked more closely at the photograph of Marcello. "Gianni's likeness to Marcello is uncanny." He sighed, thinking he finally understood Raffaella's friendship with Gianni.

"We named our son Gino after Gino Bartoli, the champion Italian cyclist. A vocal anti-Fascist. Marcello's hero. A year or so after our Gino was born, Marcello crossed paths with Gino Bartoli who was smuggling false documents to help Jews and known partisans leave Italy. By then, Italy had entered the war.

"Marcello was then a known and wanted partisan. I saw less and less of him. He never returned to his mother's house for fear of placing us in danger. Weeks would pass, sometimes a month or more, and then I'd receive a message to meet him in one of the caves in the nearby mountains. I'd bring food, sometimes a package left in the barn behind the Noti's house.

"We grew hopeful when Mussolini was arrested. There were rumors of peace talks, but then Germany invaded Italy, took control of the north, and they freed Mussolini. The Nazis and Fascists hunted down Jews and partisans."

Raffaella's breasts rose with a deep sigh.

"I received a message that a package was left in the barn and I should meet Marcello but not bring any food. Carrying food might draw attention. Not to wake Gino when I left, he slept with Angelina that night instead of me. I hid the small package under my skirts, walked through the vineyards and then up into the mountains. We spent the night in a cave."

Raffaella paused. She looked toward the yard where shadows pressed against the French doors. "We woke to blinding flashlights and the sound of German and Italian. Nazis and squadristi—the Blackshirts."

Shadows seemed to sigh and darken. Raffaella turned away from the doors and brought her hands to her face. The lamplight sharpened the numbers on her arm. "'That's him!' someone shouted in Italian. 'And that's his Jew wife.'"

Hanns leaned forward. "No more, Raffaella."

But Raffaella didn't stop. She lowered her hands. "Who knows how they knew Marcello was there, knew I was his wife, knew I was Jewish? By then, most Fascists had turned against Mussolini and Fascism, but not all. I heard a shot. But I was still alive."

Puzzled, Raffaella looked at Hanns, as if this was the first time she heard her own story. As if it were as shocking and unimaginable to her as it was to Hanns.

A single rose petal fell from her sweater onto the oak floor. A brief distraction. She lifted the petal and pressed its cool velvet between her fingers.

"Another shot, and a squadristi yelled, 'Morto!' and spit on Marcello. And then that horrible death rattle. Marcello choking on his own blood."

Raffaella stared past Hanns, looking at the scene that she could never cut from her memory.

"They dragged me out of the cave. Maybe I was screaming. I don't remember. If Marcello was dead, what did I care about living? But I also had a son. And for him I had to learn how to survive."

Gently, Hanns pressed Raffaella's hair away from her face. She looked into his eyes. "What's there to say about Buchenwald? I have no words to describe hell.

"After liberation, I found my way back to Italy. I learned that only a few weeks after the night the squadristi and Blackshirts found Marcello and me in the cave, word spread that Nazis were heading toward our town. There were stories that Nazis raided towns and killed all the young men, believing they were partisans. Women and children were spared. So the men in our town hid in the mountains. They returned to the stench of burnt flesh."

Raffaella pressed her face into her clinched fists and screamed. "Women, all ages, children, babies, including Signora Noti, Angelina, and my little Gino had been shot by those Nazi monsters, their bodies tossed on a pile of smashed pews in the church and set on fire."

Hanns embraced Raffaella. They swayed prayerfully because words were not enough to purge the grief.

When their eyes went dry, Hanns released Raffaella. Her face had turned pale and her arms went limp.

"My father, grandparents, and whatever relatives I knew of all perished in the camps. I'm the only one to survive."

She glanced at the French doors. The shadows vanished.

Once in bed but unable to sleep, Raffaella and Hanns stared into the darkness. Hanns reached for Raffaella's hand.

"One question," he said. "If Marcello smuggled false documents to help Jews and partisans leave Italy, why didn't the three of you escape?"

Asking certain questions about the past is as futile as questioning the future, but Hanns asked so little of Raffaella and accepted so much. For his sake, she tried to make sense of what didn't happen.

"I don't know for sure if, like Gino Bartoli, Marcello smuggled false documents," Raffaella said. "Maybe the packages were of money, or maps, or some kind of communications. But I do know Marcello would not leave Italy. Some men love their hatred, their beliefs, their lofty aspirations more than their wife and son. So that leaves the larger questions I have no answer for. If I knew he would never leave, why didn't I ask him to help Gino and me escape? Did I love him too much to leave? Did I put my love for him above my son's safety? I can't count the number of times I've asked myself those questions. And what's worse, I've often dreamt of little Gino asking me the *same* questions."

Hanns turned, faced Raffaella, and slipped his arms around her.

CHAPTER 15

Gianni unlocked the door from the street to the parlor rather than enter The Orchard through the lobby. He carried in trays of biscotti and pastry, a case of Half-and-Half, and several bags of coffee beans. He arranged the biscotti, sfogliatelle, and pasticciotti in the display case, filled a half dozen cannoli shells with ricotta cream, then put away the remaining shells, cream filling, pastries, and biscotti in the refrigerator. He ground coffee beans, lined two baskets with filters, filled each with a dozen scoops of fresh-ground coffee, and added boiling water. Four days had passed since he showed Raffaella the flier. No more excuses. A cup of fresh coffee might serve as a healing potion.

Raffaella looked up from her book. She smiled. Gianni's eyes remained focused on the steaming cup.

"I'm sorry." He held out the cup of coffee.

"For what?"

"You seemed angry Sunday night. I thought it was because I tried to take your choice away."

Raffaella set her book down next to the cash register, accepted the cup of coffee, and blew across its steam. "Is that what you tried to do?"

"That's what my mother said I did. She thinks Hanns and I acted as if we knew better than you about what you can handle. I mean about the interview."

"Do you think you know better?"

"Of course not."

"Then neither do I."

Gianni stuffed his hands into his pockets. "But you seemed angry."

"Not at you. Or Hanns." She sipped a little coffee. "I was angry at the past."

A framed poster hung on the wall behind Raffaella with the words "Joan Crawford Week" in bold script. Beneath the title, photojournalist Eve Arnold's black and white photograph of Crawford filled much of the poster. The four films featured for the week: *Dancing Lady* (1933), *The Women* (1939), *Mildred Pierce* (1945), *Humoresque* (1946).

Raffaella pointed. "Have you seen these films?" She moved aside to give Gianni a clear view.

"*Mildred Pierce.*"

"Ahh—my favorite. I like the no-nonsense women Joan Crawford played. I also like Bette Davis."

"My mother also likes Bette Davis. She says Davis has chutzpah."

Raffaella laughed, then pointed to a poster of Crawford with John Garfield. "Tonight we're showing *Humoresque* again. I saw it yesterday afternoon. Hanns said John Garfield was the Jewish Marlon Brando."

Gianni looked at the black and white image of Crawford contemplating Garfield as he played a violin. "Don't think I know him, but I like Marlon Brando." Garfield reminded him of the photo of Marcello. He wondered if Raffaella thought the same. His dark curly hair, piercing eyes, and brooding expression, as if burdened by his music.

"He reminds me a little of you," Raffaella said.

Before Gianni could respond, Hanns shouldered his way through The Orchard's front door. He carried a large cardboard box filled with smaller boxes and bags of candy.

"Gianni, please grab this."

Gianni took the box, and Hanns lifted another he had set down next to the door. They placed the boxes on the candy counter.

"I was just telling Gianni that John Garfield was the Jewish Marlon Brando."

"That he was." Hanns took a utility knife from his back pocket, cut open one of the boxes, and nodded toward the picture of Crawford. "The photographer who took that was also Jewish. Her father was a Rabbi."

"My husband is a walking encyclopedia of Jewish trivia," Raffaella said, sounding lighthearted and uncharacteristically coquettish. She had always referred to Hanns by his name and never used the endearing "honey" or "sweetheart." Even calling him "my husband" sounded odd to Gianni, though Hanns had been her husband for six years.

"I had to go to three wholesalers in Canarsie to find everything we need," Hanns said. He stepped behind the counter and replenished the display case with Milk Duds, Dots, and Sugar Babies.

"By the way, I ran into Saul. He's moving to Island Park. Hard to imagine Saul leaving the Lower East Side, but a lot of Jews are leaving the city for Long Island."

About to excuse himself and unlock the street door to Sanctuary, Gianni paused when Hanns mentioned Island Park.

"I have a friend who lives in Island Park. Maura Silberman."

A dozen boxes of Junior Mints sat on the glass counter. Hanns picked up two or three at a time and placed them on a shelf beneath the glass counter.

"Silberman?" He twisted his lips to the side. "Of course. Maurie and Esther Silberman. He's a podiatrist. Saul recommended him." Hanns looked at Raffaella.

"Remember? When I had the gout. That was no picnic."

"I'm friends with his daughter, Maura," Gianni said. "She also went to Lyndon State College."

"Yes, that was terrible thing what happened." Hanns shook his head.

"You mean about her husband being killed in the Vietnam?"

"Yes, that too, but I mean what happened to the poor girl."

The poor girl? Gianni's stomach knotted. He looked at the row of Joan Crawford's no-nonsense images. The arch of her eyebrows rose in alarm.

"There are two sisters. Maura had a younger sister." Gianni said.

"I think it was the older sister." Hanns looked to Raffaella, as if for advice. He looked back at Gianni. "I'm sorry, Gianni, I'm sure it was the older sister. Saul and I visited during shiva. The younger sister was there. Your friend passed from cancer. So young. Did you know her well?"

"Yes."

When Gianni told Ezra what he had learned from Hanns, Ezra told him to go home. "I can handle things here."

But Gianni stayed. Ezra corrected his errors: the wrong pastry, too much or too little change, handing coffee to a customer who had asked for tea.

After they cleaned up and closed Sanctuary, Gianni said he wanted to wait until the last show of *Humoresque* ended and the customers left.

"Think I want a little quiet time in that dark theater. It's kind of soothing under the stars."

"Want some company?" Ezra said. "We don't have to talk. I'll just sit with you."

"Sure."

They waited then stepped into the empty theater and turned out the lights, except for the starlit ceiling. Gianni recalled walking arm in arm with Maura under a dome of stars against the velvety black Vermont sky. He looked up at the theater's ceiling and recalled his own words, *Maura, I love you*. And her response, *I know, I love you too*. He told Ezra about that night—it was the last time he saw Maura.

A sliver of light interrupted the dark. Raffaella peeked in and saw Ezra sitting next to Gianni. She closed the door, went up to the projection room, and started the film. She knew how to operate the projector in case the projectionist called in sick, and Hanns happened to be in Los Angeles.

First, a clicking sound, and then light flashed on the screen. A violin bow moving with frantic grace into Czech composer Antonin Dvarok's composition, then the credits: actors, directors, producer. Gianni did resemble John Garfield, who resembled Marcello. And Maura was no more. And Owen hadn't a clue. When the film ended, Gianni wept. Ezra placed his arm around Gianni's shoulder and they sat in the dark theater under the starlight ceiling.

Maurie and Esther Silberman sat at the edge of their bone-colored leather couch. Gianni sat on the plush white living room carpet with his legs crisscrossed under the coffee table. Pictures of Maura fanned across the table's glass top. The Silbermans were a gregarious couple, and Gianni felt at ease despite the nature of his visit. He had been in their company only twice—at Maura and Jimmy's wedding, and then at Jimmy's wake. They sipped iced tea and exchanged polite chitchat.

Maurie complimented Gianni's beard. He said it made Gianni look very wise—like a rabbi. They all smiled.

"Whichever picture you want. Your choice," Maurie said.

Esther took a bite of one of the rugalach Gianni brought from the bakery.

"Your father made these? Delicious."

Gianni smiled and nodded. He selected a photo of Maura wearing a yellow summer frock, her thick brown hair in a loose braid, her dark eyes glistening, and her mischievous smile accentuated a single dimple.

"Thank you."

"Just a picture," Esther said. "No need to thank us. Maura was very fond of you. We should have contacted you. It all happened so fast, the surgery, the chemo. All consuming. In hindsight there are so many maybes and what ifs." Esther patted her eyes with a napkin. "Maura made a party for Maurie's 50th birthday. Party hats and all. It was so hot that she took off her wig and put the party hat right on her bald head. All of her beautiful hair gone from that terrible chemo." Esther smiled through her tears.

"That was our Maura," Maurie shook his head. "Our rabbi used to visit with her. We don't go to temple often, but he's a nice man and meant well. He visited less often after Maura said she wanted a carving of a middle finger pointing up on her tombstone."

Fearing he might cry, Gianni refrained from sharing similar stories of Maura. Instead, he listened and nodded. For the most part, he remained silent.

When he called the Silbermans, they immediately knew why.

"We'd love to see you," they said. Maurie held the phone away from his ear, and Gianni heard Esther's voice in the background.

Esther rolled her tear-dampened napkin into a knot. "I envy you, Gianni. Catholics believe in an afterlife. Jimmy's mother said now Maura is with Jimmy. I wish I could believe that. I wish I could believe that someday I'll see them both again."

Maurie's eyes darkened, "Esther stop. What good will such talk do?"

Sounding surly rather than apologetic, and reminding Gianni of Maura, Esther said, "I'm sorry. I shouldn't have talked."

The Silbermans sat back, and the leather couch sighed.

Once, Gianni would have agreed with Jimmy's mother, but now he was sure of very little, except he was heartbroken about Maura and unable to stop thinking of Owen.

Squinting through his tears, he drove from Island Park to Manhattan instead of home to Queens. After parking his van on a narrow street in Greenwich Village, he headed to the piers in search of sex. The rush of the hunt might clear his head and numb his emotions, if for only an hour or two.

About to cross West Street and head under the highway, he first glanced left and spotted folks outside of Keller's. Too far away to make out features. A year passed since he last saw Gabriel at The Orchard. Some nights he hit the bars along Christopher and West Streets or cruised the piers, but he stayed clear of Keller's for fear of running into Gabriel. For Gianni, the Village was a world of strangers and one-nighters, not friendships. *Maybe it's time to change that*, he thought.

He crossed Christopher Street. He walked along West toward Barrow. Two people were leaving Keller's.

Gianni recognized Tammy from the Lena Horne Festival.

"Excuse me."

Tammy paused and looked at Gianni.

"Is Gabriel here?"

"Who wants to know?"

"I'm Gianni. Remember, we met at The Orchard? Remember, the Lena Horne film?"

"Oh, yes. I remember. You were sorry for not saying hello." Tammy and her friend resumed walking. Tammy waved her hand toward Keller's as if dismissing Gianni. "Shooting pool."

There were few people in the bar, and Gianni spotted Gabriel leaning over a pool table about to take a shot.

"Gabriel?"

Gabriel turned. Gianni's eyes widened and jaw dropped.

"Don't look so frightened, child." Gabriel set down the cue stick and fanned his long, orange fingernails against his swollen, plum-colored eyelid and cheek. "I wore full drag a few nights ago. Absolutely stunning. Some straight boys just messed with the wrong queen. You should see what they look like."

Gabriel's friends eyed Gianni and offered a chorus of hm, hm, hmms.

"Gurls, don't get your panties in a sweat. This here's my prodigal son come home to beg his mother's forgiveness after a very long absence."

Gianni shrugged his shoulders. "You're right."

"Well, I've had enough eight ball. How about you buy me a cup of java?" Gabriel waved goodbye to his friends, grabbed his white faux fur jacket, and slipped his arm through Gianni's. Given it was a Tuesday and early evening, Christopher Street felt like Coney Island off season.

"Child, you look troubled. Although you always look troubled. Part of your charm. Kind of like what's his name in that movie about rebels."

"*Rebel Without A Cause?*"

"That's it. You look like the dark-haired actor,"

"Sal Mineo."

"Child, no wonder you work in a theater."

"I seem to look like everyone."

"Not everyone, child. Only good-looking brooding guys."

Gianni laughed at that.

A man wearing a red bandana and a leather jacket stepped into the street. In the storefront window behind him stood two mannequins dressed in full leather from cap to boots, and behind the mannequins was a pegboard festooned with chains and dildos. The man smirked at Gabriel and Gianni. "Someone's having chicken for dinner."

Gabriel flipped him the bird, and pulled Gianni close. "Don't mind that ole chicken hawk."

They turned the corner, walked a few blocks, and entered Tiffany's Diner. The abundance of pink—pink Formica, pink vinyl booths, pink frosted glass—suggested a flamboyance of flamingos descending upon Sheridan Square.

Gianni took his coat off.

"Don't you look dapper." Gabriel removed his jacket.

In Gianni's neighborhood, a long-haired, white, twenty-year-old (barely a) man, wearing a white button-down shirt and tie (given his visit to the Silbermans) would draw a lot of attention sitting across from a muscular, fortyish, Black man with a shiner, who wore a T-shirt with the Marilyn Monroe quote "Give a girl the right shoes, and she can conquer the world." At Tiffany's, they were simply two more customers.

Over bacon and eggs, home fries, toast, and several cups of coffee, Gianni told Gabriel about visiting Maura's parents. Gabriel's animated responses—shaking his head and punctuating his words with, "terrible—mercy—hm, hmm, hmmm"—prompted Gianni to go on. By the time the waitress cleared their plates, he spilled details from first meeting Maura and Owen to not being able to erase Owen from his thoughts.

"You got it bad, but first love can be like that," Gabriel sighed. "It's like imprinting, child. When baby ducks first see their mama, all they can think of is Mama. She moves, they move. She jumps in a pond, they jump in a pond. If she jumped off a roof, they'd follow her. Sounds like you got a serious case of imprinting." Gabriel pushed his empty cup to the edge of the pink Formica table for the waitress to fill. "You want more, child?"

"No thanks. This is going to sound weird, but I don't think it was an accident that Hanns ran into Saul, and then mentioned to Raffaella and me that Saul was moving to Island Park. It's like Maura wanted me to know what happened to her. Kind of her way of saying goodbye. But more than that. You know, the way I'm stuck on Owen, I think Owen is stuck on Maura. And Maura wants me to let him know she's gone so he can move on with his life. Like I'm supposed to be a messenger."

"Could be." Gabriel added milk and three packets of sugar to his coffee. "Sometimes we're asked to do the work of angels."

Gianni looked at Gabriel. "Angels? Are you religious?"

"My daddy was a preacher. So let's say I got religion. Too, too much religion. The only thing I liked about church was the choir director's package. Talk about amazing grace."

Gabriel arched his broad shoulders back, turned his face to the right, and his fingers fluffed his scarf. The harsh restaurant lighting accentuated Gabriel's bruised eye and cheek. "I wasn't always this ebony goddess. I was once an ashy, little sissy who had the Holy Ghost beat into him and then right out of him."

Gianni recalled Raffaella lighting candles in church. He recalled his own reflection in the bakery window while he watched a moving van drive away. He looked at Gabriel and saw in him what he recognized in Raffaella, what he now understood others recognized in him. He saw beyond Gabriel's bruised eye and cheek, beyond his taut ebony muscles, beyond his drag. He saw Gabriel's trauma.

"I'm sorry," Gianni said.

"Child, that was a long time ago."

Gianni assumed this wasn't Gabriel's first shiner. He figured Gabriel had a lot of them before he learned how to defend himself and gave as good as he got—even better.

"No," Gianni said. "I'm sorry for not saying hello right away when you came to The Orchard."

"You already apologized for that."

"But I'm apologizing again. I know what it is to feel invisible, to feel like you're not seen, to feel like you're not even real. I was very wrong not to say hello to you as soon as I saw you. Very, very wrong. I'm truly sorry."

"Thank you, child. You're sweet."

Gianni picked up the check. "My treat."

"I ain't gonna argue."

The cashier handed Gabriel a shopping bag. She snapped her gum and rattled off a list of sandwiches. "You got some ham and cheese in there, some pastrami, a little corned beef—"

"Thanks, Sylvia. Tell Danny he's a doll."

Shopping bag in one hand, Gabriel took Gianni's arm with his other hand, and they headed to the river front.

"Hey, Gabriel." A lanky light-skinned boy, his hair in cornrows gone nappy, appeared out of a dark alley that smelled of piss.

"You hungry, child?"

"Sure."

Gabriel held out the open bag.

"Close your coat, child. It's November."

The boy flashed a smile that could melt a glacier. "Johns gots to see the merchandise."

Gabriel shook his head. "Careful your merchandise don't freeze and break off."

The boy laughed and bit into his sandwich. "Thanks! You the best, Gabriel."

By the time Gianni and Gabriel reached the piers, one sandwich after another had been claimed by hungry teenagers, some barely thirteen. Gabriel tossed the empty bag and lit a cigarette. Gianni considered what Gabriel said about imprinting. Gabriel was a mama hen and this brood of young queer boys, what Sister Joan Marie might have once called "wretched souls," were his baby chicks. And Gabriel didn't call them sinners, didn't tell them to repent, didn't have any agenda except to feed them because they were hungry.

"You always do this?" Gianni said.

"Do what?"

"Give out free food."

"Not just me. These children has to eat. Restaurants throw out more food than they sell. I just collect it before it hits the dumpsters."

"Are they hustling? I might have seen a couple of these guys around before."

"Hustling. Selling weed. Some pick up a few bucks with little jobs here and there, washing toilets or sweeping up after bars close. What they got in common is being queer, and their families threw them out."

Gianni wondered what his parents would say or do if he came out to them. "Where do they sleep?"

Gabriel swept his hand across the view of the riverfront, boarded up warehouses and the empty parked trucks.

"The Ritz," Gabriel said. "And for a couple of bucks, some bars also let the children sleep in back rooms. The Stonewall used to do that before it closed. There's also a place in the East Village a couple of sister-friends started. Some kids stay there on and off. I used to keep a couple of mattresses on the floor where I live, but then one or two kids ripped off some of Gunter's stuff. I get it. You do what you can when you don't know what's coming next. But Gunter was getting old. Better not to have kids coming and going, especially if I wasn't there."

Gianni didn't ask who Gunter was. He figured Gabriel would tell him if he wanted him to know.

"Once I went with someone for money," Gianni said.

"Only once?"

"Yeah. I was curious. Like the time my friend Colleen and I stole cardboard airplanes from the Five-and-Dime. Not that we wanted them. We put them together and flew them from the top of the El steps. A bus smashed them."

"So did you throw the john off the El after you were done with him?"

Gianni laughed. "No, but I did meet him in the subway. It's like I knew he was gay."

"Gaydar."

"What?"

"Gaydar. It's how we recognize each other. A look that lingers a second too long. Although you don't have to use gaydar to know I'm a friend of Dorothy."

"A friend of Dorothy?"

"Oh honey, you need a gay-boy introduction course. So tell me about your subway john."

"He kept looking at me, and then just before he got off the train, he kind of jerked his head for me to follow him, and I did. Turned out he was in town on business and staying at the Algonquin Hotel. I told him I charge. I figured that would be the end of it, but he said okay. Beautiful lobby. Looked like something in an old movie. A lot of dark wood, fancy furniture, plants that looked like palm trees. The rooms were small. After I left, I saw this down-and-out guy sitting by the subway and holding out a cup for money. I put the money I got from the subway guy in his cup. I didn't need it."

"You're like a queer Robin Hood. You fuck the rich and give their money to the poor."

"Yeah, but only once. I'll stick to baking in my parents' shop."

A full moon appeared, vanished behind clouds, then reappeared like a child playing peek-a-boo. Gianni preferred when it hid. Gabriel's bruised eye and cheek were less visible.

"Earlier you said sometimes people do the work of angels. People like you. I mean, ya know, giving out food and all."

"I'm no angel," Gabriel said.

Gianni laughed. "That's a Mae West movie."

"Mae West. I know a drag queen who does a better Mae West than Mae West. Where do you think she got her material? Black drag, child. Only difference is she got the big bucks for it. What else is new?"

Gabriel's banter turned serious. "I've been where these children are and survived. At least so far. Not everyone does." Gabriel pointed to the Hudson. "That river eats a lot of queer kids. Especially queer Black kids. Sometimes nobody else wants them except the river. And sometimes they don't go willingly."

Moonlight reflected on the rippling Hudson.

Gabriel stamped out his cigarette. "I'm heading back to Keller's. What's your poison?" Gabriel held out both of his hands, palms open like the statues of Madonnas at Gate of Heaven. He held one hand toward the piers and one toward Keller's.

"I'll probably head home soon. Thanks for listening to me. You know. The whole thing about Maura and Owen."

"Anytime, child. Anytime. That's what mothers are for." Gabriel fluttered his fingers goodbye and walked toward Keller's.

Again, passing clouds obscured the moonlight, leaving the Hudson to churn without sparkle. Gianni walked out to the end of the pier. He ignored the surrounding shadows. He sat on a piling that rose slightly above the pier's rotted decking, and he stared at the water. How much pain must someone feel to find these pitiless waters seductive? He saw hands reach up, slap at the river's current, grab at the cold night air. He pressed his palms against his cheeks and wiped away tears. This had been a day for grieving. For Maura and for the boys whose parents had thrown them out like pottery that didn't glaze the way the potter expected.

Gianni stood. Before he turned away from the river, he made the sign of the cross. Something he hadn't done for some time. He thought of the parable of the loaves and fishes, but he saw it differently. It was about the lie of scarcity. Few have much and so many have little. Dumps behind American restaurants devour enough loaves and fishes to feed the multitudes. "That's really fucked up," Gianni called at the river.

"Amen!" Someone responded from the shadows.

Gianni laughed. He left the pier, walked under the highway, crossed West Street and up Christopher Street. He ignored the guys passing him, and he thought about times he was with someone he just met, would probably never meet again, and then ride the subway to Saint Patrick's Cathedral. He'd sit among hundreds of lit vigil candles, not to beg forgiveness from marble statues, but to think and make some sense of it all. Making sense of nonsense was his prayer. So much he had let go of. Was there anything left to cling to?

Walking to the garage, he recalled a *Tonight Show* where the guest jokingly called herself a recovering Catholic. *Exactly*, he thought. *Yup! That's what I am. A recovering Catholic.*

Driving home, Gianni, the recovering Catholic, remembered the day at Figaro's when Ezra handed him a copy of *The Village Voice*. *The forces of faggotry*, is how *The Voice* described the Stonewall Rebellion. Back then Gianni hated that sentence. But now he smiled at the memory of it. It reminded him of Gabriel. Gabriel definitely made faggotry a force. Gianni pictured Gabriel handing out sandwiches, which could just as well be loaves and fishes. Gabriel called each kid child, and when they came upon someone Gabriel didn't know, he introduced himself, and then asked if they were hungry. That's all Gabriel asked. Are you hungry? Nothing transactional. No quid-pro-quo. No demand for repentance. Just, are you hungry? And if the kid said yes, Gabriel gave them a sandwich.

CHAPTER 16

All seats were taken in Sanctuary at The Orchard for a *Casablanca* talkback. Several younger folks sat with their legs crisscrossed on the wooden floor or stood and leaned against walls, careful not to disrupt the movie posters or photographs. Hanns looked very Rick Blaine in a black bowtie and white dinner jacket. He stood in front of the cheek-to-cheek Humphrey Bogart and Ingrid Bergman poster and talked about his friendship with Conrad Veidt, the highest paid actor in *Casablanca*, who played Nazi Major Henrich Strasser.

Because of Casablanca's iconic final scene, Hanns considered wearing a trench coat, but Raffaella mentioned that she overheard women speak of a neighborhood flasher. A fib. But it worked. Raffaella preferred the bowtie and dinner jacket.

Behind the near-empty pastry display case, Gianni and Ezra stood with their arms folded and their long hair tucked up under fedoras, tilted Bogey style. For two free tickets to The Orchard, Hanns had procured the hats from a second-hand pushcart salesman on Delancey Street.

Raffaella motioned for Hanns to straighten his bowtie. He did it in an inconspicuous manner and continued his talk. "I met Conrad Veidt when we were in the film *Nazi Agent*."

Hanns held out his right arm and pointed. "Fanny, please raise your hand."

An elderly woman, her hair teased into a translucent blond bouffant, raised her hand and wiggled her chubby fingers. The one carat diamond in her engagement ring atop her wedding band glittered beneath the track lighting.

"Thank you, Fanny. Right above Fanny's hand is a black and white photograph of Connie and me taken on the set of *Nazi Agent*. I had a minor role, but Connie played both a Nazi spy and the character's twin brother, an anti-Nazi American."

Through a haze of cigarette smoke, the audience craned their necks and squinted at the photograph.

"We became fast friends and frequented Salka Viertel's salons."

Regulars knew of Salka Viertel from past talkbacks or chatting with Hanns after films. For newcomers, Hanns explained.

Gianni heard only snippets of what Hanns said. Earlier, while he and Ezra prepared for the talkback, filling the display case with biscotti and pastry, he stewed aloud over whether or not to contact Owen about Maura. Ezra listened, but offered no advice beyond, "Wow, that's a tough one. Don't know what I'd do. What do you think?"

Stories of Casablanca, Veidt, or Salka Viertel didn't interest Gianni. Hanns irritated him with his silly dinner jacket and name dropping. And he hated the stupid hat Hanns asked him to wear.

Again, Hanns tapped at his bowtie to make sure it was straight. "The most telling aspect of Connie's character was that when he worked in the German film industry and was required to list his race. Connie wrote Jude. He wasn't Jewish, but his wife was, and he refused to renounce her. Needless to say, that was the end of his acting career in Germany."

"Wow, that took balls," Ezra whispered, but Gianni remained lost in his own concerns.

Hanns closed his final remarks with Ingrid Bergman's lines, "Play it once, Sam. For old times' sake"

Ezra poked Gianni. "Push the button."

Ezra pointed to the boom box.

"Oh, yeah." Gianni pressed the play button.

Applause, boisterous chatter, and chairs scraping against the wooden floor overwhelmed Dooley Wilson's crooning and piano playing. Those who had seen the 6:30 show left through the front door to Orchard Street. Hanns directed those attending the 9:30 showing out of the parlor, through the lobby, and into the theater, so the projectionist could begin the film. As usual, Raffaella held court with a few stragglers.

Ezra picked up stray paper cups, plates, napkins, and he emptied ashtrays. Gianni removed his fedora, shook out his hair, and swept the floor. A hand on his shoulder startled him.

"Missed your cue." Hanns stood next to him smiling. "But no big deal. It worked out."

Gianni kept sweeping. "Maybe I would have taken my cue more seriously if Ingrid Bergman had called Sam a man instead of a boy."

"What?"

"That movie has a lot of famous quotes like, 'We'll always have Paris,' and 'Here's looking at you kid,' but no one remembers Sam being called a boy. At least no white people remember it."

Ezra, Raffaella, and the two stragglers looked back and forth between Gianni and Hanns.

Hanns unclipped his bowtie and opened the top button of his shirt. "I don't remember anyone calling him boy."

"Exactly! When Bergman first entered Rick's she said, 'The boy who's playing the piano. Somewhere I've seen him.' Only problem is the *boy* was probably twice her age."

Hanns smiled and nodded. "Sure, but you have to consider the time."

Gianni paused and looked from the broom to Hanns. "It's not time that's the bigot."

Hanns held up his hands as if surrendering, turned, and walked back to the lobby.

The two stragglers found their way out of the parlor without saying goodbye to Raffaella, and Ezra tossed a stack of paper cups into a garbage can. "Damn, Baker Man. That was fierce."

"Not as fierce as all the shit Black actors had to put up with. Still have to put up with."

"Easy Baker Man. I agree with you."

Raffaella lifted a near empty beverage dispenser of orange water and walked toward the sink behind the display case. Gianni dropped the broom and attempted to take the dispenser from Raffaella.

"I'll do that," Gianni said.

"No need. I can carry it."

"Maybe I shouldn't have snapped at Hanns."

Raffaella shrugged her shoulders, dumped the remaining water into the sink, and wiped out the orange slices with a paper towel.

In the lobby, Hanns fished through a drawer under the cash register for a pen. He tossed out three that had gone dry.

"Need help?" Raffaella reached around the cash register, lifted a pen that sat right in front of Hanns, and handed it to him.

"Gianni can be a pain in the ass. He turns everything into an issue," Hanns said.

Raffaella nodded.

"Not saying he's wrong. But all I wanted him to do was press a button. I didn't write the damn script."

Raffaella leaned over the counter and gave Hanns a peck on his cheek. "Wonderful talkback tonight. Everyone enjoyed it."

"Not quite everyone," Hanns said.

In the parlor, Gianni turned out the lights, including the neon Sanctuary sign. He looked at the poster of Bergman cheek-to-cheek with Bogey, and then said, "Mr. Wilson to you, bitch."

Ezra laughed. "Damn, you're on a roll."

"Yeah, this whole thing with Owen got me in a mood. Makes stuff that usually pisses me off that much worse. Should I apologize to Hanns before we leave?"

Ezra removed his fedora and picked at a few specks of lint. "Up to you." He popped the hat back on his head. "I might keep this."

"You look like an asshole."

"Yeah, but an asshole with class."

They left through the front door from Sanctuary to Orchard Street, as to avoid walking through the lobby and passing Hanns. If he didn't have to drive Ezra home, he might have headed to the Village.

Sleep didn't come easy. If not feeling guilty for snapping at Hanns, Gianni thought of Maura, of Owen, or of the hungry boys stepping out of shadows for leftover sandwiches. He thought of the parable of the loaves and fishes. He pictured Gabriel tossing a champagne cocktail in Ingrid Bergman's face. That made him laugh. Then he thought of Marcello.

Since the night Raffaella had told Gianni that she and Marcello had had a son, they spoke more of Marcello. Not often, but more. Gianni gathered that Marcello was driven by lofty ideals, but he could be thoughtless, even unkind to those who were closest to him.

He thought about what Fina said about his grandfather. His

grandfather, like Marcello, hated injustice. But maybe they hated more than they cared. Maybe they loved hate more than they loved justice and no matter the efforts of a person or a people or a society, it could never be enough. Ultimately it wasn't about righting wrongs, but outlets for anger.

Maybe this is what Raffaella means when she says I remind her of Marcello, Gianni thought. *Not just appearance, but temperament. I'm too self-righteous. What the hell do I do to make change aside from mouth off? Ezra does a hell of a lot more than I. Hanns did nothing but show a fucking film, tell a story, and give the audience at The Orchard a nice evening like he gave me the opportunity to do something worthwhile, something besides sit around sulking and feeling sorry for myself.*

Gianni reasoned that his obsession with Owen and whether or not to tell him about Maura contributed to his outburst as much as his outrage over a racist comment made in a 1942 Hollywood film. Just about every film that included Black actors had racist content. There was nothing uniquely racist about *Casablanca*.

Gianni yearned to hear pebbles against his window. It was very late when he finally fell asleep. Regardless, he woke at 7:00 to get an early start on baking. At last night's talkback the pastries had sold out, as did most of the biscotti.

The kitchen was warm and smelled of the fresh bread and coffee cake and Danish that Liberato sold to the customers he now waited on in the bakery. Gianni worked nonstop until it was time to leave for The Orchard. He loaded the van with the usual baked goods. One exception. A chocolate torte for Hanns with I'm Sorry piped across the top.

After much deliberation, Hanns chose a film for The Orchard's Tenth Anniversary Gala. Initially, he thought something light and festive, a screwball comedy, maybe a Preston Sturges farce like *The Palm Beach Story* or *The Lady Eve*. But then he pictured Liberato's wife, Fina, knotting up her mouth because she'd think either of those films were stupid. Not that he cared what Fina thought, but he was fond of Liberato, one of his most longstanding and loyal customers.

Hanns wanted him to enjoy the celebration, rather than endure Fina's complaints.

He chose the satirical romantic comedy, *Ninotchka*. Years ago this film lured Raffaella to The Orchard and eventually to Hanns. It brought him good luck then. Why not now? Another ten years of sell-out festivals.

The photographs of Hanns with the film's co-star, Greta Garbo, and with screen writer Billy Wilder, would make useful props when he addressed his guests. By way of introduction through a mutual friend, Hanns charmed the sophisticated stage and film comedian Ina Claire, who had a secondary role in the film, to attend the gala. She would provide a touch of panache. Though a private person, not one prone to the limelight, Claire agreed to make a brief appearance. Not exactly Greta Garbo, but still a coup. In fact, Hollywood gossip claimed that much of Claire's performance was edited out of the final cut, since she often outshone Garbo. Hanns would include that tidbit of gossip when introducing Claire.

He and Raffaella mailed gold embossed invitations to The Orchard's most loyal customers:

The Orchard's Tenth Anniversary Gala
Saturday, August 28th, 1971
Catering by Katz's Delicatessen
Festivities begin at 7:00 pm
Our Esteemed Guest, Ninotchka's Grand Duchess Swana, Ina Claire
Followed by Ernst Lubitsch's Ninotchka

Wearing chef's hats and bib aprons with the words *Sanctuary at The Orchard* stenciled across the front, Gianni, Ezra, and Colleen oversaw stations at several buffet tables. Gianni, the platters of pastrami, corned beef, brisket, hard and soft salami, baskets of Kaiser rolls and sliced rye bread, and bowls with condiments. Ezra, the chopped liver, white fish salad, latkes, knishes, and kishka. Collen, the desserts, including babka, cheesecake, and rugelach.

The previous spring Colleen had graduated from her two-year community college, broken up with her boyfriend and, unsure of what to do next, moved back home. "A temporary predicament," she reminded everyone, especially herself.

Saul Rosenthal's nephew managed the open bar at the pastry display case, where he served wine and beer. Wearing his Bogie dinner jacket,

Hanns greeted guests at the front door, and Raffaella milled about chatting and directing guests to the bar and buffet tables. She wore the simple crepe black dress and the long black beaded earrings she had worn the night Hanns had proposed and looked just as stunning now. The only change was a few wiry threads of silver in her hair, which made Raffaella more captivating and the adages comparing people as they age to fine wines credible.

When not replenishing meats, breads, or condiments, Gianni glanced at the front door. Raffaella had asked him if he wanted to invite someone special. He nodded and she gave him two tickets, which he offered to Gabriel.

He and Gabriel met regularly for midnight breakfasts at Tiffany's. After they ate and talked, sometimes for hours, they made their sandwich runs. Gianni bought extra sandwiches to supplement Tiffany's day-olds. He also bought underwear, socks, soap, and deodorant—items Gabriel said the children always needed. "And condoms. If they'd only use them," Gabriel said. "But you know how children are. They rarely listen to Mother."

It turned out that Gabriel was quite the authority on the Harlem Renaissance. He lent Gianni several books by Black authors and they'd discussed them over coffee, eggs, and home fries.

Whenever Gianni called their midnight breakfasts, "*Gabriel 101* at the University of Tiffany's," Gabriel laughed and his eyes sparkled under glitter eyeshadow.

Besides discussing the work of Langston Hughes and Zora Neal Hurston, Gabriel spoke more about his childhood in Mississippi. Fifteen when he left home for New Orleans.

"Momma died giving birth to my kid sister. Granma Eugenia Myrtle eventually told me to leave home. She knew my daddy was beating me. First day or so she'd put cold compresses on my bruises, and then after the swelling went down warm compresses. She said, 'When a white man looks at you all he sees is his own hate, his own prejudice. And when your daddy looks at you the same thing happens. Different reasons, but hate is hate.' She said, 'God don't make no mistakes. People do. I don't know where you gotta go, child,' she said, 'but it's gotta be far from here.'

"My kid sister was the only one who knew where I went, and she contacted me when Granma Eugenia Myrtle passed. I took a bus back to Money, Mississippi, for Granma's funeral, and then took a bus the next morning to New York City. See, I know what a lot of these children here went through—go through. I got by however I could. I'm in no position to judge these children, but I do judge those who hate them."

Gabriel also mentioned his friend Gunter again, several times. Gunter gave Gabriel a place to stay when Gabriel was about Gianni's age.

"He's the one who first told me about the Harlem Renaissance and gave me a bunch of books to read. At first, it took me forever to read a few pages. I only had a few years of schooling. But when you're interested in something, you learn fast. In school, teachers taught me about white men like George Washington and Thomas Jefferson. I already knew all I needed to know about men like them. And what I knew, I didn't like."

Gabriel still lived with Gunter. He once helped Gabriel find work: desk clerk in several seedy hotels where guests paid by the hour or in bath houses, handing out towels.

"And then I won a drag contest. I even had a few gigs at the Continental Baths. Got to meet Bette Midler."

"I saw her on Johnny Carson," Gianni said.

"Oh, Bathhouse Betty toned it down for Johnny."

Gianni didn't know if Gabriel and Gunter were lovers now or in the past. He didn't ask, but he gathered that Gunter was now elderly and in poor health.

Gabriel accepted the tickets to The Orchard anniversary gala.

"Gunter will love this. He has a big poster of Garbo in the living room. Next to Mae West, Judy Garland, Marilyn Monroe, and Barbara Streisand. He calls it the wall of divas."

Gianni's parents would wonder how he knew Gabriel and Gunter, as would Ezra and Colleen. *Let them connect the dots, or not*, he thought. Since Gianni said hello to Gabriel at the Lena Horne Festival talkback, he assumed that Raffaella already knew he and Gabriel were friends.

The crowd of guests chatted over their wine or beer and plates of food. Some sat on the mismatched settees, easy chairs and ice cream parlor chairs, or on folding chairs Saul borrowed from a neighborhood synagogue, in exchange for gala invitations for the rabbi and his wife.

Others stood and rested their plates on the pub tables Saul borrowed from a neighborhood bar in exchange for invitations for the bar owner and his mistress.

"No need for the Missus to learn about this," the bar owner said.

"No need," Saul agreed.

Saul tapped his wine glass against his plate to get the guests' attention. No luck. He tried again, a little louder, and he also cleared his throat. Still no response. Fina watched his failed antics. She rolled her eyes and banged a tin serving tray against a radiator. Liberato startled and spilled a drop of red wine on his burgundy tie. Everyone went silent and looked in Fina's direction. She pointed to Saul. "He wants you to listen."

A bit flustered, Saul thanked Fina, and pulled a sheet of paper from his jacket's breast pocket. Again, he cleared his throat. His jowls jiggled.

"Ten years ago, I persuaded my good friend, Hanns Schein, to leave sunny California and move East to open The Orchard. You all know Hanns and his beautiful wife Raffaella—"

As Saul went on about Hanns and Raffaella, mostly about Raffaella, Gabriel and Gunter entered. Gabriel wore full drag. He glowed in a white, satin turban, a white, satin, midcalf dress, and white stilettos, which added another four inches to his stature. Everyone's eyes turned from Saul to Gabriel. Gianni smiled. A queen had just entered the room.

To Gabriel's left stood Gunter. Not nearly as tall as Gabriel in heels, and stooped. Gunter wore a white linen suit and lavender paisley ascot. He wore his sparse, colorless hair in a comb-over. Had Gabriel not had his arm securely through Gunter's, Gunter might have blown away on the slightest breeze.

"As I was saying," Saul began again. This time with more force.

"As I was saying—" Guests gradually turned their attention back to him.

Raffaella approached Gabriel and Gunter. Gabriel reminded her that they had met at the Lena Horne Festival.

"Of course. You were with two friends, and one of your friends was an expert on Lena Horne."

They spoke softly so as not to interrupt Saul.

"This is my friend, Gunter. I'm fine standing, honey, but Gunter's a little wobbly."

In his high, thin voice and heavy German accent, Gunter said, "Hello, dear. Lovely earrings. Not everyone could wear them, but you have a long, graceful neck. Absolutely lovely. Absolutely—" His words trailed as if they lost their way.

Raffaella stared at Gunter, and the faint lines around her eyes deepened.

"Maybe one of those chairs." Gabriel pointed to the few folding chairs leaning against the wall behind one of the buffet tables.

"Of course. I'm sorry. I'll get chairs, and then after they finish talking you can get something to eat."

Raffaella grabbed two chairs from behind where Gianni stood. He leaned toward her and whispered. "Do you remember Gabriel?"

"Yes, yes I do." She sounded curt, as if annoyed.

Maybe inviting Gabriel was a mistake, Gianni thought.

"Now I will introduce you to the man behind the magic," Saul said. "Hanns Schein!" The guests applauded. Those sitting stood.

"Thank you. Thank you."

Raffaella opened the two folding chairs. Gabriel helped Gunter lower himself onto one of chairs, and then Gabriel sat next to him and crossed his long legs. His size fourteen white satin stilettos flashed under the track lighting.

Gianni heard little of what Hanns said. Instead, he focused on Raffaella. She stood behind Gabriel, occasionally glancing at Gunter. Her eyes shifted, as if in search of a memory.

Done with his planned remarks, Hanns looked at his watch. "I had hoped our guest of honor would be here by now. Maybe her car is stuck in traffic. You know Manhattan traffic."

Hanns filled the gap with Hollywood anecdotes and pointed again to the Garbo and Wilder pictures, which most of the guests had already seen.

The front door opened. In walked Ina Claire with her husband. The guests turned, then gawked at her wide-eyed. Not because they saw the Grand Duchess Swana in the flesh, but because she wore a white turban and white dress. Simpler than Gabriel's—tea length with a button jacket—but the likeness to Gabriel's outfit was uncanny.

Colleen dropped the rugelach she was about to stuff into her mouth.

On her husband's arm, the seventy-eight-year-old actress made her way to where Hanns stood holding a microphone, his mouth opened as if in mid-sentence.

"And here's our esteemed guest now," Hanns said, sounding a little unsure.

The guests looked from Claire, to each other, to Gabriel, and then to Hanns as if expecting an explanation. Some chuckled. Maybe the similarities between Ina's and Gabriel's outfits were a theatrical stunt to underscore the glitzy character Ina Claire had played in *Ninotchka*. After all, Hanns was a pro at embellishment.

Gunter leaned toward Gabriel. In a whisper that came out louder than he intended, Gunter said, "I didn't know this was going to be a drag contest." He patted Gabriel's hand. "Don't worry dear, you'll win. She's too pale to wear white. She looks as if she were embalmed."

Hanns proceeded with his introduction, listing Ina Claire's stage and screen credits and explained she was more at home on the stage, beginning with her work in Vaudeville and the Ziegfeld Follies. Guests applauded. Claire spoke briefly and kindly of Greta Garbo, Melvyn Douglas, the other actors in the film, and of the director, Ernst Lubitsch.

"Thank you for inviting me to your lovely anniversary party, but I must depart. We came here right from the airport. Staying with friends uptown you know, and we're expected. Our car awaits."

Again, the guests stood and applauded. Claire took her husband's arm, and they walked slowly back to the door to Orchard Street. She turned from side to side, giving a royal wave until she neared the door and noticed Gabriel towering above the other guests. Ina Claire's hand remained raised and still, as if she were requesting permission to use the little girl's room.

Gabriel wiggled his fingers at Claire. In his high thin voice, Gunter said, "Next time more color, dear. Maybe an emerald green or an azure blue. Better with your complexion."

Ina Claire and her husband left.

"Wasn't that wonderful?" Hanns exclaimed. He waved his hand toward the buffet table. "Please enjoy seconds or dessert. Our film will begin in a half hour."

Several guests gravitated toward Raffaella and, as soon as she excused herself from them, she was waylaid by others.

Gabriel picked up two plates while Gunter remained sitting.

Gianni smiled a broad, full faced smile, "Glad you made it. You look beautiful. What's your pleasure?"

Gabriel fluttered his false eyelashes. "Now, I know you don't want me to answer that question, child."

Gianni laughed. "I mean. What kind of meat do you want?" Again he laughed. "Never mind, just help yourself."

"I'll need help with the second plate. My friend's a little wobbly." Gabriel pointed one of his plates in Gunter's direction, but the many guests in line for seconds obscured the gesture.

"Is he ill?"

"No. Just shaky, and his mind runs out of juice sometimes. Nothing serious."

"I'll help."

Gabriel handed Gianni one of the plates. "Just a little of each. He eats like a bird. I, on the other hand, am famished. Glad my turban sister didn't gab much."

Gianni slid a slice of corned beef and a slice of brisket on the plate. "That was a riot. Did you and Ina Claire coordinate your outfits?"

"Child, we were on the phone all morning."

Guests shot quick glances at Gabriel, especially those close enough to hear his conversation with Gianni. Gabriel moved on to Ezra's station.

"Ezra, this is my friend, Gabriel. Please help with this plate for his friend, Gunter."

"Sure! Cool."

Gabriel smiled. "Ezra. I had an Uncle Ezra back in Mississippi. More of a great uncle or great-grand uncle. He was over a hundred when I left. Although, he didn't really know what year he was born. Uncle Ezra used to say, 'Bout a hundred, give or take a few years.'"

Gianni watched Gabriel tell the Uncle Ezra story. Inviting Gabriel wasn't a mistake. He admired Gabriel's courage and his don't-mess-with-me demeanor. No one was going to make Gabriel invisible.

Gabriel stretched out his pointer finger with its long glitter-painted nail. "What's all this, child?" He rotated his finger as if drawing circles in the air.

Ezra described each dish.

"Hmm—I'll take one of those pancakes and a knish, but I'll pass on the other stuff. You can put a tiny bit of each on Gunter's plate. I'll be back later for dessert."

Gabriel looked at Colleen. "Gurl, love your feather earrings. Don't go giving away all that cheesecake."

"Thank you. I'll save a slice just for you."

"One slice? Honey, I ain't watching my figure. I leave that to others."

Some guests had had their fill of food and drink and moseyed into the theater. Gabriel and Gunter took a seat at one of the tables. Gunter picked at his food.

The tide of guests continued to ebb out the parlor. Gabriel ate the two slices of cheesecake Colleen had set aside. He scooped up a taste on a spoon and held it out toward Gunter.

"Umm, delicious," Gunter said. "But I'm stuffed."

"Honey, you barely ate enough to stuff a canary."

Hanns announced the film was about to begin.

Finally free of her admirers, Raffaella helped Gabriel escort Gunter into theater. He took their arms and smiled at Raffaella, a slight quiver in his thin lips.

"Lovely earrings my dear. Not everyone could wear such long earrings."

Fina stacked dirty plates.

"Ma, go watch the movie," Gianni said. "We'll do that."

"Your father's saving me a seat. I've already seen this movie. Being married to your father, I've seen just about every movie ever made."

"We just have to put the dirty plates, silverware, and glasses into these crates," Hanns said. "All rented. Just scrape whatever food is left into the trash. They'll run everything through a dishwasher."

Saul entered the parlor wearing the same stupefied expression he wore when Gabriel's appearance interrupted his welcome. "I have only one question," he said, sounding like an angry teacher about to reprimand his students.

Gianni froze. He knew what was coming.

"Who the hell invited those two—"

Saul hadn't noticed Raffaella behind him. Before he could utter whatever epithet he was about to bellow, Raffaella cut him off with cool surgical precision.

"I invited them. I assume you're asking about the two who came in while you were talking."

Turning from bulldog into toy poodle, Saul looked at Raffaella. "Well—yes I was just wondering."

"Are there any other guests you're wondering about?"

Damn! Gianni thought. *I love you, Raffaella.*

"No, no, it was a very nice evening." Saul looked at his watch and turned to Hanns. "Well, I'm going to head out. I have to drive my nephew home, and then drive home to Island Park. You know how busy the Sunrise Highway can get."

"Why did you do it?" Gianni said.

He and Raffaella sat in the same chairs they once sat in when Raffaella first suggested that Gianni sell coffee and biscotti at The Orchard. Fina had joined Liberato in the theater. Ezra and Colleen rode the subway home. Hanns was on the phone in the lobby.

"Do what?"

"Say you invited Gabriel and Gunter."

"I don't know. So Saul would be quiet."

Gianni nodded.

Raffaella pressed her finger at a loose bobby pin in her hair. "You once asked me if I thought that you tried to take my choice away. Remember, about whether or not I should be interviewed for the Holocaust film?"

"I remember."

"Did I take your choice away tonight?"

"My choice?"

"Yes. Opportunity might be a better word than choice. Did I steal your opportunity to say you had invited Gabriel and Gunter?"

"Is that what you tried to do?"

"No."

"Then I don't think you did."

"Sometimes when we care about people," Raffaella said, "we're too quick to protect. Maybe that's not such a good thing."

"Like I tried to protect you from doing the interview, and tonight you thought I needed protection from Saul. I mean, what he was about to say."

"Something like that. Maybe you were making a statement by inviting Gabriel and Gunter."

Gianni fingered the hem of his bib apron. "Or maybe I invited Gabriel because he's not only a friend, but I greatly admire him."

Raffaella leaned forward in her chair and tilted her head toward Gianni. One of her beaded earrings lay against her neck. The other dangled away from her. "Do you know much about Gunter?"

"No, tonight's the first I met him. Gabriel has spoken of him some, but I've never met him before. He sounds a little like Hanns. I mean his accent."

"Yes, he does."

Raffaella turned toward the refrigerator behind the display case. "I don't know what we'll do with all the leftover food."

"I have an idea. Gabriel gives sandwiches to homeless kids." Gianni didn't elaborate, and Raffaella didn't ask questions.

"A wonderful idea."

By the time *Ninotchka* ended, Gianni and Raffaella had filled two large shopping bags with sandwiches and another shopping bag with desserts.

Gianni waited outside with Gabriel and Gunter for their cab to arrive.

Gunter placed his slim trembling fingers on Gianni's arm. "A lovely evening, young man. What did you say your name is?"

"Gianni."

"Yes, that's right. Gianni. When I was your age, but not as handsome as you, I often vacationed in Italy. Italian boys are beautiful. No wonder the sculptures. Such inspiration."

Gianni felt himself blush.

The cab arrived.

Gianni held the bags while Gabriel helped Gunter into the cab.

"Will you be able to handle all this and help Gunter?" Gianni said. "I could always bring the food tomorrow."

"I'll be fine, child. I'll just flip Gunter over my shoulder."

Gianni heard Gunter laugh—a thin, breathy laugh. He handed Gabriel the bags of food, closed the car door, and watched the cab until it disappeared around the corner.

Driving home in Gianni's van, Liberato praised the evening—the food, the film, the opportunity to speak with people he only nodded to over the years. Fina said that Saul Rosenthal should have helped clean up instead of running off.

"He treats Hanns like a servant," she said.

"I thought you don't like Hanns," Liberato said.
"I don't. But I dislike padrones more."
No one mentioned Gabriel or Gunter.

Gianni became increasingly short-tempered after his *Casablanca* blowup with Hanns. This included snapping at Sanctuary customers.

Now I'm turning into my mother, he thought when he told a an elderly woman wavering between buying a cannoli or a sfogliatelle to buy a cheese ring. "It goes with everything," he said.

The stunned woman peered at the display case. "I don't believe you have cheese rings, young man. But even if you did, I couldn't eat a whole cake."

Either call Owen and tell him about Maura, or spend his life apologizing for his cantankerous disposition. Gianni called. Owen had been drafted and was in Vietnam.

"We're praying he'll be home by the end of July," Mrs. West said. "That's when his tour ends. But if you want to write him, I'm sure he'd love to hear from you."

"Yes, yes, I will write. Thank you." Gianni scribbled the information down, hung up the phone, and taped the address to a poster in his bedroom of an army soldier's helmet propped on a cross and the bolded question, "**Your Son Next?**"

Many nights, Gianni sat up in bed or at his desk while the A train rattled by his bedroom window. He wrote letters to Owen about Maura, about listening for the sound of pebbles, about missing him. He wrote that he feared Owen's fate might follow Jimmy's, that Owen's nightmare was an omen. He ended every letter with, *I love you. Please come home.* The crumpled unmailed letters filled his trash can while the address taped to the poster remained a fatalistic reminder of the terrible phone call he'd eventually receive. "He's dead," Maura's words about Jimmy haunted Gianni, but her voice spoke of Owen.

Gianni filled many empty trash cans. They just disappeared like dirty tissues or long-ago homework assignments. He never imagined that Fina would read them. That wasn't her way until she noticed the salutation, "Dearest Owen."

Fina pressed out the crumpled paper. She read it, and then read the others. She tore the letters into tiny pieces, and then she stuffed the evidence of Gianni's love for Owen into a large garbage bag. Now, whenever she emptied Gianni's trash can, she checked for the words "Dearest Owen," and then tore these letters into tiny pieces without reading them. What purpose would reading them serve? She already understood.

Two weeks after The Orchard's Tenth Anniversary Gala, Gianni received a phone call.

"Hey, Gianni. Mom said you called back in January. I've been home a little over a month. Been meaning to get back to you. Come visit," Owen said. "It'll be good to see you."

At dinner that night, Gianni was exceptionally cheerful. He told his parents that Owen called, that he was home and safe and didn't mention anything about any injuries. "He invited me to come see him in Vermont," Gianni said. "Maybe Saul's nephew will work Sanctuary for me."

"Wonderful news," Liberato said. "And you can use a little vacation."

Fina nodded and cleared her throat. "These cutlets are dry. I must have over cooked them."

CHAPTER 17

Scarlet and rust-colored leaves peaked among evergreens. An umber haze gave way to distant slate-colored mountains, and beyond those mountains rose a fainter, higher, and more craggy range that vanished below cumulus clouds.

"I wonder if those distant mountains are the White Mountains in New Hampshire or just taller Green Mountains in Vermont," Ezra said.

Colleen rubbed her left thumb against one of her many silver rings. "You're from Queens. How the hell do you know the names of those mountains?"

"He reads," Gianni said, and he eased up on the gas pedal as the car approached a steep, sharp curve.

"Oh yeah. I forgot about that," Colleen said.

They arrived at Owen's family's farm at dusk. Gianni got out of the van, grabbed his backpack, and Colleen slipped behind the steering wheel. "We'll pick you up in the morning. Not too early."

Gianni stood on the road and watched the van until the rear bumper stickers calling for an end to The Vietnam War, Nixon's Impeachment, Flower Power, and— a gift from Colleen—"Eve Was Framed" became a blur.

He looked at Owen's house, the deep front porch, steep pitched roof, white clapboards, and rows of lighted windows. Reminiscent of the farmhouses he often watched speed by while he rode in the back of a Greyhound bus. Houses at once familiar and foreign. By the time he left Lyndon State, he perceived them to be sets on a studio lot. A form of hallucination, his therapist said. Movies were once his only exposure to farmhouses. Until going to Lyndon, he lived in a flat over a store beside the rattling El. Farmhouses were on the *Million Dollar Movie* or shows like *Bonanza*. They weren't real.

The hint of manure wafted on the slight breeze. Gianni's Timberland boots scraped against the gravel driveway, and then against the porch's tongue-and-groove planks. Moths beat against the front screen door, and Gianni knocked at the door's wood frame. It rattled.

"That you, Gianni?" Wearing a print apron over her jeans, and a light flannel shirt with the sleeves rolled up past her elbows, Owen's mother pushed the screen door open. She wore her graying blond hair in a ponytail. She had the same smile as Owen.

"Come in. Come in."

Gianni stepped into the house and Brenda West pulled the door closed behind him.

"Good to see you again, Gianni. Last time was at Parents' Weekend at Lyndon. Seems like ages ago."

"Yes, nice to see you again, Mrs. West."

"We already ate since we weren't sure what time you'd get here. Mr. West and the boys are used to eating dinner at 5:30, but Owen said he'd wait for you. He's out in the barn now. You leave your backpack right here. I can ring the bell on the porch for Owen unless you want to go up to the barn."

"Yes, I'll do that."

"Not sure which one he's in, but there's only two, and they're right next to each other."

As Gianni approached the barns, the earthy scent of manure became more potent, and the twilight blue of a Maxfield Parish painting framed the barns' silhouettes.

No sign of Owen. Just the harmony of contented dairy cows munching hay and chewing their cud.

"Owen?"

"Up here."

Thump! A bale of hay landed a few feet from Gianni. He looked up.

"Just let me pitch a few more bales, and I'll be right down."

"I'll come up."

Gianni paused before stepping from the ladder onto the loft. Owen stood shirtless, legs apart, twisting his torso to the right, grabbing another bale of hay, twisting to the left, and hurling the bale off the loft. Thud! The waning rays of twilight blinked through chinks in the barnwood and shimmered on Owen's sweaty chest, shoulders, and arms.

"Hey, Gianni."

They hugged. Lightheaded, Gianni inhaled Owen's musk made sweeter with the scent of hay. No way Owen could miss how glad Gianni was to see him. When they stepped back from each other, and Gianni got a closer look at Owen's face, he recognized what strangers once saw in him, what he often saw in Raffaella, and occasionally glimpsed in Gabriel. Owen carried the weight of the world. The light was dimmed in Owen's blue eyes, and his voice sounded flat, monotone, his words rehearsed and stilted, as if an internal voice distracted him, shook his footing, and whispered that everyone and everything is unfamiliar. Gianni once knew and feared that internal voice, but it no longer taunted him.

Vietnam, Gianni thought. *Of course.*

What did Gianni expect? Owen's still-beautiful shell lacked Owen's sparkle and enthusiasm.

Owen slipped on a sweat-stained T-shirt, and he and Gianni walked from the barn to the house. Owen looked toward the empty driveway.

"Where's your car?"

"Friends dropped me off. They're staying at a commune outside of Burlington. My friend Ezra knows some of the folks who live there. You'll meet Ezra in the morning. And Colleen."

Owen nodded. They entered the house through the back door into a mudroom, and went into the kitchen. From the living room came the sound of a television. Owen's parents and his younger brothers sat before the Zenith color console while Edith and Archie sang, "Those were the days." Owen's dad stamped out his cigarette in a melamine ashtray, stood, approached the television, and adjusted the color so Edith and Archie looked less orange.

"Ma made turkey," Owen said. "I can heat up the gravy and we can have open turkey sandwiches."

"Sounds good."

Neither Owen nor Gianni spoke of Lyndon. Between stretches of silence, Owen talked a little about 'Nam, guys he met there, USO shows, his R&R at Vung Tao beach. He didn't mention combat. Gianni talked a little about Sanctuary at The Orchard. Opportunities to mention what happened to Maura slipped away between comments about turkey, whether or not the gravy and mashed potatoes were hot enough, if apple pie is better with or without ice cream, and more silence.

The screen door into the mudroom slammed. A young woman, neither tall nor short, heavy nor thin, her hair lighter than brown but not quite blond, walked into the kitchen. Someone who would be a great extra in a film because she'd never distract the audience from the lead characters. She bent down behind Owen, wrapped her arms around his shoulders, and pressed her cheek against his.

"Gianni, this is my girlfriend, Lolli."

Gianni heard Maura's voice, *As in pop? He's got to be kidding.*

"Glad to meet you, Gianni," Lolli said. "Owey's told me all about you."

Again, Maura's voice: *Owey? Now I know he's kidding.* Gianni doubted that *Owey* told Lolli *all* about him.

"Nice to meet you too, Lol—li." Her name stuck in the curve of his tongue.

"Looks like I'm just in time for pie," Lolli said.

She grabbed a plate from a cupboard, a fork from a drawer, cut herself a piece of pie, and sat on Owen's lap. No more silence, which annoyed and relieved Gianni. Lolli jumped from one topic to another, and then described in detail the people she waited on in the post office, the packages they mailed, and the number of stamps they purchased. Owen nodded, while Gianni replayed images of Owen shirtless and pitching bales of hay.

Later, television off, Owen's parents and brothers joined Owen, Lolli, and Gianni in the kitchen. Lolli continued to do most of the talking. Owen's dad excused himself, then Owen's younger brothers, and then, after she washed the few dishes, his mom also said goodnight. Finally Lolli said she had to get up early for work, and Owen walked her outside.

Gianni listened to the refrigerator's hum. *Too mousey,* Gianni thought. *Too clingy. Too gabby. Too unlike Maura.* He glanced at the clock on the stove. *She probably won't let go of him for a while.*

Twenty minutes passed before the screen door to the mudroom slammed.

Owen entered the kitchen yawning. "We don't have a guest room, so I set up a tent. Hope you don't mind."

"No, no problem," Gianni said, though he did mind. He had hoped to be sharing a room if not a bed with Owen. He grabbed his backpack. Owen picked up a Coleman lantern. Gianni followed the lantern's light. A barred owl in a shagbark hickory tree made its baritone monkey call.

Owen unzipped the tent. Two matts lay side by side. Turned out Gianni wouldn't be sleeping alone after all.

Owen turned off the Coleman lantern. He reached for Gianni's shoulder. Gianni turned to Owen, and Owen pressed his soft open lips against Gianni's.

Gianni woke first. He stared at the shadowy mural made by morning sun and leaves that had fallen on the canvas tent. He lay still not to disturb Owen's sleep. He thought of last night. He and Owen were no longer the awkward fumbling boys they once were. Gianni learned about sex with men on the piers or with men he had met in gay bars. But how and where did Owen learn? *Vietnam.* Making do, or more?

There was always a strong physical component to Gianni, Owen, and Maura's friendship, whether they curled together before a fire in Vail Manor, watching television in the dorm lobby, or walking across campus with arms draped over shoulders. Like triplets floating in the same amniotic fluid. Touch reassured them. They weren't alone.

And then the wrestling. Not a day passed without Gianni and Owen engaging in at least one friendly tussle—physical without being carnal—until that night in Gianni's bedroom, and now last night sealed it. No more pretending that their friendship was platonic. Once spent, Owen hadn't turned away.

Owen opened his eyes and stretched. Gianni thought, *Am I the closest you can be to Maura? Is that what this is? Maura's gone, Owen.* Before Gianni's thoughts became words, Owen leaned up on one elbow and brought his finger to his lips.

"We have to be quiet. My dad and brothers are probably up already. I have the morning off because you're here."

Owen reached for Gianni's cock, which was already hard. They came quickly and quietly.

"Shower time," Owen said.

They slipped on their jeans. Gianni grabbed his backpack and followed Owen to an outdoor shower. Owen held open the door, and Gianni joined him, barely enough room for two. Their soapy bodies touched under the running water. Steam condensed on the cool autumn air.

"Rinsed off?" Owen said.

"Yes."

Owen grabbed two towels from a cupboard within the shower stall. He handed one to Gianni. Gianni shivered. They rubbed down. Their shoulders and arms touched. They bent to dry their legs and feet. Their buttocks touched. Gianni savored it all. He memorized even the tiniest details. Last night: the sound of the barred owl, the touch of Owen's hand, the taste of Owen's sweat. And now, the way sunlit water beaded on Owen's shoulders.

"You don't like Lolli," Owen said. He wrapped the towel around his waist.

Gianni stumbled over his words.

"No need to explain. She missed her period. Looks like we might have to get married. But that's okay."

"I don't know Lolli."

Owen laughed, but it wasn't his life-loving laugh. "It's okay, buddy. You don't have to like her."

"What happened, Owen?"

"What do you mean what happened? I should have used a condom."

"I'm not talking about that. I'm talking about you. Where did you go?"

Owen's eyes filled. "I went to 'Nam, Gianni. That's where I went. I saw what Jimmy and too many others saw. I survived what too many didn't survive. At least I think survived. The jury's still out on that."

Survived. Gianni thought of Raffaella, Gabriel, the homeless boys. He searched for the right words. "I'm sorry," was all he came up with.

"Yeah, I'm sorry too. Let's grab some breakfast."

Gianni opened his backpack, slipped on clean underwear and a T-shirt, then put on the jeans and sweatshirt he had worn yesterday. Wearing only a towel, Owen walked back to the house. Gianni recalled

Owen in skivvies and sitting in his dorm room, winter air blowing in an open window. Maura used to call him a human furnace.

Owen paused before opening the screen door. He spoke without turning to Gianni. "Lolli wrote to me every day while I was in 'Nam. Her letters saved me. She's more than just nervous chatter. She knows, Gianni."

Knows what? Gianni thought. *Knows about Maura? Knows about me?*

Owen's brother Jacob—a brown hair, brown-eyed version of Owen—filled a thermos with coffee. He nodded toward Owen and Gianni. "I was just going to come get you. Mom drove the boys to the dentist, and her car battery went dead. Dad's been in the barn for several hours. One of the calving Holsteins is having a hard time. You bring Dad this thermos. I'm gonna take the pickup and jumper cables and drive into town to meet mom."

"Why didn't he call the vet?"

"You take that up with Dad."

Owen slipped on coveralls. Thermos, mugs of coffee, and doughnuts in hand, Owen and Gianni headed to the barn.

Ethan West looked up at the boys from a tub of soapy water. "The calf is breech."

"I'll take over Dad," Owen said. "You've been at this for a while. You must be tired."

"I'm not the only one. This poor girl's exhausted. I've been taking it slow not to hurt her. Finally had the two rear hooves aligned, but look what just happened. Now we have to move fast."

The cow stood in a chute. One of the calf's hind legs, still in the amniotic sac, protruded out of the cow.

Gianni stared hard, a doughnut in his mouth and a mug of coffee in each hand. Owen rolled up his sleeves, scrubbed his hands and arms, and slipped on a long blue plastic glove. He lubricated the glove and slowly pushed the calf's leg back into the cow.

"Okay, I have both hooves." He pulled them out far enough for his dad to make a double loop with a rope on one of the calf's legs, above and below the ankle joint. Then Ethan West wrapped the rope around Owen's back and made a double loop on the calf's other leg. Owen reached into the cow to make sure the calf's tail wasn't hooked back. He tucked the tail down between the calf's hind legs.

With the rope wrapped around him like the anchor in a game of tug-of-war, Owen stepped back. He paused, stepped forward then backward two or three times, and then finally the calf was out. Ethan West grabbed it before it hit the ground.

Owen stepped out from under the rope. They hung the calf over the top railing of the calving pen, its head low enough for fluid to drain. It lay still on the railing. Owen cleared its nostrils and mouth, pounded its sides and chest while his dad held its hind quarters, so it wouldn't fall.

"She's breathing," Owen said. He looked at Gianni and smiled. "How long you gonna stand there with a doughnut sticking out of your mouth?" Gianni saw a glimmer of the Owen he once knew. Owen removed the blue plastic glove and scrubbed his hands and arms in the soapy water.

"You boys go drink your coffees," said Ethan West. "I'm okay here."

On the east side of the barn, Owen and Gianni sat warming on a haybale and drank their lukewarm coffee. Owen pulled a doughnut from his coverall pocket. The sun, high in the cloudless sky, turned the cool morning into a pleasant autumn day. Owen pointed to an ancient gnarled oak tree, about a hundred feet from where they sat.

"A wolf tree," he said. "It once stood like a lone wolf in a sheep pasture back when Vermont was almost totally deforested."

"Wow, can't imagine Vermont without trees."

"Yup, mostly sheep pastures back then. When I come across wolf trees in the woods, all huge and twisted, unlike any of the trees around them, I think it's not only years that left them bent, but what they've experienced. Wolf trees remember when they were the only ones left standing.

Owen spoke of more than wolf trees, but Gianni didn't know how to respond. He remained silent and let Owen's words hover like fallen leaves caught in an upward draft, as if trying to reclaim their branches. Just returned from Vietnam, Owen was yet a youthful wolf tree, in the grieving stages of loss. Too soon to accept what had happened.

The wolf tree's physical and mystical appeal—it's impressive girth, limbs like arms reaching to embrace and support, shaggy bark like the shakes on a vintage doll house, hollows where woodland creatures like opossums and fairies take shelter—and Owen's mournful but reverential tone when he spoke of a wolf tree's significance reminded Gianni of an aphorism from Nietzsche's *Twilight of the Idols*: "Out of life's school of war—what doesn't kill me makes me stronger." He also thought of Raffaella and Gabriel. They were like the wizened wolf tree near Owen's barn, and Gianni had found shelter, healing, and strength in their branches and hollows. He wished he could do the same for Owen. Instead he simply said, "You're amazing."

Owen turned to Gianni. His brow furrowed. Was he confused by Gianni's words or so lost in thoughts that he was surprised to find Gianni sitting next to him?

"How so?" Owen said, sounding as if he were in a trance.

"Well, let's start with how you saved the calf."

"Oh that. More fate than skill. We've probably lost more breech calves than we've saved."

"Does that happen a lot?"

"Sometimes, but not a lot."

"I love you, Owen."

"I know, I love you too."

Wine-colored leaves stirred beneath the wolf tree.

Gianni recalled his final words with Maura. Now would be the perfect time to tell Owen about Maura, if there were any perfect time. He heard the sound of his van.

"Probably your friends," Owen said.

Gianni called out and waved. He thought about how out of place Ezra and Colleen would look, and he realized he also looked out of place, as if a lost tribe from Woodstock had been wandering the hills of Vermont and came upon the West Farm. But only Ezra approached the barn.

"She's staying at the commune" Ezra said. "Found true love. You know Colleen."

Gianni shook his head.

After introducing Ezra to Owen, Gianni described what had happened with the calf.

"Let's see how the calf's doing," Owen said.

Ezra bent down next to the calf and it sucked on his fingers.

An hour or so passed. Casual conversation about Vermont and the commune where Ezra spent the night and Colleen found true love (again). Gianni snuffed out any talk of politics. Not easy to do with

Ezra.

Gianni picked up his backpack, and stopped in the house to say goodbye to Owen's family while Ezra waited in the van.

Owen walked Gianni to the van. They hugged. A long hug. More of an embrace than a hug.

Gianni missed Owen's sparkle. He hoped it was only dormant, and something or someone would soon wake it up. *Maybe Lolli is pregnant*, he thought. As much as that idea distressed him, he hoped that Lolli and the new baby would help Owen find what he lost.

"I'll write and let you know," Owen said. "Ya know, when I marry Lolli and stuff."

"Yes. Do that."

Owen looked at the bumper stickers on the back of Gianni's van.

"You were right, Gianni."

"About what?"

"About Vietnam. About a lot of stuff."

Gianni climbed in the van. Ezra drove. They waved as they backed out of the driveway.

"Nice guy," Ezra said.

Gianni stared at the outside rearview mirror. Owen grew smaller. Ezra asked about how Owen reacted when he learned about Maura.

"He didn't react," Owen said.

"Really. That's weird."

"I didn't tell him."

Once home, Gianni also told Raffaella that he neglected to tell Owen about what happened to Maura

Raffaella gathered the dead canes she pruned from a climbing rose and dumped them in a bucket. She joined Gianni at the table beneath the arbor pregnant with deep purple concord grapes.

"But isn't that why you went to visit him?"

"That's what I told myself. But few opportunities came up, and then I thought if Maura wants him to know, she'll have to find another messenger. He has a girlfriend. She might be pregnant. They might get married. No one needs to compete with a ghost. Someone who will always be young."

"That's true, Raffaella said. "Very true."

Gianni swatted at a mosquito. He didn't notice Raffaella move one of the lit citronella candles closer to him. He was thinking of Lolli and how unfair for her to have to compete with the memory of a never-aging Maura. He didn't realize that having to compete with a ghost could also be said of Hanns in relation to Marcello.

"Nice girl?" Raffaella said. "His girlfriend."

"She's okay. Owen said she wrote to him every day while he was in 'Nam. Not sure if he loves her or feels he owes her. He said her letters saved him."

Raffaella pulled pruning shears from one of the large pockets in her gardening apron. She stood and snipped a few clusters of grapes, then rinsed them under the garden hose.

"That would be terrible, if you married someone because you thought you owed them something," Gianni said. He didn't mention the way she clung to Owen, or that she didn't shut up long enough for anyone else to talk. Or that he envied how freely she wrapped her arms around Owen and sat on his lap.

"Grapes?" Raffaella said. She handed him a cluster, and then sat across from him again.

Gianni plucked a grape from its bunchstem and sucked at the grape's sweet skin. He pressed his tongue against his teeth to expel the grape's tiny seeds, and his lips puckered at the pulp's tartness.

"When you married Hanns, did you love him?"

"You asked me that a long time ago. Remember?"

"I remember you didn't quite answer me."

"You were in eighth grade."

"I'm not in eighth grade anymore."

"No you're not. I was fond of Hanns. Very fond of him. But I've grown to love him."

"The way you loved Marcello?"

"I was a girl when I loved Marcello. In time, not right away, but in time, I might have fallen out of love with Marcello. Being who I am now, I'd have difficulty living with a man like him. But then he might have also changed over time. He might have mellowed. And there might be more room for me to be me."

"Do you mean that you were too different from each other?"

"It's not that we were so different. It's more that he was so sure of everything. There was no room for questions. No room for me to come into my own. Are you very different from Owen?"

Gianni was stunned by Raffaella's question. Was she suggesting that his feelings for Owen were the same as her feelings for Marcello? But then, why wouldn't she? He never spoke of crushes on girls. He hadn't dated since high school. He went on and on about Owen numerous times. *Of course she knows I'm in love with Owen,* Gianni thought. *She's not an idiot.* He delayed answering, scratched at a mosquito bite, and inhaled the scent of citronella.

"I thought we were different," Gianni said. "I mean our political views. But maybe not. When I left, he said I was right about Vietnam. At college he never took part in protests. We never talked about politics. I guess we knew not to."

"War changes people." Raffaella took a tissue from her apron pocket. She laid a small hill of seeds and the bare bunchstem on the tissue. Gianni did the same.

"When you're older, does love make more sense?" Gianni said.

"I think so. More time for the head to understand the heart and the heart to listen to the head. Does that sound dull to you?"

"No. In fact I like the thought of it."

Raffaella folded the tissue around the grape seeds. "Good." She slipped the seeds into her apron pocket, and they resumed clearing autumn debris.

That night, Gianni heard the sound of pebbles against glass. *Can't be*, he thought, but he got out of bed and went to the window. Below, under the glow of the streetlight, Owen looked up and waved.

"Just let me find my keys," Gianni said.

Gianni searched his jeans, which lay on the floor next to his bed. No luck. He searched his desk, under his desk, tore the bedclothes from his bed.

"Where the fuck are they?"

He went back to the window, but only an empty sidewalk shone beneath the streetlight. He leaned out the window, shouted Owen's name, lifted his right foot, then his left, and stood on the sill outside of the window. "Owen!" he shouted. "Owen, Maura is dead. She wanted me to tell—" then he slipped, and falling woke him with a start. His heart raced and his pillow was drenched in sweat.

CHAPTER 18

When Raffaella told Gianni that she had decided to do the interview for the Holocaust documentary, she said she wanted it filmed at The Orchard. She asked him to invite Gabriel and Gunter. An odd request, Gianni thought, given she had met Gabriel briefly only twice and Gunter once. But he agreed. Ezra also told Gianni that Raffaella invited Golda, and then Gianni learned that his parents were invited. Filming was set for a Monday when the bakery was closed, so both Fina and Liberato planned to attend. Gianni and Ezra lined up two settees and several upholstered chairs to accommodate the guests. They moved the rest of the furniture toward the street-side of the parlor and intentionally blocked the front door, so a stray customer wouldn't knock and interrupt the filming. They moved a single table and two chairs beneath a poster of Charlie Chaplin in the *Great Dictator*.

Jennie, the film's director, her crew (fellow students from NYU), the interviewer (Jennie's lover, Melissa, and an Equity actor), and Raffaella sat among the clutter of furniture near the front windows discussing the shoot. Outside, Hanns shoveled a path through the snow.

Short and slight, wearing an army green fiddler cap covered with antiwar buttons and a pencil above each ear, Jennie rolled up her sleeves past her elbows as if she were about to strike an amusement park high-striker with a mallet.

"No script," she said. "Organic is what I'm looking for. It's all about the editing. That's my art—what to keep, what to discard, what to splice together. Maybe you have some old photographs that survived the war, Raffaella. I'd like to include stills. Later Jimmy here will take pictures of you selling movie tickets, or just doing things you normally do." Jennie pointed to a tall lanky guy with a red 'fro who held a Nikon camera.

Raffaella didn't mention her pictures of Marcello and Gino. She'd have to think about that.

"My vision," Jennie said, "is a montage of interviews, personal photographs, and period news photographs and videos. Point is, don't stress out about the interview. I'm not re-taking anything. Melissa's questions won't be scripted. Some of it will work. Some of it won't. As I said, organic. I'll decide what works. Trash what doesn't. I'm interviewing four people. Two men and two women. All Jewish. You're the first. Next week, I interview a rabbi in Brooklyn. The week after, a woman in a nursing home on Long Island. And finally a shoemaker. His shop's not far from here. He lives on Essex. Roger, do Raffaella's makeup. Nothing fancy. Just so the lighting doesn't wash her out. Ya hear that, Roger. I don't want her to look like a drag queen."

Fortunately, Gabriel was yet to arrive. Gianni imagined Gabriel's response. Something swift and sharp.

Two crew members set up lighting. "Hey, you guys mind sitting at the table?" one of the crew members said. "We want to see what this looks like. Talk about anything."

Gianni and Ezra sat beneath the Chaplin photo.

"So what do you think of David Bowie's Ziggy Stardust tour?" Ezra said.

Before Gianni could answer, the red head with the Nikon said. "Man, are you a Bowie fan? The guy's a genius."

A cold rush of air blew in from the lobby carrying the sound of boots stomping off snow and Hanns greeting Gianni's parents.

"Ok, Gianni is sitting where Raffaella will sit," Jennie said. "Shift the light a little. Too much shadow. Look up, Gianni. I'm not filming the top of Raffaella's head. Roger, you done with that makeup? Raffaella and Melissa exchange places with Ezra and Gianni. Raffaella, you sit where Gianni is sitting."

Fina, Liberato, and Golda entered the parlor, along with a woman who looked familiar but Gianni couldn't quite place. Hanns followed them.

"Everyone, take a seat" Jennie said. "Gianni, I brought china cups for Melissa and Raffaella's coffees. They're in that box."

Raffaella wore a simple pale lilac dress. Melissa wore navy blue. Raffaella smiled at her guests and mouthed the words thank you. They took off their coats and sat down.

"Melissa, move your chair a little to the left," Jennie said, and then she moved the table. "Raffaella, pull your chair closer to the table."

Jennie stepped back and looked at them. "I want the Chaplin poster center."

Gianni thought the poster was a distraction and wondered if others in the crew felt the same. Jennie didn't seem to be someone who'd welcome dissent.

"This is going to be a one-shot interview. In other words, filmed continuously. As I mentioned, organic, organic, organic. I'll edit later. If you stumble Raffaella, don't worry. Just keep talking. No such thing as mistakes. With this topic, my goal is not to make something pretty." Jennie turned to those sitting down. "I'll need everyone here to be quiet. Gianni, is that coffee ready?"

Gianni poured coffee in the two cups on the table between Melissa and Raffaella. He held up the pot to others. Except for Fina, they all shook their heads no, looking as if Jennie might disapprove.

A camera stood on a small dolly. Jennie spoke with the camera operator, who moved the dolly around according to Jennie's directions. Jennie stepped behind the camera, moved in close to Raffaella and Melissa, and then back.

"This isn't a part of the shoot. I just want to see how things look and get a feel for the best places to shoot from. Don't get distracted by the camera. This is your chance to practice ignoring it and everyone, especially me.

"Good luck with that," Fina mumbled.

"No talking," Jennie said.

Gianni smiled and shot a glance at Ezra who covered his mouth with his hand.

"Are we expecting anyone else?"

"Yes," Raffaella said.

"We'll give them another five minutes, but once I start shooting no one can enter."

"Then you won't start shooting until they arrive," Raffaella said.

Damn! I love you, Gianni thought.

Another rush of cold air blew in from the lobby with the sound of Hanns talking to Gabriel, then Gunter's high thin voice. Gabriel and Gunter entered, wearing winter coats. Gabriel's only distinctive attire was an African print head wrap.

"We're just about to start," Jennie said.

"In a minute," Raffaella stood and approached Gabriel and Gunter. "Thank you so much for coming on this cold day."

Gunter looked at Raffaella. He cocked his head and smiled. "Thank you for inviting us, dear. I don't believe we've met."

"Well, it's good to meet you now," Raffaella said.

She and Gabriel helped Gunter out of his coat, and Raffaella escorted him to his chair. At first, the attention Raffaella gave Gunter baffled Gianni, but then he understood. At least he thought he understood. While Gunter pulled his arm from his winter coat, the sleeve of his too-large blazer remained in the sleeve of his coat. He wore a short sleeve, button down shirt. Before Raffaella helped Gunter slip back into his blazer, Gianni spotted numbers on his arm.

Raffaella must have noticed the numbers when Gabriel and Gunter came to The Orchard's Tenth Anniversary. That's why she kept looking at him oddly, Gianni thought. *Why she asked if I knew anything about him.*

After everyone sat down, Raffaella spoke.

"Thank you for coming. Some of you helped welcome me to America. Golda, you were very generous with your time. Fina, you helped me with my English. And Liberato, if not for your biscotti, I would not have the loving and kind husband I now have."

Hanns caught a tear before it dampened his cheek.

"And Sister Joan Marie, if not for your good council and your example, I doubt that I would have given life a second chance."

Gianni's eyes widened. *That's who that is. Holy crap. No more habit.*

"Father Marlo is on retreat, or he would have also been here. His generous efforts brought me to America. I don't know how many of you know this, but during the war, Father Marlo helped Father Rufino Niccacci save many Jews through the Assisi Underground. Father Marlo is a humble man with a generous spirit. An unsung hero."

Gianni recalled that Sister Joan Marie had told him that Father Marlo helped Jews gather in secret for Seders.

Raffaella introduced Gabriel and Gunter to the rest of the guests. "I had the pleasure of meeting Gabriel at one of our film talkbacks, and Gunter and Gabriel came to our tenth anniversary celebration. I'm honored and deeply moved that they are here today."

She didn't explain why she asked Gianni to invite them.

Gianni considered the people he sat among. *Only Raffaella would assemble such a group,* Gianni thought.

"Now Jennie, whenever you're ready."

"Okay, please take your seat." Jennie lowered her voice and took on a more courteous tone. She had met her match in Raffaella.

"We'll check the lighting again and film a little just to make sure positions are okay, and then we'll begin. Please, remember just a conversation, as if you're telling a friend your story. Start where you wish. Include and leave out whatever you want. When you feel like a sip of coffee, please drink. Organic. Nothing scripted. Even if someone belches, we'll just keep shooting."

Raffaella spoke briefly of Turin and her mother's passing, but at great length of her father and how she loved and admired him.

"We had a small apartment in Padua with a lovely yard," she said. "When my father wasn't reading or grading papers, he enjoyed gardening. We took picnic lunches to the Orto botanico di Padova, a botanical garden managed by the university where he was a professore. It was said to be the world's first botanical garden. My father took great pride in that. He valued bringing beauty into the world. 'For animals, it's about survival,' my father said. 'Even the most aggressive predator can't be faulted. It's his nature. And his nature serves a purpose. If not for the wolf, deer would destroy all flora. But for humans, it's different. We have choice to be kind or cruel.'"

"He sounds like a wise man," Melissa said.

"He was, and cordial. Yes, that's a good word to describe him. Very cordial. Often his students joined us for a picnic. I was not the only one who loved and admired my father. His teaching, like his parenting, was Socratic. A dialogue of questions and answers, which generated more questions. He loved Italy and said the culture of modern-day Italy was an amalgamation of many peoples from Europe, North Africa, and the Middle East. Though Rome is the seat of the Roman Catholic Church, my father said Jews and Muslims also had a tremendous influence on Italy and that many Catholics were unaware of their own Jewish and Muslim roots. Regarding my grandparents, great grandparents, et cetera, he said our ancestors probably dated back to ancient Rome. We were Italians until Mussolini allied himself with Hitler and turned anti-Semitic.

Raffaella shrugged her shoulders. "Maybe losing my mother at such a young age, a very gentle woman, made my father that much more precious to me. I don't know. But he was a remarkable man. I can still hear him asking, 'Who brought more beauty into the world? Modigliani, the Italian-Jewish artist, or that empty barrel, Il Duce.' Then he'd say, 'Always, always hold your head high, Raffaella.'"

Melissa commented, more than questioned. As Jennie wanted, a conversation between friends, Melissa being the excellent listener slipping in well-placed prods. She was very skilled at what she did.

Raffaella explained that when the Racial Laws were enacted, her father insisted she move to the Tuscan countryside with the Noti family. Catholics.

"My father was not someone to insist," she went on. "He allowed me to choose whether I'd stay with my mother's family in Turin or move to Padua with him. He made suggestions, even about little things like bedtime, or food to eat, or books to read, but never insisted. I wasn't used to being told what to do, and I resisted the move. But my father said, 'On this, you have no choice. You must obey.'"

"And you listened," Melissa said.

"Yes. It was the first time he had ever used the word 'obey.' I was sixteen. I listened. We kept in touch by word of mouth. Nothing written. In time, I learned he lost his position at the university. Months passed and when no one had further information for me, I wanted to go to Turin, but I was several months pregnant."

Raffaella talked about Marcello and Angelina. She explained her involvement in the resistance and her relationship with Marcello. She told Melissa about the night she and Marcello were discovered in the cave. She spoke of his murder.

"They took me to a transit camp, where I stayed for several weeks, and then on to Germany. Like animals, we were crowded into freight trains. No sense describing. Read Primo Levi or Elie Wiesel. They explain it better than I. We arrived at Buchenwald."

Gunter, who until now had been glancing around the room and

smiling vaguely at the framed posters, looked at Raffaella. His smile vanished. Raffaella glanced at Gunter then held his gaze briefly. She looked back at Melissa.

"After a brief stay at Buchenwald, I was sent to a satellite camp with other women. Slave labor to build armaments. Imagine building armaments for our enemies. The work was grueling. Many died or were shot if they could no longer work. There were also horrible experiments. Buchenwald was a chamber for mad scientists. But I don't want to dwell on that. Again, there are authors who found the words to describe. Levi, Wiesel, even Dante, although Dante would need to create a new circle for Nazis. You don't need me to repeat what's already been written. However, I do want to speak of someone who gave me the words to survive."

Now Raffaella looked only at Gunter, and he stared at her. His expression quizzical like a mouse in a maze and unsure of which way to turn.

"When I first arrived at Buchenwald, I or we—there were many of us—they dragged us from the train. They lined us up. Those who could barely stand, they shot immediately. Then even the elderly and weak found the strength to stand straight. Prisoners in striped uniforms carried baggage from the train. They looked like walking dead and they had pink triangles sewn to their shirts."

Gunter leaned forward. His brow furrowed. Gabriel took his hand. By now everyone, including Jennie, looked back and forth between Raffaella and Gunter. Had Jennie known this would happen, she would have had the camera take a wider view to also include Gunter, but she couldn't without permission. The camera moved in on Raffaella's face capturing the weight and tears in her eyes.

"The SS guards separated the men from the women. They told us to undress. Our clothes would be burned. Two hands were not enough for us to cover ourselves, but we tried. The guards laughed and made remarks in German I didn't understand. Just as well. Guards examined us, looked in our mouths, as if we were horses. When a guard came to me, I looked beyond him, over his shoulder. One of the men who carried the baggage appeared in my vision. I concentrated on him to distract myself from humiliation. The guard shouted orders at me in German. I knew only Italian and French and a little English. Someone translated his words. I ignored them. I was still my father's daughter and didn't take well to being told what to do. The man I stared at held up a finger and shook it quickly like a parent scolding a child, and then he walked back to the train and unloaded more baggage. The guard shouted louder. This time I followed his orders. No need for translation. He moved past me, but I could sense that even while examining the other women, his eyes remained on me. His leer disgusted me. Next, the guards marched us to be disinfected.

"By now some of the men with pink triangles walked next to us pushing carts with baggage. I heard a man whisper, 'Sei Italiano?' I said, 'Si,' but I didn't look at him.

"And then in Italian, but with a German accent, he said, 'Even Dante would have no words to describe. Live, live no matter what you have to do. Live!'

"The guards let the men pulling the carts go ahead of us. I saw that the man who spoke to me was the same man who shook his finger like a concerned parent when I didn't listen to the guard.

"My father was a Dante Scholar. Sometimes a Dante critic. But when I heard, 'Even Dante would have no words,' I believed this poor man with the pink triangle delivered to me a message from my darling father, a message to live no matter what."

Gabriel squeezed Gunter's hand. He looked at Gabriel, and then back at Raffaella. Except for Gunter, everyone's face, including Jennie's, shone with tears.

"At the time I didn't know what the pink triangle meant, but I found out. I also learned that even in hell there are hierarchies. The men wearing pink triangles were outcasts among outcasts.

"I never saw him again. Or at least I never noticed. Everything and everyone became a blur, but I carried his words, 'Live—no matter what you have to do. Live!' After all, I had a baby to come home to."

Raffaella looked back at Melissa and closed with the story of her liberation and learning the fate of her infant son, Gino. Fina passed out her endless supply of tissues. Gunter sat composed again, looking about the room at the many posters and pictures hanging on the walls.

"My father had been deported to Auschwitz. I'm the only one in my family to have survived."

Jennie motioned for the cameraman to turn off the camera.

One by one Fina, Liberato, Golda, Ezra, and Sister Joan Marie hugged Raffaella, mourners paying respect at a long overdue shiva.

Gianni and Gabriel remained sitting next to Gunter. Jennie also hugged Raffaella.

"Thank you," Jennie said. "My parents were also at Auschwitz. They were very young and survived. My grandparents and many other relatives didn't. I am sorry for your many losses." Jennie's voice cracked. Raffaella kissed Jennie's damp cheek.

The crew took down the lighting. Hanns offered people coffee. A few accepted. They gave Raffaella space to speak with Gunter. Raffaella pulled her chair over and sat facing Gunter. Gabriel and Gianni remained sitting on either side of him.

"Should we leave?" Gianni could barely get his words out.

"No, please stay," Raffaella said.

She took Gunter's hand.

"Do you remember Buchenwald?"

"Yes, not a very nice place to remember."

"Do you remember me?"

"Were you there, dear?"

Raffaella showed Gunter the numbers on her arm.

"Yes, I have those too. But we lived, dear. We lived."

Gunter placed his hand on Raffaella's cheek. She held it there. Tears streaked her face.

"No, no, dear. You'll spoil your makeup. And you look so lovely."

Words lingered like echoes, especially those exchanged between Raffaella and Gunter. The furniture was back in place, Gianni and Raffaella sat in their favorite easy chairs and drank the last of the coffee. In the small projection room above the theater, Hanns set up the two projectors for Tuesday's matinee, George Cukor's *The Philadelphia Story*.

"He remembered being there," Gianni said to Raffaella.

"Yes. If it was him, good. If it wasn't, it's still good. Meeting Gunter reminded me that a stranger cared enough to risk his own life for me. Something in Gunter's eyes and voice when I met him at the anniversary gala brought back that memory. But Buchenwald was a very long time ago, and memories of it are best forgotten."

"Whether or not it was Gunter, do you really believe that the message came from your father?"

"I don't know. I don't know if Gunter was the man who spoke to me. I don't know if the words were my father's. But those words kept me going. I repeated them like a prayer when the horrible became unbearable. And whether the words came from Gunter or my father or some other poor man with a pink triangle, I know my father wanted me to live. So meeting Gunter now is a blessing."

"Blessing? Funny you use that word often, but you're not religious."

"True. But we don't know what we don't know. And sometimes we get a glimpse of what we don't know. Maybe that's also a blessing. Yes?"

"I like that." Gianni glanced at the Charlie Chaplin poster. Beneath Chaplin's comic but foreboding image, holding his right hand up in the Nazi salute, was the bold-print title *The Great Dictator*. To the right of the poster hung two smaller black and white photographs. One showed Chaplin staring longingly at a large globe. Below that a photograph of Chaplin balancing the globe above the tips of his fingers.

"Chaplin was a genius," Gianni said. "Maybe I'd like to study film or maybe I'll just keep baking. Honest work. Right?"

Raffaella followed his glance and also looked at the poster. She smiled and nodded. "Honest work. Yes."

"I was surprised to see Sister Joan Marie here. I didn't recognize her without her habit."

"Did you get to talk with her?"

"A little. She called me Gianni instead of 'child of grace.'"

"You're no longer a child."

"Nor filled with grace."

Raffaella let that comment pass, and she finished her coffee.

"I didn't know about Father Marlo," Gianni said. "I never heard of the Assisi Underground. You invited quite a group. Gabriel at one end and Sister Joan Marie at the other."

"I like Gabriel."

"So do I. Gabriel also likes you."

Now Gianni finished his coffee, and the afternoon's echoes faded. Silence settled like evening fog. It lingered. The shuffling of feet in the apartment above and the wind shaking the front windows and door replaced words until Gianni asked Raffaella why she had come to

America.

Raffaella pressed the empty paper cup between the palms of her hands. "Too much loss. Too much anger."

"Anger?"

"Once the war was over, no one talked about it. Marcello, his family, my family, Gino—all murdered. No one asked for forgiveness. Suddenly everyone considered Mussolini a buffoon and a brutal dictator, but he didn't come into power by waving a magic wand. For that matter, neither did Hitler. Many people supported these monsters or they closed their eyes. But no one took responsibility for what they did or what they allowed. The people Marcello wished to liberate didn't mourn his death. I grew tired of saying 'Buongiorno' as if nothing had happened. As if no one was guilty."

Raffaella folded the pressed cup in half and folded it again. A few drops of coffee stained her fingers. "My father thought Italy was beautiful. So much for beautiful. In Rome, I'd look at the Fontana di Trevi or the Four Rivers in Piazza Navona, and I saw blood running instead of water."

"So you'll never return? Even to visit."

Raffaella stretched out her fingers and wiped away the stains. "No. Not even for a visit."

Hanns called from the lobby, "My love, ready to go?"

Raffaella stood and slipped on her coat. "Are you leaving?"

Gianni shook his head. "In a little while. I'm just going to wash the coffee pots. You did great tonight, Raffaella."

Hanns stepped into the parlor. "See you Wednesday, Gianni."

"Yup. Wednesday."

Raffaella kissed Gianni's cheek. "Ciao."

Gianni knew much of Raffaella's story, but not all of it. Until today, he heard it in knits and purls, as his mother would say.

He considered Raffaella's comment, *We don't know what we don't know.* Raffaella meeting or reconnecting with Gunter gave new purpose to Sister Joan Marie suggesting that Gianni help Raffaella move, and also new purpose to his meeting Gabriel. His friendship with Raffaella and then with Gabriel became a conduit for Raffaella and Gunter to reconnect, assuming they did cross paths at Buchenwald. Like stitching together patches of a quilt, one patch fitting neatly into another and surrounded by more patches, which are surrounded by more, and more, and more. Fina's knits and purls. *Nothing happens for one sole reason,* Gianni thought. There is no singular experience or story. Did he learn about Maura's death so he would know, or for Owen to know she was gone? Or was it so Gianni would discover that, in fact, Owen's feelings for him were more than fraternal. Even Gianni's understanding of his own trauma, the way he learned he was adopted and then losing his cousins, came out in knits and purls: comments his therapist made, Ezra made, Colleen made, and then finally his outburst toward Fina. Gianni's trauma didn't have the gravity of Raffaella's or Gabriel's or Owen's, but he saw that it gave him the insight and capacity to recognize sorrow where other people just saw a striking woman, or an unapologetic drag queen, or a small-town Vietnam vet.

Or maybe everything that happens is random, Gianni thought. *And it's up to us to create purpose if we need to create purpose.* Life was easier when the good sisters gave Gianni all the answers.

He mulled over his opinions about the way Jennie shot the film. *The Chaplin poster was a distraction. It was unfortunate that Jennie didn't get footage of Raffaella talking to Gunter. But she hadn't asked Gunter or Raffaella's permission. It would have added so much to the film. Should I go back to school?* Gianni thought. *Study film?*

Almost three years had passed since Raffaella suggested selling biscotti at The Orchard, but she also said, "Until you're ready to move on."

I might never be completely ready, Gianni thought. For all her abrasiveness, Jennie inspired Gianni or at least sparked thoughts of life beyond Sanctuary. Despite scenes he detested, sometimes whole movies he hated like *Gone With the Wind*, he still loved film. *The trick is to shed light and liberate, while entertaining,* he thought. *But most of all to create magic.*

With his academic history at Lyndon, NYU wasn't realistic. *But there are other film schools,* Gianni thought. He put the clean coffee pots away on a shelf, turned out the lights, and left for home.

During the news that evening, an NBC reporter announced, "Three-hundred and twenty-three American soldiers were killed in action. Fifteen-hundred and thirty were wounded and thirty-two were missing."

The clicking of Fina's knitting needles grew louder. "What was it Raffaella mentioned that her father said? That humans have a choice to be cruel or kind. Too many chose cruelty. It's always about money and power."

Gianni turned from looking at the television to looking at Fina. "I had never heard of the Assisi Underground."

"Me neither," Liberato said.

"There are always angels," Fina said.

The image on the television changed from the reporter to Nixon. Fina held her knitting needles out toward the television.

"But angels don't become president."

With Raffaella's permission, Jennie included Marcello's photograph and the photograph of Raffaella holding baby Gino in the documentary. Jennie invited Raffaella, Hanns, Gianni, and Ezra to the film's showing. Raffaella sent Jennie a letter thanking her for the invitation. She ended her letter with, "Regretfully, I cannot attend. Maybe someday I'll be able to watch your very important film, but not now. Respectfully, Raffaella."

PART 4

I may be crazy, but that don't make me wrong.
—Marsha P. Johnson

CHAPTER 19

Gabriel's friend Tammy burst into Tiffany's, spotted Gianni, rushed to where he was sitting, shoved him over, and sat next to him. She took a moment to catch her breath. Panting as if she had just run a marathon, she said she was glad Gianni was still here.

"We're waiting for Gabriel," Gianni said.

Tammy placed her hand on her chest. "I know. Just give me a minute. Too many damn cigarettes."

She squinted at Raffaella. "I remember you." Tammy took a deep breath. "You sat with us in that movie theater."

"Gabriel asked that I invite Raffaella," Gianni said.

"Well, that's why I'm here. Gabriel ain't coming."

A waitress dropped a third menu on the table. "Gurl, you look a mess. Where's Gabriel?"

"Arrested!"

The waitress shoved in next to Raffaella. "Not again."

"What do you mean, arrested?" Gianni said. "And not again? What happened?"

Raffaella moved her coat from the banquette to her lap to make room for the hefty waitress.

"Me and Gabriel was walking." Tammy took a gulp of Gianni's water. "Gabriel was coming here, and I was gonna take the 1 uptown to the Continental. We seen a cop car stopped in an alley with its high beams on another car. Two cops was in the alley hassling these kids."

Tammy dropped her voice to impersonate the police officers: "Suppose we bring you in and call your parents and tell them their boys are nothin' but little cock-sucking faggots."

The waitress shook her head. "Fucking pigs."

Tammy and the waitress leaned across the table, their faces a few inches apart, as if they had forgotten about Gianni and Raffaella. The waitress's ample bosom pressed against the pink Formica table top.

"The poor kids was about sixteen or seventeen." Tammy said. "One of them was crying."

"Fucking pigs," the waitress said again.

"Then Gabriel yells, 'What the fuck are you doing?'"

Gianni's jaw dropped. "At the cops?"

"Damn right at the cops," Tammy said and turned to Gianni. "Don't you know Gabriel? We see this shit all the time, and Gabriel don't know how to walk away. Some kid from wherever. You know like Valley Stream or Oyster Bay or Stony Brook. You know those towns that sound like they're in soap operas. And a kid drives his daddy's car to the Village, meets someone, and they get busted in the backseat of the car. You got psychos murdering folk, but the cops hassle kids getting their rocks off."

"Fucking pigs," the waitress said a third time with great emphasis on "pigs."

Gianni's ears turned red. He didn't look at Raffaella.

"I tried to pull Gabriel away, but that's like moving a brick wall. One of the cops yells, 'Keep walking faggot.'"

"Oh boy," the waitress said. "He must a been a rookie. What did Gabriel say?"

"Yeah. I never seen him before," Tammy said. "Gabriel yelled back, 'Why don't you go harass some straight kids fucking like rabbits in drive-ins. This here's our lovers' lane.'"

"Mm-hmm. That's Gabriel."

Gianni looked from Tammy to the waitress, back to Tammy, back to the waitress... Raffaella kept her eyes lowered.

"Then one of the pigs came up to Gabriel with his nightstick, and Gabriel slugged him. Next thing, the two cops are on Gabriel, and he's in handcuffs and getting the shit beat out of him. Worse than last time."

"Last time?" Gianni said.

"Yeah, when Gabriel's eye and cheek got all swelled up and purple."

"He told me some white kids tried to give him grief because he wore full drag," Gianni said.

"And you believed that story? What white boys are gonna be stupid enough to pick a fight with Gabriel? I don't care what Gabriel was wearing. He's built like Muhammad Ali and then some. Delores was with Gabriel then. You remember Delores?"

Tammy looked at Raffaella, who looked up and nodded. "She came to the movie that night too. Anyway, they was on Grove Street and a cop car passed. Two kids was walking in front of Gabriel and Delores. Delores said they was kissing or holding hands or something. The cop rolls down his window and called the kids faggots. Gabriel yelled at the cop, 'I saw your daddy giving this young faggot a blow job last night.'"

Gianni shook his head. "How does Gabriel get out of jail?"

"That's another story. I'll let Gabriel tell you those details. But the reason I came here is before the cops pushed Gabriel into the police car, Gabriel yelled for me to tell you Gunter is home alone. I gotta get up to the Continental. I'm already late for my gig. You got a pencil, Sylvia?"

The waitress pulled a pencil out of her beehive and handed it to Tammy. Tammy wrote Gunter's address on a napkin.

"What happened to the kids?" Gianni said.

"Oh, the cops let them go. That's Gabriel's strategy, honey. Gabriel's like a human decoy. He takes the lumps. He don't want no more parents throwing their kids out. He says he's got more children than a mother can handle."

"That's Gabriel," Sylvia said. "If I don't get back to work, I'll lose my job and Gabriel's gonna have to give me sandwiches."

"Isn't it too late to just show up at the apartment?" Gianni said. "I don't want to frighten Gunter."

"He don't go to bed until Gabriel is home," Tammy said. "Gabriel is always forgetting his keys, so just ring the apartment, and Gunter will buzz you in. Their phone was disconnected months ago, so we can't call. Okay, I gotta get to the Continental for my gig." Tammy stood and looked at Raffaella. "Nice seeing you again. Love your earrings."

Gunter and Gabriel's apartment—a walk-up, prewar low-rise—was a short walk from Tiffany's. Gianni pressed the doorbell. Just as

Tammy said, Gunter buzzed them in. Gianni and Raffaella climbed the three flights to apartment 4C.

Gunter cracked the door, but left the chain latched.

"That you, Gabriel?"

"It's Gabriel's friend Gianni. Remember you came to The Orchard a few nights ago with Gabriel?"

Gunter peeked through the space between the edge of the door and the doorjamb. "Where's Gabriel?"

"He's been arrested, Gunter."

"Again?"

"He wanted us to check on you to make sure you're okay."

"Us?"

"Yes, remember Raffaella?"

Raffaella stepped forward so Gunter could see her.

"Ahh yes, the lovely lady who told that sad story. How are you, dear?"

"I'm well," Raffaella said. "How are you?"

"I've been better, dear, but no sense in complaining."

Gunter unlatched the chain. "Come in, but please excuse the mess. I wasn't expecting company."

A high-back chair faced the only light in the dark room. On *The Late Show*, Susan Hayward was getting strapped into an electric chair. Gunter turned on a lamp with a fringed Victorian shade, and then turned off the television. The lamp provided less light than the television.

"Poor Susan, such a drama queen in movies like *I'll Cry Tomorrow, I Want To Live, My Foolish Heart*. She plays a great lush, you know."

An almost empty bottle of whiskey and an empty glass sat on a dusty, mahogany pie crust wine table next to Gunter's chair. He looked at Gianni and Raffaella. "I'm sorry, what did you say your names are?"

They answered.

"Yes, of course. Please sit down." Gunter looked around the room. "Oh my. No, I wasn't expecting company."

Tattered movie magazines occupied chairs. Raffaella placed a stack on the floor and took a seat. Gianni followed her example.

Raffaella turned on another lamp, this one with a tiffany shade of cobalt blues and reds. There were many lamps on tables and shelves: Victorian, Art Deco, Italian bisque or French Provincial bisque porcelain lamps with fringed shades. Some stood on the floor, despite not being floor lamps. Crystal pendeloques hung from several lamps. Antique curio cabinets held Goebel Hummels and music boxes of little fair-haired boys and girls under umbrellas, skiing, playing with animals and birds, reading books, or singing Christmas Carols. The posters Gabriel told Gianni about hung on walls. The room resembled a mini and more cluttered Sanctuary at The Orchard.

"Isn't this nice?" Gunter said. "Too bad Gabriel isn't here. Hopefully he'll be home soon."

Gianni looked at Raffaella. Raffaella leaned in closer to Gunter. "Gabriel's been arrested, Gunter. Nothing serious, but he won't be home tonight."

Gunter sighed, "Not again."

Gianni scanned the room. His eyes paused on a poster of Vivian Leigh as Blanche Dubois in *A Street Car Named Desire*. Blanche appeared at home among the clutter of movie magazines, worn furniture, vintage lamps, knickknacks, and the smell of weed, whiskey, and dime-store perfume. *I have always depended on the kindness of strangers*. Gianni recalled the iconic line from *Streetcar*, and then looked at Gunter.

The upholstery on Gunter's chair barely covered the horsehair stuffing, and the diaphanous skin on Gunter's face and hands barely obscured the blue veins beneath. His frail body all but vanished beneath his quilted robe. *Gabriel*, Gianni thought, *is direct. His drag reveals more than it conceals. But Gunter is all smoke and mirrors.*

Gianni considered the way Raffaella looked at Gunter. *She's nothing like him, but she understands him, or at least what he's been through.*

"Have you eaten?" Raffaella said.

"Oh, I don't require much sustenance, dear."

"I can go buy you something."

"Don't trouble yourself."

"We can bring you groceries tomorrow," Gianni said.

"Yes, tomorrow would be nice."

"Well we just wanted to let you know about Gabriel. I can stop by tomorrow with groceries."

Gunter smiled and Gianni stood up. He and Raffaella walked toward the door. Gianni sensed Raffaella's hesitation.

Once they were in the hall, before Gianni pulled the door shut, Raffaella laid her hand on his arm. "I don't like that he doesn't have a phone. Maybe I can have it connected tomorrow."

"Would you rather I stay here with him tonight?" Gianni said.

"Would you mind?"

"No, it's okay."

"I'll call your parents in the morning and explain," Raffaella said.

Gianni stepped back into the apartment. Gunter remained in his chair before the blank television.

"Gunter, do you mind if I stay in Gabriel's room tonight?"

"If you like." Gunter pointed to an open door. "I do fall asleep in front of the television. I'll keep the volume low. I hope you don't mind."

"I don't mind."

"Buona notte, amore mio," Gunter said. This made Gianni uncomfortable. Sometimes, older men, though not as old as Gunter, offered to buy him drinks in bars. The other young gay guys called the men "trolls." Gianni didn't understand their disdain for older gay men. Once fed up with a young guy coming on to him and complaining about all the old trolls, Gianni snapped, "Do you think you're never going to get old? If you don't want a drink, just say no thank you. Like I don't want you flirting with me, so fuck off."

Regardless, Gianni bristled at "amore mio."

He wiped the wigs and stockings off of Gabriel's bed. *Probably just Gunter's way, like calling everyone dear*, Gianni told himself. He glanced at the dressing table, cluttered with creams and cosmetics. Taped to a heart-shaped mirror above the table were two black and white photographs. Gianni looked closer at the pictures, one a distant shot of an elderly woman sitting in a rocking chair on the front porch of a small, clapboard, shotgun house. Her white hair a halo around her dark complexion. In the second picture, two small children—shirtless and barefoot, their baggy shorts cinched at the waist with cords—posed on tiptoes. One child clasped her fingers above plaited hair, tied with ribbons, the other child's fingers clasped above a shaved head. Both children had Gabriel's beautiful smile. Gianni thought the first picture must be Gabriel's Granma Eugenia. And the second, Gabriel and his younger sister. Granma Eugenia must have taken it. Who else was loving enough to take a picture of her grandson posing like a fledgling ballerina?

A bookshelf stood next to the dressing table. Some of the books Gabriel had loaned to Gianni, others were unfamiliar, all by Black authors: Countee Cullen, Alice Dunbar Nelson, Wallace Henry Thurman, Ralph Ellison, Richard Wright. He paused at James Baldwin's *Giovanni's Room*. He took the book from the shelf and lay down on Gabriel's bed.

Gianni turned to the first page and read, "I stand at the window of this great house in the south of France as night falls…" A dozen pages into Baldwin's poetic prose, Gianni looked up and glanced at the closed door between Gabriel's room and the room where Gunter now dozed.

CHAPTER 20

Fina rolled her eyes when Mrs. Colombo said, "I know a cheese ring goes with everything, but I want something more refined. My future daughter-in-law's parents are coming to dinner. They're not Italian. My son says they're WASPS. Maybe they don't like cheese rings."

Fina put her hands on her hips. "Buy a torte. Tortes are very refined. WASPS love them."

Gianni laughed, waved to his mother, then pushed through the swinging door from the bakery into the kitchen. He slipped on a bib-apron and tied the strings around his waist.

Fina set the hands on a cardboard clock for 11:15. Across the top of the clock were the words "Be Back Soon." She turned it to face out.

Whenever Fina did this, customers complained to Liberato. They knew better than to complain to Fina.

"Having to come back a few minutes later for loaf of bread or a box of pastries is not a catastrophe. We're not running an emergency room," Fina said when Liberato tried to convince her to trash the cardboard clock.

In a large mixing bowl, Gianni creamed granulated sugar and butter with a wooden spoon. He heard the creak of the swinging door. Fina poked her head into the kitchen.

"Papa up already?"

"No, I turned the clock on the door."

"Something wrong?"

"No, I wanted to tell you that Raffaella called."

"Yes, that's good. I didn't want you to worry."

Fina entered the kitchen and the door closed behind her. "How's Gunter?"

"Okay, I guess. Sound asleep when I left. I'll check on him later. I think Raffaella is getting his phone connected today. That's why I stayed last night. No way to reach him or for him to call." Gianni scraped the creamed butter from the sides of the bowl with a rubber spatula. "Did Mrs. Colombo buy a torte?"

"Yes. Every time she comes in, she makes a production. Refined? She thinks she's Pearl Mesta. She and her torte are gone. So that's nice of Raffaella. Strange how she met Gabriel at The Orchard, and then met Gunter. As if it was meant to be."

Gianni knew his mother was fishing. He put down the spatula and looked at her.

"It's true that Gabriel first came to The Orchard by chance," he said. "That's how Raffaella met him, but I already knew Gabriel from a bar in Greenwich Village. And I was the one who invited Gabriel to The Orchard's anniversary gala. That's how Raffaella met Gunter. I know she told Saul that knowing Gabriel and then Gunter was all her doing. But that's not the whole story. Although, 'meant to be' might be exactly what happened."

"I see."

Gianni nodded, took a deep breath, and then cracked eggs into the creamed butter.

A customer banged at the bakery door. Fina yelled into the air, "Hold your horses." She looked back at her son. "Gianni, I'm not stupid, and I'm not small minded. I've told you that all kinds of people visited our apartment in East Harlem when I was a girl. What they had in common was their politics. But they were different ethnicities, races, religions—although, except for my mother, no one was actually religious. But some were different in other ways. It wasn't discussed, but people knew."

Gianni nodded without looking at Fina. He folded the eggs into the creamed butter. His ears felt warm.

"There were two women," Fina said. "They shared an apartment downtown. Everyone understood they were more than roommates."

A second bang at the bakery door. Fina waved her hand at the air.

"Your father, he grew up different than me, but he loves you more than life, as I do."

Gianni's eyes filled. A third bang.

"Uffa!" Fina yelled. "I better open the door before that stugats breaks the glass."

When Fina left the kitchen, Gianni exhaled a heavy breath of relief. In a separate bowl, he whisked together flour, baking powder, and salt. Now wasn't the time for a heart-to-heart with his mother about being gay. Now was the time to make biscotti. A much-needed distraction. He didn't want to think about Gunter or Gabriel or Raffaella. Nor did he want to think about Owen. But that was impossible. Not even baking erased thoughts of Owen.

While Gianni stirred a bit of vanilla into the butter and egg mixture, he recalled showering with Owen in the outdoor stall. He recalled their soapy shoulders and thighs and buttocks touching. He saw the sunlit water on Owens muscular shoulders. Gianni gradually added flour to the mix, and the sheen of Owen's lips turned to drool spilling out the corner of Gunter's slack and toothless mouth. He also couldn't erase what he saw earlier as he left Gabriel's room, careful not to wake Gunter who was snoring in front of the television. Gunter's blanket lay in a pile on the floor, and he had slid down low in his chair, his legs splayed and his robe parted. Gianni lifted the blanket. Below sparse gray pubic hair, Gunter's penis hung limp between skinny, varicose-veined legs. It wasn't what Gianni saw that disturbed him, but what he didn't see. Gianni paused before covering Gunter. With its dirty windows, the room wasn't bright, but light enough to see that Gunter didn't have testicles. As Gianni covered Gunter with the blanket and tucked it around his shoulders, he recalled what he once read in a book at the library after Raffaella told him that she was at Buchenwald: "Medical experiments including castration were performed on homosexuals."

Gianni appreciated Fina's attempt to say that she knew he was gay and that she loved him. But all he could think of was that he didn't want to think, which was impossible, and no amount of mixing and stirring and baking could erase what he had seen. His hands shook. He wondered if Gunter had an Owen before the camps. He wondered if there were moments in the camps, despite the stench of emaciated, unwashed bodies, when there was no baggage to carry from another train, no munitions to build for enemies, after the lights went out, when Gunter found passion with someone who also wore a pink triangle. Like the passion found in shadows on the Christopher Street piers? A reminder that he was real. And visible. And alive.

Gianni tried to block out the image of Gunter. He thought of Owen, but Owen turned into Gunter. He thought of Ezra, but Ezra turned into Gunter. He thought of folding the flour mixture into the egg mixture, but whatever or whomever he thought of turned into Gunter screaming while a Nazi butcher took a knife to Gunter's balls.

Gianni pressed his floured palms against his closed eyes, but he couldn't unsee.

Given that Tammy said Gunter was a night owl, Raffaella waited until mid-afternoon before she returned to Gunter's apartment with two bags of groceries. She set one shopping bag down on the stoop, balanced the other bag on her hip, pressed the bell to 4C and, once Gunter buzzed her in, she pushed open the front door with her shoulder.

The hallway reeked of weed, and from apartment 2B came the sound of Janis Joplin belting out *Me and Bobby McGee*. At the open door to 3D, a shirtless man wearing red corduroy bellbottoms, his white belt hanging open, placed a paper bag filled with empty whiskey and gin bottles in the hall. He winked at Raffaella. She ignored him. His eyes followed her as she climbed the steps to the fourth floor.

Gunter stood at his slightly open door.

"It's Raffaella, Gunter. Remember I was here last night."

"Oh yes, we had a lovely chat." He unlatched the chain.

"I brought groceries. Not much, but I thought you might be hungry."

Gunter wore the same robe he wore last night and his breath had a sweet fermented odor.

"I'm not that hungry, dear." He smiled.

"I can make you eggs or a sandwich or—"

"Yes, eggs would be nice."

Raffaella looked around the room.

"Behind the screen, dear. It's a pullman's kitchen. Might be a little messy. I don't cook much anymore. Gabriel brings me take-out."

Raffaella stepped behind the tapestry screen. A compact stove, sink, and refrigerator lined a small alcove. She opened the refrigerator and tossed out several moldy containers. She washed the few dirty cups and dishes in the sink, refilled the dishpan with clean soapy water, and wiped the refrigerator shelves before putting away perishables.

So Gunter could hear her above the droning television, Raffaella raised her voice.

"Do you like mozzarella?"

"What's that, dear?"

"Cheese! Do you like cheese in your eggs? An omelet."

"Sounds scrumptious."

"Toast?"

"What?"

"Do you want toast?"

"No, thank you. I'm not a big eater."

Raffaella cracked two eggs in a small bowl, and then mixed the eggs with a fork.

On television, Bert Bauer from *Guiding Light* grieved the loss of her father. Gunter pressed his finger to his cheek and shook his head.

Butter melted in a small cast-iron frying pan. Raffaella added the eggs, gave them a moment to solidify, and then added two thick slices of mozzarella. She covered the pan just long enough for the cheese to soften, removed the lid, and folded the omelet with a spatula.

"Almost ready."

"Yes, I'm ready, dear."

"No, I mean—Never mind." Raffaella smiled, poured a glass of orange juice and turned the omelet onto one of the plates she just washed. She set the plate of eggs and juice on the table next to Gunter, and picked up the empty whiskey bottle.

"Aren't you eating, dear? I've become a terrible host."

"Of course I'll join you. I brought a thermos of coffee and biscotti. Do you like biscotti?"

"Yes, very much." Gunter pierced the omelet with a fork. Like a cosmic power from a genie's lamp, a small cloud of steam swirled above the melted mozzarella.

"I do hope Gabriel comes home soon," Gunter said.

Not one to speak of what she didn't know, Raffaella didn't answer. She sat on the chair, she cleared of movie magazines last night, and poured coffee from her thermos into the screw-on lid. She dunked a biscotti in her coffee and said, "Bon appetito!"

"The omelet is delicious, dear. How is your biscotti?"

"Molto bene. Gianni made them."

"Gianni?"

"Yes, the young man who was with me last night."

"Oh yes, such a handsome young man. He reminds me of the men I met in Sicily."

"I'm from Turin, but I once visited Sicily with my father."

"I used to vacation in Taormina" Gunter said. "But that was ages ago."

Sunlight shone through the grimy windows and caught the pendent crystals on lampshades and Gunter's clouded blue eyes, which seemed to be searching memories. Rainbows from the crystals danced on the faded wallpaper, on curios, and on stacks of movie magazines.

Gunter smiled. "I had a friend named Pancrazio Buciuni. His lover was a renowned photographer. Maybe you've heard of him. Wilhelm von Gloeden."

Raffaella shook her head.

He waved his hand, his fingertips fracturing the rainbows. "Well, the photographer had recently passed and Il Moro was much distraught. Il Moro was Buciuni's nickname, Ahh—the things I remember and the things I forget. Long ago just happened, but yesterday is too distant to recall."

A single tear slid from one of Gunter's clouded eyes. "They say getting old isn't for sissies. But even sissies get old, dear. And we make the best of it. But then isn't it better to remember my youth in Taormina?" Gunter looked down at his robe. "Rather than this wrinkled bag of bones I've become."

"I don't recognize the photographer's name," Raffaella said, trying to steer Gunter back to happier memories. "I was very young when my father and I vacationed in Sicily."

"Gloeden died the year before my first trip to Taormina," Gunter said. "The summer of 1932. I went to see his photographs. That's how I met Il Moro. Then the next year and for several years after, Mussolini's Fascist police confiscated Gloeden's prints and negatives. Too scandalous for the very moral Il Duce and the Vatican. As if either were the example of morality. One summer, I learned that Il Moro had been imprisoned, but he was cleared."

Gunter sighed. Again, he pressed his fork into the omelet, now cooled. "I no longer visited Taormina. Everything got worse and worse. No sense in reliving that."

"I have a little surprise for you," Raffaella said. A phone sat on the table next to Gunter's half-eaten omelet. Raffaella lifted the receiver.

"I don't think that's working, dear. Sometimes we have a hard time meeting our expenses."

Raffaella held the receiver next to Gunter's ear. His eyes widened.

"Goodness. Who paid the bill?"

"It wasn't much."

Gunter placed his fork on the plate. "But why? Very generous of you. The groceries. The phone bill. Are you an angel disguised as a lovely Italian woman?"

Raffaella laughed. She placed the receiver back on the phone. "I'm repaying a long over-due kindness." Raffaella repeated the story she had shared during the interview at The Orchard. She removed a pen and paper from her purse then wrote two phone numbers on the paper.

"There were so many people, dear, and so much baggage," Gunter said.

Clouds obscured the sunlight, and the rainbows vanished. Gunter picked at lint on his robe. "So, so much baggage," he said. "Some filled with clothes. Some with tools. Some with kitchenware and food. It was the photographs that broke my heart over and over, until my heart was nothing but crumbs. They made us burn all the photographs. Family stories going up in smoke. Not only did the Nazis want to kill people, but they wanted to erase their history. As if these people never existed. Sometimes I dug holes and hid photographs like a buried treasure. I thought maybe, someday. But who knows?"

Gunter's eyes met Raffaella's. "I'm sorry dear, but I don't remember your story. There were so many stories. Like so much baggage. Too much to carry. At some point, I had to let go."

"I understand," Raffaella said. "But I'll tell you something wonderful. When I returned to the town and house where I lived before I was arrested, I found a picture of my husband and one of me holding my baby. So maybe someday someone will find the treasures you buried."

Gunter smiled. "So the bastards didn't erase everything."

"No, not everything."

Raffaella set the sheet of paper with the two phone numbers on

Gunter's lap. "I'm going to tape this paper next to the phone. One phone number is to my home, the other is The Orchard—where I work. You call me anytime. This is what you have to remember now, Gunter. We can't change what happened years ago."

Gunter lifted the sheet of paper from his lap. He read the numbers aloud.

Weeks later, Gianni learned where Gabriel was held, and then another few weeks to negotiate the obstacles for a visit at Rikers. The visit itself involved several bus rides, check points, inspections, and hours of waiting.

A guard escorted Gianni to a room resembling a small work-place cafeteria with square tables and plastic chairs. The guard stood with Gianni at the entrance until another guard opened a door across the room, and a third guard escorted Gabriel to one of the tables.

Had Gianni passed Gabriel on the street or in a subway, he wouldn't have recognized him. It wasn't just the green T-shirt, khaki pants, and slipper shoes, or the lack of accessories, eye shadow and glitter, but the alpha way Gabriel carried himself, pulled a plastic chair away from the table, and sat with his legs spread apart and his feet planted firmly on the hard tile floor. He folded his arms across his broad chest. His biceps strained against the short sleeves of his T-shirt.

Since caged at Rikers, Gabriel either read or did pushups. No one was going to mess with his head or body. Gianni took the seat across from him. Their eyes locked. Gabriel spoke quietly.

"Welcome to New York's finest bullpen," he said.

Gianni chewed the edge of his thumb and glanced at a man and woman sitting at a table across the room. He recognized their Spanish accent, but not their words.

"How's Gunter?"

"Okay, I guess. He's worried about you, but Raffaella and I are taking turns. You know getting him food and stuff."

"I figured she'd help out."

"She's even gotten him to shower and wear clothes aside from his bathrobe. Sometimes she takes him to The Orchard by cab to watch movies. He forgets our names. Raffaella is that lovely lady, and I'm the handsome Sicilian boy."

"You could be called worse things."

"Sure, I just meant that except for his memory getting a little foggy sometimes, he's okay."

Gabriel nodded. "I appreciate it."

"Tammy said you're usually out by now. She said you—" But Gianni paused. Despite their low voices, Gianni thought it dangerous to mention that Gabriel knew people or had connections since a guard stood a few yards away from their table and might overhear them.

"Tammy's right."

"So, you'll be out soon."

Gabriel shrugged. "I'm not sure why I got out quickly in the past. I have an idea, but—" Gabriel leaned into the table. "I've had closeted mobsters and closeted cops. Only difference is their uniforms. Some wear sharkskin suits and some wear blue, but they're all the same. Bullies and crooks."

Gabriel formed quotes with his fingers. "Straight guys. Married, but they like dick, especially drag-queen dick because they can still think of themselves as macho. Make it a Black drag queen, and these white guys are in heaven. Some kinky slumming, and then they go home to their tidy neighborhoods and Doris Day wives. Thing is they come back and sometimes—" Gabriel shifted in his seat. The guard looked at him. Gabriel lowered his voice to a whisper. "Sometimes one-night turns into a week. Sometimes months. And they tell me things they later regret. I know a lot of shit, Gianni. I know who gets laid and who gets paid."

Gabriel ran his fingertips along his bottom lip, and his eyes shifted to the left. "Ain't no way I'm gonna let those pigs harass queer kids on our turf. It's the only few streets they got. They're pushed into the shadows, and then the pigs are gonna bust them for doing what straight kids do in alleys outside their church socials. Not while I'm around."

Gabriel sat back and folded his arms again. "Now? Who knows? Maybe the shit I know will help me get out of here soon. Maybe it won't. Might be just the opposite this time. Ya know, maybe I'm too dangerous to be free."

"Have you seen a lawyer?"

"I'll get to talk to a lawyer five minutes before trial. But who knows when that will be."

"Isn't there some kind of time limit?"

Gabriel's right cheek knotted and he spoke out of the side of his mouth. "Gianni, this is a Black and Puerto Rican bullpen. Those rules are made for white folk with connections and bail money."

As if to underscore what he said, a door opened, and the same guard who escorted Gianni stood next to a young Black woman holding a toddler. They both looked terrified. The door Gabriel came in also opened, and the same guard who escorted Gabriel now escorted a young Black man to a table. Twenty years old—if that. The woman and toddler joined him. She pressed the palm of her free hand against her cheek and wiped away tears. The toddler cried, "Daddy."

Gabriel glanced at the couple, and then looked back at Gianni. "As I was saying. That child's in here for weed. Busted for weed. Ya know, Nixon's war on drugs? Guess what color the casualties will be in this war."

Gianni shook his head. He chewed his top lip. "Thank you, Gabriel."

"For what?"

"For doing what you did that night. For sticking up for those kids. For doing what you always do. You're a fucking hero."

Gabriel chuckled. "Well, your hero is in the slammer for now, but I'm butching it up." Gabriel spread his arms and flexed his muscles. The guard shot a warning glance.

"Are you afraid?"

Gabriel shook his head. "No. No, I ain't afraid. Just doing what it takes to survive. It's not my first time here. I know the game."

Their conversation shifted to less serious matters. Gabriel talked about a visit from Tammy and Delores and a volunteer from a prisoner advocacy group. Gianni talked about Ezra and Colleen. Ezra had just graduated from Columbia and been accepted in several journalism programs.

"Pretty sure he'll go to Berkeley. He talks about it a lot. I'll miss him, but California definitely sounds good. You know, a change."

"Change sounds good," Gabriel said. "California. I'd head right to the Castro."

Gianni paused. He listened to the buzz of the overhead florescent lights. "Yes, change does sound good. When you get out of here, let's go to California. A vacation. We can drive cross country in my van. I haven't taken a long break since I opened Sanctuary. Maybe Ezra would go with us. He could check out Berkeley. See if he'll like it."

Gabriel laughed. "Two white boys and a Black man driving a van across America. We'll see every jail in every Podunk town, unless the Klan gets us first."

"We could camp."

Now Gabriel really let out a laugh. The guard shot him another glance.

"Honey, the only camp I do is on a stage in stilettos."

Gabriel's sparkle shone through the macho act, and Gianni felt grateful. Jail hadn't hardened Gabriel. He simply turned down the camp and dropped talking of himself in third-person. He wore armor to survive. In Gabriel's smile Gianni still saw the little boy from Money, Mississippi, who Gabriel sometimes talked about during their midnight breakfasts at Tiffany's. Several times, in his best Aretha Franklin impression, Gabriel crooned, "Ain't no way I was gonna let them beat the sissy out of me. I was the most fabulous little sissy to come out of the Mississippi Delta."

But Gabriel was right. The two or three of them driving cross country would tempt white-hate.

Gianni sighed. "America's one fucked up place, Gabriel."

"Honey, you just figuring that out?"

"No, but sometimes I try to forget."

"I hear ya. Now tell me more about Colleen. You said she got herself knocked up."

"Yup. Last Fall, when I stayed at Owen's, Ezra and Colleen stayed on a commune with Ezra's friends. Since then, she kept driving back and forth. Each time she stayed a little longer. I guess she fell for some guy."

"What's a girl to do?" Gabriel said. "The heart wants what the heart wants."

"Guess so. She's marrying the guy next week. I assume it's the baby's father. But with Colleen, who knows. Ezra and I will be her best men."

"No maid of honor?"

"She said Ezra and I can flip for who's the maid of honor."

"I liked that girl, first I saw her with her feather earrings."

Gianni cleared his throat. "I've been wondering something. And if you don't want to answer, that's okay. How'd you meet Gunter? I mean, you told me he gave you a place to live. It's none of my business. I was just curious."

"No problem. When my Granma died I left NOLA and went back home for her funeral. My kid sister had called me. She was the only one who knew where I was, but I think you knew that part already."

Gianni nodded.

"After that, I went to New York City. Harlem. Gay life was pretty open, at least compared to Mississippi, but then the police started their faggot busts, and me and some friends shifted locations. We spent more and more time in the Village. I was hustling, doing drugs, sleeping wherever I could sleep. Sometimes in Harlem. Sometimes in the Village. I met Gunter at a food pantry. He volunteered there. He was friendly and talked with a lot of us while we ate. Sometimes he'd sit across from me and ask how I was doing. I was probably your age. One morning I woke up in his apartment. I did that a lot. Waking up places with no memory of how I got there. He said he found me under the highway puking my brains out. He said I could stay if I got clean. Not easy, but I did.

"He owned a little antique shop at the time. That's why we have all that old crap in the apartment. He'd also take in kids now and then. Give them a place to sleep for a night or two. But I put a stop to it. Sometimes they'd steal his stuff. One kid even got a little rough with Gunter. I didn't blame them. That's how they learned to survive. But Gunter was getting old, and I couldn't be home all the time."

"You never mentioned that Gunter was in the camps."

Gabriel nodded.

"You must have seen the numbers on his arm."

He nodded again. "My Great Aunt Mitlide had scars on her shoulder from a branding iron. And she wasn't the only elder with scars. We didn't talk about it. It wasn't polite."

Gianni looked down at the table. He explained that he stayed with Gunter the night Gabriel was arrested. He explained what he saw the next morning, or what he didn't see.

Gabriel sucked at his teeth and remained silent. Gianni was about to let the matter drop, but then Gabriel said, "I don't know if that happened in Buchenwald or in prison after Buchenwald."

"After?"

"Yep, Gunter said he went to Buchenwald from prison and, after the war, gay men were sent right back to prison. The war ending didn't do shit for faggots. Lopping off gay men's balls like they was neutering swine was a punishment. He said the doctors at Buchenwald were butchers. Remember, Raffaella talked about them when she was interviewed?"

"Yes, she mentioned that they carried out terrible experiments. I read about it too."

Gabriel nodded. "Gunter was always stinking drunk when he talked about this stuff. I never asked him questions. I just let him rant, so I don't know where it happened. Prison? Buchenwald? What difference does it make? It just happened."

"Horrible." Gianni shook his head.

"Those Nazis sure were butchers, but we got a lot of our own home-grown butchers. We don't have to look across no ocean. Walk up along Central Park East to 103rd Street. There's a statue of this doctor named Sims. He's called the father of modern gynecology. He experimented on Black enslaved women without using anesthesia. Some father."

Gianni's jaw dropped. "Holy crap."

"Most of the monuments in America are to white folk who fucked over Black folk. Nothing new about that. And it's still going on. You think prisons are built to get criminals off the street?"

Gabriel looked around the room. His eyes paused at the young couple and child sitting across the room from them. He looked back at Gianni.

"Granma Eugenia's funeral was on August 28th, 1955. Doubt your teachers taught you about that date, but I was standing outside Granma's house smoking a cigarette when I saw white men drag Emmett Till out of his great uncle's house. Just another night in Mississippi. I'm still waiting for Till's murderers to do time. But I ain't holding my breath."

The guard stepped forward. "Times up, Gabe."

Gianni looked at Gabriel, his brow wrinkled. *Gabe?* he thought.

Gabriel stood. "See ya at Tiffany's."

During the bus rides from building to building across Rikers Island and the bus ride off the island back to Queens, Gianni thought hard about his visit with Gabriel. Probably because that's all he wanted the guards and inmates to see, Gabriel wore the veneer of a large, dark-skinned, muscular Black man. But Gabriel was like the ocean—calm and cool enough to nurture a desperate queer youth, but stormy enough to mangle a bully, whether the bully was from the Mob, the NYPD, or some john getting too rough with the trade.

Despite the macho posturing there had been glimmers of the old Gabriel. Gianni liked that he no longer called him child. It wasn't demeaning coming from Gabriel, but calling him by his name or even "Honey" felt like a milestone in their relationship, a graduation from being one of Gabriel's queer children to a friend and confidant. He felt honored.

Gianni adored Gabriel as he adored Raffaella. *Wolf trees*, Gianni thought. And then he thought of Gunter who was instrumental in both Raffaella's and Gabriel's survivals. Neither Gunter nor Raffaella was positive that Gunter really was the man with the pink triangle who gave Raffaella the words that kept her alive, but Gianni was sure. He had shed many of his Catholic beliefs, but not his magical thinking.

Emmett Till, Gianni thought. The name sounded familiar. Someone he had read about in books his teachers never assigned. He'd check the microfiche of old newspapers kept on the bottom floor of the 42nd Street Library. After Lyndon State, he went there to fill in the gaps that conventional teaching left. The library morgue where news goes to die, especially news that white America wanted to bury.

Getting off the bus at the Jamaica Bus Terminal, the last stop from Rikers, Gianni looked about the bus as other passengers disembarked. Except for him, they were all Black or Puerto Rican. He overheard a snatch of conversation: "If only we could come up with the bail money to get him out."

Shit, Gianni thought. *Bail money. Of course.*

CHAPTER 21

Gianni turned off the paved road about ten miles outside Burlington. Hardly a road, but more than a path, mostly beneath spruce and fir trees. An occasional white pine bough brushed the van's windshield. Ezra fell asleep after they crossed the New York-Vermont border. The sights, sounds, and smells of Vermont brought Owen to mind, but so did the sounds and sights of New York City traffic and the smell of bread baking or coffee brewing. Everything sparked thoughts of Owen. Since Ezra was asleep, there was no conversation to distract Gianni from remembering Owen shirtless and sweaty and throwing bales of hay from the loft in the barn. No conversation to distract Gianni from memory of Owen's seductive musk made sweeter with the scent of fresh hay. No conversation to distract Gianni from the feel of Owen's muscular body and rising erection. No conversation to distract Gianni from the memory of sundrenched droplets on Owen's broad shoulders. Silence evoked memories. Distractions distracted, but they didn't replace. Not a day passed without Gianni remembering—the way he might remember a favorite movie, and he could pause his memories at will and savor a particular frame.

Ezra yawned and stretched. "Where are we?"

"Kansas," Gianni said.

"Far out. Must have slept longer than I thought."

Ezra looked out the window. "Yup, we're here. Just keep following this road."

"Calling this a road is a stretch. Did you know Vermont was once nothing but sheep pastures, with very few trees."

"Hard to imagine," Ezra said. Several low-hanging evergreen boughs brushed the windshield. "We'll pass a few tents and houses, then come to a vegetable garden."

"What?" Gianni said.

"Vegetable garden. Colleen and Equine live on the other side of the garden."

"Leave it to Colleen to marry someone named Equine. Can't be his real name."

Ezra shrugged. "What's in a name?"

"Okay, Juliet, how much farther?"

"Almost there."

Gianni spotted a few tents and trailers through the trees. Ezra removed his T-shirt, unzipped his jeans, and slipped them down to his ankles.

"What the fuck are you doing?"

"Getting ready."

"For what? A bath?"

"Didn't I tell you, Baker Man? This is a clothing optional commune."

Gianni slammed on the breaks. Ezra wound up sitting bare-assed in the footwell, his jeans still wrapped around his ankles."

"No, you didn't tell me."

Gianni took a closer look out the van window. Towheaded youngsters appeared then disappeared behind an understory of berry brambles. A young woman followed them with an infant at her breast. All of them in the buff.

"You gotta be fucking kidding me," Gianni said. Then he noticed folks weeding a vegetable garden, a smattering of bare bottoms soaking up the sunshine. "Looks like most everyone is ignoring the clothing option."

Ezra climbed back onto the bench seat and pulled his feet out of his pant legs.

"Come on, Baker Man. It's not like you've never seen anyone naked. We had to swim nude in high school gym. Remember?"

"Don't remind me."

But Ezra was right. Nudity wasn't new to Gianni, at least same-sex nudity. But at the baths you wore a towel around your waist—until you didn't. But you also didn't frequent the baths to weed a vegetable garden.

"So much for me bringing a suit jacket to be Colleen's best man."

Ezra laughed. "Who said you're the best man? We still gotta flip for best man or maid of honor."

"You're an asshole."

Gianni undressed after they came to a stop.

"Hurray!" Colleen yelled and ran toward the van. She wore an India print wrap around skirt, but her bare engorged breasts bounced above her very pregnant belly.

Gianni and Ezra stepped out of the van. Ezra walked over to the driver's side and Colleen pulled them both toward her. Gianni imagined Sister Joan Marie shaking her head and saying, *Colleen, you must be more appropriate*.

Colleen stepped back, looked at Ezra and Gianni from head to toe. "I love both of you. You're absolutely beautiful."

Gianni restrained himself from covering his crotch with his hands.

"Come, I'll introduce you to Equine."

When Ezra first told Gianni that Colleen's boyfriend was named Equine, Gianni said, "You mean as in horses."

"Yep," Ezra said. "Guess he grew up in Kentucky. His family bred horses. Colleen goes by Clover."

"As in four-leaf?"

Ezra nodded.

Gianni had laughed so hard he almost dropped a tray of pastries.

"Working in the bakery, guess I'm out of step with the times" Gianni had said. "If I lived there, they could call me Cannoli."

"And me Matzah," Ezra said, also laughing.

Holding hands, like kindergarteners on a school field trip, Colleen, Gianni, and Ezra walked to the far side of the garden and stopped at a corn patch.

"Equine, you already know Ezra, but you have to meet Gianni. These guys are my twin flames, although I guess we're triplet flames."

A tall man with broad hairy shoulders turned around, and Gianni couldn't help but notice that being called Equine wasn't because he was born in Kentucky.

"Welcome, brother." Equine embraced Gianni. Gianni recalled

Father Kelly lecturing the boys at Saint Mary Gate of Heaven about impure thoughts: *Never look at your nude body in a mirror or the bathroom tiles.* Picturing Father Kelly's green teeth was the turnoff Gianni sought while hugging well-endowed Equine.

Equine asked about their trip, and Gianni tried his best to keep looking Equine in the eyes.

The commune soon grew on Gianni. *Just a big outdoor locker room, which happened to include women and children*, he thought. Until he noticed a guy gaze at him bit too long, and Gianni's gaydar among other things rose. He thought of Father Kelly's green teeth.

At midnight, under a clear sky and full moon, as Pachelbel's Canon D played on a Celtic harp, Gianni and Ezra escorted Colleen down a path strewn with colorful petals. Like Equine, Colleen wore a crown of yarrow and asters and a long gauze kaftan. In the moonlight and the glow from tiki torches, Colleen appeared other-worldly with the yellow and lavender wild-flower crown atop her wild auburn hair. She carried a bouquet of sunflowers. Gianni and Ezra wore gauze pants tied at their waists, garlands of echinacea, and Queen Ann's lace in their hair. On either side of the path stood the adults and children of the commune, some partially clothed in India print or tie dye wraps, many completely nude except for garlands of flowers. A host of woodland faeries and sprites gathered among evergreens before a moonlit pond. Equine stood next to a shaman, a priestess called Aine.

The names Equine and Clover were no longer comical to Gianni, nor the varied levels of nudity awkward. The moonlight dancing on flowers and flesh, the harp's resonance, Colleen's hand in his and knowing that Ezra held her other hand, all felt lovely, childlike, and innocent. He grieved for the men on the Christopher Street Piers, for Gabriel and his children. He wished they were here and could experience what he experienced at that moment. *Just be who the fuck you are*, he thought. *Without hiding, without threat, without guilt.*

Gianni and Ezra released Colleen's hands and she took Equine's. They looked into each other's eyes, and she recited what she later explained to Gianni and Ezra were Celtic wedding vows, "You cannot possess me for I belong to myself. But while we both wish it, I give you what is mine to give—"

Equine paraphrased Kahlil Gibran's poetry on marriage, "We will love one another but make not a bond of love. Let it rather be a moving sea between the shores of our souls—"

They untied the butterfly knots at the tops of their kaftans and let the gauze fall to their ankles.

Aine wrapped braded hemp around their joined hands. She recited a First Nation's blessing, "Now you will feel no pain, for each of you will be the shelter of the other. . ."

Aine looked up to the moon and released a howl. This startled Gianni but when everyone followed, so did he. Howls diminished, and then turned to silence. Aine said, "I now pronounce you partners in this life."

Lively fiddling followed everyone's applause. A tray of shrooms made its way through the crowd. Equine popped a sliver of the psychedelic mushroom into his mouth. Colleen shook her head no and patted her pregnant belly. Ezra lifted a sliver, but then put it back on the tray.

"I'll pass." He looked at Gianni. "We'll keep Colleen company."

Colleen kissed Equine. "Go dance. I'm going to sit with my brothers by the pond and contemplate the moon."

Equine smiled, hugged Colleen, Ezra, and then Gianni. Despite feeling more relaxed than he had when he first stepped out of the van, Gianni still resorted to imagining Father Kelly's green teeth when Equine hugged him, just to make sure his body didn't salute. Equine lifted a brownie from another tray, popped it into his mouth, and then disappeared among the dancers and fiddlers.

"Are the brownies loaded?" Ezra said.

Colleen nodded.

"Far out. Equine is going be flying."

"He'll have plenty of copilots," Colleen said and lifted a blanket from a stack near the pond.

"Help me spread a few of these out," she said.

This was the first the three of them were alone since Gianni and Ezra arrived.

They sat in a circle, inside a ring of tiki torches, their knees touching, hands held, and whatever time had passed from sitting on the lawn in Washington Square or on stoops beneath moth-luring lights or kneeling beneath a larger-than-life crucifix waiting for Jesus to wink and turn his head vanished. Should they not see each other for another fifty years, then meet in the eleventh hour of their lives, those fifty years would also vanish. Their friendship transcended time. Gianni wondered if losing Michael and Peter so suddenly made his friendship with Colleen and Ezra more precious and whether his relationship with Maura and Owen was an attempt to recreate that familiar comfort of being one of a trio. What he had with Colleen and Ezra was rooted in childhood and nourished with malted balls, Bit O Honey, and licorice wheels. Irreplaceable.

"Too bad your family's not here," Gianni said.

"That would be something. They said I'm not married until it's in a church with a priest. I didn't buy all that crap when we were kids. I definitely don't buy it now. The big three were about controlling women. Robbing us of our spiritual power."

"The big three?" Gianni said.

"Yup. Judaism, Christianity, and Islam. All rooted in misogyny. No offense, Ezra."

"No offense taken."

"Mary's big in Catholicism," Gianni said.

"Of course she has to be a fucking virgin. Again, controlling women."

"Fucking virgin is an oxymoron," Ezra said.

The trio laughed.

Gianni shook his head. "I bought it all bigtime. You know, all the magical thinking."

"Who's knocking magic?" Colleen said. "It's religion I'm not crazy about."

Colleen released Ezra's hand and plucked a Queen Ann's Lace from his hair. "It's hard to see in this light, but if you look closely you'll notice a purple flower at its center. The story goes that the purple flower represents a drop of Queen Ann's blood. Interesting, since daucus carota have been used to induce abortion. I don't have anything against myths either. It's the thou shalts and thou-shalt-nots that cause problems."

"Daucus carota? Guess you're the new brain among the three of us." Gianni said. "Sorry Ezra, you've been outdone."

Colleen's tummy gave a slight jolt. "Danu is awake."

Colleen pressed Gianni and Ezra's hands against her tummy. Their eyes widened.

"Far out," Ezra said. "Danu?"

"Yes, named for the Celtic goddess. Divine mother of all."

"And if it's a boy?"

"It's a girl. Aine told me. The priestess who officiated the marriage. She lives in a commune near Brattleboro. All women. She's named for the Irish faery queen and goddess of summer, love, protection, and fertility. I've gotten into Irish lore. Funny, my family considers themselves to be so Irish, but they act as if Ireland began with Saint Patrick."

Colleen asked if Gianni had seen Gabriel lately, and he told her about the arrest and the visit at Rikers.

"Bummer," Colleen said. "The pigs think they own the fucking streets."

"I have to find out how to bail him out. I have some money saved. Guess it depends on how much it is."

"I bet it's not too much," Ezra said. "It's not like he killed someone. I know folks who were arrested at protests. I'll check with them. Bummer is right."

"Did you ever hear of Emmett Till?" Gianni said.

Ezra nodded. Colleen shook her head no.

Gianni explained to Colleen that he recently read in the library morgue about the fourteen-year-old Emmett Till. While visiting family in Money, Mississippi, he was accused of flirting with a white woman, and the white woman's husband and his brother bludgeoned Till and gouged out his eye, tied him to a cotton gin fan with barbed wire, shot him in the head, and threw his body in the Tallahatchie River.

"Gabriel saw Emmett Till being dragged from his uncle's house. 'Just another night in Mississippi,' Gabriel called it. And those fuckers are still free. Gabriel is in jail for defending gay kids. All we heard about when we were at Gate of Heaven was what happened to Jesus two thousand years ago or to white saints or white nuns and priests in the missions. No one ever told us about the Emmett Tills of the world."

Ezra nodded. "You know there was a time, in some cultures, when Gabriel would have been a shaman. Venerated. Not arrested and thrown in jail."

Gianni took a deep breath. "In my culture, Gabriel *is* a shaman. I can't tell you how many kids he saves. How much he's saved me."

Not that he told Ezra and Colleen something they didn't understood already, but this was Gianni's way of coming out to his friends. A step further than he went with Fina when he told her he met Gabriel at a bar in Greenwich Village. Insinuating rather than saying he was gay. Next he shared the more honest story about Maura and Owen.

"We knew this," Colleen said. "Not the details, but we knew how you feel about Owen. It's all good. We love you."

Colleen pressed the palms of her hands against Gianni's cheeks, and then kissed him full on the lips. She did the same to Ezra. "I love both of you. Now I better look for Equine. After all, it is our wedding night. I hope it doesn't hurt."

The three of them laughed. Colleen stood and tossed a blanket over them. It was getting a little chilly. She also wrapped a blanket around her shoulders and walked toward the merriment.

Lying beneath a blanket with Ezra—maybe because it was Ezra—suddenly felt too intimate.

Ezra touched Gianni, and Gianni responded in kind. The gauze pants were easy to remove. Gianni felt at ease. This surprised him. Ezra was playful and passionate. Totally uninhibited. This also surprised Gianni. When it was over, Ezra said, "That was fucking hot, Baker Man."

Gianni laughed out loud. How novel and wonderful to laugh after sex! It seemed right to have a joyful, humor-filled afterglow. There was something humorous about all the panting and grunting. Why not laugh? *That was fucking hot*, was the honest thing to say. Gianni wondered about the fraternal love of the ancient Greeks or Romans, which went beyond the platonic. The comradely love of men in war when they feared an evening might be their last. He wondered if this is what Owen had experienced in 'Nam. If that was why Owen became a more knowing lover. Gianni loved Ezra, not the way he loved Owen. But who's to say which way is truer or more important? Had he lifted his love for Owen from the pages of an Emily Bronte novel or from the screen of a William Wyler film? Gianni was Heathcliff chasing the unattainable. *And maybe*, Gianni thought, *I'm more in love with the story than the man.*

He wondered what Ezra was thinking as they lay in each other's arms beneath the full moon. If Ezra thought at all about what had just happened. Maybe it meant little more than getting his rocks off with a friend. When Gianni left college, and stepped back into the kitchen behind the bakery, he also stepped out of the counterculture revolution brewing on college campuses across America. He understood little of free love. Sure he knew of anonymous sex, but that had nothing to do with love. Or did it?

Gianni and Ezra fell asleep in the moonlight and to the music of a Celtic harp and they woke at sunrise to the sound of mourning doves and hermit thrushes. They left a note for Colleen, "We love you. See you soon," and then they drove back to Queens.

CHAPTER 22

Raffaella asked Hanns about a lawyer. Ezra checked with his friends about bail. Gianni checked his savings. But then the prison advocate who visited Gabriel called Tammy, and Tammy called Gianni. No need for a lawyer or bail.

The police report stated that Gabriel and another inmate came to blows. They were each placed in solitary confinement. Gabriel's body was found in the morning. Cause of death: suicide.

"It's a fucking lie," Gianni said, his face soaked with tears, his nose running, his hands balled into fists. "They killed him. He knew they were all liars and crooks, and they killed him."

Raffaella rested her hand on Gianni's arm. She knew what happens behind concrete walls.

"He never would have killed himself. Never!" Gianni said. "They're a bunch of liars. All of them."

Instead of driving the van or taking a cab, Gianni and Raffaella, arms linked, walked from Raffaella's place in Chelsea to Gunter's apartment in Greenwich Village. Gianni repeated the same words over and over: "Liars. They're fucking liars and murderers."

They walked along the tree-lined streets, in the shade of slim, pale green honey locust leaves, past prewar low-rise apartment buildings and brownstones with black wrought iron railings. Passersby glanced at Gianni, and several gave him and Raffaella a wide berth or stepped between parked cars and crossed the street. Raffaella suggested they buy coffee, a muffin, or a sandwich. "Have you eaten today?"

Gianni shook his head no. "I'm not hungry."

Raffaella now had her own key to the street door of Gunter's building. She knocked on his apartment door once, and then a second time and called his name.

Gunter opened the latched door. One clouded, blue eye peeked through the narrow space between the door and the jamb.

"It's Raffaella and Gianni, Gunter."

"Oh, the lovely lady, and the handsome Sicilian boy."

There are worse things to be called. Gianni thought of Gabriel's words.

The door opened to a shock of light. Gunter's apartment no longer resembled the bleak, crowded hovel they found him in on the night they came to tell Gunter of Gabriel's arrest. The windows sparkled and the curtains were open. Raffaella had helped Gunter sort through his movie magazines, and they disposed of most of them. She kept the apartment clean, including his many lamps and tchotchkes. She replaced Gunter's tattered high back chair—more stuffing than upholstery—with a new recliner, which looked misplaced among Gunter's antiques, but it was comfortable and clean.

Raffaella turned down the volume on the television, helped Gunter to his recliner, and then sat next to him. Gianni stood by one of the windows. Two shirtless boys, engaged in animated conversation below. Their shoulders and backs shone alabaster and onyx in the sun. Maybe two of Gabriel's children. Gianni couldn't see their faces. *Mother's gone*, Gianni thought.

Raffaella took Gunter's hand. "We have very sad news. Gabriel has died, Gunter."

As if his bird-like bones no longer had the strength to carry his skin, Gunter folded into himself.

"The pigs say suicide," Gianni said. "But it was murder."

Gunter didn't respond, he didn't cry, he just sat in the recliner—a pile of withered flesh and clouded eyes, which looked inward.

Gianni turned away from the window. "Gunter, did you hear—"

"Gianni!" Raffaella's voice had an edge. "He heard."

"What do we do?" Gunter said.

Raffaella squeezed his limp hand. "What can we do?"

"Bring Gabriel home."

Gianni pulled a chair next to Gunter. He struggled to compose himself. "It's not so easy, Gunter. Tammy said we have to find family to claim Gabriel's body." The word body turned Gianni's stomach.

"I'm Gabriel's family," Gunter said. He lifted his head and raised his shoulders.

"They mean legal next of kin."

"And who are *they*?" Gunter's voice sounded years away. "The men who murdered Gabriel? The keepers of unjust laws?" Gunter pressed his hands against the arms of his recliner. He stood but then paused and brought his trembling fingers to his lips, as if trying to recall his purpose for standing. Then he nodded and shuffled toward his bedroom.

"Gunter," Raffaella said, but Gunter held up his hand.

"One minute," he said.

He returned carrying a Chinese black lacquer box with figural and landscape scenes. He flopped back into the recliner and stared at the box for several moments. He appeared to be wondering who had put this lacquer box in his lap. Then he ran his fingers across its sheen.

"Ah, yes, I bought this in Chinatown. We had just had dinner."

"Gunter," Raffaella said. "We were talking about Gabriel. Do you have a family member's address?"

"Maybe Gabriel's sister," Gianni said. "Gabriel has a younger sister."

"Had," Gunter said. "She died in childbirth."

"That was his mother," Gianni said.

Gunter looked at Gianni. His lips moved, but no words.

Gianni repeated, "Gabriel's mother died in childbirth."

"And so did his sister," Gunter said. He opened the box, removed an envelope, and handed it to Gianni. "I'm Gabriel's family."

Gianni removed a paper from the envelope and unfolded it: *In the matter of adoption of Arnold Gabriel Moore, on the petition of Gunter Meyer.*

"Is this real?" Gianni said.

"Of course it's real. I'm Gabriel's next of kin. We did this so that if something happened to me, Gabriel wouldn't be homeless. He'd inherit succession rights to my rent-controlled apartment."

"I don't understand," Gianni said.

"What's there to understand? I'm Gabriel's closest next of kin. Bring Gabriel home."

Hanns showed the adoption papers to a lawyer friend. They were legit. The lawyer explained that he knew of a few gay men who adopted a partner or a friend, to protect their inheritance and their last wishes.

Gianni told Gunter that the prison advocate suggested an independent autopsy. "'Justice for Gabriel,' she said."

"They took Gabriel's life, dear," Gunter said. "They can't have his body. No coroner is going to risk his own life to tell the truth for a Black drag queen? Gabriel's body will suddenly disappear. Justice?" Gunter shook his head and looked from Gianni to Raffaella. "To bring Gabriel home is the only justice we'll get."

Raffaella nodded. The next day Raffaella brought Gunter to identify Gabriel's body. Gabriel's wrists were slashed. A ruse to suggest suicide over murder?

"Aren't people checked thoroughly before placed in solitary confinement?" Raffaella said. "What would Gabriel have used to slash his wrists?"

The coroner shrugged his shoulders.

Gunter leaned forward. Raffaella held his arm so he wouldn't stumble. He kissed Gabriel's lips. "You were stunning, my dear. Absolutely stunning."

A traffic light turned red, and drivers pressed on horns while mourners crossed West Street, found their way through the shadows under the Westside Highway, and walked toward Pier 45. More than a few mourners shot their middle fingers up at the impatient drivers. They gathered at the far end of the pier where seagulls mewed atop rotted pilings, waves lapped below, and if you listened with your mind's ear, you heard queer youth, who once sought peace in the Hudson's turbulent waters, prepare to welcome Gabriel.

Below a clear blue sky came Tammy's rendition of Lena Horne's *Stormy Weather*. "Don't know why, there's no clouds up in the sky. Stormy weather, since—" Her voice cracked like the scratches on worn 78 RPM vinyl.

Wearing a wide-brimmed hat, sunglasses, and one of his linen suits, Gunter sat in a wheel chair. In his lap he carried an urn he decorated long ago with baubles and seashells from Provincetown. He and Gabriel spent a week there each summer before Gunter's antique shop folded. The urn was meant for his own ashes, but life ignores plans. Raffaella stood on one side of Gunter, Gianni the other, and Ezra next to Gianni. As if reading braille, Gunter ran his fingers across the shells. Stories from a time when his mind was sharp, his body strong, about a magical sandspit at the end of Cape Cod, like a long finger, curved into itself and beckoning exiles.

One after another, Gabriel's children paid tribute. They remembered his gifts of food and clothing and toiletries and condoms, but they also spoke about love and support, about Gabriel replacing the parent or parents who abandoned them because their wrists were too limp, their voices and movements too feminine, because one way or another their parents learned of their affections for other boys.

A young man, Esteban, spoke next. Slightly older than Gianni, similar build, his complexion a shade darker, his black hair pin straight. Esteban worked at the Strand Bookstore on Twelfth and Broadway. He related the day his parents found him with another boy on a secluded alley fire escape outside their apartment in East Harlem. He was thirteen at the time and thought his parents were visiting his abuela several blocks away. He lifted his shirt and showed the scars his father left. He recalled pleading with his mother, but she made the sign of the cross and turned away from him.

"Papi told me to get out. What could I do? Like a lot of us here, I hustled. What difference did it make? I was going to hell anyway."

Understanding nods spread among the mourners like the heads bowing to the name Jesus at Saint Mary Gate of Heaven.

"One night, a john got rough with me in the Meatpacking District. I was a puny kid. He tried to pull me into his car. I had a bad feeling. There were stories about boys disappearing and turning up on meat hooks like sides of beef."

More nods.

"I heard this booming voice. 'Boy! Grab his nuts and twist them.'"

Nods tuned into to laughter and remarks, "You know that was Gabriel—Gabriel would have torn them off—Gabriel was the best."

Esteban waited out the remarks, ran his fingers through his thick, black hair, and then continued, "That white guy saw Gabriel coming, and he let go of me, jumped in his car, and sped off like his life depended on it."

"His life did depend on it, honey," Tammy said.

Everyone laughed.

Gianni caught Esteban's eye as Esteban was about to end his tribute. They exchanged smiles, not joyful smiles, but consoling smiles of recognition. And then Esteban looked back at the crowd, "You all know the rest of the story," he went on. "It's your story too. After that, Gabriel was there for whatever I needed. We sat on the curb that night and talked for hours. Never knew someone so buff who could be so gentle. I laid my head in Gabriel's lap and cried like I was a baby." Esteban shook his head. "I didn't feel stupid crying. Nope! I felt safe. Safer than I ever felt."

Next, three drag queens dressed in full Supremes' regalia stepped forward, clicked on a boom box, and lip-synched *Ain't No Mountain High Enough*.

A boy, barely thirteen years old, approached Gunter. Gianni recognized him from late-night walks with Gabriel. His name was Hiram. A skinny, pretty boy, with a café au lait complexion. Hiram lifted the urn from Gunter's lap.

"Please leave some ashes to someday mix with mine," Gunter said.

The boy took off the lid and handed it to Gunter.

The Diana Ross look-alike forwarded the tape on the boom box to *Reach Out And Touch*.

While the boy poured some of Gabriel's ashes into the Hudson, mourners wrapped their arms around each other's shoulders and swayed. Some sang. Most cried. A few managed to do both.

"Lovely, simply lovely," Gunter said to Tammy. "You gave Gabriel and all of us a beautiful afternoon. You really outdid yourself, dear."

Tammy kissed Gunter and left smudges of red lipstick and wet mascara on Gunter's cheek.

Tammy picked up the boom box and a few feather boas and left. The rest of the mourners followed, except for Gunter, Raffaella, Gianni, and Ezra who stayed awhile. They watched a small tugboat pull a large barge along the Hudson, while sun bathers in cut-off jeans, speedos, underwear, or less, replaced the mourners and spread towels among Gabriel's sprays of flowers.

They stopped at Tiffany's for lunch and talked about Gabriel.

"We're sitting shiva," Ezra said. Raffaella nodded.

Gunter told many stories of trips to Provincetown. Then, as if losing his way, he grew silent and glanced about the pink booths and mirrors. Raffaella gently guided him back whenever this happened.

"Is your hamburger overcooked?" Or she said, "That was a wonderful story," even if he stopped in the middle of telling it. "Tell us another."

Gunter smiled and began another story, often one he had already told.

After lunch they walked to Washington Square and sat near the fountain. The four spent the day together, Gunter dozing on and off in his wheelchair.

Later, they walked to Yonah Schimmel on East Houston Street and, except for Gunter, they each had a knish for supper. Gunter said he was still full from lunch.

Gianni spent the night at Gunter's. It didn't seem right to leave him alone. He turned on the television.

"What channel do you want?"

Gunter yawned. "Not tonight, dear. It's been a long day. I'll just go to bed."

Once in Gabriel's room, Gianni knew that his motives for spending the night weren't just for Gunter. He wanted to feel close to Gabriel. He undressed down to his underpants and got into bed. He stared at the ceiling and saw the first night that he and Gabriel met. He could see again how Gabriel shone under the colored lights over the bar at Keller's. How Gabriel smiled and called him over with the curl of his finger.

"Welcome to Keller's. I'm Gabriel."

Gianni heard Etta James singing. He heard himself tell Gabriel about Owen. He recalled what the young man, the one with the handsome smile who worked at the Strand Bookstore had said earlier, "We sat on the curb that night and talked for hours—I felt safe."

That was Gabriel's magic. You could say anything. Stories you would never tell anyone. Things you did that you barely acknowledged to yourself and it made no difference. Gabriel loved you unconditionally.

The nuns told Gianni that Jesus loved everyone unconditionally, but then they always added a long list of conditions. They called them sins, which caused you to fall out of Jesus' favor—venial sins a little, mortal sins a lot. A venial sin was like covering a light with a sheer cloth. A mortal sin was like covering a light with a blanket. Your soul was the light.

If there were a Jesus, Gianni thought, *maybe he was more like Gabriel than the nuns gave him credit for.*

Gianni heard Gabriel say, "You'll be okay, child. I got a feeling you're gonna be better than okay."

Bang! Gianni jumped out of bed, ran to Gunter's room, and found Gunter trying to pick himself up. The only light came from a small bulb on a bedside lamp, which lay on the floor next to Gunter.

Gianni squatted down next to him. "Are you alright? What happened?"

"I don't really know."

Gunter was easy to lift, and Gianni helped him to sit on the edge of the bed. Then he knelt on one knee and picked up the lamp and a framed photograph. He put them back on the nightstand. The lamp and bulb were intact, but the fringed shade had not fared as well and sat bent and lopsided on its harp.

Gianni looked at the photograph. He touched its frame with the tips of his fingers.

Like bits of sky obscured by cirrus clouds, Gunter's eyes met Gianni's clear brown eyes, as bright as volcanic glass.

"It was taken at a cabaret in Berlin," Gunter said. "Before the war."

Gianni pointed to a slim, fair, and pretty boy on the cusp of adulthood who could have been a model for Thomas Mann's Tadzio in *Death in Venice*. "Is that you?"

"Yes."

"And you have your arm around a friend?"

"A lover. But that was a hundred years ago, dear boy."

"How did the picture survive the war?"

"My sister. She gave it to me when I was released from prison. That's what they did to us back then, you know. But let's not speak of sad things. We had enough sadness today."

Gianni stood before Gunter in the dim lamplight. Gunter looked at him. His eyes traced Gianni's hair and features, then neck, shoulders and chest, then—and Gianni felt the blush rise from his neck to his face. Gunter's expression wasn't the furtive side-glance Gianni grew accustomed to in Greenwich Village gay bars, or on the piers, or in bath houses, but rather a childlike look of astonishment.

"Have you ever been to the Uffizi in Florence?" Gunter said. His gaze turned inward. "Or to the Accademia Gallery? It houses Michelangelo's David."

"No. Only pictures in books or postcards."

"Youth!" Gunter said. "When we're young we're unaware of youth. We think ourselves inadequate, not measuring up. Foolish. It's like a lily comparing itself to a peony when all flowers are magnificent."

"Are you feeling better, Gunter?"

Gunter nodded. "I don't know what happened," he said. The timbre of his voice suggested that he spoke of something weightier than a fall.

"Would you like if I stay here with you?" Gianni said. "At least until you fall asleep."

Gianni's words surprised Gianni as much as they surprised Gunter.

"That would be lovely," Gunter said.

Gunter stood, and Gianni turned down the bed covers, helped Gunter into bed, and then lay next to him. Given it was a warm night he pulled only the sheet over them, and then slipped his arm under Gunter's bird-like shoulders. Gunter turned toward Gianni and rested his head against Gianni's shoulder. His trembling hand moved across Gianni's strong, smooth chest, and then paused on Gianni's stomach.

Did you plan this, Gabriel? Gianni thought. *You probably knocked over the damn lamp.*

When Gunter's hand grew still and his breathing turned to snoring, Gianni stayed a bit longer, but then slipped out of bed and went back to Gabriel's room.

No need to turn on a light. His eyes had adjusted to the dark. He lay on Gabriel's bed. *Goodnight, Gabriel. I'll miss you terribly.* His tears dampened Gabriel's satin pillow case. He drifted off to sleep.

Vince Sgambati

CHAPTER 23

Hanns rested an elbow on the small mosaic topped table outside the row of French doors. Fingers extended, he ran the palm of his hand across his chin, and his wedding band shimmered in the light of a citronella candle. Raffaella sipped wine from a stemmed glass.

"I don't think the only reason you want Gunter to come and live with us is because Gianni said he fell. At least I don't think that's the only reason. Old men in New York City fall all the time. We can't take them all in."

Raffaella said, "Of course we can't. But we're speaking of Gunter."

"And who is Gunter?"

Raffaella shot Hanns a warning glance. He approached a line that might provoke her retaliation, but he crossed it nonetheless. They were married for eight years. Didn't that give him some rights to express what he felt?

"Gunter is someone you barely know," Hanns said. "Even if he was the man you met briefly at Buchenwald who spoke of Dante, he's not your father, Raffaella. And Gianni is neither Gino nor Marcello." Hanns rehearsed saying this countless times, but held his tongue. Why say it now? Maybe Raffaella suggesting that Gunter live with them also crossed a line for Hanns. He long felt and accepted that his place in Raffaella's affections came after the memory of a young husband. Then he learned of a son, and of course there was Gianni. But now to fall behind an old man Raffaella barely knew, especially an old faggot, was too much for Hanns. He said nothing, but Raffaella acted as if she had read his mind. Despite the warm evening, despite the light and heat from the candle, Raffaella froze in shock. Had she been able to move, she would have balled her fist and slammed Hanns across his face.

"All I'm saying, Raffaella is—"

Raffaella cut him off, "All you are saying means nothing to me."

She stood. Hanns reached out and knocked over both their wine glasses. Wine spilled on the table, dripped onto the patio, and glass shattered. Raffaella shoved her chair back, stood, stamped on the already shattered glass, and left Hanns to sit with the mess he created.

Could Hanns rewrite the scene, he would have. His lines simpler, less accusatory. Something like, "Might there be an alternative? A home aid to look in on Gunter?" Hanns would pay for that. No need to speak of Gianni, Marcello, and Gino. Another time he could mention how he felt—how his role in Raffaella's life seemed to keep getting smaller and smaller, how he feared that soon he might shrink to an occasional walk-on role. Hanns searched the kitchen for a broom. He swept the shards of glass into a dustpan.

Upstairs, in their bedroom, Raffaella packed a suitcase. When Hanns emptied the dustpan into a trashcan, he heard the front door slam shut.

PART 5

When I grew up, I put childish things away.
— 1 Corinthians 13:11

CHAPTER 24

The roar of arriving and departing planes and the loudspeaker announcements made it difficult for Gianni and Ezra to hear each other. Their heads were so close that Gianni could smell Ezra's shampoo and the coffee on his breath. Despite the noise, Gianni spoke softly. He didn't want others to hear what he was saying.

"About what happened that night after Colleen's wedding. I mean between the two of us. We never talked about it. I wanted to, but I didn't know what to say. And now, with you leaving, it's like. Well, if I don't say something now—I mean we can't just pretend it never happened."

Gianni stumbled over his words, and finally he pushed Ezra's shoulder. "Are you just going to sit there and let me go on and on?"

Ezra smiled and nodded.

"Asshole," Gianni said.

"Look, Baker Man, what happened, happened. No regrets. I wanted it to happen since we were kids looking for the Afikomen."

"Are you shitting me?"

"No, man. Guess I didn't understand it back then, and when I did we were in high school, and you were hanging out with the guys in the neighborhood, and I hid in books. I figured I was just some kind of weirdo, and then you went away to college. And then, and then. There's a ton of and-thens. By the time I figured out you were also a weirdo, you had a thing for Owen. Colleen and I figured that out long before you told us. Turned out we were right."

"What do you mean Colleen and you?"

"We used to talk about it. She knew how I felt."

"Now I know you're shitting me."

"No, man! You were going through heavy shit when you came home from college. I wasn't going to add extra pressure and mess up our friendship. We got history, man. Look, you're not responsible for my feelings. Just like Owen's not responsible for yours. Life's not like the movies at The Orchard."

A voice over the loudspeaker announced: "Flight 605 to Oakland now ready for boarding at Gate 43."

"That's me, Baker Man."

Eyes wide, Gianni watched Ezra stand and slip his arms through his trademark backpack.

"You going to walk me to my gate, or you going sit there like you're stoned, which I'm pissed if that's true, since you didn't share the joint."

Gianni stood and Ezra threw his arm around Gianni's shoulder. They walked toward Gate 43.

"I'll see you during winter break, unless you want to fly out to California before. Some great film schools out there. Baking is honest work, but just in case you change your mind, you know where I am."

Change my mind about what? You? Owen? School? Gianni thought. They hugged.

"I'll miss you, Ezra."

"Miss you too, Baker Man."

Gianni watched Ezra hand his ticket to the agent at the desk and get in line to board the plane. *He's wrong*, Gianni thought. *Sometimes life's exactly like the films at The Orchard.*

Gianni smiled and nudged his way through the crowds at La Guardia Airport. *Ezra, the brainy ever-changing enigma*, he thought. A quiet, shy kid who occasionally spurted out something profound. Then a recluse, bookworm teenager. And once he hit Columbia, Ezra turned into Abby Hoffman. *Definitely unpredictable. Not like Colleen.* No surprise that Colleen married a well-endowed guy named Equine in a nudist commune. Colleen always ignored parochial constraints. But Ezra? Well, it depended on which Ezra and at what age.

Gianni couldn't shake Ezra's comments about feelings and

responsibility, but then he thought of Scarlet O'Hara's line: *I can't think about that now. If I do I'll go crazy. I'll think about that tomorrow.* He hated the movie *Gone With The Wind*, and especially hated the character Scarlet O'Hara. But her signature refrain was sage advice for this moment.

"At least that racist bitch was good for something," Gianni mumbled louder than he meant to. A security guard frowned at him.

Gianni smiled and his ears turned red. "Just rehearsing a line for a play I'm in."

The security guard watched Gianni until he left the terminal.

Once home, Gianni found his parents sitting at the kitchen table over cups of coffee and a cheese ring, chatting with Uncle Leo and Aunt Liviana. Over the years, Leo occasionally stopped in the store. The two brothers would sit in the kitchen behind the bakery and catch up, while Fina waited on customers. But Gianni hadn't seen Liviana since she stood at the top of the stares telling his not-real cousins to get away from him. And there she was, much smaller than Gianni remembered, her mouth full, and a dab of icing at the left corner of her lip.

"What are you doing here?" Gianni said. The words spilled out, not in anger but shock. Gianni caught himself. "I mean I'm surprised to see you. How are you, Uncle Leo and Aunt Liviana?"

What happens between adults doesn't involve the children. Fina's words echoed in Gianni's head. *Always show respect to your elders.*

"We're good," Uncle Leo said. "How's your shop?"

"Fine. It's doing fine."

He thought to ask about his cousins. He occasionally overheard his parents or his uncle and father speak of them. He knew Peter had to get married and Michael went to college in Florida. But then he thought, *Why ask?* It wouldn't change the past or erase the loss he felt as a child. Truth was, now he didn't care where they were or what they were doing. Far too late. Why pretend?

"Do you want some coffee?" Liberato said.

"No, thanks. I just stopped by for a minute. I have to bring trays to The Orchard."

A lie, but there was no way Gianni could sit and exchange small talk. It wasn't only about the way he learned he was adopted or losing his cousins. For years Fina kept Liviana on a pedestal from hell—a satanic Madonna who took pleasure in his ruin. When his grades dropped, when he played hooky, when he came home too late, Fina said that Liviana was getting her way. Liviana became Gianni's invisible nemesis, always waiting for him to flounder. And flounder he did. No, he couldn't sit at the kitchen table with the four of them and pretend all was well. Some situations even a cheese ring can't fix. It wasn't about forgiveness. Liviana never asked his forgiveness. Neither had Fina. Gianni wasn't interested in being a part of let bygones be bygones nonsense, until the next time Liviana and Fina would fight, which Gianni figured would be inevitable. He had better things to do, like turn his own life around.

"If you'll excuse me." He thought of Gabriel. *What would he say?*

"By the way, Aunt Liviana." Gianni pointed to the corner of his mouth. "Some of your frosting stuck."

On a side table in the foyer between the kitchen and the door to the apartment, Gianni used the phone to call The Orchard to find out if Raffaella was working. She was.

Fina called to Gianni from the kitchen. "There's mail for you next to the phone."

Gianni lifted the envelope with Owen's return address. He could barely wrap his thoughts around Ezra's comments, and then seeing Liviana. Owen's letter had to wait. He slipped the envelope into his back pocket, left the apartment, and then walked three blocks to his parked van. After passing a stop sign and almost sideswiping a car crossing the Williamsburg Bridge, he took the first parking spot he could find, pulled the envelope from his pocket and tore it open. No letter, just a small, slightly mangled photograph of Owen and his four-month-old son. Carefully, Gianni flattened it. Maybe it was the way the sunlight reflected on Owen's blue eyes when the picture was taken, but they again appeared lit from within. The picture slipped from the steering wheel onto the floor beneath his legs. He reached down, picked it up, and noticed writing on the back. "Gianni Mauro West." Owen named his son after Gianni and Maura.

Gianni burst into the Orchard. The baby's name, seeing Liviana, Ezra comments—Gianni felt overwhelmed. Too much to absorb.

Raffaella sat on the stool behind the cash register. She was reading Sylvia Path's *The Bell Jar*.

"Did you ever notice there's something weird about the number three?" Gianni said. "The Three Little Pigs. The Three Little Kittens. Even the Nina, Pinta, and Santa Maria. Like the ocean couldn't handle one more boat. Not to mention the Trinity."

Raffaella laughed. "Or you, Ezra, and Colleen."

Gianni looked at Raffaella and his frenzy turned solemn. "Or me, Owen, and Maura."

Raffaella folded down a page in her book. "Are you alright?"

"It's just been one crazy day." He pressed the palms of his hands against the candy counter. "It's time, Raffaella."

"I agree."

"But you don't know what I'm about to say."

"You're about to say, it's time to move on."

Gianni stared at Raffaella. She was right. Those were his exact thoughts, despite his inability to articulate them. But leaving without direction? He did that already when he left Lyndon. He wasn't about to do that again. So many times, Ezra encouraged Gianni to give film school a try. He just mentioned it again at the airport. Maybe he was right. Ezra's director friend Jennie irritated yet inspired him. At Gabriel's memorial, Gianni wished he were filming the eulogies, Gunter holding the urn decorated with shells, the boy pouring Gabriel's ashes into the Hudson, Pier 45 strewn with flowers. He wanted to capture Gabriel's story on film.

"At some point, a sanctuary becomes a prison." Raffaella said.

Gianni shoved his hands into his pockets. "You once said there's magic at The Orchard. You were right. And maybe I want to have a larger role in making magic than selling pastries. I don't know if I want to make films, or teach, or write about film, but maybe college will help me sort it out. I'd have to start with a few courses to prove myself. Doubt that I could even get into clown school with my records from Lyndon State. If I have a purpose, maybe I can ignore all the bullshit I once hated about school. Back then it felt like a lot of lies and hypocrisy. Or maybe that was my excuse because I couldn't see beyond my own crap. Maybe now I can keep my eye on a goal. Not go off track so easily. Who knows? But Ezra's moving on with his life, Colleen's doing her thing, even Owen, after all he went through in

'Nam, is beginning a new life."

Gianni pulled the picture from his pocket and handed it to Raffaella. Raffaella looked at the picture. "Very sweet."

Hanns came down from the projector room. Raffaella handed the picture to Gianni and looked down at her book.

"Hi, Gianni. What's up? Monday. You don't work today."

Might as well get it over with, Gianni thought. "I'm going back to school."

Hanns paused. "And Sanctuary?"

Raffaella looked up. "He never said he'd do that forever. We can get someone else to work."

"I'm not saying that. I'm just saying—"

Gianni sensed a tension between Raffaella and Hanns.

"Wait a second. I didn't say I'm leaving tomorrow."

"And I'm not saying you should or shouldn't," Hanns said. "What I am saying, if you'd both give me a chance without biting my head off." Hanns glanced at Raffaella, and then looked back at Gianni. "You've built a business. Sure Saul didn't charge you rent, but it benefitted The Orchard, so it's not just that we find someone else to take it over. You deserve some kind of financial compensation. Not sure what that would be, but I'll talk to Saul, and we'll work something out."

"Wow! That would be great but, like I was just saying to Raffaella, I'd start with a course or two in film. It's probably too late to sign up for classes this semester, so the earliest we're talking about is January."

"Maybe it's not too late." Hanns pointed to a framed poster of Jean Harlow gazing up at Clark Gable's profile. "This month, we're showing pre–Code movies. A professor in filmmaking at NYU will speak about censorship at the talkback this Friday. He wrote a book about Joseph Breen the head of Production Code Administration."

"I read about Breen," Gianni said. "Bigtime anti-Semite."

"Yes, that's the guy." Again, Hanns glanced at Raffaella. She didn't meet his eyes, but the tension had left the corners of her lips. He looked back at Gianni. "You'll be working Friday during the talkback, so I could introduce you to the professor. Maybe he'll have some advice. I know him fairly well. He's done a few talkbacks. With your dad, it's no surprise you're interested in film. The apple doesn't fall far from the tree."

Gianni pictured Liviana sitting at the kitchen table. He felt the sudden urge to knock her out of her chair. "Except I'm adopted," he said. "So the apple metaphor doesn't apply."

Hanns squinted and pulled at his mustache, now gray. "Doesn't matter. Grafted trees produce the best apples."

A smile spread across Gianni's face. "I like the sound of that, Hanns." He pictured Liviana standing at the top of the stairwell. He pictured his child-self outside the door of his apartment, looking up at his aunt. But this time, when he heard her say to his cousins *I told you to stay away from him*, this time, in the sanctuary of his thoughts, he rewrote the scene and gave voice to his child-self: *Fuck you, Liviana. You miserable bully.*

As if releasing an albatross he'd been carrying for far too long, Gianni took a deep breath, and then slowly and calmly exhaled.

"You're right, Hanns. I never thought of it that way, but you're right. I've inherited my dad's love for film. And, like him, I make damn good pastries."

Hanns, the consummate promoter, convinced his professor acquaintance to allow Gianni to enroll in the professor's *Introduction to Film* course and convinced his wife to move back home. Until the fall semester progressed and Gianni's two courses became more demanding, he and Raffaella took turns spending nights with Gunter.

"The kid's a hard worker and sharp as a tack," Hanns said to the professor, loud enough for Raffaella to hear him. "He built this business on his own." Hanns pointed to the Sanctuary sign. "And he knows as much about film as I do." This of course was a lie. But with the tenacity of a Coney Island carny, Hanns persisted, and the professor yielded.

Saul overheard that conversation and, while the professor talked with Gianni, Saul whispered to Hanns. "That's why I wanted you to manage the theater. You could sell feathers to a duck."

Gianni also registered for Expository Writing, and Saul's nephew Ethan worked at Sanctuary. "Not so reliable," Saul said. "But in a pinch. No sense complaining."

Gianni baked, delivered the baked goods to The Orchard, attended classes, studied, and wrote papers. He aced both his classes. He also planned to retake his SATs, and then apply to NYU Tisch School of the Arts. Come fall, he hoped to be a full time, matriculated student.

"Damn, Baker Man," Ezra said. "You're on a roll."

Ezra was home for winter break. The theme at The Orchard was "Firsts: A Director or Actor's First Feature Film." He and Gianni had just watched Martin Scorsese's *Who's That Knocking At My Door*, and Gianni told Ezra that he registered for two courses in the spring semester, one of them with Scorsese.

"So you're not letting the bullshit in academia get to you this time?" Ezra asked.

"No time for distractions. If I'm not writing papers, I'm baking sfogliatelle. Guess that's the trick. Stay busy. I also think having a goal makes a difference. Maybe I'm one of those guys who needs a reason. Just getting a degree wasn't enough. Or maybe I was just too fucked up to stick with it."

"It's not like you've been sitting around since you left Lyndon," Ezra said.

Gianni scooped fresh ground coffee into baskets while Ezra transferred pastries from the refrigerator to trays in the display case. When classes ended, Gianni resumed working at Sanctuary, and Ethan, who preferred watching television to working, took a break. Ezra also helped out.

"I might still be just sitting around if not for my parents and for Raffaella and Hanns. Their support made a big difference, starting with my mom's back going out, so I'd have to help my dad with baking. I'm sure that was bogus. My mother never had back trouble before or since. She's a trip, my mother."

Gianni unlocked the front door. On the windows, Ethan had taped cardboard cutouts of menorahs and dreidels, Christmas trees and Santa Clauses, and Happy New Year signs. More tape than cardboard. A strand of color lights hung across the tops of the windows on either side of the door. Gianni plugged them in. At least half the bulbs were burned out.

"Nice effect," Ezra said. "Kind of a gritty Haight-Ashbury feel. Coffee's done. Want a cup?"

"Ethan's a work in progress," Gianni said. "But who am I to talk?"

They sat at a table, drank their coffees, and talked about Scorsese's film, Ezra's first semester at Berkeley, Gianni's course work, and

Colleen—whose daughter Danu was now four months old.

Raffaella was at Gunter's, and Hanns worked the box office. A slow wintery Wednesday afternoon. Only a few ticket sales. Martin Scorsese and the actor Harvey Keitel, who stared in *Who's That Knocking at My Door*, were unknown to the general movie-going public.

After the handful of movie-goers entered the theater and the projectionist started the film, Hanns joined the boys at their table. From where they sat, he could keep an eye on the lobby.

"There's coffee, Hanns."

"No thanks." He shrugged. "You win some. You lose some. Tomorrow night we're showing *Bad Sister*. The debut film for Bette Davis. We'll get a better crowd. Guess I was too hasty with Scorsese. Wait until *Mean Streets* comes out in October, Scorsese will become Hollywood gold. He's got a young actor in it, Robert De Niro. Believe me, he's going to be big too. Real big."

"I'll be taking Scorsese's course this semester."

"Good! Take a picture with him. We'll hang it on the wall. Maybe he'll do a talkback in the spring. You know, he can talk about being an up-and-coming director."

"I'll let you negotiate that," Gianni said.

"Tough business, Gianni. If you're going to make films, you have to learn how to schmooze."

Ezra glanced at Gianni, who sucked at his bottom lip and held his cup of coffee tighter than necessary.

"You're probably right, Hanns," Gianni said. "But I'll take it one step at a time."

"Of course I'm right. Half of anything is who you know." Hanns glanced at the lobby. "Ezra, do me a favor in case some straggler comes in or someone comes out to buy candy. Mind standing at the box office for a few minutes? I want to ask Gianni something."

"Sure." Again, Ezra looked at Gianni. Gianni nodded.

"How can I put this," Hanns said, "without sounding like I don't care about Gunter, but sometimes we have to make hard decisions. I'm worried about Raffaella. She's doing too much."

Raffaella alternated sleeping in Gabriel's room at Gunter's apartment and going home to Hanns, but lately she spent more nights at Gunter's. She also worked fewer hours at The Orchard. Some days Gunter appeared lucid, and then there were days that if Raffaella didn't nudge him to eat and drink and wash, he'd sit in front of the television staring vacantly. Mostly he slept. Raffaella bought him adult diapers and placed a rubber mat with a folded sheet over it on his chair. On very good days, they took a cab to The Orchard and watched a film. Those days grew increasingly rare.

"I tried to explain this to her, but I didn't say it right. She got mad so I don't bring it up anymore. You know Raffaella. I understand, but—"

"Maybe you *don't* understand," Gianni said. "How could we understand? We weren't there."

Hanns folded his hands and a vein pulsated near his right temple at his receding hairline. He kept his eyes focused on his hands. He wasn't about to listen to Gianni lecture him about Holocaust survivors.

"Gianni, I never asked you for anything, but now I am. Taking care of Gunter is a heavy weight on my wife. It's a weight on our marriage. She doesn't talk much about it, but I can tell that Gunter is getting worse. I'm afraid this will turn into twenty-four-hour care. He was your friend too, Gianni. Maybe if you talk to her. You know, about Gunter going into a nursing home."

At first Gianni didn't answer. He thought of the time he showed Raffaella the flier about the interview for the Holocaust film and what Fina said—that he and Hanns tried to take Raffaella's choice away, that they tried to protect her from something neither one of them knew anything about, that they assumed they knew better than Raffaella about what she could handle.

"I'll think about it, Hanns," Gianni said.

But Gianni never mentioned to Raffaella that she was doing too much, and he never suggested that Gunter should be in a nursing home. He did help out more. During the semester break, he and Raffaella took turns again staying with Gunter and, once the semester began, unless a paper or project was due, or he needed to study for a test, he continued to help. Hanns was right. Gunter's physical and mental health were declining. Gunter balked at seeing a doctor. Hospitals terrified him.

Had Gianni suggested a nursing home to Raffaella, she wouldn't agree anyway. She especially wouldn't agree after the night she and Gunter watched Alfred Hitchcock's *Foreign Correspondent* on television. A spy thriller set in Europe at the onset of World War ll. Gunter didn't fall asleep. He watched the whole movie.

When it ended, Gunter said, "I remember."

Raffaella took Gunter's hand. The room was dark, except for the television and a light in a curio cabinet containing the Hummels Gunter couldn't part with.

"I remember too," Raffaella said.

Gunter looked at Raffaella. Tears fell from his clouded eyes. Raffaella didn't ask Gunter what he remembered specifically, but she imagined him saying, *I remember the train. I remember the tall, girl. Her shoulders back and head held high despite their insults. I remember the way the Nazi guards looked at her. I knew what they were thinking. I remember you, Raffaella.*

After that night, whether or not Gunter was the kind man with the pink triangle, they'd have to kill Raffaella before she allowed anyone to take Gunter from his apartment. Had Hanns suggested the nursing home idea to Raffaella, she would leave Hanns for good.

CHAPTER 25

Two dragonflies quivered then darted, a synchronized rite around the fountain that geysered upward at least twenty feet above the small pond. In winter it froze and Lyndon students called it the phallus.

"Been waiting long?" Gianni asked.

Owen lifted his arm from across his eyes and propped himself up on his elbows. "Not long. What's in the case?" Owen pointed to the camera bag hanging from a strap that crossed Gianni's chest. After Gianni's course in cinematography, the camera became an appendage.

"A super-8 camera." Gianni sat next to Owen on the fresh mowed grass. They gazed at the dragonflies.

Two weeks earlier, Owen called Gianni. "My dad knows this guy on the board at Lyndon. He said they're leveling Vail Manor. Safety is the excuse." Owen suggested they meet there one last time before the demolition—to say goodbye.

Gianni agreed. He explained to Owen that he was taking courses. After one last assignment, he could drive to Vermont.

"We can meet next to the phallus," Owen said.

Of course, Gianni thought, and they set a date and a time.

"One more thing, Owen. I wanted to tell you this before. I wanted to tell you a ton of times." Gianni told Owen about Maura, how he learned of her passing as if Maura wanted him to know, how he visited with the Silbermans.

"I intended to tell you. That was my reason for visiting last fall, but then I met Lolli, and I got all confused—Owen, are you still there?"

"I'm still here," Owen said. Without any mention of Maura, he wished Gianni good luck on his assignment, said he looked forward to seeing him, and then he hung up.

The pair of dragonflies hovered in the wheel positions, their sex organs briefly locked.

"Imagine doing it while flying," Owen said. He leaned across Gianni and kissed him.

A college campus above Lyndonville, Vermont, in 1973, wasn't the Christopher Street piers or a clothing-optional commune outside of Burlington, but Owen gently pressed his lips to Gianni's, as if it were perfectly acceptable. Then sat up and said, "I missed you."

Stunned, Gianni looked at Owen, his blond hair platinum in the sun, his broad shoulders, the blades of grass that clung to the back of his shirt, the exposed skin above his belt loop. Gianni placed his hand on Owen's back and thought if they could stay like that forever, if time stopped and the moment became eternity, if everything fell away except his hand pressed against Owen, he'd be at peace.

Owen turned and looked down at Gianni. "I knew."

"You knew what?"

"I knew about Maura. I didn't know the specifics until you told me. But I knew she was gone. I sensed the emptiness she left behind. Remember when we used to search for ghosts in Vail? We walked along balconies with our arms extended and suddenly our hands turned cold as if we came upon an icy void, someone no longer there. That's what I sensed—Maura's absence. And then that feeling got mixed up with so many feelings in 'Nam. Loneliness, fear, hate, grief, until I stopped feeling at all."

"I also know what it's like not to feel," Gianni said. "Or to feel disconnected. If, in fact, that's a feeling, or lack of feeling. I didn't go through what you went through. I mean Vietnam. No comparison. But I know what you mean about not feeling. Everyone and everything became a prop, including me. As if I hovered above myself, I watched empty characters go through meaningless motions, like a movie without a plot. That's where my head was when I left Vermont. I went to a therapist for a while. He called it disassociating. And when I explained to him that people and buildings and trees looked distant and flat, he said it was a type of hallucination brought on by extreme depression. The guy was a bit of a nut, but what he said made sense.

There was something reassuring about having someone understand. Even if he really didn't understand, but knew how to say the right things."

"Did he help?"

"I think so. I also took antidepressants. I don't anymore, but I did for a couple of years."

"So you're better?"

"I'm not frightened. I don't think everyone is distant. I'm not stuck in my head, bouncing from one panic attack to another. Right now I'm here with you. I'm present and, except that I wish this moment could last forever but know it can't, I'd say I'm better. A lot better."

"That's good. That's very good."

"Are you better, Owen?"

"I'm getting there. How about we say goodbye to old T.S. Vail's ghost? He must be rambling around those old buildings fretting that they will soon come down around him?"

They stood and walked toward Vail Manor. Only a few students remained at Lyndon State after the spring semester ended—procrastinators, but also several seniors who lived out of state and thought it foolish to travel home, and then return in a week for commencement.

"Pick a door," Owen said.

"Door number three."

They entered the closest door, which opened into one of Vail Manor's twin towers, a library turned bookstore in 1965 after the library moved to one of Lyndon's featureless new buildings. In the circular room, three students packed books into cardboard boxes, then stacked the boxes in the oversized opening of a brick fireplace.

"Shame they're tearing this all down," Owen said.

One of the students looked up from her work. She wore cutoff jeans and a tube top. Her black hair long and ironed straight, and her eyes heavily made up—very Cher-like. She looked from Owen to Gianni as if trying to place them. Given the small student population, even if you didn't know everyone, you at least recognized them.

"Did you graduate from Lyndon?" she said.

"No," Owen said. "But we went here for a while."

"Yes, a lot of people went here for a while." The girl laughed. "I was almost here for a while, but then I stayed. Not such a bad place.

It grows on you."

"Like a mole," one of the other students said.

They all laughed, except for Owen whose eyes traced the circle of large windows, the empty bookshelves, the fireplace's brick facing, the threadbare oriental carpets, as if searching for a book he had misplaced, or a memory.

"Do you think the building's really not safe?" Owen said.

"No." This time a student with thick, black-rimmed glasses answered. He spoke without making eye contact and continued to pack books into boxes. "It's about expense. These old buildings cost a lot to maintain. In the long run, it's probably cheaper to raze, than in years to come to repair roofs, pay for heat, a new furnace, et cetera."

"They're also afraid of fires," the Cher look-alike said. "You know, kids coming in the building after hours and holding seances with lit candles."

"That was us," Gianni said. "Bigtime poltergeist hunters."

Now all three students stopped working and looked at Gianni.

"Any luck?" said the student with thick glasses. His eyes appeared disproportionately large like the forlorn children in a Keane painting.

"Some weird shit happened, but who knows."

"In fact," Owen said, "we're here to say goodbye to a special spirit, if we can find her."

Gianni looked at Owen. *So that's why we're here.*

They wandered from building to building, through the labyrinth of hallways, and endless rooms, ignoring do-not-enter signs. If doorknobs didn't turn, Owen slipped a piece of plastic between the door and door jamb or jimmied the lock with a screwdriver.

"Where did you learn that?" Gianni said.

"I was in 'Nam. Remember?"

"And you just happen to be carrying pieces of plastic and a screw driver."

Owen didn't answer.

As if looking weren't enough, Gianni and Owen ran their hands along wainscoting, balustrades, and leaded mullion windows. They inhaled the mustiness in some rooms and the smells of wax and furniture polish in others, so that either of them, long after they had last seen the other, or long after only one of them be left, could recall—in great detail—the three of them, including Maura, sitting in one of

Vail's many window seats looking out through the diamond shaped panes of glass at new fallen snow, or reclining before a fire in one of Vail's many fireplaces and inhaling the comfort of woodsmoke, or pressing their fingertips to a planchette on a Ouija board to spell out their futures—back when they all had futures. Gianni caught some of it on film. He lingered behind and shot Owen walking away from the camera. Then he walked ahead of Owen and shot Owen walking toward the camera. Owen paused and stared, and Gianni zoomed in until Owen's face filled the frame, his eyes looking left and his knuckle pressed against parted lips, as if he suddenly stumbled upon a memory.

"You're really into this stuff," Owen said.

Gianni remembered Ezra once said something similar to him about baking. "Not sure cinematography will be my thing," Gianni said. "Thinking directing, if I stick with this, but we'll see. Maybe I'll go back to baking biscotti."

"Can't go back," Owen said. Gianni knew that Owen wasn't talking about baking.

In the carriage barn and shrouded beneath tarpaulins, they found Vail's deep-winged and canopied, porter-styled chairs—the chairs Vail had made for himself and President Taft, where Gianni and Owen once sat, pressed next to each other with Maura curled onto their laps.

"There they are," Owen said with the enthusiasm of a child finding treasure. He slipped off one of the tarps. Gianni shot a close up of the chair. Owen held out his hand, and Gianni put the camera back in its case. Gianni took Owen's hand, and they sat, their shoulders and thighs and hands pressed together. They closed their eyes.

"Do you think she's here?" Owen said.

"I don't know."

"I think she is," said Owen. "I feel her against my lap. I feel her breath on my cheek."

Owen turned and pressed his lips to Gianni's. Gianni didn't respond. Owen pressed harder, but still Gianni didn't respond. Owen sat back.

Through the many chinks in the weathered siding, sunbeams formed a continuous pattern of crisscrosses illuminating the leisurely rise of airborne dust, which turned disserted spiderwebs into cobwebs, dulled the sheen of sleeping bats, and settled on rafters and other surfaces in the carriage barn. Dust marked the passage of time.

"What about Lolli?" Gianni said.

Owen looked perplexed. "I told you she knows."

"You meant about Maura."

"I mean about everything."

Gianni looked about the barn. To ask what Owen meant by everything seemed redundant. He knew what he meant. "Do you love Lolli?"

"Yes. She's my wife and the mother of my son."

"That sounds like a justification, Owen. I mean, are you in love with her? The kind of love that doesn't have a reason. The kind of love that doesn't even make sense."

"You mean the kind of love you feel for me?"

Gianni's eyes widened. He could have called Owen arrogant. He could have been embarrassed or angry, but Owen was right. "Yes, that's exactly what I mean."

Owen slipped his arm behind Gianni's shoulders. They curled into each other.

"I'm in love with what we had," Owen said. "The three of us, before everything went wrong. Before Jimmy died. I thought it could be saved, but I was wrong. There was honesty among us. Maybe all our playing in the spirit world made our own spirits touch."

Gianni's head lay against Owen's chest and rose and fell with his breaths. "But it wasn't being honest," Gianni said. "My feelings for you were more than platonic."

"So were my feelings for you," Owen said. "We were always physical. Sure, Maura and I had sex, but you and I were also physical. It was only a matter of time before wrestling became something more, and even more wouldn't have been enough. I wished to press through the skin that separated us. For the three of us to become one. I felt most complete when we were together in this chair. That's when I was the happiest. I hated when you left Lyndon, but I understood you were in a bad way. I didn't say anything to stop you. Maybe I should have. Gianni, you don't want to know what I saw in Vietnam. You don't want my nightmares. But when I'm reminded of before, of what could have been, I'm most at—"

"I'm not Maura," Gianni said.

"No, but you're who I have left."

"I'm not sure I understand."

"Neither do I," Owen said. "Guess it's the kind of love that doesn't make sense."

Gianni turned his face up to Owen's. Owen pressed his lips to Gianni's, and this time Gianni responded.

At a table, next to a bay window trimmed with Irish-lace café curtains, they ate bowls of steaming, steel-cut oatmeal with maple syrup. Embers in a woodstove took the chill out of the cool spring morning. Gianni and Owen were silent, except to ask the other to pass the cream for coffee or if the oatmeal tasted good or to comment on the chickadees and goldfinch perched on feeders outside the window. What more was there to say? They had spent the night at a small bed and breakfast and talked until they ran out of words. Owen talked about his son and how he hoped to be a good father. He said that Lolli was an excellent mother and wanted more children. Gianni spoke of coursework and how he hoped to matriculate in the fall. Film was his interest, but he was unclear about what aspect of film, except that whether he directed, held a camera, wrote scripts, critiqued films, or taught, he wanted to expose the lies of the past and tell the stories of those left in the margins. He told Owen about Gabriel and the homeless queer youth Gabriel cared for. "If I do make films, those are the stories I want to tell."

"Maybe you'll make a film about us," Owen said.

"What would I say?"

"That I tried to be a good husband and father. That you went on to make honest, important films. And that, without hurting anyone, we occasionally spent time together. Maybe once or twice a year. Maybe more often."

"And do what doesn't make any sense," Gianni said.

"Yes."

"Suppose I meet someone else?"

"I hope you do, but that will be the part of your life that does make sense. It won't replace what we have."

Would once or twice a year be enough for Gianni? Sometimes it worked in movies, but years on film lasted only a couple of hours.

That's when they ran out of words. There's no making sense of what's senseless. *The heart wants what it wants*, Gabriel once said. Owen sat naked and cross–legged on floral bedsheets. To Gianni, Owen was more perfect than anyone or anything he had ever seen. Gianni embraced Owen, they made love, then fell asleep—flesh pressed against flesh. That sweet, contented, unbroken sleep of young lovers when all that matters is their embrace.

After they finished eating breakfast, Gianni slipped his arms through his backpack straps and Owen lifted a small gym bag.

"You have your camera?" Owen said.

"Yeah, I put it in my backpack."

"Don't want to lose those memories. Next time we'll look at them together."

"It's a date."

They stepped out into the morning mist, heavy with the smell of wood smoke and balsam. Gianni's van sat next to Owens's truck. He tossed his backpack in the van, and then lifted a gift from the front passenger seat and handed it to Owen.

"For little Gianni Mauro. My mom bought it. I'm not familiar with babies."

"Neither am I, but I'm getting the hang of it. Thank you."

Gianni wondered if he should give Owen the copy he had made of Maura's photograph. A snapshot of a time when Maura will always glow, her hair will always be dark and thick, her eyes will always glisten, and wrinkles will never diminish her single dimple. Photographs don't age. Unlike Lolli, Maura's youth will remain. How does a woman compete with a photograph of a girl? But Owen said Lolli knows everything. Either Gianni had underestimated Lolli, and she was a confident, strong woman, with progressive views about sex and relationships, or she was so hopelessly in love with Owen and insecure about herself that she'd tolerate anything. For all Gianni knew, Owen might already have a framed photograph of Maura perched on a dresser with candles before it like Fina's mini-shrine on her dresser. Gianni recalled Fina's words about not thinking he knows what's better for others. He handed Owen the envelope with the photograph. *His choice*, Gianni thought.

"I had this copied for you."

Owen slipped the photograph from the envelope. Maura, the girl Owen had never met anyone else like, just as he never saw a day as wonderful or a sunrise as awesome. This said more about who Owen was than it said about any girl or day or sunrise. But that was then. Now, Owen slipped the photograph back into the envelope. He looked at Gianni. "How about you save it for me?"

Gianni took the envelope. "Yes, I'll do that."

They hugged. Mist settled on their hair and shoulders.

"I'll be in touch," Owen said.

"You do that," Gianni said, unsure that Owen would, unsure that he wanted him to.

Gianni sat in his van and waited for Owen to pull away. He slid the envelope with Maura's picture into his backpack.

"What's done is done," Maura told Gianni when he last saw her. *Not always* Gianni thought. *Sometimes a new and unexpected beginning happens. Not only movies have sequels.*

CHAPTER 26

On the morning of June 24th, 1973, Raffaella sat on a bench in Washington Square. A book lay open and ignored on her lap. Rather than read, she people-watched. An old man who fed crusts of stale bread to pigeons, the elbows of his cardigan sweater worn thin. Two middle-aged women walked arm in arm and chatted as if they hadn't seen each other in years. Dozens of young people, holding signs, most too far for Raffaella to read, milled about near a raised stage in front of Washington Square Arch. She caught a few bold and brightly colored words like Liberation, Pride, Gay, Transvestites, Lesbian. Music and chanting grew louder. Then, following a CHRISTOPHER STREET LIBERATION DAY banner, thousands paraded onto Washington Square Park.

Stonewall was not the first time queer folk fought back, but it was a critical point of no return, when enough was truly enough and a renewed level of organizing and activism exploded. On June 28, 1970, activists in New York City held the first of what would become annual worldwide parades to commigrate the Stonewall Uprising and LGBTQ (plus) Pride. Today was the fourth anniversary.

The old man feeding the pigeons laughed and looked at Raffaella. "We got every kind of nut there is." He threw the rest of his breadcrusts into the air, as if tossing confetti to mark the festivities, and a band of pigeons surrounded his feet. A few caught the crusts in mid-air. The old man applauded, lit a De Nobili cigar, and waved to Raffaella.

"Ciao, signora."

"Ciao," Raffaella said.

She closed her book. She had shopping to do before visiting with Gunter. She didn't notice Gianni with Ezra, Colleen, and eight-month-old Danu in the crowd. On the way out of the park a young man wearing a T-shirt with the words REMEMBER STONEWALL handed Raffaella a pin.

Raffaella smiled and said, "Grazie." Without looking at it, she slipped the pin into her pocket.

As usual, she found Gunter sitting in front of the television, his head tilted to the right. Several months ago, Raffaella bought Gunter a color television set. On its screen a lighthouse shone against a turquoise sky. Above the background theme music of *The Guiding Light*, a voice-over actor said, "Presented by Zest, the deodorant bar that leaves you feeling cleaner."

Gunter's head tilted a little too far and he didn't snore. His chest remained still. Raffaella placed the bag of groceries on a table, and then knelt next to him. She said his name, placed her hand on his chest, moved her hand to the side of his neck and pressed her fingers into his diaphanous flesh, and then into his spindly wrist.

She promised him no hospitals. Never. Should he have a heart attack or a stroke she would let nature take its course and not call an ambulance. Gunter now spared her that difficult decision. She sat back on the heels of her shoes and rested her head in his lap. She thought it odd to savor such a moment, but it was the peaceful end to a long life. She was denied quiet, end moments with her father or grandmother or any of her family who perished in the camps. She couldn't hold Marcello as he lay bleeding or cradle her baby as he took his last breath. Her mother passed years ago, and she remembered the warmth of her grandmother's hand in hers as they entered her parents' bedroom. Her father at the bed's edge, next to her mother—a single, tall narrow window open to the morning light. As untimely as her mother's passing was, Raffaella was there to bear witness and to grieve.

The rest of her family vanished en masse. Brutal tales too horrible to fully comprehend. Even Marcello's death—though she heard the gunshot and his death rattle in the dark cave, she often entertained thoughts of his survival. When she worked in the orphanage in Rome, she searched every child's face to find Gino's familiar smile.

Marcello and their son and her father lived in the happy endings of The Orchard's vintage films. Sitting in the dark theater, beneath the dome of imaginary stars where reality was immaterial, Raffaella sat between her father and Marcello, and baby Gino slept at her breast.

So Raffaella savored this moment with Gunter, his body still warm. She stood, took a comb from her purse and tidied his wispy hair. She went to the kitchen sink, held a dish towel under the faucet, and then wiped crumbs from Gunter's chin and rubbed at a stain on his robe.

She remembered the pin the young man had given her before she left the Square. She reached into her pocket and thought to fasten the pin to Gunter's robe. But the black pin with a pink triangle and the word PRIDE confused her. What could a symbol meant to malign have to do with pride? And then she looked at the numbers on her arm and the numbers on Gunter's arm intended to shame, to strip away their real names and their humanity. But now the numbers spoke not of their shame, but the shame of those who enforced such inhumane laws and closed their hearts to brutality. The numbers spoke of survival. They spoke of never again. Raffaella recalled the chance a man with a pink triangle took to speak to her when she had arrived at Buchenwald, to give her the words to live. Maybe it was Gunter, maybe not. But whoever it was, he turned his pink triangle into a badge of honor. She fastened the pin to Gunter's robe, and it flashed boldly against his burgundy collar.

"Ciao, mio caro amico," Raffaella said.

She picked up the phone's receiver and dialed 9-1-1.

At the sound of the door to their apartment closing, Fina stuffed her knitting needles and the mittens she was knitting for the upcoming church bazaar into the canvas bag next to her rocking chair. Gianni noticed the light coming from the living room.

"Ma, you're still up? It's after midnight."

"Yes Gianni. Sit down. I have to tell you something."

Gianni sat on the couch. This felt vaguely familiar, but back then it was his father who said, "I have to tell you something." Then he asked Gianni if he knew what adoption meant.

"Raffaella called," Fina said.

"Is she okay?"

"Yes. It's Gunter. Raffaella said Gunter passed away peacefully. She found him in his chair. No sign of struggle."

Gianni sank back into the couch. He rubbed his hand against the back of his neck. His fingers settled at his jawline and he stared at the blank television.

"I hope he was watching a Susan Hayward movie," Gianni said. "He loved Susan Hayward. He used to say, 'Poor Susan, such a drama queen.'" Gianni shook his head and thought, *Poor Gunter, such a drama queen.*

"You and Raffaella have been very kind. Few old people get the care the two of you gave him," Fina said.

"Raffaella, not me. I just stayed at his place a few times. He was once in the camps you know."

"Yes, I was there for Raffaella's interview."

Gianni leaned forward. He rubbed the palms of his hands together. "Gunter feared that he'd wind up in a nursing home or hospital. Raffaella said it would be like he was returning to the camps or prison."

"I imagine that's right, but he no longer has to worry. No one does."

Gianni looked at his watch. "It's late. Did Raffaella call from Gunter's? Maybe she's still there."

"No, she was home. She left as soon as they came and took—well, you know. There will have to be an autopsy because he died at home."

"I hadn't thought of that." Gianni shook his head again. "I'm glad Raffaella is home with Hanns. He worried that taking care of Gunter was too much for her." Gianni sucked at his bottom lip. "Now Hanns doesn't have to worry anymore either."

"Are you alright?" Fina asked.

"I'm alright." He looked at Fina. "You know, Ma, if I had lived in Germany in the 1940s, what happened to Gunter could have happened to me."

Fina leaned forward and took her son's hand. "That was a long time ago, Gianni. Should anyone ever try to hurt you, they'd have to get through me first. Your grandfather, me, and now you. We're not people who stand for bullshit."

Gianni hugged Fina. "You're the best."

Their eyes spilled tears.

Propped against two pillows and his arms folded behind his head, Gianni stared at the flashing train lights outside his bedroom window. He rode a rollercoaster of emotions. The highs and lows of his first gay parade, and then learning of Gunter passing.

Marching with thousands of people from Central Park to Washington Square and shouting, "Out of the closets into the streets." It felt like a door shattering, and his lungs filled with possibilities. In time, his disparate lives, an A train ride apart, would become integrated. Maybe celebrated.

Gianni found the day's bold visibility, sense of unity, and solidarity exhilarating. But unity is a fragile bubble. When it burst, the air in Washington Square turned fetid and reeked of anger. A clash ensued, mostly between drag queens and lesbian feminists. Both shouted foul, cruel words. Ezra said the issue was larger and more complicated than drag.

"It's about misogyny, classism, and racism," Ezra said. "Oppression competition. I've seen this many times in other progressive movements."

What did Gianni know? This was his first gay march and rally. Except for his brief stay at Lyndon, he was never involved in organizing anything except a tray of pastries. This was also Ezra's first gay event, but he was the seasoned activist, especially regarding protests against the Vietnam War. He also took part in the Poor Peoples March in D.C. Since then, he returned for other D.C. marches and protests. He knew how internal squabbles unravel movements.

"The establishment loves when this shit happens," Ezra said. "And it always does."

Gianni recalled the boos and vehement cries from women and men. Having blond hair with two-inch black roots and wearing a jumpsuit, similar but less glittery than Gabriel's, the speaker shouted, "Ya'all better quiet down." Gianni recognized Sylvia Rivera.

One night when Gabriel and Gianni had entered Tiffany's for a midnight breakfast, Gabriel introduced him to Sylvia and Marsha P. Johnson.

Sylvia's speech was passionate and pointed. She spoke of gay brothers and sisters in jail. "Ya'll don't do a God damn thing for them–

—"

Another speaker, more restrained but just as determined as Sylvia, also troubled Gianni's memory. A small woman with close cropped hair and a tailored appearance.

"It's very hard for me to be gay and proud because there's another side of me that's a woman," Jean O'Leary said. "And I'm disgusted by this mockery up here in these costumes by these people," referring to drag queens.

O'Leary stressed that her opposition was not to the way people dressed, but the "exploitation of women by men for entertainment or profit." She referred to Sylvia as a man and Sylvia's speech as a ruckus, and then read a statement signed by one hundred lesbian feminists.

Finally, Bette Midler performed. She both raised and lowered the crowd's temperature.

"I heard a little on the radio and it sounded like you were beating each other up out here," Bette said. "So I came to sing this song." She sang *Friends* and the crowd, moments earlier at each other's throats, cheered, sang, danced, and hugged. By the end of her performance, thousands of people in Washington Square sang along. "You've got to have friends—"

Like a continuous loop, Gianni replayed Rivera's words, then O'Leary's, then what Ezra had said about internal squabbles undermining movements, then Colleen's comment that O'Leary was right-on when she said, "Men have been telling us who we are all our lives." But Colleen also thought O'Leary had a stick up her ass about drag. These thoughts morphed into thoughts of what Fina once said about his trying to take Raffaella's choice away, and that his grandfather, for all his noble causes, didn't hold women's opinions in the same esteem as he held men's. Raffaella also insinuated that Marcello too was a man of noble principles, especially when the principles were men's.

Then Gianni recalled the rumblings of the folks who stood near him at the rally, especially two middle aged men dressed as if they just played a round of golf and complained that drag queens create a bad image. "Not all gay men are a bunch of nelly queens," one shouted. Next, Gianni again heard Rivera's words, *Ya'll don't do a God damn thing for them*, and so on and so forth until Midler's rollicking song became Etta James's soulful *At Last*.

Gianni pictured Gabriel in his white shimmering jump suit beckon him at Keller's. Overwhelmed, confused, but most of all missing Gabriel, Gianni's dark bedroom turned flamingo pink, he sat across from Gabriel in a booth at Tiffany's, over eggs and hash browns and enough coffee to wake the dead.

Gabriel felt pained and angry by the way Sylvia was treated. Gabriel said, *That white girl, O'Leary, like almost all of the white boys and girls at the rally don't have a fucking clue. They never stepped foot in the Stonewall or slept in the back of a truck on West Street, or an abandoned, rat infested, condemned building. They never slugged a cop because they don't know what it is to have been through enough. Most of the folks in Stonewall couldn't get into other gay bars. Stonewall was about a hell of a lot more than who you slept with or how you dressed.*

Gianni struggled to sort out his own feelings about what had taken place.

O'Leary was critical of female impersonators. But the only time Gianni saw Gabriel perform was at Rikers where Gabriel impersonated the stereotype, society-imposed image of Black men—not for entertainment, but for survival. Gabriel was always an enigma with a muscular body and glitter eyeshadow. Gabriel could punch out a cop while wearing stilettos. Gabriel defied categories and blurred boundaries. Gianni recalled that four years ago *The Village Voice* had described the Stonewall Rebellion as, "The forces of faggotry."

Is faggotry what O'Leary and others, women and men, wanted to erase? Gianni thought. But to erase faggotry was to erase Gabriel, and Gianni couldn't bear the thought of that. Then Gianni recalled someone else Gabriel had once introduced him to: Storme DeLarverie, a lesbian and drag king who sang with the Jewel Box Review.

There were drag queens and drag kings. There were lesbian feminists. There were men who seemed to hate "nelly queens." Sylvia and Marsha founded an organization called STAR, a radical collective focused on the needs of trans and gay youth, many of them sex workers. Gianni knew there were schisms, but he didn't understand the depths and anger until today. He both loved and hated his first gay march.

To the distant rumble of another A train, faint footsteps in the apartment above, and the dim glow of the streetlight below, Gianni recalled an elderly speaker who mentioned Buchenwald. He too said,

"Never again." Exhausted and grateful that Gunter was at rest, maybe celebrating with Gabriel, Gianni feel asleep.

"There's nothing I want," Gianni had said, but then he remembered the photographs. The two taped to Gabriel's heart-shaped dressing table mirror and the framed photograph on Gunter's night stand, taken when gay men filled cabarets, before they filled prisons and concentration camps.

"I'll be at the apartment by noon," Raffaella said. "A dealer is coming at 1:00 to bid on anything of value."

In one of Gunter's more lucid moments, he asked Raffaella if she knew of a lawyer. He designated Raffaella to dispose of his remains—he wished to be cremated. There was no money. For years, Gunter and Gabriel lived on his social security, whatever money Gabriel made and, when bills piled up, Gunter sold antiques left from his shop. He hoped that Raffaella selling his remaining possessions would at least pay for his cremation.

Gianni found the door to the apartment slightly ajar, and Raffaella was in Gunter's room boxing clothes. She looked up and smiled.

"Gunter was quite fashionable. Some things I'm leaving for the dealer. The rest I'll donate to a thrift shop."

A partially filled plastic bag with a slight smell of urine sat next to Raffaella's foot. The bedroom windows were open. She was diligent about tossing soiled mattress pads, pajama bottoms, and underwear. She also scrubbed Gunter's apartment regularly, reminiscent of her days working in an overcrowded orphanage after World War II and at the Gate of Heaven convent. Raffaella wasn't a stranger to hard work—she found comfort in it. Where another person might seek a warm bath or sitting in a lotus position to relax, Raffaella scrubbed or planted or pruned. The exception being vintage movies at The Orchard. They did for her mind what physical work did for her body.

"Yes, folks are into vintage clothing," Gianni said. "I bet a theater company or playhouse or something like that might want them."

"That's a good idea."

Gianni lifted the framed photograph from Gunter's nightstand. "This is one of the photographs I mentioned." He held it out to

Raffaella. Light from the open windows reflected off the glass. "That's Gunter."

"Yes." Raffaella didn't look. She folded a pair of striped pajamas and placed them in a cardboard box on top of other folded pajamas.

"Does he look familiar?"

"You mean from the camps."

Gianni considered Raffaella's question. "Yes, I guess that's what I mean."

Raffaella took the framed photograph from Gianni. She stared at it for a few moments then handed it back to him.

"If it was Gunter I met at Buchenwald he had already been there long enough to look like everyone else. Like walking dead. Whoever I met years ago looked more like the frail, old man you knew than the young man in this picture. But it was Gunter's voice I had recognized more than his face."

Raffaella turned and opened an ornate cherry armoire. She pulled out a box from beneath the hanging suits, sport jackets, and slacks. Gianni ran his hand across the glass covering Gunter's photograph. He remembered coming upon the pictures of Marcello and young Raffaella and Gino when he helped Raffaella move.

"So you're sure it was Gunter who talked to you when you arrived at Buchenwald."

"I don't know. Once, when Gunter and I watched a movie about the war, he said he remembered. But what he remembered, I don't know. What does it matter now? Come sit, Gianni. You might want some of these."

With one hand, Raffaella pushed Gunter's clothing aside—shirts, ascots, underwear, and socks Gunter once wore while conversing with antiquarians in his shop, or dining with friends in Little Italy or China Town, or walking his long-gone standard poodle, Dietrich, on the sidewalks in Greenwich Village. In her other hand, she held the shoebox she pulled out of the bottom of the armoire. They sat on the bare space of mattress, and Raffaella handed Gianni the box.

"I found this a few days ago when I started to pack clothes."

Gianni lifted black and white photographs: pictures of same-sex couples dancing, holding hands, kissing. Some wearing work clothes, some in bathing suits, some dressed to the T, and some in uniforms.

"These are wonderful. I recognize Gunter in a few of these, but

I wish I knew the others. I wish I knew their stories." He paused at a picture of a young Gabriel—maybe Gianni's age. He handed the picture to Raffaella. There were many pictures of Gabriel—either alone or with friends—on the piers, in Central Park, at the Bronx Zoo, Coney Island, and several taken on a beach that didn't resemble any of the New York City beaches that Gianni knew—an archive of Gabriel's life after meeting Gunter.

Gianni held several color beach snapshots out to Raffaella.

"I wonder where these were taken. There are no sand dunes at the Rockaways or Coney Island or any of the beaches I've been to."

In several beach photographs, Gabriel, Gunter, and a woman appearing to be somewhere between Gabriel and Gunter's age stood with their arms around each other's shoulders. Next Gianni came across color photo proofs of young Gabriel wearing a white thong taken by a professional photographer in the same coastal setting. Gabriel rising out of beach grass or wading in meandering rivulets surrounded by sea lavender. In some, Gabriel struck a relevé or an elevé pose, and Gianni thought of the picture taped to Gabriel's mirror. Little Gabriel posing like a fledgling ballerina. The barefoot sissy from Money, Mississippi, wearing baggy shorts cinched at the waist with a cord, had grown into a stunning, ebony force of faggotry. Gianni lowered his eyes when he handed them to Raffaella.

"Che bello," Raffaella said. "Like a Rodin sculpture."

Gianni looked at Raffaella and smiled. She never ceased to amaze him.

"Gunter told me about a friend he and Gabriel visited in a place called Provincetown," Raffaella said. "His friend was a photographer. Maybe she took these pictures of Gabriel. See, there's a name in the corner of these pictures."

"Yes, Gabriel also mentioned Provincetown," Gianni said. "Do you mind if I keep this box of pictures?"

"Of course not. I thought you might want them."

"And there are two more pictures in Gabriel's room."

"Hello!" A voice came from the door to the apartment.

"It must be the dealer," Raffaella said.

"Sounds like you're buying drugs," Gianni said.

They both laughed. They left Gunter's bedroom and found a man who looked more like a truck driver than an antique dealer standing in the living room and examining a press back nursing rocker.

Raffaella introduced herself. "You're Mr. Rapp, yes?"

Stanley Rapp eyed Raffaella, his eyes pausing at her breasts.

"I think you're here to look at antiques," Raffaella said. "I'm not one of them. At least not yet."

Gianni laughed. His heart filled with love for Raffaella. Fina, Raffaella, even Colleen—Gianni admired and relished their no-nonsense ways, like the female actors in pre-Code movies before the Catholic Church's campaign to dictate morality in motion pictures and turn all women into Doris Day characters.

"Yes, of course," Mr. Rapp said. He went about his business of tipping chairs, turning over cushions, picking up knickknacks, and turning lamps on and off.

Gianni left Raffaella to deal with Mr. Rapp while he went to Gabriel's room. Except for the few boxes piled on the floor and the two photographs Gianni wanted, still taped to the heart-shaped mirror, Gabriel's room was a stark contrast to its once jamboree chic. He thought of Jean O'Leary speaking in Washington Square and, for a moment, he hated her, because it was easier than dealing with Gabriel's near-empty room. But it was the landlord who wanted to renovate the apartment and rent it as soon as possible, not O'Leary. Raffaella asked Gianni to contact Tammy who, with other friends, took Gabriel's boas, wigs, gowns, makeup, and costume jewelry. Gianni asked Tammy to leave the two photographs and Gabriel's T-shirt with the Marilyn Monroe quote "Give a Girl The Right Shoes, and She Can Conquer The World." The T-shirt lay folded on Gabriel's mattress. Gianni took his T-shirt off and slipped on Gabriel's. He spotted a feather from one of Gabriel's boas on the floor beneath an empty clothes rack. He picked it up, sat on Gabriel's bed, and stared at the feather—flamingo pink. And he felt that Gabriel sat next to him. *I miss you Gabriel—I know you do, child*. He liked that Gabriel went back to calling him child.

Raffaella followed Mr. Rapp as he nodded and cleared his throat and made other odd noises that were probably code for the worth of a particular item. He jotted notes on a yellow tablet. Raffaella knew how to negotiate with men and women selling wares from pushcarts on Delancey Street. In those situations, she was the buyer and could just walk away if she felt the price was too high. She had no experience being the seller. Regardless, if Gunter's possessions didn't cover cremation expenses, Raffaella would pay the difference. She never asked or expected Gunter to repay her for any of the money she spent. How do you put a price tag on the risk a man with a pink triangle took at Buchenwald? "Even Dante would have no words to describe. Live, live no matter what you have to do. Live!" Words that she's clung to ever since. To Raffaella, it had been Gunter who gave her those words. That's all that mattered.

Gianni pressed his ear against Gabriel's bedroom door, waited until he heard the front door close, and then joined Raffaella in the living room.

"So how did you do? You sounded like a pro."

Raffaella showed Gianni the check. "I don't know what anything is worth, but this will cover the cost of cremation, and there will be money left to donate to a charity in Gunter's name."

"I know an organization that Gunter and Gabriel would want to support," Gianni said. "It's called STAR."

"Good. Very good. Then that's what we'll do."

Raffaella folded the check and slipped it into her pocket. Gianni laid the two photographs he had taken from Gabriel's room in the shoebox on Gunter's bed before he helped Raffaella box the rest of Gunter's clothes.

"Do you think Gabriel and Gunter were ever lovers?" Gianni asked. "I mean, I know what happened to Gunter, and I'm not sure if—well, it's a stupid question. They were family. That's all that matters."

As usual, Raffaella waited quietly while Gianni thought aloud. They boxed the rest of Gunter's clothing.

CHAPTER 27

Irregular hours and poor service is not the way to keep customers happy. Even The Orchard's long-time and most ardent movie-goers complained. Saul's nephew Ethan had to go. Hanns met with Gianni and Raffaella and posed several options regarding Sanctuary's future. With each option, he looked sheepishly at Raffaella, but Raffaella sat with her eyes fixed on her folded hands. Hanns also kept glancing at a poster of Susan Hayward screaming behind prison bars, as if it were a leaky faucet getting on his nerves. Earlier, Raffaella added two movie posters from Gunter's apartment to the already busy walls at The Orchard. One of Greta Garbo in *Camille* and one of Susan Hayward in *I Want To Live*. Hanns thought screaming *I Want To Live* looked crass among the vintage and, according to Hanns, more tasteful posters, but he kept this opinion to himself.

Finally, Raffaella looked up. "Hanns, if you don't like the poster just take it down. You look as if you're sitting on a broken bottle."

Gianni covered his grin with his hand.

"No, no, it's not the poster. I'm just distracted by trying to come up with the best Sanctuary solution." He cleared his throat. "What do you think of this, Gianni?" But when Hanns said Gianni, he looked at Raffaella. "I know a guy at Ferrara's Bakery in Little Italy who's interested in taking over Sanctuary." Now Hanns looked at Gianni. "They'd change the name from *Sanctuary at The Orchard* to *Ferrara's at The Orchard*," so it's not like they're buying the business. They'd pay Saul rent for the space, but I told Saul that you should receive some compensation since you created a business, which then made the space appealing to Ferrara's."

"What's the compensation?" Raffaella said.

"Well that's yet to be decided. When I meet again with Saul, you should join us. You have more sway over Saul than I do," Hanns said without a tone of sarcasm. He simply stated a fact.

"I will," Raffaella said.

Though hesitant to interrupt, Gianni finally jumped in. "Sounds good to me, and you should have heard Raffaella negotiate with the guy who bought Gunter's stuff. She was amazing."

"That she is," Hanns said.

It was true that Gianni worked hard and Sanctuary benefitted The Orchard, but Hanns and Saul took money out of The Orchard's finances to pay for the café renovations. Gianni never paid rent and, after reimbursing his father for whatever baking supplies he used and paid Ezra for his hours, Gianni still made a fair profit. He had offered to pay his parents for room and board, but they balked at the idea.

"You're our son, not a border," Fina said.

Gianni used some of his savings to pay for his four courses at NYU, but a fair amount of savings remained. Whatever Saul agreed to would be gravy. He wondered if Hanns really believed that he deserved compensation for Sanctuary or if he said this to please Raffaella. Since Raffaella began to spend time at Gunter's, Gianni noticed that she grew quiet when Hanns was around. Not always, but occasionally Gianni sensed tension. With Gunter gone, he hoped that whatever riffs emerged between Raffaella and Hanns would heal. If Saul coughing up a few bucks for Sanctuary would hasten the healing, Gianni wasn't about to complain. Should he continue to take courses at NYU and pursue a degree, he had a lot of expenses ahead of him. Fina and Liberato offered to help, but at twenty-three Gianni hoped to pay his own way, and it was time to find his own apartment.

"So, Gianni, I take it you're comfortable with this idea?" Hanns said. "You're okay if Raffaella and I meet with Saul? Would you like to be at the meeting? Maybe make a case for how much you think you should get."

"Whatever it is, I'm grateful," Gianni said, though he was being a bit disingenuous. He knew that Raffaella would be much better than he at persuading Saul as well as Hanns to pay a fair price.

"Good, then that's settled," Raffaella said. She stood up, walked toward the Susan Hayward poster and removed it from the wall. "Now you can take the broken glass out of your ass, Hanns."

Damn, Gianni thought, *Hanns must have done something big to piss Raffaella off. She's turning into Fina.*

CHAPTER 28

Pier 45 was quiet. Cruising ended before sunrise when some men returned to their respectable lives. They showered and left for their work in retail, construction, teaching, prosecuting, defending, judging, serving Mass, or arresting the men they had blown or fucked the night before. Some men claimed they worked a double shift, but before they kissed their wives good morning, they scrubbed away the smell of the night.

Gianni and Ezra walked on either side of Raffaella, the morning sun behind them, and their mournful shadows stretched out on the pier before them and foretold of their reason for being there, while homeless men and youth slept in secluded spaces among the fetid crumbling structures of rusted metal and rotted wood. Earlier, when the sun rose on the East River but was yet to reach the Hudson, rats claimed their spoils. They knew that the fermented, sweet stench of alcohol meant a deep sleep, and they tore at pockets for a forgotten chunk of Danish or bagel. They also knew the fetor of death and, when they smelled it, they chewed at fingers and ears, anything fleshy, and then gnawed at bone until the sun reached the Hudson and a cop on patrol came upon the bloodied body. Once someone's child but now carrion for fish if the cop chose to kick the body into the Hudson, or medical students' anonymous cadaver if the cop called an ambulance.

Raffaella carried Gunter's urn. No fanfare. Gunter's wishes.

"I've outlived everyone," Gunter had said. "Even Gabriel."

Raffaella asked if there were relatives in Germany he'd want her to write to, but Gunter shook his head: "I doubt that any young people, nieces, nephews, their children, whomever, know of me. Germans have a way of erasing our unpleasant past."

"Not only Germans," Raffaella said.

They paused at the pier's edge, and Raffaella handed the urn to Gianni. She reached into her pocket and retrieved a yellow sheet of paper. She unfolded it and handed it to Ezra.

"Gunter asked that we read this," she said.

He must have written Pastor Martin Niemöller's iconic quote before his tremors began, before he met Raffaella, maybe before he met Gabriel.

In a solemn voice, Ezra read, "First they came for the socialists, and I did not speak out, because I was not a socialist. Then they came for the trade unionists, and I did not speak out, because I was not a trade unionist. Then they came for the Jews, and I did not speak out, because I was not a Jew. Then they came for me—and there was no one left to speak for me."

Then Ezra read the words Gunter had added to the quote, "For my silence, I am deeply sorry."

Raffaella nodded mournfully. Gianni removed the lid and tilted the urn until Gunter's pale gray ashes, speckled with bone and mixed with Gabriel's remaining ashes, rained into the Hudson. Gulls gathered, then whined their disappointment.

Back at The Orchard, a man, wider than tall, wheezed and puffed on a cigar as he scraped at the word "Sanctuary," one letter at a time. First, he dipped a sponge into soapy water and soaked the window. Next, he scraped with a professional grade razor, and then rubbed the spot with fine grade steel wool, careful not to scratch the glass. When no flake of the letter remained, he began the process again, dipping the sponge back into the bucket of soapy water.

Two neighborhood women, wearing babushkas and weighted down with stuffed mesh shopping bags, paused and watched him work. They shook their heads.

"Didn't they just paint that sign?" one woman said.

"Not too long," the other said. "Change. That's the only thing you can depend on. Change and death. Taxes too. But I don't take care of taxes, my Larry does that."

The first woman agreed.

The man puffed harder on his cigar, creating a noxious cloud of smoke. The women coughed, waved the stench away from their faces, and then hobbled to Essex Street where they'd squabble with a shopkeeper about the cost of kosher dill pickles. The cigar-puffing man scraped at the letter Y, while two carpenters replaced the small pastry display case with a larger one and an electrician rewired the prep area, adding more outlets.

Raffaella, Gianni, and Ezra crossed West Street. Once back at The Orchard, Raffaella placed Gunter's seashell and bejeweled urn on a shelf she had the workmen install behind the candy counter.

Ezra returned to Berkeley, Saul agreed to split the income from Ferrara's rent with Gianni while Gianni was in school, Gianni began classes fulltime at NYU, and he moved into a one-bedroom apartment in an East Village four-story walkup on Twelfth Street, a block away from the Strand Bookstore. Track lighting recently installed, Gianni hung the photograph Raffaella, Ezra, and Colleen gave him as an apartment warming gift. Raffaella contacted the photographer in Provincetown who took the beach photographs of Gabriel that Gianni found in the shoebox from Gunter's closet. The photographer had been a longtime friend of Gunter's, and Gunter and Gabriel often stayed with her during their Provincetown vacations. She had lost touch with Gunter, as friends often do, but was heartbroken to learn of his passing and of Gabriel's tragic end.

"Those photos you have are proofs," she said. "No doubt, I have them on file and can make a larger picture for you."

Beneath the new track lighting and in vivid color, Gabriel waded in rivulets, surrounded by sea lavender and beach grass. The photographer had signed her name beneath the words *Angel Gabriel Blessing the Backwaters*.

Perfect, Gianni thought.

There was another gift to hang. Something Raffaella had given him this morning at The Orchard after they drank their cappuccino, and

Gianni told her he called Angel Guardian Home to inquire about a visit.

"Angel Guardian scheduled a tour of the campus for the first week in November," Gianni said.

Raffaella added cinnamon to the froth on her coffee. "Will you go?"

"Yes, I'm looking forward to it."

Gianni glanced at the words *Ferrara's At The Orchard* spelled in reverse across the window, and then looked back at Raffaella. A lot had changed, except for Raffaella. She'll be one of those women who regardless of her age will turn heads like the formidable dowagers who played supporting roles in vintage films but always upstaged the younger star. Maybe it was her poise and stature. Maybe it was her eyes and gypsy-like hair. Maybe it was something from within. What chance did years have to diminish a woman who survived what Raffaella had survived but remained apart or even above the physical humiliation and degradation. "Always hold your head high," her father told her. And she held fast to his counsel.

"Would you like company?" Raffaella said. "I'll go with you if you want."

Gianni remembered that Raffaella had told him working in an orphanage made her miss Gino all the more. One of several reasons she left Italy for America. He feared a visit to Angel Guardian might resurrect painful memories. Despite Fina's ever-lingering words, *You assumed you knew better than her about what she could handle*, Gianni declined Raffaella's offer.

"Thank you, but I think visiting Angel Guardian is something I should do alone. Kind of a rite of passage. A quest."

"I understand."

Raffaella lifted a package wrapped in brown paper and handed it to Gianni.

"You already gave me the picture of Gabriel,"

"This belongs with you. A keepsake. I think that's the word." Raffaella said. "Be careful opening it."

Carefully, Gianni unwrapped the gift.

"I stood right next to the electrician when he took it down to make sure he didn't break it," Raffaella said.

Gianni's eyes filled. He set the neon Sanctuary sign down on an empty table next to them, stood, pulled Raffaella up from her chair, and hugged her.

"I love you," he said.

Raffaella's eyes also filled with tears. "You have no idea what a gift you are to me."

Gianni hung the sign in one of his apartment windows facing Fourteenth Street. Beneath the sign, on a bookcase were Gunter's photograph taken at a club in Berlin, the snapshot of Maura in her yellow summer frock, and a snapshot Gianni took of Owen at Lyndon. Gunter's shoebox of photos sat next to books on film. He looked back at Gabriel's photograph and thought of the snapshots of Marcello and Raffaella with Gino. *So many stories,* Gianni thought. *These are the films I want to make. I'll be a contender after all.*

CHAPTER 29

The first Saturday in November turned out to be one of those misty, chilly reminders—not only was summer a memory, but fickle autumn will soon surrender to winter. On the large Angel Guardian campus, between Sixty-Third and Sixty-Fourth Streets in Dyker Heights, Brooklyn, several visitors in Gianni's group stood beneath the lingering yellow leaves of an old beech tree. A spotty canopy so large and sprawling that Gianni wondered if the beech might be a wolf tree. Some visitors also stood under umbrellas and close to a long, low building, distinguished only by the lichen and rust that stained its weathered bricks. They pressed their fingers to the bricks, as if they were reading brail and retrieving the preludes of their lives, discovering backstories, finding answers to countless questions.

But for the absence of an ominous smokestack rising above the building's peak, it reminded Gianni of pictures in library books of Dachau's gas chamber and crematorium. He was glad Raffaella hadn't come. He neither stood beneath the beech tree, nor pressed his fingers against the building. He stood alone between the two groups of visitors.

A very young social worker and tour guide said of the building, "This is where we keep our files and adoption records."

One man, tall and stoop shouldered, frowned—his blue eyes and lined face haloed by thick white hair and a beard—kept his free hand pressed against the building, and with his other hand, he held his umbrella out toward the social worker—an indication that he would interrupt her.

"*Your* records?" he said. "What you casually call files are *our* roots pressed between sheaths of cardboard. And, by the way, the roof's shingles are in urgent need of repair."

The social worker cleared her throat and looked toward the people beneath the beech tree. "As of this year, we no longer house orphans and foundlings here. We have a medical clinic for the children in Mercy First, our foster-care program, and a convent for nuns."

The man released a slight grunt and shook his head. Gianni recalled Sylvia Rivera at the gay march and event. Not that the man resembled Rivera and his tone was much more subdued. If anything, he sounded defeated. But, like Rivera, there was a subversive truth in his words. A truth that ruptured the status quo of sealed adoption records hidden away in derelict buildings like rotting tissue from so many lobotomies.

The tour guide directed the group toward a building along Sixty-Third Street. Only two stories, but its architecture no less intricate than the conspicuous main building that faced Twelfth Avenue. An Italian Renaissance Revival Style with Beaux-Arts elements that loomed above the modest homes in the surrounding residential neighborhood.

"This was our nursery," the social worker said. Trimmed in the greenish blue of copper patina, its façade spoke of the many years that passed since it was built in 1905. In 1907, a second nursery was built to quarantine sick infants. Gianni scanned the roof line of peaks and the second-story groupings of three large windows beneath each peak. Fifteen windows in all, another row of fifteen windows on the first floor. The social worker said that thousands of children were adopted from Angel Guardian, founded by the Sisters of Mercy in 1899. Gianni wondered if he once slept in one of the cribs behind one of the windows. He felt an affinity for the campus, for its buildings, for the trees and shrubs, especially for the huge old beech tree that surely predated Angel Guardian and witnessed the endings and beginnings of countless families. He looked at the larger-than-life statue of an angel and child at the heart of the campus. One of the angel's hands rested on a child's shoulder, the other hand open and held up as if guarding the child from harm. Gianni thought of Raffaella and Gabriel. They had been real-life angel guardians, not only for war orphans and homeless queer youth, but also for Gianni.

As if Gianni were back at Gate of Heaven and lost in one of his daydreams, he saw himself standing on the landing outside his parents' apartment, digging his bare toe into the cracked tile floor, as Michael said, "You're not our real cousin." Next Peter said, "Our mom said you were adopted." Then Michael said, "Uncle Liberato and Aunt Fina are not your real parents. They adopted you." And Peter added, "Because your real mom didn't want you." Finally, in unison, they said, "That's why you're not our real cousin." Then he saw the door open on the floor above them, but Liviana was not the imposing adult he remembered looking down on the child Gianni. She was the small, insignificant woman sitting at a table in his parents' kitchen with cheese ring frosting stuck to the corner of her bottom lip. She no longer had power over him, just a vile, frosted mouth.

"And now if you'll follow me into the chapel," the social worker said, which sounded to Gianni like Sister Joan Marie calling him from a daydream.

It was ten years since Gianni had been in a church. It felt like coming home, even if home was not all it boasted to be. It was familiar: the stained-glass windows, the arches and pillars, the marble altar and statues, and the faint scent of candles and incense. And these features evoked memories of stories: the poor in spirit, those who mourn, the meek, those who hunger, the merciful, the pure in heart, the peacemakers, those who are persecuted, and the least of these. Even among the marginalized there are always the least of these. Maybe it was some preconscious memories of having once been in this chapel or in the nursery or on the surrounding grounds, but Gianni felt at peace. He felt real. He felt visible.

He recalled walking along the balconies in Vail Manor with Owen and Maura, their hands extended searching for the cold spaces they believed were ghosts. Had he the nerve to extend his hands in the chapel, he would not have felt the cold of ghosts, but instead the warm tides of goodbyes and surrenders—memories too potent to dissipate.

Gianni handed his camera to a young woman and asked if she'd take his picture. He stood next to a smaller version of the outside angel-and-child statue. After a few clicks, the woman returned his camera and asked if he was from Angel Guardian. He thought it an odd way to phrase the question as if she were asking if he was from Brooklyn, Queens, or Mars, but he knew what she meant.

"Yes," he said. "Guess I was a year old when I was adopted."

"I was older," she said. "About four."

"Do you remember living here?"

"A bit. Shadowy memories."

A husband and wife, fiftyish, medium height and build, and smartly dressed, approached Gianni and the young woman.

"These are my parents," the young woman said. "Carl and Mildred Walsh."

Gianni extended his hand. "Nice to meet you. My name is Gianni."

After he shook hands with Carl and Mildred, the young woman extended her hand. "And my name is Verna. How old are you, Gianni?"

"Twenty-three."

"So am I. Maybe we were neighbors. You know, my crib next to yours."

Gianni smiled a half smile, only one corner of his mouth rose giving his face a quizzical expression. As far as he knew, Verna was the first adoptee he had met, certainly the first adoptee to pose questions about what's unknown and most likely unknowable. Maybe someone once noted which infants were in what cribs, but names changed and records most likely lost.

Carl and Mildred Walsh remained quiet, but their daughter's musings didn't fluster them. *Why should they?* Gianni thought. Why hadn't he asked Fina and Liberato to join him at Angel Guardian? He told Ezra about the open house before Ezra left for Berkeley and also Raffaella, but he didn't say anything to his parents. He hadn't given it a thought. He long knew that his adoption was a source of consternation for his parents. A fact better to ignore, though ignoring sharpened the edge of his cousins' words and rendered Gianni invisible and not real. But he was real. It took time for him to believe it, to feel it, but slowly at Sanctuary in The Orchard, at his midnight breakfasts at Tiffany's, and in Owen's arms, Gianni became real. He was really relinquished as an infant, he really was adopted, he was really gay, he was really in love with a married man.

"Nice meeting you, Gianni," Verna said, and then she and her parents left before Gianni had the chance to ask her questions. Not that he knew what he would ask. *Why weren't you adopted until you were four years old?* felt intrusive. But he regretted that she left so quickly.

He ambled about the chapel, past a statue of Mary, a statue of Joseph holding the baby Jesus, a stained-glass window of another guardian angel. This angel surrounded by several children. While wandering, Gianni overheard snippets of conversations: "I wonder if she had prayed in this chapel—Maybe she brought me here before she left—Did my father know about me?—Were they young?" And their questions became his and his theirs. He confused what he heard with what he thought. But what did it matter? All versions of *Who had I been before?*

Gianni once told Raffaella that he didn't know anyone aside from himself who was adopted, and now he stood in this chapel with at least a dozen adoptees, maybe more.

He spotted the man with the white hair and blue eyes sitting alone in a pew. Gianni sat next to him.

"I like what you said."

The old man turned to Gianni, his eyes bluer than Owen's and also lit from within. For the briefest moment, they took Gianni's breath away.

"What did I say?"

"Something about *our* roots being pressed between sheaths of cardboard."

"Oh, that?" And the man turned back and stared at his large, gnarled, clasped fingers.

He's daydreaming, Gianni thought. Gianni stood and began to leave, but the man said, "Angel Guardian started to accept young boys in 1906. That's when I came."

At first, Gianni remained silent. Maybe a bit of Fina and Liberato's doings. Better not to talk about adoption. He forced himself to ask, "How old were you when you were adopted?"

"I wasn't."

"You grew up here?"

"On and off between foster homes until I was old enough to be on my own." The old man looked back at Gianni. Gianni felt as if he could wade in the blue of the old man's eyes and be completely at peace. Clouds hadn't dimmed the tranquility as they had in Gunter's.

"I'm called Abe," the old man said.

"I'm Gianni."

And as Abe appeared to slip back into himself, Gianni imagined the adoptees present gathering around the altar. Abe could easily play the role of a sage and, like Ezra's father, Joseph, lead a sacred meal. *A Seder*, Gianni thought, which Gianni now understood to be a ritual of acknowledging collective trauma. *But adoptees have no such rituals. We can't express our feelings without fear of appearing ungrateful or hurting those who adopted us or disrespecting the memory of those who relinquished us. It's always about them. Always about us making it okay.*

Gianni imagined Abe breaking unleavened bread and passing it to the next adoptee, who in turn did the same until all held a piece of the bread, and shared their varied stories. Some longed for their birth families, some felt indifferent or angry, some felt deep connections to their adoptive families, some were estranged, some—like Abe— had grown up in and out of foster homes, some found love, some abuse. But the common thread that connected all the stories, no matter how wonderful or terrible, was that of a diaspora. No matter what information they might someday learn about their roots or biological family they meet, growing up as children in diaspora was the bond adoptees shared. Without viewing adoption as positive or negative, good or bad, enriching or damaging, being severed from biological, and, in most cases, natal roots is central to who adoptees are as a people. Gianni thought, *It's the prelude to all of our stories.*

The young social worker's voice startled Gianni. "Our tour has ended. Please leave through the same door we entered. Thank you."

Gianni and the old man stood. The social worker lowered her eyes when the old man walked past her. He nodded and thanked her.

"Might I take picture of you," Gianni asked.

"Sure."

Gianni pointed to the beech tree.

Abe stood beneath the broad reaching canopy. He looked wizened– –a wolf tree with roots pressed between two sheaths of cardboard.

Gianni snapped a few pictures. They left the campus together, exchanged small talk, mostly about Gianni's course work at NYU. They stood at the campus entrance—a tall green, iron gate with the words The Angel Guardian Home across the top.

Gianni extended his hand. "Nice to meet you, Abe."

Abe took Gianni's hand, pulled Gianni toward him, and wrapped his free arm around Gianni. Not only did Gianni allow Abe's embrace, but he returned it. Tears welled in his eyes.

"You'll be okay, Gianni," the old man said.

Gianni recalled Gabriel's words: *Better than okay.*

Back home, Gianni turned on the Sanctuary sign in the window. It was only 4:30, but already getting dark. Below, Esteban, the young man who said Gabriel once saved him from an aggressive john in the Meatpacking District, noticed its glow. He had seen the sign before, after leaving his shift at the Strand Bookstore, and it made him smile. He had also noticed Gianni leave the four-story walkup once or twice and spotted him at the Strand, browsing through books about film. Gianni looked familiar, and then Esteban recalled seeing him at Gabriel's farewell on Pier 45. They had smiled the kind of smiles that ask, *Don't we already know each other? And, if not, shouldn't we?*

Gianni heard the faint sound of pebbles against a window pane, more memory or notion than actual sound, but he looked out the window onto 12th Street. Snow flurries vanished beneath streetlights. A passerby paused and looked up at his window.

pg. 225
Anger